What Gold Buys

Books by Ann Parker

The Silver Rush Mysteries
Silver Lies
Iron Ties
Leaden Skies
Mercury's Rise
What Gold Buys

What Gold Buys

A Silver Rush Mystery

Ann Parker

Poisoned Pen Press

First Edition 2016

10 9 8 7 6 5 4 3 2 1

Library of Congress Catalog Card Number: 2015957981

ISBN: 9781464206238   Hardcover
     9781464206252   Trade Paperback

Map Credit: Map created by Michael Greer, Greer Studios

Poisoned Pen Press
6962 E. First Ave., Ste. 103
Scottsdale, AZ 85251
www.poisonedpenpress.com
info@poisonedpenpress.com

Printed in the United States of America

To the readers—

Especially those who waited patiently and encouraged me as I completed this, the next installment of the Silver Rush saga.

This one's for you.

Acknowledgments

When a book takes this long for a writer to write, it's almost a guarantee that the acknowledgments will stretch back in time. As someone who is a little fitful when it comes to taking notes (and keeping track of them), I apologize to anyone who has helped me along the path and is left out of this list.

First and foremost, I am grateful to Barbara Peters and Robert Rosenwald and their staff at Poisoned Pen Press, especially Barbara and Rob for their patience with my long absence from the world of fiction and their encouragement once I "hopped to" and dove into writing this, the fifth in the Silver Rush series.

Further thanks go to my long-standing critique partners, who provided inspiration, comments, and edits: Camille Minichino, Carole Price, Colleen Casey, Janet Finsilver, Penny Warner, Priscilla Royal, and Staci MacLaughlin.

A special tip of the hat goes to Camille—who provided a "write-away guest room," kept my spirits up as I thrashed, and did a blazing fast and focused beta-read on the draft—and to Colleen, for her above-and-beyond legal sleuthing, digging up and helping me understand the arcane legal precedents, laws, statutes, and summaries for "divorce, à la Colorado 1880." A tip of the hat goes to Jane Staehle, Bill McConachie, and Mary-Lynne "Persnickety" Pierce Bernald for a close read of the ARC version for errors, hiccups, and oopses.

A special shout-out goes to the Leadville folks who "aided and abetted" my trip to the past, including Lake County Public Library's Janice Fox, *research librarian and historian extraordinaire* (who deserves accolades galore) and beta-reader; library director Nancy Schloerke; and staff. You are all amazing! Libraries and librarians rock the world! Many thanks are also due to Marcia Martinek, editor of Leadville's *Herald Democrat*. Marcia took me on a tour of the "underbelly" of the newspaper building, which once housed a mortuary. Great fodder for fiction lie within those walls. All of Leadville's museums are amazing, but this time I want to give a special nod to The House with the Eye Museum and its curator for keeping Leadville's history alive.

Experts who helped me along the way include Steven and Amy Crane for background into Civil War medicine and weaponry, James Lowry for timely insights into historical undertaking and embalming, and others who wish to remain anonymous— you know who you are! (NOTE: If you supplied expertise and I didn't list you, forgive me. Send me a note and I'll rectify as best I can.) Of course, any errors found within these pages are mine.

Thank you, Francoise Alexander, for lending me your melodious name. I love the serendipitous connections between certain elements of this story and your family history. Your inclusion was clearly meant to be!

Finally, there are many others in the writing community I am grateful to—writing is both solitary and a group effort. Thank you, Dani Greer (Yeah! Now finish that book, girl!), the folks of the Colorado Writers and Publishers Facebook group, and the communities of Poisoned Pen Press authors, Women Writing the West, Mystery Writers of America, and Sisters in Crime.

A wave to the folks at the various cubicle farms (brick and mortar as well as virtual), who made it possible for us to not only keep body and soul together but also pay the mortgage and college tuition. They include S&TR staff, Jeff Sketchley (holding the LDRD whip), and TRE's Laurie Powers, who as supervisor and a published author herself performed the exquisite balancing act of shoveling plenty of work my way to keep the wolves from the door and then holding back the projects during those intense last few months of finishing the draft.

Last, but *never* least, my dear family, who, along with my closest friends, must deal with the ups, downs, and sideways of having a writer amongst them. My "core group" Bill, Ian, and Devyn—who cheer me on, cheer me up, and give me hope—as well as the farther-flung Colorado clan of Joel, Kim, Jake, Dave, and Elly, who feed me, house me, and inspire me, as well as Alison back East, Steve out West, and all the McConachie clan. We live but a blink of the eye, and aspire to shed a little light into the corners of our own family history mysteries. Every life has a story, and from that, other stories are created. Love you all!

"Thinking to get at once all the gold the goose could give, he killed it and opened it only to find—nothing."

—Aesop

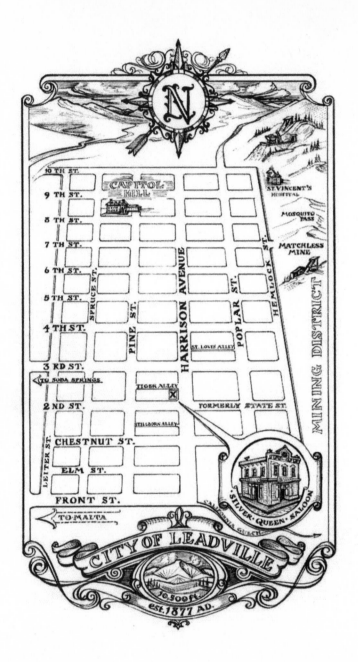

N

10 TH ST.
9 TH ST.
8 TH ST.
7 TH ST.
6 TH ST.
5 TH ST.
4 TH ST.
3 RD ST.
2 ND ST.
CHESTNUT ST.
ELM ST.
FRONT ST.

CAPITOL HILL

SPRUCE ST.
PINE ST.
HARRISON AVENUE
POPLAR ST.
HEMLOCK ST.
LEITER ST.

ST. LOUIS ALLEY
TIGER ALLEY
STILLBORN ALLEY

TO SODA SPRINGS

FORMERLY STATE ST.

TO MALTA

MINING DISTRICT

ST. VINCENT'S HOSPITAL
MOSQUITO PASS
MATCHLESS MINE

SILVER · QUEEN · SALOON

CALIFORNIA GULCH

CITY OF LEADVILLE

10,500 ft.
est. 1877 A.D.

Chapter One

It was hard to find somewhere close by the crowded silver mining boomtown to practice killing a man, but Antonia was nothing if not determined.

After trudging up hills and skittering down slopes, the dusty smell of broken sage chasing her all the way, she'd arrived at her place—*her* place—where no one would find her. Here, Antonia felt safe. She had the targets. She had the gun. She had the rounds. Now, to practice, so that she'd be ready. Ready when the time came.

Three cherished glass bottles stood side by side on tree stumps in the clearing. Antonia knew them all. One was a soda bottle she'd pulled out of the trash behind Schmidt and Aldinger's soda water manufacturing on East Chestnut Street. One was a cracked whiskey flask given to her by Mr. Jackson from the Silver Queen Saloon. The last was her mother's tonic bottle snitched from under the bed.

One, two, three. Like soldiers lined up on the firing line.

Or maybe like her maman's clients, who came to the one-room shack with the sign FUTURES AND FORTUNES TOLD nailed to the eaves, hoping for a glimpse of a brighter tomorrow. The first ones to arrive each day were the women, many of them hungover, misused, abused, who crept out of their tiny shanties or out the back doors of the bigger brothels when the sun was high. Clutching pennies, they often came in twos or threes. They crowded around her mother, the fortuneteller, squeezing young Antonia back into the corner behind the curtain that hid the single bed she shared with her maman. They all wanted the well-worn cards or tea leaves to yield up promises of future husbands—tall, handsome, but most important, *rich*. Men who would love them and never leave them.

Later, when dusk fell and candles were lit, the men showed up. Most had clothes bleached colorless from endless prospecting, or powdered red from hard-rock mining, and faces gnarled and creased as old pieces of wood. The men never asked about love. What they wanted was for maman to take their hands, first left, then right, trace the lines across their callused palms, measure the fleshy hills and valleys across the span, calculate the shape of their fingers, and from this swear to them that they'd make it rich, if not today, then tomorrow, or maybe next week, but no later.

They all waited calmly enough, but weren't so calm when maman didn't tell them what they wanted to hear.

Antonia's fingers curled tight around the pistol. She clicked the cylinder from chamber to chamber, timing the small snap, snap, to the distant pounding of the stamp mills. Mind inward, she thought about the mysterious Mr. Brown and her mother.

Antonia had never met Mr. Brown. In fact, if it weren't for the hard reality of the gun, she'd have doubted his existence.

When Antonia and maman had lived in Denver, Mr. Brown had been a regular client. While Antonia was learning her sums at school, he'd slip into the hotel where they lived to have his fortune told. When maman talked to Antonia about his visits, her eyes would shine and the small lines between her straight dark eyebrows would smooth out. And she always smiled. "He's kind, Antonia, always polite, wears a top hat and fine clothes. A beautiful voice—he comes from over the sea, same as we did. Ah, but you were so young, a baby, you would not remember before we came to America. He listens and takes care of us. You know he pays for us to stay here, in this nice hotel? Someday, I believe, we will be a family. How can it be otherwise? He wants to meet you, soon. Then, you will see what I say is true."

Antonia didn't want to meet Mr. Brown. She and her mother were already a family. They didn't need a stranger in a top hat. They had each other. But Antonia couldn't say this to maman's shining face. She could only swallow hard and nod, hoping that, Mr. Brown or no Mr. Brown, they could stay in Denver forever so she could keep going to school.

But it was not to be.

In fact, it was Mr. Brown who sent them to Leadville. He *made* them leave Denver. Her mother said Mr. Brown had provided the gun for protection until he could join them, just as he'd provided the train tickets to Leadville, and the money for staying in the hotel until he could come for them. The hotel had been expensive, and so had the food. It wasn't long before the money was gone and no more came. After that, all they had left of Mr. Brown was the gun, a carpetbag of his clothes, kept under the bed, and her mother's unshaken belief that he would come for them…someday.

When Antonia had pressed her mother, maman had only caressed the gold and silver engraving on the revolver and gently touched the initials WPB carved into the ivory grips. "Why would he gift us with such a powerful means of protection, and so valuable, if he was not going to follow? Besides, I have seen it. I have seen you, *ma fille*, in a blue dress, so pretty, so rich, stepping from the train, and the men bowing to you like a queen. It will be so, because of Mr. Brown."

Antonia couldn't stand it when her mother said, "I have seen it." She always said the words as if there was nothing more to say, as if those were the final words, words that sealed the future. She hated her mother's faith in her second sight. That faith never wavered, even as they starved and lived in filth and even when the men hit her maman when she said things they didn't like and when some of the women shunned her—*she's a witch, she's a fake, she's a Gypsy.*

She hated it most when her mother talked about her own, Antonia's, future as if it was sealed and done, and there was nothing she could do about it. So, when one of the men, smelly and dirty, had come into their one-room shack while Antonia was there, and said, "Such a purty girl you got there, got such purty hair, all growed up, I'll bet, and eyes jest like your'n," and grabbed Antonia's long black hair with one dirty hand while he'd tried to grab the top of her dress with the other, she'd kicked him. Maman had leaped up, screaming, and the candle on the table had leaped as well, almost toppling to the dirt floor. The sudden tallow flare had flashed on the knife in her mother's hand.

And Antonia ran.

Pushed her way through the startled men waiting outside the shack and kept going, into the warren of shanties and cribs that clustered hodge-podge in the State Street alley. She kept running even when she heard her mother's screams change in pitch and volume. Later, when she crept back and saw her mother, face beginning to bruise and swell, Antonia burned with guilt for not running back to the shanty and beating the dirty man with her fists. Her mother had not scolded, but hugged her. "What could you have done, little girl that you are? You were right to run from danger. The other men, they came in and beat him, then took him away."

Always the men, that was who Antonia's mother turned to for help. Well, it would be different now.

That terrible night, while her mother slept deep under the spell of something from a bottle, Antonia had slid the worn carpetbag out from under the bed. Her mother didn't stir when Antonia extracted the shears and chopped off her own long, dark hair. Nor did she stir when Antonia dug deeper into the bag and pulled out Mr. Brown's togs.

Antonia could hear her mother's voice in her head as she undid the buttons and set them on the small table in the dark: *"He gave us his money, his clothes, his gun. He will come. I have seen it."* Her mother's voice ceased when Antonia ripped off her own bedraggled sweat-stained dress, and donned Mr. Brown's clothes: three shirts, no collars or cuffs, two pairs of trousers, one pair of suspenders, a belt she had to wrap twice around her waist, and a thick gray wool jacket, warm, soft, long enough to be a coat. She rolled the sleeves and trousers up, but the pant cuffs still dragged in the dust. Later that night, she stole a hat and boots from a drunk passed out behind the Silver Queen.

Or maybe he was dead?

Antonia didn't know or care.

He was a small man, but she still had to stuff the toes of the boots with paper and rags. There were always dead or dead drunk fellows in Stillborn and Tiger alleys, behind the saloons, dance halls, and houses. And, if you were sneaky and fast—she was both—you could snitch a pair of gloves, a copper penny, even a pocket watch, if you were careful.

She'd traded the pocket watch for a cap and a nickel from one of the newsboys, Ace, that little thief, who really should have paid her more. She'd taught him a lesson, though, by going to the newspaperman he worked for and getting herself hired as a newsie. Still, being a newsie didn't pay as well as emptying the spittoons at the State Street saloons, so she did both, and swept up the floors too, if asked. That was always good for finding coins in the sawdust, dropped and overlooked. Antonia wanted to buy a carpet for maman to cover the shanty's bare floor. And then, someday, she'd buy them both train tickets back to Denver, and buy a nice house, too, and they wouldn't need Mr. Brown or anyone, because they'd have each other.

A bird screeched from a tree, shattering her daydream. Antonia shook her head. She hadn't taken this precious time, when she could have been hanging around the newspaper office with the other newsies, or selling newspapers at the train station, or tipping buckets of spit into the alley behind the Silver Queen, to go off woolgathering about the future. Nope. She was here to practice on how best to kill a man with one shot.

She brought up the gun, sighting on the first bottle. The initials on the grip pushed against her palms: WPB. "Worthless Pisspot Brown," she whispered. "You ruined our lives. You made us leave Denver—for nothing. If you ever show up, I will kill you."

Sighting carefully, deliberately, from one bottle to the next, Antonia cocked the hammer and pulled the trigger, three times. One by one, the bottles exploded in a rain of sparkling glass.

Chapter Two

Inez Stannert paused in the process of disembarking from the passenger car at Leadville's Denver & Rio Grande station, one gloved hand gripping the hold bar, one foot planted on the step, and surveyed the scene. A tide of people poured out of the depot toward the train, pushing and jostling against a river of arrivals who pushed in the other direction.

Beyond them, the haze from coal- and wood-fired commerce blanketed the town. The miasma thickened to the east, shrouding the mining district that covered the rolling terrain below the Mosquito Range. A faint smell of new-hewn timber, still seeping from the station hastily erected the previous month, tickled her nose and mixed with the dust churned up from rutted thoroughfares by thousands of wheels, boots, and hooves. The noise of the train station rang in her ears—the sighs and clanks of the engine at rest, the rumble of carts full and empty rolling this way and that, passengers shouting to be heard above the racket, and the laughter of "well met!" greetings.

The familiar sights, smells, and sounds of the silver rush boomtown that was Leadville enveloped her. It was a place of constant movement, shifting dreams, and phantom schemes. Of silver wealth, pulled from underground by backbreaking work and tenacity, wealth that poured easily into the pockets of the silver barons, and squeezed to a grudging trickle for those whose hands brought it to the surface, to the stamp mills, and to the railroad for transport. The profits pulled from that mineral river also fed the businesses of the town, much of it finding its way to State Street businesses of entertainment, ease, and ill-repute. This was Leadville.

A home where fortunes were made and lost, often at dizzying speed. Where dreams were created and destroyed, sometimes in a toss of the dice or an assay of a claim. Where life could be snuffed out with cruel suddenness, in the dark of an alley, in the depth of a shaft, in the dusk of opium, morphine, or alcohol… or in the pain of childbirth. Leadville. It pulsed with energy, with drive, with purpose.

It was a mountain metropolis. Colorado's City in the Clouds.

It was—Inez took a deep breath, and filled her eyes and ears yet again—it was *home.*

As she allowed the familiar symphony of sights and sounds to settle over her, she detected a faint, discordant note. She cocked her head, still, listening intently. *That sounded like…*

Then again.

A shot. Distant. Not a rifle, most likely a revolver.

And again.

Well spaced. Deliberate.

She looked down at her husband, Mark Stannert, who had stepped off first, and was holding out his hand, patiently, waiting to help her descend.

"Did you hear that?"

"Hear what, darlin'?"

"Gunshots."

Mark glanced around the chaos of the station, giving the cacophony of people, animals, and machinery time to sink in.

A volley of shots boomed out, punctured by energetic hoots and hollers from the far end of the platform. People scattered away from the vicinity, leaving a clear view of a clutch of men, guns being reholstered, slapping one of their own on the back, then hoisting him into the air and bearing him away, with raucous cheers. "Sounds like someone's train's come in, in more ways than one," observed Mark. "Let's hope they stop by the saloon to celebrate."

"I know what I heard, and that wasn't it. Three shots. Deliberately spaced." She looked at Mark, who had removed his sober-as-a-judge black bowler and was knocking the travel dust from it. "Whatever happened to that ordinance forbidding the discharge of pistols within town limits?"

He shrugged. "It's not as if someone shootin' a gun is an unusual happenstance, even in town."

Inez shook her head, annoyed at herself, annoyed that the three even shots lingered inside her mind like an insistent echo.

Letting her gaze wander the forward length of the train, she saw that the outward flow of disembarking travellers had slowed to a trickle. Those impatient to board pushed in the other direction, maneuvering onto the train. Toward the rear, the baggage porters who had just finished emptying the cars were now busy dealing with an inward flux of boxes, trunks, crates, and mail bags.

A carriage, draped all in black and pulled by two black horses topped with black head-plumes advanced slowly toward a baggage car hitched two cars down from where Inez stood. A pathway opened up as if by magic as the funeral coach moved up alongside the sliding doors. Two somber-faced black-coated men, black crepe armbands visible over the sleeves of their coats, clambered out of the back. Up front, another man, dressed in a formal frock coat of similar midnight hue, looked around briefly, his eyeglasses catching a brief flash from the sun. He removed his bowler to dab at his high square forehead with a handkerchief, before replacing his hat. He climbed down from the funeral coach and walked to the baggage car to talk to the handlers, who had whipped off their peaked caps, in deference to the departed. The driver remained in place, holding the horses steady as the handlers jumped out of the car and began sliding the coffin from the back of the carriage under the direction of the man in charge, who Inez surmised was the undertaker.

Inez lingered on the top step, mesmerized by the sight of some soul departing for the last time from Leadville. "No more dreams and schemes for that one," she said half to herself. As if in agreement with Inez's assessment, the sun flashed off the sides and top of the coffin, just as it had from the undertaker's spectacles. It was, she realized, a metal casket, polished to a high, mirror-like shine, with gleaming gold fittings.

Inez noted the dearth of mourners: the two men who had accompanied the funeral coach appeared to be the only ones who were present to see the dearly departed on this final journey. They stood, hats removed, heads bowed. From their appearances, she surmised they were young, still approaching their prime, as opposed to the undertaker whose dark beard and hair was shot with silvery undertones. *Perhaps they are here to say farewell to a friend, a business partner. Someone wealthy, but new to town, and felled by violence or disease. Called home by grieving family on the sunrise side of the continent, or even over the ocean.*

Mark turned to look at what had captured Inez's attention. He shook his head, said, "I'm guessing no one we know. Those fellows don't look familiar to me. New to town, maybe, and one of them met with misfortune. So many, they come and they go, one way or another, right, darlin'?" The funeral carriage pulled away with a squeak and a rattle, to be replaced by the next of several baggage wagons, anxious to disgorge their own contents.

Mark resettled his hat and held out his hand. Inez accepted. Once she reached the platform she withdrew her hand, and gave her traveling skirts and cloak a good shake. Soot and cinders floated away on an October breeze that had an icy snap to it, a reminder that winter was stepping over the threshold to make itself at home in the high mountain city. She glanced covertly around the station as she fussed with her hat, tilting it a bit more to one side and straightening the travel veil. Mark caught her shifting gaze and his mouth twisted beneath his well-groomed mustache. "Expectin' someone special to arrive and deliver the eulogy, Mrs. Stannert? Or maybe a welcoming committee from church?"

She parried smoothly. "I thought Mr. Jackson might be coming to pick us up."

Her statement was a lie. He knew it. She knew he knew it. It was all part of the game they had been playing—thrust, parry, riposte—ever since they had reconciled in Colorado Springs. *If,* Inez thought, *reconcile was even the proper word for their uneasy marriage-bound truce.* And even that period hadn't lasted long. A few good days, a week, and they'd slowly, surely, started slipping back into their old ways. It had been, Inez concluded, an "interlude," and little more than that.

Nothing had really changed.

Any warmth that had ignited between them during their stay in the Springs with Inez's Eastern seaboard relatives had slipped away as the time to return to Leadville had approached. It wasn't just the air that got colder and thinner as they traveled from the Springs to Leadville, at the top of the Rocky Mountain range. The temperature between them had plummeted as well, growing frostier with every mile of track that clickety-clacked under the parlor car.

"Hmmm." Mark made a noncommittal sound. But its very neutrality indicated that, reasonable as her explanation was, Mark wasn't taken in.

The shadowed knowledge of Inez's lover—the Reverend Justice B. Sands—walked between them like a ghost, accompanied by the phantom presence of Mark's most recent paramour, an actress who had spirited him away from Leadville more than a year and a half ago.

Ignoring the chill cast by their shared infidelities, Inez pressed forward with her line of inquiry. "You did telegraph Abe that we were arriving on the afternoon train, didn't you? If he's coming from the saloon, he would need to be sure Sol is there to handle the bar. Otherwise, heaven forbid, he would have had to close it for the afternoon."

They began to walk together, side-by-side, but not touching. They paused to watch the regurgitation of innumerable Saratoga, steamer, barrel-stave, and flattop trunks from the baggage cars. The mountain of luggage was accompanied by a flurry of smaller hat trunks as well as more business-like industrial boxes and crates. Inez noted with satisfaction that her possessions were all present and accounted for.

"I sent word to the saloon yesterday, as to which line and when," said Mark, after he directed a baggage handler to their trunks and boxes so that they could be brought to the front of the station. "But I'd put bets on Sol bein' the one to pull greeting duty at the station. Abe likes to keep a personal eye on the goings-on at the saloon when we aren't around. Sol's good behind the bar, but still a bit of a greenhorn. Gets rattled when there's trouble brewing, not sure whether to step in or step back. Still, he's got a steady pouring hand, a good listening ear…just needs a little more time to age."

He placed his hand at the small of Inez's back to guide her toward the station door. Inez slipped away from his touch and began walking toward the station door at a brisk pace, remarking, "Too, with Mrs. Jackson still *enceinte*, I imagine Abe would prefer to remain at the saloon. That way, everyone knows where to send him a message when her time comes. I'm surprised that—" She cut herself off, not wanting to discuss such indelicate matters in public. But privately, she worried that Angel Jackson had yet to give birth. By late July, shortly before Mark's surprise return, Inez and Abe had teamed together to insist that Angel stop waiting tables at the Silver Queen. Although Angel's energy never flagged and she still moved about with astonishing speed and grace, her gravid body strained the fabric of her apron, and Inez feared she might go into labor right there on the sawdust-strewn plank floor. Apparently some of their customers feared the same thing: Inez had spotted them averting their eyes and shrinking into their chairs with shoulders hunched as Angel passed behind them, as if they were afraid that any slight touch would induce childbirth.

And then, there were the others, the drunken or not-so-drunken louts who leered and commented, acting as if she couldn't see or hear. Or worse, acting as if Angel was still one of the "working girls" at Frisco Flo's parlor house at the end of block, instead of being the proper married woman that she was. When the stares got too bold and the comments too loud, or if behavior moved beyond "look, don't touch," the perpetrators quickly discovered that Angel could more than hold her own. What's more, the owners of the Silver Queen did not suffer them or their foolish ways any longer than it took to toss the culprits into the ever-present mud and muck of Tiger Alley behind the saloon.

Inez's musings were interrupted by a small voice at her elbow. "Posy for a penny, ma'am?" It was a tiny girl of indeterminate age—Inez guessed four? Maybe five?—muffled in layers of rags against the cold, looking up at her through a tangled nest of hair. The flower held tight in her rag-wrapped fist was drooping and fading fast as the day's residual warmth. Inez bit her lip, then dug out a penny from her no-nonsense black reticule and placed it in the small palm, closing the tiny dirt-crusted rags over the coin with her own suede-gloved hand. She smiled at the urchin, shook her head at the proffered flower, and watched the girl scamper off. "Is it my imagination or are there more ragamuffins around now than two months ago?"

"Most likely you're seeing true." Mark opened the station door for Inez. "The train makes it easy for folks of all kinds to get here now. They land in town, families and young ones in tow, dreaming of easy pickin's. When the weather's kindly, hopes are high, and every one of them is sure they'll be walking around town like Horace Tabor, a bonanza king of Leadville, inside of a week. When reality sets in and summer disappears, then it's all shoulders to the wheel, from youngest to the oldest."

He glanced sideways at Inez. "Any pennies we hand out'll just circle on back to us when the head of the household comes in to the Silver Queen hankering for a shot of Jig Juice or Blue Ruin, a bowl of beans, or a lucky turn of the cards. It doesn't help to go sermonizing or fussing about it. If we turn them away, sayin' use those coppers to put food on the table for your family, well, those pennies will move on down State Street to some other saloon or a gaming hall or whorehouse. Money has no morals."

"No need to lecture, Mr. Stannert," snapped Inez. "I wasn't born yesterday, and I ran the saloon just fine during your absence. Abe and I kept the saloon a going concern and turned a tidy profit while you were gallivanting down in Denver with that floozy of an actress, Josephine What's-her-name. Besides…"

She looked him up and down, openly taking his measure: impeccable bowler, precisely waxed mustache, silver-and-gold-thread embroidered waistcoat, fine worsted sac coat and black trousers, gold-headed cane in hand. All topped off with a slight smile that invited confidences but didn't reach calculating blue eyes that took in everything. Mark looked every inch the prosperous businessman or cardsharp, which he was, on both counts.

"…Sermonizing isn't your strong point," she continued. "Leave the soul-searching to those who have a soul."

"Ah, could you be referrin' to Reverend J. B. Sands? The preacher who, before he found God, spent a fair portion of his life sendin' any number of souls to the afterlife to earn his living?"

The conversation, carried on in low but increasingly tense tones, was interrupted with a crash as the station door flew open to shouts of "Mr. Stannert! Mrs. Stannert! I say, hold up!"

Inez turned her back on Mark, bestowing a brilliant smile on the handful of nattily dressed nobs descending upon them and exclaiming, "Why, it's the merry Lads from London! You all appear relatively sober. How can that be?" Privately, Inez thought of the five top-hatted dandies heading their way as the "Lost Lads of London." The Lads, British remittance men living in the Colorado Springs area, had been shipped off from the seat of "the empire on which the sun never sets" by their well-heeled families. As to why they all ended up in Colorado, clustered in the Wild West of the New World, Inez had her theories.

At the first of every month, their living allowances or remittances rolled in—over the Atlantic Ocean, across the Mississippi River and the wide-open prairies, to renew the accounts of each highborn black sheep and second son. Such payments ostensibly allowed each castaway to keep body and soul together, in some fashion or other. In practice, however, come the first or second weekend of each month, they all bought tickets from Colorado Springs to Leadville, arriving in Leadville with wallets stuffed with banknotes and the devil in their eyes.

The result?

A bacchanal of high living in the City in the Clouds—spending freely on expensive cognac, oyster-stuffed quail, high-priced prostitutes, and high-stakes games of chance—until pockets and wallets were empty. As part of this routine, they made the Silver Queen their first and last stop. At the start, they all handed over to Inez any pocket valuables they didn't want to lose to chance or thievery, as well as enough cash to pay for return tickets. She would deposit everything in the Silver Queen's safe so that, at the end of their debauchery, they at least retained the means to return to the Springs. Usually Tuesday, although sometimes it was Wednesday or Thursday, they would straggle in, hung-over and depleted in more ways than one, collect their goods and their ticket monies. Down from the peaks they'd rumble to live meagerly on beans and beer, counting on the goodwill of the sizeable English émigré community in the Springs to keep them solvent and sated for the remainder of the month.

In the station, Inez held out her hand, wiggling her gloved fingers meaningfully. "Tickets, gentlemen." As they all began to pat down waistcoats and check pockets, she added, "I wasn't certain you would make it off at the stop. It rather looked as if you were intent on depleting the parlor car of all the high-quality firewater at their disposal, even if it meant traveling to the end of the line. Sir Daniel? You have your chit?"

Daniel Tipton dressed in an olive-green ensemble from boots to top hat, held his paper payment for return aloft between two fingers. "Much as I love the old D&RG—the founder is a good friend of the *paterfamilias*—there's no chance I would deplete my monthly remittance before bestowing a goodly portion upon the Silver Queen, the fairest drinking establishment in all of Colorado. Bloody perish the thought, Mrs. Stannert."

She slid the bills from his two-fingered grasp. "Why, thank you, Mr. Tipton. Rest assured we'll keep a stock of our best under lock and key until you gentlemen grace the bar. And I shall take good care of this, per usual."

One of Tipton's companions stepped forward, removed his top hat, pulled his safe-passage-home money from the lining, and handed it to her with a mock bow. His sleek blond hair glinted, putting Inez in mind of a light-coated otter, emerging slick from a river, while his mustache, waxed to sharp and vicious points, could have been whiskers.

"Thank you, Mr. Epperley," said Inez.

As the others jostled forward to hand in their paper and specie, Epperley tipped his hat back on his head, calling out the name of each in turn, "Balcombe, Percy, and Quick...sounds like a bloody bunch of barristers."

"Shut it, Epperley," said Balcombe. "Tipton and Epperley could be wool exporters or accountants, so don't be so snub."

"Enough," said Inez. "You all start squabbling and scraping now, the law will step in and you won't have an opportunity to sample the wares of State Street. I'm sure you all recall what happened last June, yes?" She tucked the money into her purse.

"Oh, June." Quick shuddered. "Perish the memory. Twenty-four hours under the auspices of the county gaol."

"Could have been longer," Inez noted. "None of you were being particularly forthcoming as to what happened in that suite in the Tabor Grand."

"That's because none of us could remember," countered Percy.

Inez waved a hand. "Off you go, gentlemen. I know you have your plans, and I do believe I see Sol—at last!—trying to squeeze between that nice cabriolet and the ore wagon. I hope he brought a large enough wagon to carry all our baggage."

The Lads headed off only to have Percy peel away from the group and circle back to Inez, rummaging through the inner pockets of his waistcoat. "Almost forgot." He pulled a rabbit's foot dangling from a silver chain from his waistcoat, saying as he always did, "Mind, you keep this locked up tighter than a State Street virgin. It's the left hind foot of a rabbit killed in a country churchyard at midnight, during the dark of the moon, on Friday the thirteenth of the month, by a cross-eyed, left-handed, redheaded, bowlegged Negro riding a white horse."

Inez rolled her eyes. "Of course. And I'll have it ready for you Saturday, should you deign to grace the Silver Queen's poker table with your presence."

He grinned, always jolly. "Right-o! And one more thing…" He glanced at his companions. They were busy appreciating the anatomical attributes of a young matron, who was bending over to straighten her toddler's skirts. From an innermost pocket of his jacket he pulled out a crumpled, sealed envelope and handed it to Inez. "Please slide this in your safe with the rest of the stuff. If I'm insensate when it's time to leave, perhaps you could keep it for me for a while, if you don't mind."

"Certainly." Inez weighed the envelope, curious. "Not empty, is it? Feels that way."

Percy gave her a sneaky smile and mimed twirling his small, neatly trimmed black mustache, even though there wasn't much to twirl. "Ah, that envelope holds a weighty matter. Inside, a fortune hangs in the balance. Wouldn't want it to fall into the wrong hands. Now, please tuck it away and out of sight in that reticule of yours, dear lady, and let's not mention it again."

He sneezed. "Oh dear. That's either a sign of good fortune or bad luck ahead. Surely the former."

"Bless you," Inez said, willing to encourage his superstitious optimism.

He beamed. "Good fortune it is. Thank you, Mrs. Stannert."

"Percy!" bellowed Balcombe. "Shake a leg. We're behind schedule. Mustn't keep the lovelies of State Street waiting."

He shouted back, "When we get to State, you must save one for me. I'll join you fellows after I have my fortune told."

Much grumbling from the others, and Epperley, the sleek blond impecunious otter, said, "Bother! Waste of money, Percy. Save it for better things."

With an approving nod and a parting wink to Inez, Percy sauntered away to join his brethren, saying, "Ah, but I just sneezed and was blessed by Mrs. Stannert. And don't forget the penny I found on our way to the station in the Springs. Heads up means good luck. I need to consult an expert who can divine what this all portends. If Lady Fortune is smiling, I must attend to her come-hither looks."

Inez slid the envelope into her purse. The Lads paused as they piled into a hired hack to hoot encouragement at the Silver Queen's barkeep-in-training, Solomon Issacs. Sol, straw hat askew, was attempting to maneuver a flatbed wagon toward the Stannerts and their luggage. It was only as he drew closer that Inez saw his face, red with exertion, held an uncharacteristically agitated expression.

"Mr. and Mrs. Stannert," he wheezed, sounding as if he'd pulled the wagon himself from the Silver Queen Saloon to the station. He jumped down, gave each Stannert a brief shake of the hand. "Welcome back, but…hurry!" He grabbed the nearest hatbox and looked around at the station and traffic, wild-eyed. "We've got to get back to the saloon and quickly!"

Chapter Three

Inez grabbed one of the hatbox strings before Sol could toss the box into the back of the wagon. "Stop! This isn't mine. Our luggage is over there." She gestured to the loaded cart behind them, and pried the hatbox from Sol's white-knuckled hands. "Now, what's wrong?"

"It's, it's…" He removed his derby hat and ran a sleeve over his forehead. His red hair stuck out wildly in all directions, although Inez caught the faint track of a part on one side and the wet, shiny look that indicated he had used pomade earlier in the day to tame the unruly waves. "Sorry. Didn't realize the traffic would be like this when I started out. Last night's snow melted away during the day and now it's tough going in the streets."

Mark gripped his arm, steadying him. "Hold on. Let the experts toss the bags and such while you tell us what's got you runnin' like a pack of wolves is at your heels." He caught the attention of one of the station's baggage handlers loitering against the batten walls of the station and waved him over.

As the handler obligingly loaded the flatbed of the small wagon, Sol stuttered into speech. "M-m-Mr. Jackson took off a couple hours ago for home. Mrs. Jackson, you know." He flushed even more. "Well, he thought he'd just be peeking in, not taking very long. But, he hasn't come back. And I knew you'd be waiting. I decided, well, actually, Bridgette came out of the kitchen and ordered me to come get you. She's holding the fort until we get back. It wasn't too busy when I left, so seemed a reasonable thing to do, only I hadn't counted on the jammed streets…"

Inez interrupted. "You could have sent a runner to tell us, and we would have just hired a hack, but no matter. We should get going." The wagon was loaded, Mark had tipped the handler.

Mark handed Inez up into the front bench and spoke to Sol, who had taken the driver's post, reins at the ready. "Sol, you take Mrs. Stannert and the luggage to the saloon, and I'll walk." He glanced down Poplar, calculating. "Shouldn't take me more'n fifteen minutes. I should get there quicker 'n you can in this traffic." Then, addressing them both, "I'd not worry too much about the Silver Queen. Bridgette's capable of pourin' a shot and chaser if someone's dyin' of thirst." With an encouraging nod at Sol and a tip of his hat to Inez, Mark set off at a brisk pace, his gold-handled cane swinging, his limp barely detectable.

For some reason, the fact that his limp—evidence of the broken leg that had set him flat on his back in Denver with the actress Josephine Young—had nearly vanished over the past two months now annoyed Inez almost beyond measure. That, added to the ease with which Mark took control of the spiraling situation, poured oil on the troubled waters of Sol's panic, popped her into the wagon and set off, not even consulting her as to her preferences or opinions, made her seethe. *He walks so carefree now, setting everything to rights with a snap of his fingers. And yet, he couldn't figure out a way last summer to send me a message that he was alive, couldn't figure out a way to get to Leadville until a year-and-a-half had passed?*

Sol clucked at the horse in harness. It pricked its ears and obediently moved forward a few steps, only to stop as a carriage swerved in front of them, its door swinging open before the apparatus had creaked to a stop, and disgorged a man—a traveling drummer, by the look of his wear-ever checked sack jacket, weathered brown bowler, and the small multitude of exhibit trunks and cases that tumbled out after him. He commandeered the empty cart the Stannerts had left behind, and began slinging carpetbags and small trunks into it with the help of the carriage driver. The train whistled a warning, and Inez heard the inevitable announcement, "All aboard that's going aboard!"

"Damn it!" shouted the drummer, throwing his hat to the ground.

Inez heard the inexorable chug-chug-chug of the train locomotive and the screech of metal on metal as the great wheels slowly gained purchase and momentum on the steel rails.

The hatless drummer clutched his hair in both hands, looking the picture of defeat and frustration. He said, "Devil take the *infernal* street traffic in this confounded town! The roads! The roads! The dang-nabbit roads!" It was hard to tell whether he spoke to the hired driver, who stood by shaking his head, or to the few still on the platform, or to the universe at large.

With the drummer's curses ringing in her ears, Inez stared at Mark's retreating figure. He'd crossed the track and was nearly down to Eleventh Street. It wouldn't be long before he'd cross over to Harrison Avenue, the main business street in town. From there, it was a straight shot to the saloon on the corner of Harrison Avenue and Second Street, which was still referred to as State Street, its original appellation before the city fathers had tinkered with the street names earlier that year. Center of the red-light and entertainment district of Leadville, West Second was still called State Street by all who had any acquaintance with its infamous commerce.

Sol tried to steer the horse around the hired carriage, even as the driver, apparently not wanting to be left behind with the cursing salesman, was back in his seat, urging his own team back into the sluggish flow. All was for naught, as the equine-powered traffic struggled at cross-purposes: some vehicles fought their way uphill to the mining district while the rest, Inez and Sol's wagon included, attempted to move downhill and into town.

The whole situation—the shouting, the carriage, the traffic, and seeing Mark recede, so carefree, moving forward without a backward glance—it was more than Inez could bear.

"Give me the reins!" she snapped at Sol. She snatched them from his astonished hands, and with an unladylike "Gee up!" gave the horse a stern slap. The animal, no doubt astonished itself, lurched to the left, angling past the carriage with inches to spare.

"We are *not* going to be left behind," she said through gritted teeth. "Did you come up Harrison to get us?"

"Well, sure, it's the straightest route here, ma'am." Sol clutched the front rail of the wagon.

"Straightest, but not the fastest. I'd think you'd know that by now. Side streets, downhill from the mines." She encouraged the horse, which increased to a trot, veering further to the left to round the outside of an empty ore cart, heading in the opposite direction. The wagon lumbered around a corner onto sparsely populated Fourteenth Street. "He's not going to get there first," she said, almost to herself. "Once he reaches Harrison, he will slow down, palaver, shoot the breeze. He's not in a hurry."

"Who?" Sol sounded confused. "Mrs. Stannert, do you want me to drive and you just tell me where to go?"

A warm destination in the afterworld popped to mind as a response, but Inez bit it back. Obviously Sol hadn't considered the ramifications of leaving the saloon with no one but Bridgette to tend to things. It was not really his fault. Sol just did what he was told.

With a more or less open road before them, the horse was happy to increase its pace to a trot at a flick of the reins.

"I'm sorry, ma'am. I thought of maybe sending for Mr. Jackson, but Bridgette, she said we shouldn't, that without knowing how things were going with Mrs. Jackson." He gulped back any further words as the horse, ever obedient to her hand, jerked around the corner onto Harrison. A wagon wheel bumped sharply over a rock. The trunks and boxes jumped on the flatbed with a thud and rattle. Inez scanned the road ahead. "It's not bad right here." She transferred the reins to one hand so she could adjust her askew hat. "Where did things clog up?"

"Well, it was bad all the way to the station, but the worst was around Seventh."

"Of course, a major route up to the mines." Inez directed the wagon to the left, passing several meandering souls on horse and mule. "We'll turn on Ninth and take Pine or Spruce."

She relaxed a bit. She knew now they would arrive first. That way, she could take measure of the situation before Mark arrived. She could talk to Bridgette and perhaps obtain a picture, untinged by Mark's asides and interruptions, of how business had been the past two months. Inez suffered a sudden pang of guilt for having extended her stay in the Springs so blithely. Until now, she had not spared much thought as to what the extended time away from the business might mean to Abe, Bridgette, and Sol. When she arrived, she could see if their usual customers were in their usual places for this time of day. Find out who had been by recently.

"Has Reverend Sands been by?" The casualness she injected into the loaded question sounded forced to her ears. A sideways glance at Sol told her she wasn't fooling even him. His face revealed consternation, and maybe a touch of terror. He shifted on the wooden seat, then grabbed it tight as they hit one of many ubiquitous potholes that graced the city's streets.

"Well?" She didn't mean that single word to sound as sharp as it did.

Clamping down on her own nervousness, Inez added a soothing note to her words. "I expect he's been back, oh, a month or so, maybe more. I also expect that he would have been by the Silver Queen to find out about our arrival." She took a deep breath. "He certainly knows Mr. Stannert has returned. I left him a letter."

Apparently her matter-of-factness did the trick and Sol's tongue was loosened—at least, in part. "Yes, ma'am. He has been by. A few times at least, mostly to talk to Mr. Jackson and Bridgette, uh, Mrs. O'Malley. He didn't stick around."

No, he wouldn't.

As the Right Reverend Justice B. Sands had told her, he'd given up guns, gambling, and liquor when he found God. Or maybe when God found him. She was not entirely clear who found whom, but it was apparently a mutual discovery of the spiritual sort. Inez had heard Reverend Sands preach forgiveness, tolerance, temperance, and understanding from the pulpit more times than she could count since he'd arrived in town almost a year ago. Yet, she still wasn't entirely sure what manner of God would countenance one of His chosen sharing a bed with a married woman—much less a married woman who ran a saloon, liked a "little something" in her coffee in the morning and a glass of decent brandy before retiring, ran a regular high-stakes card game with some of the wealthiest men in town, carried a gun, and didn't hesitate to use it.

But then, her own conversations with God tended to be of the "Where is the fairness? Where is the justice? Why does good get punished and evil rewarded, the innocent suffer and the sinners prosper? Where is the rightness in the world?" variety. Well, not discussions, really, they were more one-way rants on her part—often liberally sprinkled with the kind of language that was more associated with hell and damnation than heaven and salvation—because God never deigned to answer her back, at least in any way that she could ascertain.

It was a point of tense theological debate between her and Sands, but one that had not lessened the passion and fierce tenderness and longing they shared between the sheets.

"…and Mr. Jackson has brought in musicians during the week in the evenings, to draw in more of a weeknight crowd."

Inez realized that Sol had been rattling on while thoughts had swirled through her head darkening her mind like storm clouds over the sun.

"Musicians?" She turned onto Pine, encouraged to see that traffic was light.

"Mr. Jackson has been trying to find a good brass band for hire. One that isn't already working one of the other saloons and such."

Inez winced, imagining hour after hour of trying to hear and make herself heard over the energetic squawks, trumpetings, and oompah-pahs of the typical State Street brass ensemble.

State Street was just ahead. And, she knew from experience, that it would be as crowded as Harrison…its crooked boardwalks and streets pulsing with pedestrians and four-wheeled conveyances, men looking to celebrate or to forget by spending on liquor, cards, or women, while others schemed to increase their pockets and purses by supplying the same. With a sudden decision, she stopped the wagon, just short of Pine and State Street, threw the reins at Sol, and climbed down from the seat.

"I'll walk from here," she announced. "Sol, please bring the wagon and my bags to the saloon. Mr. Stannert's luggage can then be delivered to wherever his lodgings may be."

She snapped her parasol open to ward off the late fall afternoon sunlight and set off with a firm step toward the saloon.

Chapter Four

Turning the corner to head up State Street, Inez passed Frisco Flo's brick "pleasure palace." It sat, quiet and serene, waiting for longer shadows and later hours. Another saloon or two followed, then a couple of more-or-less respectable boardinghouses, and a gaming establishment with questionable "lodging rooms" above. The Silver Queen Saloon, splendid in her two-story glory on the corner of State and Harrison, was just visible over the false fronts of the neighboring buildings.

Inez decided to bypass the entrance that fronted the red-light district on State and enter by the Harrison Street door instead, to give her arrival a little extra gravitas.

She turned the corner just in time to see Mark slowing to a stop by the door on Harrison. He spotted her at the same time, smiled, and waited.

"Took the long way around, Mrs. Stannert?" he asked, reaching to open the door for her. "Where's Sol and our luggage?"

Before she could answer, a swirl of newsboys banged out the saloon door and converged on them. Mark grabbed for Inez's arm instead, to keep her from being knocked over. "Whoa boys, what's your hurry? You could mow someone down, travelin' at speeds like that, and lose a payin' customer."

"Mrs. O'Malley threw us out," grumbled the tallest, pushing his oversized bowler back on his head and clutching his stack of newsprint to his checkered jacket with a skinny arm. "Said we was makin' too much noise. Too much noise in a spit-and-sawdust? How we supposed to sell papers, just with a please-sir and a thank you? It ain't natural!"

"*Carbonate Chronicle!* Get your news from us!" chanted two other boys, each attempting to thrust a copy into Mark's hands.

Another urchin, wearing a straw boater several sizes too large, a little ragged around the rim, and dented in the crown, wiggled between them with "*The Herald!* Latest news from around the world and Cincinnati!"

An elbow-tussle ensued only to be disrupted by a fifth with ragged curly black hair tufting from under a faded red cap. He batted the boater off *The Herald* newsie, sending it to the filthy boardwalk, and announced, "*The Independent* tells the news with truth and integrity! We don't print lies. And we don't just repeat the party line of politicians, local or national!" A pointed glare with this last statement sent the *Chronicle* ragamuffins scurrying after easier prey.

Mark laughed, a touch of admiration coloring his surprise. "Looks like your silver tongue out-shamed the competition, son. Jed Elliston'd be mighty proud of your hawking on his behalf."

The boy looked more suspicious than gratified at the praise. His eyes, shadowed by the cap's brim, narrowed. "You know Mr. Elliston?"

"Of course. I happen to be part-owner of this here spit-and-sawdust, along with this fine lady you almost knocked into the street."

The urchin pushed up his cap, giving them the once-over. "You Mr. and Mrs. Stannert?"

With the daylight now full on his face, the newsie, Inez noticed, had very disconcerting eyes—one brown, the other greenish, almost hazel. Inez bet the newsie got constant grief and comments about the oddity, which probably explained why he wore his hat yanked down.

"We are." Inez disentangled her arm from Mark's grip and dusted off the side of her traveling coat where the newsies had bumped into her. "Any self-respecting businessman or woman in town better know all the publishers and chief editors of every one of the local papers."

"Doesn't hurt to know the scribblers and newsies as well." Mark winked.

The boy shook his head. "I didn't start no trouble. Just want you to tell Mr. Jackson that. Mrs. O'Malley, she can't tell us one from another. So's I just want you and Mr. Jackson to know that Tony Deuce—that's me—didn't start the bother and didn't cuss out Mrs. O'Malley when she said to shush. That was Ace that done that."

So, we have an Ace and a Deuce. Inez guessed "Deuce" was probably for the eyes, unless he was second in command of the ragtag band. Inez was tempted to ask if the other three who had scurried off might be nicknamed Jack, Trey, and Four-Spot.

Tony darted a glance at Ace in his checkered jacket, thrusting a paper under the hawk-like nose of a bespectacled gent. "Mr. Jackson, he's always nice to us. Lets us in to hawk our papers and sometimes gives us biscuits 'n pennies for emptying the spitboxes when they get full-like and it's really busy."

Inez stifled an urge to roll her eyes. *Abe. Always a soft touch for orphans and strays—or those asserting to be such.*

Mark nodded "It's a deal, Tony Deuce. So, how much?"

"Two cents, and a bargain at the price."

Money and paper exchanged, the boy tugged his cap lower over his forehead, mumbled a barely intelligible "Thank you Mr. Stannert" and beelined toward his companions. The newsies were now hustling a cluster of well-dressed gentlemen that seemed to be contemplating the odds of crossing Harrison to reach the Merchants and Mechanics Bank on the other side of the street.

"You shouldn't encourage them," Inez said. "It sounds to me like Mr. Jackson is letting kindness overrule good sense. I'd wager of the five at least two are pickpockets and probably a third is acting as someone's outside man, looking for an easy mark to steer to some shell game."

"Darlin', you are possessed of a magnificently devious and suspicious mind. No doubt they are just trying to make an extra couple pennies to put bread on the table for their families." Mark pushed the door open for Inez and swept the folded newspaper forward with a slight bow, an invitation to enter. "After you, Mrs. Stannert."

Inez closed her parasol and stepped into the comforting gloom of the Silver Queen Saloon: her domain and domicile.

Her first thought was that it was unusually quiet. All she could hear in those first few seconds was the squeak of chairs, a phlegmy cough or two, and the clink of cutlery on dishware. As her eyes adjusted to the light, she saw it was just as crowded as one might expect on a Friday before supper and quitting time. Satisfyingly populated, far from empty—the saloon was never empty except for the few brief hours when it closed in the wee hours before dawn. When the sun rose and the workday began, the Silver Queen reopened in time to supply flapjacks and a morning chaser for those who needed to dispel the fog before their shifts began.

"Long time no see, Mrs. Stannert!" said someone in the interior gloom. A sudden scraping of chairs heralded the prompt rising of the men in the large room, accompanied by greetings that included "God save the Queen!" It was a salutation that many of the regulars had adopted early summer, and much as Inez pretended to demure, she secretly enjoyed the honorific. It satisfied her to think that others viewed her and the establishment as inextricably intertwined, almost one and the same. It was even more important that this be the case now that Mark was back and moving easily into the accepted masculine role as chief architect and public face of the Silver Queen.

A slightly rumpled fellow from the nearest table, standing with the rest, tipped his hat and said, "Glad you're back, ma'am," and added in an undertone, "and not a minute too soon. That Mrs. O'Malley, she drives a hard bargain and wields a mean stick."

Satisfied that order reigned in the absence of anyone more ferocious than Bridgette O'Malley, the saloon's cook, Inez looked around the large shadowed room, finally spotting Bridgette behind the bar. Which was odd, as Bridgette didn't hold with liquor and focused on the victuals end of the business. The other oddity was the rolling pin she held in one hand and was tapping lightly, but meaningfully, into the palm of the other.

Mark brushed past saying, "Mrs. O'Malley, everything under control?"

She turned toward him, her steel-rimmed oval glasses flashing with a stray sunbeam that snuck in the door with them. Her stern visage brightened. "Why, Mr. Stannert! And ma'am! Welcome back!" She edged out from beyond the bar, ceding her position to Mark. "No problem, no problem at all. I raised five boys by myself, and a handful they were, not to be cowed by threats of a switching. This lot are easy by comparison. A promise of special cheese biscuits if they behaved, and the threat of cutting them off of all but black coffee if they didn't, plus a knock on the head if things got out of hand." Clutching the wooden instrument of pain and cookery close to her ample bosom, she approached Inez while Mark busied himself with removing his outer coat and greeting the men who had moved forward to order something stronger than coffee.

Bridgette continued, "And where is Sol, bless the boy? He was supposed to go to the station and meet you both. Did you walk all the way here?"

"Oh, he's on his way. I left him on Pine with the luggage and walked. He's probably making his way up State now."

Inez glanced at Mark. He was smiling and nodding as Chet Donnelly, one of the regulars, regaled him with a story of how he'd just offloaded a worthless claim for a "pretty penny" to a greenhorn. "Was like takin' candy from a baby, Mr. Stannert, you shoulda seen. I'd bought that hole in the ground for a spit and a song a whilst ago, hopin' somethin' had been overlooked, and was thinkin' of lettin' it loose anyways. I'd loaded up a shell with some high-grade cerussite, turned old Bessie to the drift face and let her go."

Mark said, "You know, Chet, someday someone's going to catch you at that game and turn a shotgun on you."

"They gotta catch me first. Anyhow, no sooner done, well, I done it a bit ago, but anyways, I bump into one o' those foreigner dandy types, all bright-eyed and hopeful, just across the street here. Tells me a prognosticator said that Lady Luck was smilin' on him, but he has to act fast. Well, looks to me like he's got gold burnin' a hole in his pockets and mebbe Lady Luck was smilin' at me, 'cause, Lady Luck's the name of my claim, and that's the truth. I showed him some assay papers that might or might not have been touched up a bit and offered to take him up to the district right then for a gander. He said no need, his mind was made up."

Inez was intrigued. "He didn't even bother to look at the claim?"

"I tell you, Lady Luck, she wasn't just smilin', she was givin' me for free what fellas gotta pay for on them fancy bagnios on Fifth." Chet beamed a snaggle-toothed grin through his bird-nest beard, obviously much pleased with himself. "He didn't want to wait another minute, just said, 'How much?' I named a lowish figure—was just aimin' to get it off my hands, ya know—and he didn't argue. Paid cash. That foreigner fella, just too greedy for his own good, probably thought he'd sneak somethin' over this old-timer who don't know nothin' for nothin'. Guess it's up to me to teach fellas like that a lesson, eh?" Chet caught Inez's eye and winked. "Buyer beware, eh, Miz Stannert?"

"They should certainly beware when you are the seller, Chet," answered Inez.

Bridgette nudged Inez's elbow with the rolling pin and said in a stage whisper, "Ma'am, a private word?"

Inez nodded and turned to Mark. "I'll go help Bridgette pull those biscuits out." She regarded Bridgette. "No word from Mr. Jackson?"

Bridgette nudged her again, toward the kitchen. "There's some things better not talked about in the company of men, ma'am."

Once through the kitchen's swinging door, Inez was hit with the seductive scent of melted cheese melded with warm biscuits. Bridgette dropped the rolling pin on the scarred, massive pine table, which was littered with pans of cooling biscuits. "Mr. Jackson, he came by a wheel of cheese at a bargain price, and now I know why, because it's starting to turn blue. I'm putting it in everything I make, before the mold eats it away. Cheese in biscuits, cheese on eggs, cheese in flapjacks, cheese sprinkled on the stew…I'm of a mind to make a cheese soup and be done with it. It's getting to the point when I can't stand the sight or smell. And I loved cheese, once. No finer delicacy back in forty-nine, when Mr. O'Malley and I were new to California and the goldfields."

"You brought me into the kitchen to have a private word about cheese?" asked Inez, as she reached for a biscuit.

"Oh no, ma'am, not at all, but please, help yourself, eat a dozen if you want." Bridgette ran a critical eye over Inez, from the top of her hat to the toes of her shoes. "You know, ma'am, I think that trip did you good. You look like you put a little flesh on those bones, which you certainly needed, and there's a nice color in your cheeks. And your hair has a nice shine. My lands, I do believe it's grown several inches in those two months you were with your sister and your boy down in the Springs."

Inez touched the chignon at the nape of her neck, wondering how Bridgette could infer anything about her hair length, being that it was cranked into a tight knot. Since she'd hacked off her "crowning glory" last December, Inez had been fighting the impulse to pick up a pair of scissors and do it again. As her chestnut hair attained a feminine length, Inez found that she mourned the loss of freedom that had accompanied short hair. "They fed us well in Manitou and Colorado Springs, all that rich food for the consumptives. Lots of cheese, butter, milk, fresh meat. Now, Bridgette. What did you want to tell me?"

Bridgette cleared her throat, and glanced nervously at the door. "We're worried about Mrs. Jackson, we being Mr. Jackson and me. She's well past her time, no matter how you count the months, and we all know, don't we, that she was in a family way before Mr. Jackson married her. Didn't matter a speck to him, he makes that clear, and who knows who the father is, what with her," Bridgette flushed, "well, with her past. But that's water under the bridge."

Bridgette took a deep breath. "Mr. Jackson, he doesn't hold with midwifery, and he's been saying that all manner of *women*— I can't really say whether *ladies* or not, but I expect more not than otherwise—keep showing up at home and offering advice and potions and such. Drives the poor man crazy, he calls it 'tomfoolery of the worst sort.' I don't know that I agree, I've done my share of helping with birthings in my day and know a few things myself. I offered to do what I can, but he'll have none of it, says he'll only allow Doc to see her, now that things are getting so out of hand."

Inez swallowed the last bite of the biscuit she'd consumed during this wandering speech and said, "What do you mean things are 'getting out of hand?' Is she delivering at last?"

"Well now, we don't know, do we? Mr. Jackson left in a hurry earlier today, and he's not back yet, and there's been no word one way or another. I'm nearly beside myself with worry. Mrs. Jackson, she's such a wee thing, and oh my, last time I saw her, well, I'm surprised she's still able to walk, that's all."

Inez had started unbuttoning her travel coat in the warmth of the kitchen, but now reversed her activity. "I'll go right away and either return with a report or send a runner."

"Bless you, ma'am. I just didn't want to go into all this with menfolk present. You understand. Speaking of menfolk…" her voice lowered again, although there was none but the two of them present in the cheese-filled kitchen. "Reverend Sands, he's back in town. He came in asking about, about…Well, he didn't know that Mr. Stannert and you were…" Bridgette stopped, uncharacteristically at a loss for words. "I didn't know what to tell him, ma'am. And he came back several times, asking if we'd heard anything from you, more impatient each time."

Inez's throat closed up. It felt as if a hand had reached into her chest and was slowly squeezing her heart, forcing all breath away. She gave herself a shake. *First things first.*

"The good reverend will have to be patient," said Inez. "After all, what's that passage from the Bible?"

"Love is patient and kind?" offered Bridgette. Then, seeing Inez's expression, she tried again. "Be patient in tribulation, be constant in prayer? Blessed is the man who remains steadfast under trial?"

Inez pulled her glove on. "I was thinking 'Admonish the idle, encourage the fainthearted, help the weak, be patient with them all.' Patience is a virtue, and who better to practice it than one who preaches it?"

She gave Bridgette's sleeve a little pat. "Besides, whose side are you on? When Mr. Stannert first returned, you flirted shamelessly with him and seemed to plead his case. Now that Reverend Sands has returned from his time away, it sounds as if you are taking his side."

"That's not a question for me," said Bridgette, peering at Inez over her glasses, "but one for you." She lowered her gaze to the biscuits. "I'd better take these off the pans and get them out to the tables. They all behaved themselves in there, and I did promise cheese biscuits if they did so. Now, ma'am, you should go."

Inez waggled a finger at her. "Bridgette, don't think for a minute that you can scold me and send me away like an errant schoolgirl. And don't meddle in things that aren't your affair." Wincing a little at her own choice of words, Inez added, "Please tell Mr. Stannert where I've gone, and ask Sol to put my things upstairs in my rooms when he arrives."

With that, she left the kitchen, passed through the saloon and out the State Street door. Setting her face toward the Arkansas Valley and the high mountain peaks beyond, she proceeded at a brisk pace toward Abe and Angel Jackson's home.

Chapter Five

Shadows were stretching up the street, which was beginning to refreeze into an unstable icy mush as she paused outside the saloon. A flash of red caught her eye, and she recognized the determined newsie, Tony, nimbly dodging traffic across State, weaving in and out amongst the churning wheels and hooves. He made it to the far side of State, and then, with a quick look around, vanished into one of the small openings between buildings. That path, Inez knew, spilled out into Stillborn Alley, the older and even more disreputable sister to Tiger Alley, which ran behind the Silver Queen.

What would such a young newsboy want with Stillborn Alley?

It certainly wasn't a place where anyone would buy a newspaper. At most, the denizens of Stillborn would scavenge discarded papers to stuff in the chinks of the sad hovels they called home.

It wasn't any of her business.

It wasn't on her route to the Jacksons' home.

It wasn't even particularly safe—although, she reasoned, it was safer now in the waning sunlight than after dark.

Still…

Almost as if under by a spell, Inez found herself crossing State and marching down the well-trod path between Bedford & Reed, Lawyers, and the Grand Central Theater, straight into Stillborn Alley. The alley was a labyrinth of irregular small hovels and shanties that formed French Row at the top of the block and

Coon Row at the bottom. The occupants of these two pockets of prostitution and attendant vices were separated by color of their skin but united in poverty and desperation. Most of the quarter's denizens were not visible, either gathering strength for the business that darkness would bring or still recovering from the previous night's commerce. A small slight shadow topped with red darted between two ramshackle structures. Inez stopped in her tracks. Tony froze almost at the same time as she, and they exchanged wary stares from a distance.

He broke eye contact first, pulling his hat lower over his brow and disappearing around the corner of one of the cabins. Inez pushed herself into motion and, as she passed the cabin, she took its measure, partly out of curiosity, but also out of caution. This was not her territory, and if it was the boy's, well then, best to be vigilant. There was no telling if he might be alerting a confederate to the fact that a well-dressed woman, not of the area, was wandering about…alone.

A board nailed above the door held the carefully painted legend FUTURES AND FORTUNES TOLD. She kept walking, keeping an eye out for the easiest way to head back onto State Street and out of the row. A creak of protesting hinges caused her to back into the shadow of one of the small shacks. The ill-fitting door to the fortuneteller's abode swung open. Tony stepped out, frowning, and looked around. His scrutiny passed over Inez without stopping. He either didn't see her, or dismissed her in favor of some more pressing concern.

Perhaps, Inez thought, the youngster was simply visiting the fortuneteller, hoping to gain word of a better tomorrow.

Scooting up a narrow footpath squeezed between a residence and a laundry, Inez emerged with relief onto State. She hurried in the direction of Pine as the sun continued its slide down the autumnal sky to meet the mountaintops.

Soon after Abe had married Angel, they had moved from his snug one-room cabin on Chicken Hill to the less populated, far west end of State Street. "Closer to business, closer to home," was the way Abe put it.

As she approached the frame abode, she reflected on how it seemed that, no matter where Abe settled, even if it was for only a night, he created a welcoming place. During the ten years that she, Mark, and Abe had drifted from east to west, they had lived a flowing existence, not lingering in any one place too long. Whenever they had the wherewithal or the need to lodge in a town, whether the lowest, shabbiest inn on the wrong side of the tracks or a gilt-edged hotel, they tried to stay in the same establishment, although that wasn't always possible. Still, some places would turn a blind eye to the color of a man's skin when the color of his coin flashed gold. Whenever Mark and Inez had cause to venture into Abe's domain, she noticed he had covered whatever bed was in the room with the same quilt, worn soft and faded.

"It's the one thing I kept from my life afore the War," Abe once told her, when the three were settled by a campfire, somewhere outside of Laramie on an unseasonably warm spring night. He'd pulled the rolled coverlet out of his saddlebag, and Inez had ventured to trace one tiny line of fine stitches with a tentative finger, exclaiming over the skill of the quilter.

"My mammy said it tells a story, but I never did have a chance to find out what that story was afore she died."

Inez paused on the small patch of dirt directly before the tiny porch, overcome by the tug of her memories. She shook her head, annoyed at the patina of nostalgia that washed over those freewheeling days of footloose camaraderie. Those times, they were no picnic. Sometimes their exploits set squarely on the right side of lawful and honest. Sometimes, they wavered on the border or tiptoed over into possibly criminal—should anyone catch them at it. A few frantic interludes saw the three of them just one whistle-stop ahead of the law or a tar-and-feathering. Then, there was the sometimes explosive nature of her marriage. Mark had a wandering eye and she occasionally retaliated in kind, out of hurt, out of anger, out of a need to kick him in a way that would wake him up, out of a desire to be loose of him, if only for a short while.

She had been sick and tired of it all when they'd blown into Leadville three years previously on a chill autumn breeze. Abe, too, seemed tired, perhaps close to calling the partnership off—tired of constant moving, of living in close quarters with a man and wife who just couldn't seem to get along but also couldn't be apart. They were *all* tired of life on the road.

Then, Mark had won the Silver Queen from a fellow in a high-stakes poker game, and everything changed.

Their timing couldn't have been better. The silver rush in Leadville was rising, gaining momentum, the steady trickle of prospectors, speculators, and investors had turned into a flood.

And Inez was pregnant.

Their lives glowed with the promise of silver. Property deed in hand, Mark hadn't had to work hard to convince Inez and Abe that Leadville would be a good place to set a spell, for them to build new lives. As a further incentive, as if they needed any, Mark offered that the saloon would belong equally to them all. Two men and one woman, two white and one black, they would share in the profits and losses. That was one of the things that Inez had loved and admired about Mark: he considered them all equal partners. In fact, he viewed her female presence and Abe's dark skin as advantages, not liabilities.

"Among us, there's not a sucker we can't swindle, a game we can't play," pointed out Mark. "Whether it's ladies only, no niggers allowed, or for colored only, not a door is closed to us."

Abe had agreed to Mark's Leadville proposition, not taking issue with the unspoken fact that, as man and wife, Mark and Inez ended up with two-thirds of the stake....

As Inez mounted the two steps to the porch fronting the small house, she became aware of a rising crescendo of women's voices raised in excited tones.

"Madam," roared a familiar indignant male voice, cutting through the chatter. "This is non-negotiable!"

Doc?

She lifted a gloved hand to knock on the green-painted door.

The babble was replaced by an unholy scream, causing Inez's ears to ring.

The ladylike knock degenerated into desperate pounding. "Doc? Angel?" she shouted.

The door jerked open, falling away from her fist.

Doc Cramer stood, glaring at Inez from behind the half-open door, one arm braced against the frame, barring entry. That arm and its rolled up sleeve was splattered and streaked with blood. The screeching continued behind him, high and inhuman.

Inez's hand flew to her mouth, "Angel, is she—?"

His gaze, unusually combative, softened not at all. He cut her off. "Mrs. Stannert, move to the side. Please."

This was so unlike the peaceable, excessively polite physician that Inez knew, the physician who called her "m'dear" and was inordinately fond of good brandy, that all she could do was obey. He threw open the door wide and stepped to the threshold. A dead chicken dangled from his other hand, dripped blood onto the neat plank floor. Without ceremony, he flung the chicken into the street. He then returned inside, disappearing briefly from Inez's line of sight. The screaming wound up in volume and pitch.

Other voices, decidedly feminine in nature, joined in, spilling protests. "No! Oh, no, Doc! Don't! Please!"

He reappeared with a small iron pot. A tiny ancient woman, scrawny as the chicken, back bent into a question mark, was now attached to his sleeve, tearing ineffectually at the cuff. Ignoring this human appendage, Doc stepped onto the porch. As he passed Inez, she caught a metallic whiff, glimpsed a dark, viscous liquid in the container.

"No more of this voodoo-hoodoo-flim-flam," roared Doc.

Inez had never seen him so angry, his normally flushed face pale, the jowls framed by graying muttonchops quivering. Without ceremony, he tossed the blood into the street. The falling curtain of scarlet splashed onto the chicken and splattered into the hardened dirt street around it.

The small woman ceased ripping at his sleeve, snatched the pot away, pushed past Inez with surprising strength, and scurried into the street. A liquid language—which Inez identified belatedly as a French patois—streamed from her as she retrieved the chicken, feathers now caked with dust and blood. She faced Doc defiantly. "No voodoo!" She raised the chicken high and shook it in his direction. A few feathers fell to the road. "For soup!"

Doc uttered a loud "harrumph!" He backed into Abe's house and immediately returned, gripping a small canvas sack. "And are you going to tell me that this," he pulled a snake out of the bag, "is also for soup??"

Inez involuntarily took a step back, before realizing that the reptile in his grasp was as limp as the chicken. Doc tossed the dead snake into the street at the woman's feet. The canvas bag followed.

The woman's seamed face collapsed further as she delivered a dark scowl at Doc.

He jabbed an accusing finger at her as she started gathering the scattered objects and stuffing them into the bag. "Madam, I am a *trained physician*. Do not try to con me with your tricks! I was in New Orleans after my years of service to the Union. I saw the insanity instituted by the Widow Paris and your ilk. I brought more men back from the edge of death with science in one week during the War than all of you with your chickens, *gris-gris*, powders, and incantations. Mrs. Jackson's husband has hired me to help his wife at this time, and that I shall do, without interference from you or any of the rest! "

The rest?

As Inez approached the open door, a tableau revealed itself: Angel, half reclining on a worn blue velvet fainting couch, pillows at her back and her feet, three young women clustered around her. Abe's faded quilt was spread over what would have been her lap—if she had one. Inez winced in sympathy as Angel struggled to sit up, fighting gravity and her gravid state. One of the women, a young mulatto with fine cheekbones and hair pulled tight and high off her face, patted Angel's shoulder and furtively nudged a glass on the occasional table at Angel's elbow.

Doc limped over to them, his cane and black physician's bag abandoned by the door, and barked, "What is that, Miss April?"

April looked up a trifle guiltily. "Nothing bad, Doc. I swear. At Miss Flo's, we were talking about how to help Angel. I remembered my mam swore by this, and she birthed nine."

Doc swept up the glass and sniffed, then shook his head with a small grimace. "Castor oil? Miss April, this will cause cramping of the intestines, not induce labor. If Mrs. Jackson imbibes, she'll suffer severe cramps, diarrhea, and possibly dehydration, all of which will do nothing but weaken her for the time to come. Better to use this stuff to polish the furniture."

His tone softened at the stricken expressions on the visitors' faces. "Now, now, Misses April, May, June, I understand you mean well. The best course of action for you is to return to Mrs. Sweet's and tell her that I said you could best help Mrs. Jackson by knitting baby blankets. Winter's coming, so blankets, caps, sweaters, that sort of thing would be useful." Doc herded the three out the door as Inez headed toward Angel. "Mrs. Jackson needs quiet for now, not a flood of visitors. And no more potions, pills, and various magicks."

As Doc closed the door behind them, Inez said, "April, May, June?"

"And Mrs. Sweet has recently added a July and August as well. I believe she is trying to entice visitors by conjuring up the pleasant months of spring and summer. Not that mud-season in Leadville could be termed 'pleasant' by any stretch of the imagination." Doc picked up his bag and moved toward Angel.

Inez was trying to help her sit up, if struggling to a seated position with a boulder-sized lump from breastbone to hip could define the motion.

"It seems much has happened in my absence," said Inez, "except for the one event that I felt sure would have come to pass." She smiled at Angel and sank down on the couch beside her. "Mrs. Jackson, how are you bearing up?"

Mute by choice, Angel cradled her belly with both hands and an expressive wince.

Doc offered, "Pains?"

She nodded, then tipped her hand side to side: *A little.*

Doc nodded. "That is good news, Mrs. Jackson. Those twinges are the forerunners of the moment we are all anxiously awaiting, none more so than yourself and Mr. Jackson, I am certain." He smiled fondly at her, before turning to Inez. "If you'll pardon us a moment, Mrs. Stannert, I need to check her condition."

Angel grabbed Inez's hand, the gesture and the plea in her eyes clear: *Stay!*

Inez extracted her hand gently. "I'm not leaving, Angel. I'll just wait by the hearth while Doc performs his examination."

Doc set his bag on the end table, unlatched it, and washed his hands using the nearby pitcher and basin. "Excellent. I do want to talk to you, Mrs. Stannert, once we're finished here."

Inez wandered over to the stone fireplace and picked up the framed cabinet card showing Angel and Abe soon after their marriage. Abe sat in the high-backed chair, eyes narrowed slightly as if he was suspicious of the whole process of having his image captured and held in a frame. The pressed somber suit, the loop of silver chain across his waistcoat, all bespoke of a free black man who had successfully made his way in the world. However, the clenched fists resting on top of trousered thighs and the lines and furrows on his face—rendered a deep dark brown in the sepia tones of the photographic process—signified that this success was hard won over hard times and many obstacles. Angel stood slightly behind him and to the side, the sepia rendering her smooth, mocha skin in a palette true to life. One hand rested on Abe's shoulder, the other splayed protectively at her waist, the plain wedding ring on her finger gleaming gold. A line of buttons marched down the front of her form-hugging bodice, ultimately surrendering to an exuberantly flounced narrow skirt. It was hard to recollect that this proper young matron, every inch the lady, had once been the prime draw at the brick parlor house owned by "Frisco Flo" Sweet.

A rustling of clothes behind her and Doc announced, "Done, Mrs. Stannert."

Inez turned around. Angel still stood, loose dressing gown draping her from neck to floor, dark tresses cascading down and over her shoulders. All she needed was a pair of wings, thought Inez, and she could pass for one of God's messengers. Although it seemed unlikely that any seraph would take on the rotund form of an overdue mother-to-be.

"It won't be long now, Mrs. Jackson. If you want something to do, I recommend walking when you feel the pains. But please, stay inside. You should not be out and about. Your water could burst at any time, and at that point, you need to send word to me."

Doc walked behind the couch to a sturdy table holding a white-and-blue china water pitcher and basin. He splashed some water into the bowl and commenced scrubbing his hands, still talking. "Mrs. Stannert, I sent Mr. Jackson to Chicken Hill to bring a woman I trust and know well to keep Mrs. Jackson company while he is not here. I must return to my surgery." He swiveled around, pale blue eyes taking in Inez. "May I ask you to stay here with her until Mr. Jackson returns? Welcome back, m'dear," he added belatedly. "I trust your visit with your sister and the young Master Stannert went well? Despite what I understand were some interesting developments in Manitou." He peered at her over the top of his glasses. "By the way, I should like to hear how that story ended sometime. And would very much enjoy hearing how your son is doing."

"Certainly," said Inez. She moved to help Angel back down onto the settee, placing a needlepoint pillow at her back. "Mr. Stannert is at the Silver Queen and will be running a game tonight for newcomers. I'm assuming poker, but we shall see. As for William," Inez opened her black-beaded travel reticule, "perhaps you would like to see this, Doc?" She added to Angel, "I brought it to show you."

Inez held out the carte viste to Doc. The image taken in Colorado Springs, showed William, two-and-a-half years old, seated with William's caretaker, Inez's younger sister, Harmony. The expression on his face was somewhere between suspicious and terrified. Harmony looked serene with large luminous eyes.

The paleness of her skin and the slight darkening of flushed cheekbones gave her an ethereal glow.

Doc took the card and examined the images. "My professional opinion: young William Stannert looks a hale and hearty youngster. His move to the East Coast appears to have suited him and his condition." He gave Inez a sharp glance. "You did the right thing, m'dear, in sending him back there. He would have deteriorated here in Leadville. I have seen the condition many times before and since. I believe it was only an innate stubbornness, no doubt inherited from his mother, that allowed him to hang on long enough to be settled at sea-level where his lungs could recover and he could regain his health."

Inez nodded, unable to swallow a lump in her throat. "It was the right decision at the time."

His voice softened. "I know it was difficult for you, but it's a testament to you that you selflessly gave him up to be raised by your family. Obviously," he tapped the picture, "William thrives. If he had remained here as an infant, the altitude would have killed him. His lungs were far too weak for him to survive."

Angel clutched his arm, alarmed, and shook it. He laid a calming hand on top of hers. "Pardon me, Mrs. Jackson. What was I thinking? I should not talk about such matters around you with you in your condition. You have little to fear. Mrs. Stannert's boy was born early, undersized, and in winter. None of which applies to your case."

Doc held out the picture to Angel, who snatched it from him and proceeded to examine it closely. He moved to the door, indicating with a slight tilt of the chin that Inez should accompany him. "How is your sister?" he asked in a low voice, as he settled his top hat on his head. "Consumption, is it?"

"Yes," Inez struggled to keep her voice low and neutral. "Her husband is doing everything within his power for her. He intimated that they might return to the Springs for a longer stay, perhaps semi-permanent. As to how she is doing, she is," Inez hesitated, "I think the picture no doubt tells you what you might need to know on that account." Harmony's thinness and the high flush in her cheeks, apparent in the photograph, were the tells that accompanied the body-wracking coughs that she tried to smother behind her fine linen handkerchiefs.

He nodded soberly. "Take comfort, m'dear, in knowing that recovery can happen. It's a throw of the dice, a turn of the cards. We physicians think we know it all, but a long time in this profession only humbles me and shows me how little we comprehend of how an individual's constitution responds. I say, with complete candor, that I know any number of consumptives who have relocated to Colorado and survived long, fruitful years. I pray your sister will join their ranks."

He paused, eyeing her, as if trying to decide whether to continue speaking. He finally added, "I'd hazard, from that picture, that she loves your son a great deal. You chose his guardian well. Perhaps they will heal and save each other, hmm?" With an encouraging smile at Inez, he opened the door and glanced back at Angel, still examining the photo. "And, Mrs. Jackson?"

Angel looked up.

"No more potions and pills, eh? Trust me, they do more harm than help." He started out the door, then stopped and turned to Inez once more. "Will you still have your Saturday night gatherings, now that you have returned? I do hope so."

"I plan to. Mr. Stannert and I, we have come to an arrangement. I will continue to host the regular Saturday poker games. Mark will hold a 'Friday night special,' open to visitors and others who have expressed interest. We shall see how it goes."

Doc beamed. "Delightful! If I'm not called away," he shot a glance at Angel, "I shall drop by this evening, give my regards to Mr. Stannert, enjoy the proceedings and my customary tot of brandy." He leaned in on his cane. "I don't mean to be a busybody or interfere…but I must say, I am glad to see the two of you seemed to have worked out your differences and are now in accord."

In accord?

Inez lifted her eyebrows. "Let's just say we've come to an agreement." Her mouth tightened—a thin smile that didn't reach her eyes.

Chapter Six

Agreement.

It hardly seemed the proper word for the legal horse-trading and fancy verbal footwork that had transpired between them the last week of their stay in the shadow of Pikes Peak.

Drawn up while they were in the Springs at Inez's insistence, as a condition for presenting a front of "marital accord," the agreement outlined how they would handle different nights at the saloon. With the saloon open six days a week and closed on Sunday, she wanted to be assured of not crossing his path every night and bumping into him behind the bar.

Inez knew, from her decade-plus years with Mark, that, even when she was raging at him, his charm and the passage of time had a way of damping the fire of her anger.

Furthermore, and most important from her point of view, their "truce" stipulated Mark would not interfere with the comings and goings of her personal life, nor would she with his. She did not want him trailing her about through any daily—or nightly—assignations and appointments she might make, and she certainly didn't want to know about what he was doing when he was not in the saloon.

Originally, they had thought of drawing up the agreement with Abe as witness, but after further thought, Inez proposed that they use a local Colorado Springs lawyer, someone unknown to them, someone bound by law to be circumspect. Abe, she argued, would soon be a father, with additional responsibilities and concerns. It wasn't fair to drag him into the middle of their private affairs. Too, deep down, Inez didn't want to force Abe to have to "choose" between her and Mark. The two men had met toward the Civil War's end in a Union prison, where Mark was a prisoner and Abe a guard. Against steep odds, they identified a mutual inclination for serious, no-holds-barred gambling and teamed up after Appomattox with the common aim of making a fortune along the war-weary Eastern seaboard.

At least that had been their plan until, quite by chance, Mark had sauntered into her life—the distant cousin of the nephew twice removed of a business associate of her father's or some such convoluted connection. A New York debutante, chafing at the restrictions, conditions, and plans for her future as dictated by her industrialist father and her conniving Aunt Agnes, Inez was more than willing to surrender to Mark's considerable charms and didn't hesitate to display a few of her own. They wooed in a whirlwind and then eloped. The twist to their story, Inez often reflected, was that, upon hearing of their exchange of vows, her wealthy father had disinherited her on the spot. "If you were counting on marrying a rich heiress, you gambled wrong," Inez told Mark on more than one occasion. This remark was always followed by an embrace and something along the line of "Darlin', when I met you, the only thing I counted on was makin' you mine for life."

During their tentative reconciliation in the Springs, Mark had as much as said that he hoped she would abandon the divorce proceedings she had put into motion earlier that summer. In fact, one aspect of their agreement, hammered out in the Colorado Springs law offices of Wingfield and Schmidt, Esqs., was that Inez would suspend divorce proceedings for a year. After that, if she still wanted to proceed, Mark would not fight it. "You will agree to plead guilty of adultery, desertion, whatever charges my lawyer decides will be best," Inez had said.

Inez could still remember how Oliver Wingfield sat back in his chair at that, raising both bushy eyebrows nearly to his hairline. He'd stared from one to the other for a moment, then, without comment, had leaned forward, re-dipped his pen in the inkwell, and asked them to repeat the conditions.

However, Mark had his own agenda, and made no secret about it when he enumerated his stipulations for Wingfield's busy pen. "Mrs. Stannert and I are to spend one evening a week in each other's company." He'd turned to her adding, "Just the two of us. No ghosts of dance hall girls or men of God hoverin' over our shoulders or whisperin' in our ears. Once a week, we go over the accounts together, talk about the business. Afterwards, we go out to dinner, or the theater. Sit and talk, play cards, like old times. It's only fair, darlin'."

Fair.

Mark, Inez knew, only played "fair" when he either didn't care whether he won or lost or when he had weighed the odds and calculated that "fair" would get him what he wanted. In this case, Mark had made it clear: he didn't want a divorce. Not now, nor later. Inez suspected that, deep down, he felt he was gambling for stakes higher than any combination of coins on the table. As such, he was betting that after she had spent a year in his company, settling into a routine that embraced them both along with everything they shared—the saloon, their business, their mutual past and their son—the walls she had erected so fiercely would come down, and that she would surrender. She had to admit, if only to herself, that there had been moments in the Springs, some evenings, a few nights, when the past year and a half and all that had happened during that time had seemed a dream…

"Your son. He is well now?" Angel's soft voice, throaty with disuse, broke through her thoughts.

Inez took the cardboard-mounted image from her. "Yes, completely. He is a happy, healthy two-year-old under my sister's tender loving care." She looked into Angel's deep brown eyes. "You will be a wonderful mother. Listen to what Doc says. He helped me through William's birthing. He will do the same for you and your child." She changed the subject. "Who was the woman that Doc was so angry at?"

"Oh, her. She is…" Angel seemed to search for a word, then shrugged. "The girls turn to her for love potions, spells for luck, health." Angel sounded dismissive. She sank back on the pillow, resting hands on her belly. "I just wish the baby to come so I can sleep."

Inez decided this was not a good time to mention that sleep would continue to be elusive after the baby's arrival, unless Abe engaged a wet nurse.

A knock on the door sent Inez hurrying to open it.

She fully expected to see the promised woman from Chicken Hill. Instead, she was confronted with two women: one tall and holding a basket; the other, small and bird-like, peering around with a slightly terrified expression. The basket-holder, looking exceedingly out of place for State Street, was dressed in the deepest of blacks—a jet-beaded silk mourning mantle with full sleeves and black silk fringes above a narrow black silk skirt. The veil of her small hat was raised, revealing a pale face haunted by eyes of palest blue. Light, almost white-blonde hair was smoothed and sleeked back to the point of invisibility.

"Excuse me," she said, her soft, well-bred voice evincing an odd uncertainty in the utterance of those two words. The woman held out the basket covered by a striped napkin. "These are for Mrs. Jackson, from the church."

"The church?" Inez took the basket gingerly.

"The church. Reverend Sands?" she prompted.

Cognizant of Doc's parting dictum—*No potions! No pills!*—Inez lifted a corner of the napkin and spotted a small clutch of eggs, a cluster of graham gems, a hunk of aromatic cheese, and a small jar. Inez lifted the jar out to view its contents.

"It's *confiture de myrtilles,* blueberry jam?" the visitor said.

The French rolled out so naturally that Inez was immediately convinced that she stood before a native speaker, which might, she thought, account for the hesitancy with the English words.

Inez nodded and stepped aside to let the two women in. "Thank you, I'm certain this will be much appreciated. I am Mrs. Stannert, a friend of the family."

The woman entered and brushed her skirt with the back of a black-silk-gloved hand. "How do you do? I am Mrs. Alexander. My husband runs Alexander's Undertaking. On Harrison?"

"Ah," said Inez, a little bemused.

"Yes. And this is *Madame* Drina Gizzi."

At this introduction, Mrs. Gizzi, who had lingered uncertainly at the threshold, stepped inside, pulling her paisley shawl tighter around her shoulders, lifting her chin, standing a little straighter. Even with her ramrod straight posture, she did not top five feet, and looked almost a child next to her companion. The long black braid that wound over one shoulder only accentuated her childlike appearance. In other ways as well, she painted a contrasting picture to the somber but expensively clad Mrs. Alexander.

Shoes that had seen better days peeked out beneath a plain maroon wool skirt that looked as if it might need a good cleaning. The rust-brown suede gloves clutching the good-quality shawl were mended with thread that didn't quite match. All this ran counterpoint to a considerable number of bangles that lined both wrists and a gaily striped yellow-and-maroon satin bodice just visible beneath the point where the shawl was clutched above her breast. Her hands moved nervously and the shawl fell away a little, revealing a striking gold-threaded sash about her waist, glinting with a hint of riches from better days. It was a strange combination, almost as if she expected to be viewed only from the waist up.

She put Inez in mind of a nervous twitchy bird, perhaps a finch. Her gaze darted around the room, and Inez could have sworn that Mrs. Gizzi was noting and accounting for each and every escape route. For the briefest of seconds, her examination settled on Inez. Inez noted, with an odd shock, that one of her eyes was a deep brown, the other a light blue-green. *I've seen that combination before, only more subtle. That newsie, Tony Deuce.*

"This is Mrs. Jackson, yes?" said Mrs. Alexander, looking past Inez's shoulder.

Inez turned around. Angel had managed to achieve a standing position unaided and had approached in silent, slipper-shod feet behind Inez.

"Yes, indeed. Mrs. Jackson, this is Mrs. Alexander and Mrs. Gizzi," Inez smiled encouragingly at Angel, and stepped to the side so she could approach her visitors. "They have brought you some victuals that even Dr. Cramer would approve of."

Inez turned to place the basket on the table. She turned back to see Mrs. Alexander staring at Angel's belly in a disconcertingly direct manner. "You are so blessed," she said. "I wish you well. The very best for you and your baby. That is why I volunteered to bring the basket and also why I bring *Madame* Gizzi."

She made it sound as if Mrs. Gizzi was being offered up as a gift, something to sit on the mantelpiece or to display on an occasional table in the corner. Inez said politely, "How do you do, Mrs. Gizzi. Are you from the church as well?"

Mrs. Gizzi started, then looked down at her gloves and began to remove them, as if just seeing them for the first time and abashed of their condition. "Ah. No. No church. But I know Reverend Sands. He is a good man. Always trying to help those in need. One of the saints."

"Indeed, he is a good man, an excellent man," interrupted Mrs. Alexander. "But that is not the reason she is here. She is my idea, and mine alone. *Madame* Gizzi is gifted."

"Gifted?" Inez began to feel like the situation was sliding rapidly away from blueberry jam and eggs.

"She has helped me see my girl, my child, my darling, my only daughter," said Mrs. Alexander. "And she will help you see yours, Mrs. Jackson. If I may."

Without preamble she seized Mrs. Gizzi's bare hand and placed it, palm down, on Angel's swollen abdomen.

Sudden apprehension coursing through her veins, Inez demanded, "What are you *doing?*" and started forward.

For a second, Angel stared uncomprehending at Mrs. Alexander, as if frozen by the odd turn of events, and then at Mrs. Gizzi. Her face filled with fear and loathing, and she hissed, knocking Mrs. Gizzi's hand away, before pulling the edges of the rumpled wrapper closed around her. Inez was grateful that Angel did not have a knife close at hand.

Mrs. Gizzi was staring at her hand as if it was on fire. Mrs. Alexander seized her shoulders and shook her gently. "What did you see, Drina? What did you *see?*"

"Mrs. Alexander, I demand to know, what is going on!" Inez started toward Mrs. Alexander, then became aware that Angel had backed away, across the room. Her normally warm-toned skin had drained to ash. One hand gripped a nearby high-backed chair, the other rested where Mrs. Gizzi had touched her. Her face was now twisted in panic.

"The baby, she, she will not know her father. I, I have seen it," stuttered Mrs. Gizzi. She had an unfocused aspect to her countenance, seemed unaware of the commotion further inside the room. "Beautiful, like her mother, but so much sorrow, much hardship and sorrow. And to have no father."

"Who's got no father?" Abe stepped in through the still yawning doorway, his face like thunder. "What the good god-damn is going on here?"

Chapter Seven

"Mr. Jackson!" A woman who apparently been following in Abe's wake, stepped around his scowling presence. In a startled instant before this newcomer turned to face Abe, Inez glimpsed the ebony equivalent of Bridgette—a woman of indeterminate middle age, sturdy and round, no-nonsense steel-rimmed spectacles perched precariously at the end of a determined nose. A tiny hat perched atop iron-colored hair wound into a tight bun. Her mouth was set with the certainty of someone who knew the right and wrong of the world, and knew that she, if no one else, stood on the side of right. "I will not stay in a home that profanes the Lord," she announced.

"Apologies, Mrs. Buford, but it kinda seems that all hell done broke loose here in my home." Abe glowered around at the assemblage of visitors, until his gaze fell on Angel, who still stood frozen in place, gripping the chair, wild-eyed as a feral cat clamped in a trap.

"Damn. Angel." Those two words, spoken softly, were shot through with concern. He started toward her only to be beaten to the draw by Mrs. Buford, who had been on the move before that second "damn" had hit the air.

"Now honey, Mrs. Jackson, you remember me, don't you? I'm Mrs. Eugenia Buford, from Chicken Hill. I remember y'all, back when you and Mr. Jackson jumped the broom. Now don't you worry about a thing," she cooed, putting an arm about Angel's shoulders.

"Let's get you settled and Mr. Jackson will shoo these nice folks away so's you can rest." Mrs. Buford tipped her head toward Abe and slid her gaze pointedly from the three women to the still-open door.

While Angel was being comforted and coddled, Abe turned his attention to Inez, the woman in black, and her companion. Mrs. Gizzi appeared to have shaken off her trance and was now shifting uneasily from foot to foot, eyes cast down, twisting the ends of her shawl in both hands. He stepped toward them. "Someone better tell me what's goin' on here, and that someone better do it on the double." He said this to Inez, but by the end of the sentence, he was looking hard at Mrs. Gizzi.

Mrs. Gizzi uttered a squeak and stepped backward. She hastily burrowed her hands beneath the shawl, as if trying to hide them, ducked her head, and glanced toward the open door. Not looking at him, she whispered, "No harm. I meant no harm."

Mrs. Alexander stepped forward. Head held high. "Mr. Jackson, this is Mrs. Gizzi and I'm Mrs. Alexander, from the church."

"I don't hold with no church," interrupted Abe. "That's Mrs. Jackson's doin's."

"Yes, well, we brought," Mrs. Alexander gestured toward the basket on the nearby table, "just a small gift to wish you both the greatest happiness. A baby," her voice faltered, "the greatest blessing from the Lord to man and wife."

"That be the truth of it," said Mrs. Buford from the couch, where she was settling Angel, tucking pillows all around her as if she was a fragile piece of china. "Children's a blessing, sometimes a trial, but that's the way of the Lord."

"Didn't sound to me like no blessin' was goin' on just now." Abe turned pointedly to where Mrs. Gizzi had been hovering.

She had vanished.

Inez rushed to the door and scanned State Street for a flash of maroon. It was as if she'd disappeared into thin air, the most insubstantial of apparitions.

Inez turned to Abe and shook her head.

Abe frowned at her, arms crossed, then swiveled his head toward Mrs. Alexander.

Without further encouragement, Mrs. Alexander said hastily, "My apologies if our visit has upset you and your wife, Mr. Jackson. *Madame* Gizzi foretells that you will have a beautiful daughter, may she always be a source of joy and pride to you. As for the rest, I do not know what to say. But seeing the future, by scrying, cards, or laying on of hands, is difficult and imperfect. We see and hear, but often do not understand."

A deep sorrow and pain seared through her last words. She looked down at her gloves, straightened one seam, and then said softly, "Please do not take what was said at face value. The truth only comes from the spirits themselves." She began moving toward the door, pausing before Abe and Inez briefly. Inez caught the glimmer of tears barely held in check. "Once again, as *Madame* Gizzi said, we meant no harm."

Head bowed, she exited, the hem of her black skirts whispering softly as it brushed over the raised threshold.

Once Mrs. Alexander was out on the street, moving purposefully away, Inez let out her breath, not aware until just then that she'd been holding it.

Abe uncrossed his arms.

"I had nothing to do with that. They just showed up," Inez said by way of explanation. "If I'd known their true purpose, I'd have closed the door in their faces. They ambushed me with the basket offering and talk of the church," she finished lamely.

"Uh-huh." Abe's noncommittal response only made Inez feel more responsible for the whole scene.

"Mr. Jackson," Mrs. Buford came up to him, glancing back at Angel, who was now resting in her nest of pillows, fatigue weighing her delicate features. "I brought the makings for chamomile tea with me. I'll make her a cup, now. Nothing you need worry yourself about." She patted his worsted-wool jacketed arm. "Now, that Doc Cramer, he did right in sending you to fetch me. He's fine, as far as all them doctors go, but I always say, no one who hasn't gone through a birthin' themselves can be an expert. I've had ten myself, all born healthy, bless the Lord, and I've delivered hundreds more in my years. Now, this is Mrs. Jackson's first, and they often come late. That baby's kickin' up a fuss, one touch can tell you that. Whether a he or she, you and Mrs. Jackson be holdin' that baby in your arms by next week's end."

With those encouraging words, she turned the pat on the arm into a gentle shove. "There's nothin' else you can do here but wait, and menfolk are no good at that, so just go on and get on with your day. I'll be stayin' here and I promise to send word to you and Doc when the time comes."

Abe nodded and addressed Inez. "Time we got back, anyways, right, Mrs. Stannert?" He went to Angel, leaned over, and murmured to her. She looked up, one hand left her belly to clutch his shoulder and draw his face down to hers.

Inez and Mrs. Buford pivoted around as one to observe the dark blue sky of an October afternoon creeping toward evening. A dust devil swirled through the street, pulling bits of paper trash in its wake. Inez caught the flash of a couple of golden aspen leaves in the whirling dervish. A puff of surprisingly untainted mountain air—cold and pure as crystal—tapped Inez's face, like the gentle touch of an unseen spirit. "Gonna be a long, hard winter," said Mrs. Buford calmly.

Inez pulled her coat a little tighter around her neck. "Aren't they all up here?" she responded.

Mrs. Buford's stern round face relaxed a bit. "That they are, ma'am, that they are."

"So what was all that about no father?" said Abe as he and Inez walked back to the saloon.

Inez wrinkled her nose. "Honestly, it all went south so quickly, I can't exactly recall." That, of course, was a blatant lie. She recalled very well indeed. "No matter. Just before they showed up, Doc had tossed out a hoodoo woman."

Abe raised his eyebrows and tipped back his hat. "A who?"

"A tiny woman, not much taller than Mrs. Gizzi. Are all purveyors of hocus pocus of small stature? She looked to be at least eighty years if a day. Spoke patois," added Inez. "New Orleans, I'm guessing, from what Doc was saying."

Abe grunted and tipped his hat forward over his forehead. "Huh. Frisco Flo's girls brought her 'round? Sounds like Madam Labasilier. Don't want her 'round Angel. Doc done right."

Inez blinked. "You don't believe in that sort of thing, do you?"

"I don't b'lieve in anything I can't lay my hands on, but that don't mean I turn my back neither," said Abe. "She's got plenty that do believe, even here. I was born and raised in the Crescent City. I know that, when I meet a snake in the road, I take a wide path around it and take care not to disturb its slumber." He turned an impenetrable dark gaze back to her. "Guess your return to town kinda got off to a rough start."

"Yes, well, it's been interesting so far," said Inez drily.

"So you and Mark bury the hatchet down there in the Springs?"

Inez tipped her head to one side. "We are on speaking terms. As for the rest, we shall see."

Abe grunted. "You two aren't gonna pull a fast one and sell the saloon out from under me are you?"

"What?!" Inez was so shocked she stopped, right in the middle of a wagon rut in the middle of Pine.

Abe kept walking. Inez spurred into action, hurried to catch up, thanking her lucky stars that she wore her wider travel skirts, which allowed her to match Abe's long strides. "Heavens, no. What would even make you think that?"

"You were both gone a long time. Not a lot of word comin' up mountain on what was going on down there. Not sure if you were maybe thinking of resettlin' down there or mebbe even moving on." Abe kept his eyes straight ahead.

"No! We're partners, remember? Three. All equal."

"Yeah, but if you two skedaddle, I can't afford to buy you both out of your shares." Abe turned up his jacket collar against a brisk puff of cold and shoved his hands deep into his jacket pockets, looking grim. "I plan on Angel and me stayin' put, leastways for a good long while. Just bought that house. I'm not lookin' to pull up and go elsewhere, much less pick up on wanderin' ways again." Abe glanced at her. "So, just wanted to know straight up. Don't be bluffin' me, Inez."

"No, Abe. I swear. Talk to Mark, he'll tell you the same."

He switched topics. "That reverend of yours been by while you been gone. I let Bridgette do the talking. Didn't feel comfortable in saying much beyond my understanding was that you were extendin' your stay so's you could spend more time with your boy and sister. Still, he knows, as everyone knows, that Mark was there too. I gotta say, your reverend didn't look happy."

"My reverend," said Inez through clenched teeth. She hated that appellation. "Well, that's my business and his, so thank you for not offering up any suppositions or notions for consideration."

"Oh, I figure I'd leave notions and suppositions to Bridgette. As you say, none of my business." He paused outside the saloon, one hand on the door, forcing Inez to stop as well. "Leastways, not my business unless you and Mark decide to make it my business. We got an understandin' here, Inez? I don't care what you do with your private life. One or the other, up to you. But if things go such that you're ready to move on from the Silver Queen, I'd much appreciate a heads-up."

"Not likely to happen," she snapped. "Leadville is as much my home as it is yours…and more than it's been Mark's, given all that's happened in the past year."

Abe nodded, then pushed the door open. "After you, Mrs. Stannert. Welcome home."

Chapter Eight

Concern about her maman's disappearance had fueled Antonia's never-subtle newspaper-selling style with additional obstinacy and aggression. Her heavy armload of papers had lightened considerably and her coin pocket had increased in weight as she pestered, badgered, and cajoled passersby on Harrison, Chestnut, and up and down State to read the latest offerings from *The Independent.* Twice more, she slipped into French Row to see if maman had returned. Occasionally, posh ladies from the nicer parts of town—West Fourth Street, Capitol Hill—would arrange for her maman to come to their homes. None of the hoity-toities wanted to risk their reputations or their silk and merino finery by setting foot on State, much less by wandering through French Row. But maman always told her of such visits ahead of time, or left a note.

This time, there was no note, no hint that she'd been summoned. It was as if she'd simply disappeared.

Down to her last four papers, Antonia decided to call it quits. The hour was edging into evening, and the lamplighters were beginning their chore of lighting the gas streetlamps on Harrison. Antonia hurried back to the shanty, promising herself that if maman wasn't there, she would wait all night if necessary. She'd invent some story later for Mr. Jackson, if he bothered to her ask why "Tony" hadn't showed up to empty the spittoons that night.

The one window in the shanty showed a wan flickering light behind the purple net drape. Heartened, Tony grabbed the latch and set her shoulders to pull the reluctant door open. She staggered backwards when someone pushed on the door with equal force from inside. Catching the jamb for balance, Tony barely stopped herself from falling prat-first into the refuse that had accumulated by the front of the shack. A tall, elegantly black-clad woman, black-edged linen handkerchief pressed to her nose, paused in the act of exiting, eyeing Tony. Tony stared at her—a *lady*, most certainly, Tony thought—as dumbstruck as if a circus elephant had appeared trumpeting through the crooked passageways of this, the most desperate part of town.

"I thought Drina said she had a daughter," the lady said in an uncertain, muffled tone from behind the handkerchief. "She never mentioned a son." Her eyes examined Tony's sweaty, dust-streaked face dispassionately with what Tony thought was a tinge of disappointment. The lady untangled the black veil wound up on her hat, pulled the opaque netting down, and adjusted it. Faceless, the lady now looked like some dark wraith, a poisonous spirit from beyond, come to wreak havoc on the living. Tony suppressed a shudder. Without another word, the lady in black turned and hurried away, disappearing into the lengthening shadows of French Row.

Tony rushed inside, clutching the handful of pennies and the prized quarter that Mr. Stannert had given her. She came up short at the sight of her maman, elbows braced on the table, hands clutched at the back of her neck, chin trembling, gazing at a slim pile of gold coins glinting in the candlelight on the table before her.

"Maman?" Tony felt her elation and pride ebb away, the coins in her pocket and the determined effort she had expended to put them there shrinking in significance compared to the lustrous treasure between her mother's propped up arms.

Maman looked up, stricken. "I shouldn't have said what I saw. But, she paid, she said I was to tell the truth, that it was a way to test me. To test whether what I said was true."

Tony crept forward, hugging the few crumpled newspapers to her. "Was it the lady in black? How much did she give you?"

"A hundred dollars," her mother said, voice rising. "But it was wrong, wrong. There are things that should not be said."

Tony shushed her, alarmed. "Someone outside might hear you." She glanced nervously at the thin plank walls. A hundred dollars! A fortune!

"We can buy train tickets to Denver," said Tony suddenly. "We can leave!"

Her mother swept the coins off the table into her hand. Tony heard the muted clink of metal trapped in her fist. "We wait," said her mother, in a harsher tone than Tony had ever heard her use. "Tomorrow, we leave here and go back to the hotel."

Tony stepped back, startled, confused. "But, Maman—"

"That way, Mr. Brown can find us." Drina rose, secured the coins in the knot of her waist sash, and fussed with it, positioning the knot to one side so it was hidden under her shawl. "He is on his way here." She spoke forcefully, with a certainty that stopped all argument.

Tony blinked. "You know this, how? Did he write to you?"

In the candlelight, her mother's eyes gleamed. "It matters not how I know. I know. As surely as I breathe and stand before you. You will meet him, at last, he will embrace you and take care of both of us. This money will help us all! Mr. Brown, he understands that sometimes, a misstep is necessary so that it can lead to better times. My mistake, it was a mistake to say so much, yes, but it will be our fortune. And Mr. Brown, he will come soon. Tomorrow. Maybe even tonight, he will step off the train and be here."

Tony's breath came out in a whoosh. "Well, I *won't* be!" She was shocked at the words that flew out of her, words she flung at her mother with the force of a curse. "I *won't* be here to meet Mr. Brown! I don't *want* him to take care of us! We don't *need* the bastard!"

Drina's palm slammed across her daughter's mouth, stunning Tony into silence. "How dare you!" Drina's voice, already wound tight, pitched higher. "You are my daughter! You do as I say. And I say we will be together, like a family. I should not have let you cut your hair, put on trousers like a boy, fight in the streets over pennies. Over *pennies*! I should have *forbid* it!"

"My pennies helped. I helped!" cried Tony, the pain in her heart worse than the pain in her face from her mother's blow. "You, me, we made enough to eat. Enough for coal for the stove. I was saving to buy a carpet for our…home." Even as she said it, the dream now sounded ridiculous to her ears. How could she have hoped to save enough for a carpet such as those she saw in the window of Owen & Chittenden on Harrison with the pennies and the occasional nickel she managed to set aside? She was as bad as those women who came to hear their fortunes told, hoping for things that would never happen, never come to pass. She was as blind as they were, scrabbling through their wretched lives, hoping for something better.

"Antonia." Her mother tried to hug her. "He will save us from this hell. You don't want to stay here, you talk about leaving all the time. You want to leave? We will, with Mr. Brown."

Tony ripped herself away from her mother's embrace. "I'd rather stay here by myself than go with you and Mr. Brown!" With that, she fled, tearing open the door, not bothering to shut it behind her, not daring to look back, running, zigzagging around the hovels, running toward State Street, the crowded boardwalks, disappearing, one boy among many weaving through the anonymous crowds of men, heading toward the warm seductive glitter of the Silver Queen Saloon and the work and pennies that awaited her there.

Chapter Nine

Inez walked into a very different scene in the saloon from the one she'd left about two hours ago. It was Friday evening, and the town was stepping up to meet for the weekend.

Most of the travelers arriving by stage, train, and carriage were in, and most of those had had time to check into their hotels, residences, and boardinghouses and were beginning to wander the town in search of entertainment and excitement. Many of those who worked in and called Leadville home, at least temporarily, had received their envelopes of pay for the week's labor and were looking to unwind on their ways home. Housewives waited anxiously or expectantly for those envelopes to appear, so that tabs at the butchers, grocers, druggists, dry goods, and mercantiles could be at least partially paid. Some workers headed straight home, but many lingered on their way out of the mines, mills, smelters, banks, railroad yard, and offices. Barkers and steerers worked the wooden walks on State, looking to persuade those drifting by to lighten the weight in their pockets, pay envelopes, and wallets in one or another of the entertainment halls, music venues, or saloons—large, small, mean, or elegant.

Entering the Silver Queen after dark on the weekend was to step into another world. The sharp temperature of a late October evening vanished, vanquished by the steamy warmth of the packed room. A shifting sea of men stood shoulder to shoulder and three-deep the length of the mahogany bar. Every chair at every table was claimed, while customers unable to gain seats stood clustered around their mates, staking their spot at the table with a shot glass, beer mug, or glass bottle. The cacophony of voices—bass, baritone, and tenor—were a welcome symphony to Inez's ears. She breathed deep, reveling in the visual and audio chaos, the pungent tinge of unwashed male bodies and alcohol a welcoming embrace.

It was then she realized how her time in the Springs had flattened all her senses. Conversation there had been controlled, men's voices muted and nearly overwhelmed by the overlying soprano and alto tones of the women. The scent of perfumes and toilet water wafted over each carefully prepared meal and recital. All movements were slow and deliberate. Nothing was brash, exuberant, or overdone. Ever. Whether taking the waters, strolling one of the many manicured "walking paths," or seated at dinner, everyone presented carefully erected façades.

Any visible display of a possibly strong emotion roiling beneath the surface was confined to the lift of an eyebrow, the small, barely visible smile or frown, a discreet nod or shake of the head, a deliberate turn of the head, the coded flip and twist of the fan, or the intentional inclination of a glove. At times, Inez had felt she was suffocating, in body and spirit.

Here, on a weekend at the Silver Queen, it was a different story. The noise, the smell, the sheer energy threatened to shake and shout down the walls of the two-story building.

"Guess we'd better get hoppin'," said Abe.

"Has business been this good while we've been gone?" Inez followed Abe behind the bar.

"You could say that." He pulled a clean apron from a hook, offered it to Inez, grabbed one for himself and snapped on a pair of sleeve garters. Abe nodded to Mark at the other end. Mark gave them both a casual salute before turning his attention back to filling a line of shot glasses. Each eager drinker slammed four bits on the polished wood surface before grabbing a filled glass. Mark pocketed the silver with one hand as he continued pouring with the other.

Inez removed her travel cloak, now wilted and streaked with its long day's journey, and donned the apron, wrapping the cloth strings twice around her waist. "I don't know why I bother with the apron," she said as she followed Abe to the middle of the bar. "This outfit needs a good airing and brushing." She wished she had time to change, freshen up, but it was clear that wouldn't happen for a while. She removed her hat, set it on a high shelf on the backbar, and pinned a straggling dark lock back behind her ear.

Mark approached them both, greeting Abe with "Mr. Jackson, any news on the home front?" He stashed the empty Kessler Whiskey bottle in one of the tin tubs below bar before plucking a full one from the shelf behind.

"No change," said Abe.

Mark raised his eyebrows at that, but only said, "Well, a full moon's a-comin'. Situation's bound to change." He glanced around the room. "Speaking of changing, think y'all can handle the crowd, until Sol shows? He left to take my trunks down the street and return the wagon. Back soon, I reckon. When he comes, I'll need to check the card room and get ready for the evening game. I kept back a suit for tonight." This last was directed at Inez. "Hope you don't mind me doing a quick change upstairs, darlin'."

Inez turned, brandy bottle in one hand, snifter in the other, and leaned toward Mark with a smile that would seem to indicate sweet words were coming. "Our agreement," she said softly into his ear, in a tone of poison, "was that *you* were not to *intrude* on my living quarters. Which are upstairs."

"Ah, but surely that does not include the office, wherein business is regularly conducted by you, me, and Abe," he responded, with a smile of equal charm. "A washbasin, a few minutes, and I'll be done. At no time will I breach the wall to your boudoir, on my word as a gentleman."

A fellow at the bar, the dust of the stagecoach still on his coat sleeves, interrupted their low-toned exchange. "Pardon, ma'am. If I might." He pushed a half-dollar toward Inez. "Four bits'll cover it? I have a powerful thirst. 'Twas a long trip from Chicago to Leadville."

Realizing it was neither time nor place to engage in a marital tiff, Inez turned her back on Mark, and said, "Of course, sir," to the traveler. "And how do you find our fair city in the clouds?"

After that, time speeded up and Inez's focus narrowed to the faces on the other side of the bar. She took orders, exchanged libations for lucre, accepted enthusiastic salutations from Friday night regulars, responded to queries from newcomers about the weather (pleasant, for October), the state of the silver market (most excellent), and the opportunities for investment in the City in the Clouds (never better).

"Excuse me, ma'am." The voice to the left was exceedingly polite. Inez, who was in the act of slicing up a lemon for a hot Scotch whiskey sling, paused, knife in hand, and looked up. Spectacles flashed in the lamplight on the wall behind the bar.

The undertaker from the train.

Still dressed in his formalwear from earlier in the day, the undertaker waited patiently, hat in hand, seemingly unaffected by the jostling and press of men around him. Slightly behind him hovered a tall, thin man, almost a living cadaver, with gentle eyes and sunken cheeks. Add a chin curtain and a stovepipe hat, Inez thought, and he would be a dead ringer for the late President Lincoln.

"I am looking for Mr. Jackson," the undertaker said. "I understand he works here. It's important that I speak with him. Is he by chance available for a few minutes?" At this, Inez's attention focused on the undertaker. Behind the glasses, his eyes were a startling green. His face was lined with a lurking sadness, whether induced by his choice of vocation or perhaps some other reason, it added to the overall sense of gravity and empathy he exuded. He added, "Pardon, I should have introduced myself. I am Mr. Burton Alexander." He turned to his angular companion. "And this is Dr. Gregorvich."

Inez offered a polite smile. "And I am Mrs. Stannert, owner of the Silver Queen Saloon along with Mr. Stannert and the aforementioned Mr. Jackson." She held out a bare hand, having set her gloves aside for her bartending duties. After a pause, Alexander gingerly took her fingers with his hand, which was gloved in immaculate whiteness. Dr. Gregorvich limited himself to a single nod.

Marveling as to how Alexander could possibly keep his gloves so clean in a city that prided itself in measuring its financial well-being by how impenetrably the industrial smoke and ashes filled the air on any given day, Inez said, "Mr. Jackson is tending center. I'll take you to him." Then, recognition of the name dawned. "Mr. Alexander. Are you the owner of Alexander's Undertaking? Françoise Alexander is your wife?"

"Françoise." The name was breathed out, seeming instinctive almost in pain. "Yes, yes. And we are here to…" He stopped and glanced at Dr. Gregorvich. Some invisible communication passed between them. Mr. Alexander shook his head, and then continued, "This is a matter I should discuss with Mr. Jackson directly, as it is somewhat private in nature. However, you have my measure, madam. Alexander's Undertaking, that is my business. I am located on Harrison, next to Dr. Gregorvich's offices. That happenstance has turned out to be a situation that encourages superstition and jest, but has allowed us to become well acquainted, to the benefit of all." He smiled briefly, then said, "If we might talk to Mr. Jackson now?"

"Of course." Inez moved toward Abe, keeping an eye on Alexander and Gregorvich to be sure they were able to navigate through the crowds successfully.

Inez reached Abe first. "Abe, two gentlemen want to talk to you. One is Mr. Alexander of Alexander's Undertaking."

Abe paused in the act of counting money into the box beneath the counter. "You mean…?"

"Yes, I do believe I mean. Ah! Mr. Alexander and Dr. Gregorvich, here is Mr. Jackson."

Alexander's mouth twitched, and he glanced around the saloon nervously. "I apologize, Mr. Jackson. I need to talk with you, somewhere private, if I could. I assure you, it will not take long."

Abe nodded back and glanced around the saloon, before settling brown eyes on Inez. "Can you two hold the fort for a bit?"

Inez gave him a nudge. "Go. The office is available. Or the gaming room."

Abe removed his apron and said, "Gentlemen, follow me." The three men proceeded up the stairs. Inez followed them upstairs with her eyes, then looked at Mark. He raised his eyebrows. She nodded, pointed at him and drew a line that went from his far end to the center of the bar. He nodded back, and moved to cover more territory while she slid over to do the same.

Soon after, a faded red cap bobbed up just above the level of the bar and she heard a determined voice say, "'Scuse me sir," the three words running together in a single breath. Inez leaned over to see what was transpiring on the other side of the mahogany slab. What she saw was the young black-haired newsie with the striking eyes sliding an emptied spittoon snug up against the rail.

"Tony?"

He looked up from under his red cap, eyes shadowed and wary.

"What are you doing here?"

"Emptying the spit-pots. Mr. Jackson said that tonight was gonna be busy, and you could use the help." Tony glanced at Abe, who was coming back downstairs with Alexander and Gregorvich. After nods all around between the three, Alexander and Gregorvich appropriated a table near the kitchen door. Abe came back behind the bar, mouth set in a tight line beneath his grizzled gray mustache, but that was the only sign that something had transpired during the conversation. Inez was dying to know what had been said, but resigned herself to waiting.

She turned to Tony, while pulling out a fresh rag from beneath the counter. "Mr. Jackson said, did he? Well then, you'd better get busy." Tony touched his cap and said, almost as an afterthought, "Thanks, ma'am. Mrs. Stannert." He turned and wiggled back into the crowd, heading toward the back tables.

Inez saw a spate of top hats jostling her way, heralded by distinctive and familiar, "Pardon. Bloody *pardon*. We're perishing from lack of spirits and refined company. Damn it all, let us through, we're good friends and business associates of the Stannerts and we…Well, hullo, Mrs. Stannert."

The Lads from London jostled up to the bar, with Lord Percy acting as point man of the patrol. Once he'd attained the bar, his compatriots spread out to either side, sliding the drinks before them to make room. The displaced patrons eyed the group sourly and there were some grumbles, but the evening was young, and as yet no one was itching to start a fight. Epperley slid in next to Percy, looking more bitter and tight-lipped than usual. Inez knew the young hotelier and manager of the Mountain Springs Hotel as a non-smiler, but his fair-haired visage seemed even darker than usual. "Damn it, Percy."

"Shut it," said Lord Percy loftily. "You're simply envious that you weren't able to partake of such a *unique* investment opportunity. Poor bugger that you are, having all your funds from now to eternity pouring into that white elephant of a hotel. I told you, once summer season's over, the debts would overrun any profits. You should've listened. If you had, you would've had a chance to throw in with me. To think, silver nuggets, lying around on the ground."

Alarm pricked Inez. "Percy, what are you talking about?"

"Met this fellow, just as we left you last, a prince of a man. Showed me papers, for his claim, Lady Luck. Offered to sell. Couldn't refuse." Percy's words dissolved and he sputtered, "Absinthe, neat, Mrs. Stannert, if you please. I have a serious need to 'smother the parrot' and get half-rats."

"You have a serious need of a bloody solicitor who can dig you out of the worthless hole you just bought into," snapped Epperley.

Tipton guffawed. "You just want him to pour his inheritance into the worthless hole you call a hotel and health resort in Manitou." He pointed at the highest shelf on the backbar. "Brandy for me, Mrs. Stannert. Best you have."

Inez raised her eyebrows but held her tongue, gathering glasses and bottles to prepare the potations. She knew Mark had held discussions with Epperley while they'd lingered in the

Springs. She knew Epperley had been looking for investors, and while she privately thought there was potential, the seasonal uncertainties caused her to caution Mark against it. "Too many of these resorts overextend for the summer crowd, and then, come winter, the crowds disappear."

Mark had shrugged. "Sometimes, darlin', you need to take a chance. Back the dark horse."

"Not with *my* money," she'd said with some asperity.

Mark had smoothed his mustache, considering. "Not *our* money, then."

At that point, she'd privately congratulated herself for keeping certain of her private funds—profits from business investments that Mark knew nothing about—apart and separate.

One of the regulars who had been squeezed to one end finally abandoned his post to claim a chair vacated close by.

His space was immediately taken by a vaguely familiar figure in a blatantly checked sack coat. A repetitive squeak-squeak caused Inez to pause and lean over the counter to see what it was he was hauling with him that made such a racket. He was maneuvering a trunk that was nearly as tall as he was, hauling on its leather handle. Fastened to the two lower corners of the trunk were a cleverly mounted pair of wooden wheels. The whole was obviously engineered to make it easy to haul the trunk and contents while walking over dirt and uneven pavement.

Inez removed a grouping of dirty glasses that had been shoved aside by the Lads, pulled a clean towel from the working bench beneath the counter, and wiped the area before him clean of spills. "Welcome to the Silver Queen, stranger. What's your poison?"

The newcomer, who was not particularly tall, draped his arm atop his large trunk as one might around the shoulders of a dear, but slightly inebriated friend. "I'd jump at a sherry and egg."

"Whole or yolk?"

"Whole."

Inez pulled a clean whiskey glass, poured a small portion of sherry, barely enough to slick the bottom, hunted down an egg from the sawdust-filled ice box under the back bar, and cracked it into the glass, making sure the yolk stayed whole. She handed it to the customer along with the bottle of sherry wine. The unbroken yolk glistened in the glass, cradled by the liquor layer. As he removed his rust-brown hat and set it atop the case and measured a tot of sherry into the glass, Inez took in his overall appearance with a professional eye. He had russet hair, slightly tousled, merging into side-whiskers. Combined with a sharp chin, copper-colored eyes, and restless hands, he put Inez in mind of a woodland fox. The face was unfamiliar, but the rumpled burgundy-and-tan checked jacket was the definitive tell.

"Didn't I see you at the train station?" Inez asked.

The newcomer placed his coins on the counter, then lifted his glass in a half-salute to Inez. "To Cloud City, where trains run on time, the road traffic is infernal, and wealth and possibilities abound." He drank, the yolk sliding from cup to mouth, disappearing under the mustache.

"You missed your train," Inez persisted.

He smiled. Teeth gleaming. "I had no idea I made such an impression on such a lovely lady."

"You arrived late and your carriage cut us off," she said calmly. "While we were trapped in the 'infernal' traffic, we witnessed your...tantrum."

"Ah." He sounded regretful. "It's the curse of a choleric temperament, as passed down by my father and his father before him. Ofttimes gets the better of me. Apologies if I offended."

"No offense taken. Missing the train is easy to do, if one doesn't know alternate routes that avoid traffic." She retrieved the sherry bottle and now-empty glass. "So what business brings you to Leadville and apparently keeps you here a while longer?"

"The name's Woods." The sherry and egg seemed to have added an extra sparkle to his eyes. "As for my business, a lovely personage as yourself need only ask, although I'm certain being a woman of perception you know the answer." He gave his trunk a paternal pat. "I'm in the sales business." He leaned toward her. "Ladies' unmentionables. Corsets and stockings, the finest of materials, only." Although his voice was confidential in tone, it was loud in volume. Nearby heads swiveled instantly in their direction.

One fellow in well-worn corduroys elbowed his way next to Woods, followed by someone who could have been his shadow, except his pants were of denim, but no less worn. "Whatcha got there, drummerman? Pretty lady things? Mebbe something nice I can bring on back t' my Carole Jane? Ain't seen her all summer, and this bein' well into fall, I gotta make amends for my absence."

The speaker didn't look like he had a cent to rub against another, but Inez knew from experience that sometimes the shabbiest fellow was the one newly flush with riches. They came from the gulches and the hills outside of town, having worked hard all summer and itching to spend some of the gains before winter closed in.

With a grin, the drummer stepped to one side, flipped the latches on the trunk, and opened it from its standing position, as if revealing the contents of a magic wardrobe, revealing the contents to onlookers as well as Inez. Inez almost gasped in delight, as her initial skepticism dissolved before the corsets— washes of sky-blue, navy, orange, and scarlet in silk and satin, frothy with ivory lace. A rainbow array of silk ribbons, cords, and ties looped like small, tame snakes on hooks along one side, as if all that was needed was the sound of a pipe to bring them alive and writhing.

All conversation in the immediate vicinity had ceased. Men jostled each other to get a better look at the wares. Even Dr. Gregorvich and the undertaker abandoned their table in the back to join the crowd.

Woods took advantage of the pool of awed silence in his vicinity to launch into his patter. "All the way from the new and fashionable Coronet Corset manufactory, located in Jackson, Michigan, we have corsets such as the Madame McGee, the Ladies' Favorite. From all I hear, it is the gentlemen's favorite as well." He wiggled his eyebrows suggestively. "All of which have many recognized points of superiority, are readily adjustable and conserve comfort, health, and *convenience*," he gave that last word special emphasis, as he held one of the samples aloft for better viewing by those craning to see, "in *every particular*. Provides elegance of contour, without interfering with the freedom and comfort of the wearer." He set a few items aside, continuing, "Also, I carry the celebrated Duplex corsets which have attained so wide a celebrity by reason of their vast superiority that it seems almost superfluous to more than mention them. Double bones and double steels, they are adjustable over the *hips* by strap and buckle and can be made to fit *any form* instantly. Then we have our specialties, imported from Paris, and I don't mean Paris, Kentucky."

The man in denim gripped his friend's shoulder. "Corduroy Dan, I don't think ya got enough to buy one a of them lady's unmentionables for the missus. They look like they'd cost all your whiskey money and then some."

Corduroy Dan shook off his friend's grasp. "How much for that there blue one?"

Inez cleared her throat, and caught the drummer's eye. "If you are planning to conduct business in the Silver Queen, we must first come to an…understanding." She placed her elbows on the recently waxed surface, and leaned toward him.

Woods shut the case. A collective sigh of disappointment erupted from the crowd around him, and even Inez experienced a sudden twinge as the colorful array disappeared from sight. The drummer then placed a protective arm over the lid and leaned in toward her, copper-colored eyes anticipatory, waiting.

"Five percent of whatever you make while selling your wares in the saloon."

"Ah, madam," he sounded sorrowful. "You'll send me to the poorhouse. However, I have heard good things about the poorhouse in Leadville. Decent victuals, and sermons on the Christian virtues of piety and hard work." His smile reappeared. "Deal." He flung the lid back up, and a frenzy erupted in his vicinity.

Inez immediately wished she'd asked for seven percent.

While Corduroy Dan began mining his pockets, extracting crumpled paper currency of uncertain denominations, other men crowded around, throwing out questions. "For any size?" "Got somethin' in red, with all that there lacy stuff around the top?" "How about silk?"

Even Mr. Alexander seemed caught up in the fervor. He had somehow made his way to the front and was perusing the corset strings with great solemnity. Inez had a sudden vision of Mrs. Alexander in a black corset, gleaming silver laces crisscrossing up the satin back panels. She immediately tried to banish the image from her mind.

Lord Percy elbowed his way to the case. "You said you have offerings from the Continent?"

Woods twisted around and Inez thought his cheerful voice cooled several degrees. "That I do. Paris, as well as a few specialties from the renowned Marie Grochovska, from a Varsovie in Faubourg de Cracovie."

"In scarlet?"

Epperley leaned in past Percy to rummage through the nearby items with a negligent hand. "In a *range* of scarlets, apparently. Must be a popular shade."

Woods said with stilted courtesy, "Please, do not fondle the merchandise, sirs. Might this meet your approval?" He pulled up a confection of blood-red satin, embroidering skimming top and sides in a flourish of flowers and leaves. "I warn you, this comes dear, as it is imported from—"

"Yes yes," said Percy impatiently. "Do you have two? I'll take two. With the same color laces."

"What the bloody hell do you need with two?" asked Tipton, giving the undergarments an approving squint through his monocle.

"Guess," said Percy with a leer. He turned to the room at large and, on tiptoe, held his glass of absinthe high. The liquid, lit by the gaslight, shone translucent and ethereal, a green beacon. "Let it not be said…" he began in a loud voice. The room quieted. Faces betraying varying degrees of curiosity, weariness, or hostility, turned toward the swaying Englishman at the bar. Percy backed up and started over. "Never let it be said that Winslow Percival Brown is niggardly with his women."

The clunk of a heavy object hitting the floor in the back of the saloon echoed through the floorboards, like the beat on a drum. An unnaturally high-pitched shout of "Worthless Pisspot Brown!" was closely followed by the crash of a pistol discharge. A metallic *ting!* indicated the bullet had missed its mark, entering the tin-plated ceiling instead.

Cards scattered, chairs overturned, and men dove under tables or crouched in place.

Percy ducked, clutching his tall hat to his head. Tipton's monocle dropped from his widened eye to swing tick-tock metronome fashion from its chain. Epperley's lip lifted in a snarl, his hand reaching inside his frockcoat for what Inez suspected was a concealed hip pocket holster. Quick—anything but—looked around, befuddled, with an "Od's bobs!" Balcombe merely held tight to his hot rum and said, "Breakers ahead, Percy. Whose sister did you despoil this time?"

Shouts and curses quickly filled the room, threatening to erupt into chaos and confusion. At the first rumble of disorder, Inez started to move toward the shotgun beneath the bar, but Abe was closer and quicker. Up came the shotgun, its cold double-eyed stare directed at no one in particular but everyone in general.

"Freeze!" he said in a loud voice intended to stop everyone in their tracks.

Everyone did, except for a flurry of men near one of the back tables. Abe continued, "What's going on back there? Someone, speak up!"

Inez pulled her Smoot Remington from her hidden pocket and hastened around the end of the counter. Mark did the same from the other end of the bar, and they converged on the melee.

"Young'un pulled a pistol!" someone yelled. "He was gunnin' for loudmouth by the bar up there."

A brass spittoon, rolling listlessly across the floorboards in an arc, dribbled its remaining contents onto a now-ruined scatter of playing cards before banging into a table leg. The brown puddle on the floor was being scuffled and smeared by the boots of three men struggling to hold a boy-sized tornado at the center. Inez recognized the red cap, firmly clamped down around the boy's ears. Short arms and legs windmilled punches and kicks at the barricade of men. What grabbed Inez's attention was the fancy pistol swinging free from a cord around his neck. The flash of gold and silver from the body of the gun, combined with what looked like a pearl or ivory grip, was wildly incongruous to the layers of raggedy jackets and waistcoats now twisted and pulled from around his shoulders.

One patron finally pinned Tony's arms back while another gripped the back of the boy's shirt, lifting him up on tiptoe, so he was forced to use his feet for balance, not weapons.

Tony's squeaks and sputterings resolved into "Worthless… Pisspot…Brown! You, you worthless piece of…you…my maman."

The Lads from London had peeled away from the bar, Abe's shotgun notwithstanding, and were advancing with a united growl like a pack of wolves. They brushed past Inez, pocket pistols and a pearl-handled derringer appearing from hidden dandified pockets. Sir Daniel Tipton was pulling a thin gleaming length of sharp steel from the staff of his cane.

She quickened her step to interpose herself between the murderous Englishmen and the still thrashing youth, who didn't appear the least intimidated by the top-hatted gang with blood in their eyes.

"What did you call me, *boy?*" said Lord Percy with a menacing drawl.

"You! You're a worthless, no-good, lying—"

"Enough!" said Inez.

Tony looked up at her, eyes shrouded behind a curtain of black curly hair. "Brown's a liar!"

She stepped closer, crouched to look him straight in the face, almost nose to nose. "Enough." The word was whisper soft but the threat behind it was heavy as a hammer on an anvil. She turned to the Lads, with Lord Percy in the fore. "We'll handle this, gentlemen," she said and repocketed her revolver. "Drinks on the house, for those who were offended and for those who stepped up to help. As for the rest," she looked around the room, calculating. Sol slid in the Harrison Street door, taking in the scene with a confused air. "House whiskey is half-price per shot, for the next five minutes, starting NOW."

Eager imbibers hit the bar like an avalanche driven by a deep winter blizzard. Inez gestured for Sol to get behind the bar and get busy. She turned to Tony's restrainers, who appeared torn between letting loose of the newsie and claiming their reward and staying put to help. "Thank you, gentlemen," Inez said. She stepped carefully through the slippery ooze of sputum and tobacco juice. "Mr. Stannert and I will take over in a moment. You needn't worry about the saloon running out of your favorite brand of spirits. There will be plenty for you."

Slowly, she untangled the leather thong that encircled Tony's neck, lifting the pistol and its lanyard free. She broke the cylinder, and emptied it of ammunition.

"I will keep this," she told Tony, holding up the gun, "and these," she palmed the cartridges, "until we have a full accounting from you."

Mark stopped beside her and eyed the newsie. "Probably ought to keep this as well." He lifted the cap off Tony, whose eyes widened then narrowed.

"Could tell you put a lot of stock in that cap, given how tight it held to your head," he said. "Gentlemen, to the kitchen with the captive and we'll take it from there."

Chapter Ten

Once the captive was deposited on one of the wood chairs in the kitchen, the captors departed, eager to claim their bonus for their work. Tony sat sullenly, arms crossed protectively over the two jackets and three waistcoats wound around the thin frame. Those unsettling eyes darted from Inez, who was guarding the door to the saloon proper, to Mark, who was standing in front of the door that led out the back to the alley.

Cap in hand, Mark regarded Tony thoughtfully, stroking his mustache in a meditative gesture. Inez's arms were crossed in unconscious imitation of Tony, the offending gun held securely in one hand. She had wound the thong around her wrist, a precaution in case Tony contemplated making a quick snatch and escape with the weapon…not that it would do much good, since all of those present in the saloon had been aware of the fracas. The newsie wouldn't get far.

Too, given the look on the faces of the remittance men, Inez thought Tony was far safer in the kitchen than out where they could get their hands on him.

Tony must have been aware of that, because the small figure slouched further in the chair with a lowered head, refusing to look at either Stannert.

Inez brought the revolver closer to the guttering coal-oil lamp hanging by the kitchen door for a detailed examination. "This is a fine piece. Very fine indeed. My first question to you, Tony, is, how did you come by it?" She turned to face the newsie. "And my second question is, just what did you intend to do with it?"

Tony glared at her, tightlipped, with an expression that clearly said that was the stupidest question ever asked.

Inez waited, undeterred. She was curious to see how Tony decided to respond. Would it be a mumbled unintelligible apology accompanied by a shifty visage? Or a whimpered, insincere "I didn't mean it!" reinforced with a sad-eyed, I'm-only-a-child hangdog face? Or, a wordless spit on the floor? Or…would it be the truth?

"Well?" Inez nudged.

The silence stretched out, broken only by a single sniff from Tony, who used a sleeve to scrub a dripping nose.

"Now, son," said Mark kindly, "we aren't the enemy here. If anything, we're just tryin' to save your hide. You tangled with a crowd that, well, they may look like Johnny-come-latelies and easy touches, but they'd slit your throat in a heartbeat. Especially once they get all liquored up, which I'd say they nearly are. We aren't going to be tellin' your stories to anyone. As for Mrs. Stannert, she's not likely to give you back your piece until she knows what's what."

"And I want the truth," Inez added. "I'll know if you're lying. Through necessity, I've become adept at telling when someone is trying to pull the wool over my eyes, as I suspect that you, despite your obvious youth, are also quite proficient at doing."

Tony glared up through straggling locks of hair. Inez was taken aback by the depth of rage in the childlike face.

"I was gonna *shoot* him," Tony spat. "That…Worthless Pisspot Brown!"

Inez's brow furrowed. "Worthless?" She held the revolver up to the light again, squinting to bring the letters into focus. "I see. The initials. What did you call him?"

"WPB. Worthless Pisspot Brown."

Inez gave out a "Ha!" of discovery, then said, "I'm going to show you something, Tony. But first, you must sit on your hands."

Tony didn't move, apparently bewildered by Inez's laughter and odd request.

"I just don't want you to try to make a grab and run," Inez explained. "That would be most unwise, and I don't want you tempted."

Tony cautiously shifted, sliding balled hands under trousered thighs.

Inez approached. "Now, as to these initials." She gripped the barrel, lanyard still wound around her wrist, so Tony could see the ivory grip clearly. The light from the gas lamp threw the engraved letters into sharp relief. Inez continued, "There are a lot of added flourishes and curlicues, which probably contributed to your confusion. Look." She traced the letters slowly with a finger. "W, R, B. Do you see? R, not P."

Tony frowned.

So," Inez continued in a conversational tone, straightening up, "the gentleman you are so eager to ventilate is not Winslow Percival Brown." She turned to Mark. "I had no idea that was Lord Percy's moniker, did you?"

Mark shook his head.

Inez turned back to Tony. "So, you'll need to come up with a word that starts with R to replace the P for pisspot. Rotten, perhaps? Worthless Rotten Brown?"

Tony looked suspicious.

"Don't believe me?" Inez said conversationally. "Well, we could ask Mr. Stannert, but you might not believe him either, think we're in collusion, perhaps? How about Mr. Jackson? Hmmm. Who else might you trust?" Her brow furrowed then smoothed out again. "You are a newsie for *The Independent*, yes? Well, if you hurry, you might still catch Mr. Elliston at the office. He often stays late, then stops by here for a libation afterwards, but I don't think you should tarry here this evening. It's not safe for you. Now, how came you by Mr. Brown's weapon and why are you so determined to turn it on him?"

"He gave it to Maman!" Tony's fists shot up and slammed the table. "He told her he'd come back for us. He didn't, and he won't! We wait and wait and she says she's *seen* him coming back, and she still thinks he will, but he *won't!* He won't *ever!*"

Inez retreated a step, taken aback by the venom and agony in the tone. The small-framed figure shivered with uncontained hatred. "And I'll *kill* him if he does!"

Inez had a sudden overwhelming desire to go to the newsie, now on the verge of tears, and envelope that shaking bundle of filthy rags in a hug. She reined in the impulse and gentled her tone to buffer any sharpness in the words, "Well, if Mr. Brown doesn't come back, you might find it hard to use this against him." She offered the pistol to Tony, grip first. "Put this away, somewhere safe. Others saw it, and I can't guarantee that they might not try to wrestle it from you in the alley some night. I have to say, I'd lay odds on you getting the better of most of them, through wits if nothing else." She smiled.

Tony wiped leaking eyes with a sleeve, embarrassed, took the gun, and lowered the lanyard overhead before tucking the weapon away inside several layers of waistcoats.

Mark moved forward and set the cap on Tony's head with a firm twist, then yanked it low so Tony had to peer up through tangled bangs. "Mrs. Stannert's no fool, so best listen to her advice. Find a secure place to leave Mr. Brown's fancy firearm, maybe with Mr. Elliston, or you could leave it here with us and we'll put it in the safe for you. Find something a little less flashy to protect yourself with. Best you make yourself scarce around State Street for the next few days. Those fellas are only here through Monday or Tuesday, then they return from whence they came. By the time they return next month, they won't recollect any of this."

Mark moved to the stove, grabbed a nearby tin plate, and piled some of Bridgette's biscuits onto it and brought it back to Tony. "Now, take this along to your mama. Don't eat them all at once, got it, sport? Return the tin when you can."

Bypassing the plate itself, the newsie stuffed the biscuits into inner and outer pockets. Finally, jacket bulging, Tony glanced covertly at Inez. "C'n I have my cartridges?"

Inez frowned and looked at Mark.

Mark said, "Promise no shootin' at someone unless they shoot first?"

Tony nodded.

After a moment's close scrutiny, Mark said, "Might as well, Mrs. Stannert. No doubt there's more where they came from."

Inez pulled the rounds out of her pocket and reached to tuck them into the newsie's breast pocket. Tony shied away from her touch and held out an open hand. Inez dropped the shells into the dirty palm. Tony muttered, "Thanks."

Mark held open the back door, and Tony stepped into the alley.

Inez moved next to Mark to observe Tony disappear into the murky darkness.

She turned to her husband. "Well, Mr. Stannert. Shall we place bets? Tony's real name: Antonia, or Antoinette, or…?"

Chapter Eleven

Mark turned to Inez. "I'd wager that her name isn't even close to 'Tony.' If she's as smart as she seems, she'd choose a moniker far afield from the original. She could be a Caterina, Soledad, Mary, Sarah, Eliza."

"I'd wager not," countered Inez. "If she has family with her here in Leadville—and it sounds like there is at least a mother, so perhaps younger siblings, what-have-you—I'm guessing whatever she chooses to call herself is close enough to her real name to lessen confusion. She's young. Not some well-traveled confidence trickster."

Mark shrugged and followed Inez to the swinging kitchen door. "Ask her yourself sometime. Better yet, ask Abe, since he's the one who hired her. Maybe he knows her story."

Inez paused, hand on the door. "In fact, I believe I met her mother, earlier today. Did you notice Tony's eyes just now? One brown, the other more a green?"

Mark nodded. Unusual. Keeps that cap pulled down low when she sells papers and is working in the saloon, so they aren't obvious."

"Well, I saw a woman with a similar odd pairing today, only she had one brown eye and the other was of a blueish hue."

At the staircase, they parted ways, Mark heading up to ready himself and the card room for the evening's visitors, and Inez to the bar to talk to Abe and check on the drummer.

Woods was comfortably settled on the State Street end of the bar. One elbow rested atop his shut trunk, and he appeared to be lingering over another sherry and egg. "Mrs. Stannert," he said jovially, "thank you for allowing me to set up shop in your establishment this evening." He lowered his voice. "I almost sold out of what I had. If you would permit me to return tomorrow evening, once I've restocked my case with what I have in the hotel, I believe it would be profitable for us all."

He slid a large pile of receipts across the top of the bar to her. "All in all, I sold two hundred fifty-five dollars' worth of ladies' unmentionables. You are welcome to check my numbers and I'll pick up the receipts tomorrow at your convenience." He floated two five-dollar bills and a pair of well-used one-dollar notes atop the receipts and added six bits. "Five percent of total sales. As agreed upon, yes?"

Inez eyed the pile of scribbled bills of sale. Two hundred fifty-five dollars. In less than an hour.

"Thank you, Mr. Woods." She took the receipts and thumbed through them, curious at the chicken scratches that accompanied each numerical total. "You take notes?"

"Every place I go," he said. "I have my own system. I get the name and what they bought. That way, when I come back to the Silver Queen and Mr. Smith pops up again, I'm more likely to remember and say, 'So, how did Mrs. Smith like the silk stockings you bought last time?'" He looked a little chagrined. "Sometimes, the stockings aren't for Mrs. Smith at all. So if he doesn't say 'for the missus' or what have you, I keep it simple."

Inez took the receipts and the money, and placed them in the lockbox. "Of course, this venture is more profitable for you. I lose the space along the bar for those with a thirst for liquor and lose the attention of those who might partake of a game of chance."

He raised his eyebrows. "Ah! She looks for an increase in the house take. So, what do you propose, Mrs. Stannert?"

"Ten percent of total sales," she said promptly.

"Not enough of a profit to make it worth my while. Seven-and-a-half."

Inez regarded him as she pulled out a shot glass and set it by his hand. "Ah, but think what you'd save on shoe leather and time. You hold court at the bar, right here by the State Street entrance." She pulled out a second shot glass and set it by the first. "And, the customers come to you. Plus, no dealing with the slammed doors in your face and the 'infernal' street traffic, which as you probably know, is even more difficult to negotiate on foot. Particularly when wheeling your wares around with you." She set a bottle of the better whiskey between the two glasses. "Eight and a quarter percent."

He cocked his head, apparently pondering, reminding Inez even more of some sly check-coated Reynard from children's fables, then broke into a smile. "I cannot help but admire a woman who presents a compelling argument and drives a hard bargain. Flat eight and call it done."

"Done." She opened the bottle and tipped a measure into each glass. "Do suggest that your buyers celebrate their purchases with a liquid libation, if you don't mind."

"My pleasure."

They raised their glasses to each other and drank.

The whiskey slid down her throat, a stinging burn that melted into a warm, breathless welcome. She sighed with pleasure, then opened her eyes with a start, realizing she'd inadvertently closed them during their toast.

Woods' wildwood russet eyes were upon her, calculating, while a knowing smile played about his face. The expression shifted and disappeared. "Ah, yes. One more thing. I almost, but not quite, forgot." He dropped his gaze, rummaging through the left pocket of his jacket, and then the right. "I held these back for you, as a thank you for allowing me to conduct my business here at the Silver Queen."

From his pocket he pulled silver and gold silk, smooth but strong as steel, twined and woven into a single cord, then pulled out its twin as well. He placed the tangle of metallic-themed corset laces on top of the counter.

"I do not mean to be forward," he added quickly. "Consider it my equivalent of your whiskey offering, just now. I had exactly two pair on this trip. Sold one just now, and kept this back for you."

Inez picked up the cords, aware that the nearest customers had stopped their conversation and were eyeing the laces with interest. The laces gleamed, a whispered reminder of the two metals that brought Leadville her fame. Gold had been discovered in the early 1860s, only to be overshadowed by the enormous silver rush that followed. Inez had a sudden vision of Reverend Sands' face, up close to hers, his hands tracing the path of those laces down the length of her back stays, their breath mingling as their lips met in a kiss…

A delicious shudder raced through her, and the vision vanished. Inez closed her fingers tight around the cords. It was the clearest she'd seen his face, felt his presence, in weeks. Bowing her head to hide the flush climbing up her neck to her cheeks, she stuffed the laces into her pocket, where they tangled against her revolver. "Most kind," she said briskly. "I shall go over the accounts you've left with me, and we shall see you tomorrow. What time shall we expect you? Five? Six?"

"Six is perfect." He pulled the case off the counter, clapped his hat on his head, and paused. "That set from the continent, you know who I mean." Dislike colored his words. "After that one fellow bought two foundation undergarments, the rest decided to follow suit. They bought me out of everything I had in red, including stocking and laces. Would you say that is a popular hue among the general population? Should I come prepared for more interest in that color versus the others?"

"I'm no expert in what the ladies of Leadville wear beneath their shirtwaists," said Inez drily. "However, beyond that door is State Street, the red-light district. I'd hazard a guess that you cannot go wrong with red, and probably black as well."

He smiled, tipped his hat. "Thank you, Mrs. Stannert."

A late October wind whipped through the door as he exited, pulling the squeaking trunk behind him.

She startled to hear Abe say behind her, "Drummer's comin' back tomorrow?"

"That he is. Six o'clock. I negotiated a higher percentage."

Abe nodded. "Good thing." He picked up the whiskey bottle and began to move away toward the sea of hands holding up empty glasses for a refill.

Inez grabbed his sleeve. "What did Mr. Alexander want? And that doctor?"

Abe glanced at the clientele. "Wanted to apologize for his wife. Asked if we knew anything about the one who'd come with her."

"Mrs. Gizzi? What about her?"

Abe lifted a hand to get Sol's attention, and pointed to the clump of dry and desperate drinkers mid-bar. At Sol's nod, Abe turned his full attention to Inez, his deep brown eyes sober. "Seems the missus has a habit of falling in with soothsayers, tableknockers and such. Seems the church sent her on a goodwill visit, and damn if she didn't empty the household accounts to bring a fortuneteller along. He tries to keep her corralled between home and church, but she slips the halter sometimes. Guess this was one o' the times. Gotta say, Mr. Alexander ain't exactly happy with this Mrs. Gizzi, not to mention your reverend's preachin' texts about 'give to the poor and succor the sorrowful.' He also said that they lost a daughter soon after they came to town. She ain't gotten over it yet."

Inez experienced a pang of sympathetic sorrow. "Well, that explains a great deal."

Abe grunted. "A great deal, huh? You'll have to tell me more about that. Anyhow, I thanked the mister for his time and told him he could tell the missus that Mrs. Jackson's on bed rest and Doc said no visitors. Seemed easiest way to discourage return visits." He shot a glance down the bar at Sol. "Sol's doin' well there. I think we got things under control. You stayin' around this evening?"

Inez wiped her hands on a clean rag and took in the buzzing room in a glance. "I'd like to change out of my travel things. Mark asked if I'd sit in on a game this evening." She frowned. "I'm still trying to decide."

She grabbed her reticule and the drummer's receipts from the lockbox and took them upstairs to the office, lifting a lit kerosene lamp from a hook at the bottom of the staircase. After letting herself in to the office with a key, she paused, surveying the room. It was clear that Abe had preferred doing the paperwork downstairs in the kitchen or perhaps at home. The stray papers and files on her rolltop desk looked exactly as she left them in August, and were filmed with dust.

She walked over to the hulking black safe in the corner of the room, partner to a black walnut teacart holding a dusty, nearly depleted decanter of brandy. The accompanying brandy snifter held nothing more than an industrious spider, sitting atop a web that stretched across the open bowl and down to one of the teacart handles. Inez knelt, spun the dial one way, then back, then forward again. A last, satisfying click assured her that she'd remembered the combination correctly.

She grabbed the handle and hauled the heavy door open. In went the drummer's receipts for tomorrow's review. She scrounged an envelope from one of the desk shelves to hold the Lads from London's money for their return railway tickets. Last, was Percy's envelope. She paused, running it lightly between two fingers. Light as air, it didn't seem to hold more than a single sheet of paper, if that. What could it be, that he didn't want the other Lads to know he'd slipped it to her? She was sorely tempted to steam it open. There was no writing on the outside. Such an anonymous envelope could, she thought, easily go astray or be buried in the safe once the lockboxes from the night's take joined the stacks on the shelves. Finally, she wedged Percy's mystery envelope and the envelope holding the Lads' cash reserves tight and vertical against the wall of the safe on the topmost shelf, where they would be relatively undisturbed.

She then pushed the door shut and spun the dial randomly a few times, until assured that everything was snug and secure. "Well, Percy, your secret is 'safe' for now," Inez said aloud, with a small smile.

Standing up, she ran a finger over the top of the teacart, leaving a streak in the fine dust, and tarried a moment longer at the mullioned window by the desk. The window overlooked the false-fronted saloons, dancing halls, and brothels of State Street to the distant snow-covered peaks of Massive and Elbert. The moon was on the wane, but its pale light was still strong enough to cast a silver gleam to the mountains in the distance. *Another winter coming.* It wouldn't be long before the snow would cover not just the mountains, but also the rooftops and the boardwalks, smoothing a coverlet of white over frozen muck and mud on the streets and the alleys and burrowing beneath coat collars and sneaking in over boot tops. Those who had the wherewithal would bring out their furs, their cashmere and fine wools when going outside, and stoke the stoves and fill the warming pans and hot water bottles when inside.

Those without the wherewithal would freeze.

And many of those would die.

Inez shivered, turned away from the window, and exited the office. After locking it, she proceeded to the next door down the hall, the one that led to her private quarters. Originally, she had entered her dressing room through the office. But shortly before leaving for the Springs, Inez instructed Abe to have another door cut so she could access the two private rooms directly from farther down the hallway. "And get a locksmith to put sturdy, unpickable locks on the door that leads to the office as well as the new door," she told him.

"You trust Mark that little?" Abe asked.

"I trust him not at all," she'd answered.

She stopped in front of the new door, the sharp scent of recently sanded pine stinging her nostrils, and examined the structure. It had sturdy planks, she noted with approval, hinges on the inside, a lock that looked like it would serve to protect a bank vault. *Good.* She inserted the shiny brass key, which turned with a satisfyingly heavy feel, and pushed the door open. She hesitated on the threshold, looking toward the gaming room, farther down the hallway, its door wide open and inviting. Unlike the kitchen below, the card room was plumbed with gas lighting. Shadows, sharp and bright, flickered on the wall opposite as Mark moved about inside, preparing for the upcoming game. Inez shook herself. What was she thinking? Going in, conducting small talk with the man she'd sworn to divorce as soon as possible? Why? To what purpose?

Cursing herself, but for what she wasn't exactly sure, Inez entered her quarters, slammed the door shut, and locked the door behind her with a hard twist of the key.

◇◇◇

After washing off the grit of travel and hanging her travel clothes for a future brushing, Inez dressed in a manner appropriate for the evening. Regaining a measure of composure, she approached the gaming room.

Mark looked up from the round table where he sat, shuffling a deck of cards, alternating between overhand shuffles—undercutting, dropping—kick cuts, and faro dealer shuffles. His cigar balanced on the lip of a crystal tray, smoke winding toward the ceiling, while a snifter of brandy waited to one side. He broke into an approving smile. "You are lookin' mighty fine tonight, Mrs. Stannert. Like a million dollars."

His eyes moved over her in a friendly assessment. "Always amazed me how you could change your outfit quicker 'n the weather changes on a high summer day in the mountains, especially with all those strings, buttons, and hooks. Feminine sleight of hand that has served us well in the past, right, darlin'? Remember Chicago in seventy-five?"

She leaned against the frame and crossed her arms across the bodice of her burgundy silk brocade and purple satin dress, burgundy gloves dangling carelessly from one hand. The silk of the bodice felt cool and smooth against her bare wrists. "You remember that, do you?"

"Darlin', I remember each and every time we stepped out together from the first night we met." Mark paused and leaned back, drawing reflectively upon his cigar, eyes following the smoke as it drifted to the chandelier. "That night, you were wearin' blue. Lace over the back of the skirt. Flower in your hair, same color as the dress." His eyes lingered on her face. "What mostwise sticks in memory is the obstinate expression on your face as your cousin waltzed you around, steppin' all over your skirt hem and your shoes."

Surprised, Inez laughed. "Well, you recall correctly, Mr. Stannert. Poor Cousin Jerome, how annoyed he was when you cut in on the dance and how relieved I was to discover you didn't attempt to waltz in four-four time." Still smiling at the memory, she strolled into the room, and looked around. "So who are you expecting tonight?"

Mark straightened up and resumed shuffling, his fingers manipulating the cards so quickly she was hard put to follow them. "A couple gentlemen I met in the smoking car, from Chicago, incidentally. Sir Daniel, Lord Percy, and Balcombe would've beaten me up sideways to Sunday if I'd turned them away. I expect the others will come to egg them on or rein them in."

Inez rolled her eyes. "Epperley will *not* be happy. He seems determined that Percy assume his own miserly habits."

Mark shrugged one shoulder, the lights overhead catching the silver-gold brocade threads in his waistcoat and gleaming off his carefully styled light brown hair. "I see you're wearin' the diamonds I gave you." The quicksilver maneuverings of the cards slowed, each action deliberate, as if to prove every move was straightforward, hiding nothing. "Does that mean you'll be gracin' our table with your presence?"

"I haven't decided yet." She moved to the table. "So you anticipate five tonight?"

"A couple more might show. Gents from Texas. Big ranchers, big money. We'll see." His fingers paused, cards cradled in one hand. "Call it."

Inez pondered, then, "Five of spades."

Mark tossed the five of spades on the table.

Bracing her arms on the surface, Inez leaned forward.

"You'll play it straight tonight, yes? Best not to toy with the unknown. We don't want things to spiral out of control."

"Mr. Jackson said I could find you here." The cool voice behind Inez was as familiar to her as the crack of thunder after a lightning flash and just as heart-stopping.

Chapter Twelve

Inez's heart banged against her ribcage as if it would leap right through her steel and satin stays.

She spun around, hand at her throat, covering the diamond necklace from Mark.

Reverend Sands stepped into the room. His impenetrable gaze fixed on Inez, lingering for a moment that felt like an eternity, before moving to Mark, assessing.

The pools of gaslight seemed to dim and shrink from the reverend's black-garbed form as he advanced toward the table.

Mark didn't stand, but offered a slow smile that evaporated as soon as it appeared. "And *this* must be the Right Reverend Justice B. Sands, unless I miss my guess."

"And you must be Mr. Mark Stannert." The words were polite, but barely.

Reverend Sands looked over at Inez. Something in his expression made her want to simultaneously reach out to him and retreat at the same time.

"Welcome back to town, Mrs. Stannert."

"Reverend! I was coming to see you—" she began.

His eyes flicked over her evening dress.

"—tomorrow," she finished lamely. "We just arrived this afternoon. It's been…chaotic." She took a step toward him, empty hand raised in a gesture of reconciliation, extending to touch him.

"Now, darlin', not looking to confess are you?" Mark said conversationally. "Not like you've done anything wrong or sinful. Wife spendin' time with her husband and child after a long spell apart, it's all perfectly natural."

Spell broken, Inez spun to Mark, clutching her gloves in a stranglehold. "Stop it!"

Mark ignored her, all attention focused on Sands. "You know how it is, Reverend. Married couple, reunited after being separated through no fault but the Lord's and the fickle nature of chance. I understand you were here several times askin' after Mrs. Stannert, but we-all decided to prolong our time in the Springs. Mrs. Stannert and I, we had a lot of catching up to do. A wife on her own, she gets used to doing things her way. It takes time to reconcile the differences, mend the breach."

His hands resumed their skillful manipulation of the cards. "But then, word around town is that you've had plenty of experience with offerin' comfort to wives whose husbands are absent."

Reverend Sands, who had started toward Inez, stopped dead in his tracks. He regarded Mark. "I don't like what you're insinuating," he said in a dangerously soft tone.

"Well now, Rev. Seems you've got quite the reputation. Killed men in a broad swath across the territory, if tales be true. Seems an odd background for a man of God." Mark stopped shuffling and set the cards on the table, leaned back.

"I've paid for those days," said Reverend Sands. "And every day I pray for forgiveness and redemption. I'd say, given what I've heard about you, that your past is no stranger to the self-same sins."

Mark slid a sideways glance at Inez. "Tellin' tales out of school, Mrs. Stannert?" He turned his gaze back to Reverend Sands. "Might be. Might be. You know how stories grow in the telling, which is why I had a good look at what folks say about you. Still, there's a big difference between us."

"Which is?"

"I don't lose any sleep over it. All those sinners had it coming, one way or another." Mark leaned forward, folding his arms on the table, silver and diamond cufflinks twinkling. "Let's cut to the chase, Reverend Sands. I know all about the affair between my wife and y'all. It's not like you've been discreet about it." Mark spared a quick look at Inez, amusement flitting across his face. "I'd have expected more discretion on your part, Mrs. Stannert, but can allow how you thought I was dead and gone."

Inez pointed a finger at him. "Mr. Stannert, you never bothered to correct that impression during your absence, as you damn well know."

Mark rolled his eyes in mock exasperation. Mrs. Stannert, since I've come back I've explained myself six ways to Sunday. In fact, we've trod that ground over and over until it's nothing but a dusty rut."

"And as I've pointed out, over and over, your specious explanations hold water no better than a leaky sieve."

Reverend Sands stayed motionless through Inez and Mark's exchange, listening, watching, his face growing darker, his jaw tighter.

Mark's attention switched back to Sands. "As I'm sure you've learned by now, Mrs. Stannert's a woman who makes up her own mind and follows her own path, sometimes contrary to all evidence and advice. That's how she took to me, you know. Turned her back on her whole family for me, and not a day has gone by in our ten-plus years together that I haven't thanked the Lord for her strong-willed ways. But I have to say, Reverend," his tone hardened, "while Inez was struggling to deal with my disappearance, your behavior didn't seem quite so befittin' of a man of the cloth, offering succor by *beddin' my wife*."

Mark's last words scarcely had a chance to meet the air before Reverend Sands moved. A lunge across the table, almost too fast to see, and Sands had the front of Mark's spotless white silk shirt twisted tight in his black-gloved grasp.

Sands hauled Mark up and forward, pulling him half out of the chair, until the two men were nearly nose to nose.

The fury on the reverend's face sent a waterfall of icy fear cascading over Inez.

She managed to gasp out. "Mark! How *dare* you!"

During his speech, Mark's eyes had been half lidded, his voice drawn out with a more exaggerated drawl—mannerisms Inez associated with him maneuvering toward a desired end. All that had vanished when Sands had grabbed him. Mark's eyes were now wide, his arms out, hands open. The gesture said as clear as words: *I'm unarmed.*

Inez didn't trust that gesture for a moment. She knew Mark never entered a room unless he had something sharp and available up his sleeve, just in case.

She reached out and covered Reverend Sands' knotted fist with her free hand. All his attention was focused on Mark, deep rage and loathing hardening his features and turning him into a stranger. Yet, something in the manifest darkness of him was familiar, something she'd glimpsed in the past, lurking below the surface of his soul, like a dark shadow gliding beneath the calm surface of a lake.

When the reverend finally spoke, his words were delivered with a cold deliberation more frightening than any shout. "You do your own wife a vast injustice by maligning her, Mr. Stannert. If I ever hear of you speaking about her or to her in such a manner again, you will regret it. Am I clear?"

Beneath her hand, she could feel Sands twist the fabric tighter around Mark's neck. Mark didn't lower his gaze, despite what must have been the near stranglehold, his face the unreadable expression of the inveterate poker player in a high stakes game. Yet, as close as she was, Inez saw her husband's eyes narrow almost imperceptibly. She also sensed a gathering of energy, the approach of impending violence.

Fearing that the situation was on the verge of exploding in a way none of them would be able to control, Inez slid her hand from the reverend's fist to his arm. Pleading. Warning. "Let him go, Justice. This is exactly what he wants you to do."

Her words hung suspended, between them all. She held her breath. The tension stretched until it quivered at the breaking point. Then, the darkness in Sands shifted.

Sands released Mark, shoving him down into the chair. Mark grabbed for the edge of the table to keep from toppling over backwards.

Air crept back into the room and into Inez's lungs.

The reverend stepped back, as if adding physical distance would keep him from doing something worse.

Mark said nothing, just kept both hands on the table rim in plain view, motionless, but his gaze sharpened in speculation as he took in the reverend's retreat. Inez thought she saw respect... *and is that fear?*...flit over her husband's face. Inez had rarely seen Mark afraid of anyone or anything, so she couldn't, wouldn't swear she'd read him right.

Finally, moving with slow, exaggeratedly careful gestures as if to display his harmlessness, Mark lifted his hands from the burnished walnut and proceeded to straighten and smooth his tie.

Reverend Sands turned to Inez, the rage gone.

Speaking to her as if they were the only two people in the room, he said, "I'm glad to see you are returned and hope your visit with your sister and son went well. We need to talk, in private, but I can see this isn't a good time. We'll do so later." His tone was as intimate as a caress, a brush of his hand down her cheek and neck.

Inez started toward him. "Justice, wait. I'll walk down with you. I'm done here."

Mark interjected, speaking to Reverend Sands as if nothing more than words had been exchanged between the two of them a moment ago. "Now, Reverend, Inez and I, well, we're a pair of black sheep. I know her weaknesses, she knows mine. We're two of a kind, and a pair of any suit beats a high card in any game I've ever played. I understand you used to turn a hand to cards now and again, Reverend?"

Already at the door, Sands turned around to regard Mark. "You seem to have gone through a lot of trouble to unearth my past," he said, not without irony.

Mark picked up the scattered cards, riffling them, tapping them into an orderly pile. "Well now, I figure it's always a good idea to know who my opponent is. And make no mistake, Reverend. We are opponents. Way I see it, we can handle this like gentlemen, without resorting to fisticuffs or guns."

"Or knives," said Sands. "Which I understand *you* favor, Mr. Stannert."

Mark half smiled, his equanimity returning. "Sounds like you've been doin' your homework too. In any case, the law's on my side, being that Inez's married to me still. But Mrs. Stannert's made it plain she's intent on divorce, just as I've made it clear I'm intent on keepin' the matrimonial bond intact. Now, you and me, seems we're both gamblers in life and love, so why don't we let the cards decide? That way one or the other of us doesn't end up bleedin' out in Tiger Alley some moonless night."

He placed the neatened deck of cards in the center of the table. "High-card draw, with Mrs. Stannert the stakes. Loser steps aside and winner gives it his best shot to win her affections. If six months hence, she spurns him, then winner retreats like a gentleman, no harm done and no offense taken."

Incensed, Inez backtracked to the table and slammed her hand on the deck, covering it. "You will *not* do this. I will not be placed up for bid like a, a side of beef!"

Mark didn't even look at her. "Aces high." He slid his hand beneath Inez's, extracted the deck from her grip, and flipped over the top card: nine of clubs.

Mark leaned back. "Go ahead, Reverend. By my reckonin', you've got a decent chance of comin' out as the man on top."

The reverend's coldly polite expression transformed into one of disgust. "I won't demean her or myself."

He turned and left.

His footsteps retreated down the hallway until they were washed out by the sounds drifting up from below. She started to follow him but couldn't restrain her anger.

She turned and pointed at Mark, her arm shaking. "That was completely uncalled for," she snapped. "I know what you were trying to do. Try something like that again, odds are, your son will grow up fatherless."

Mark shifted in his chair. "He got the drop on me that time. Won't happen again. But what makes you think he'd go to the wall for you or that I'd just sit back and take whatever whipping he's got in mind to deliver?" Mark eyed her, curious.

She opened her mouth to argue, to say that Mark had no idea what the reverend was capable of, to demand Mark explain himself and his despicable behavior…and stopped. *This is exactly what Mark wants, to hold me here, trading words with him. I will not play into his hands.*

Without another word, she left, slamming the door hard behind her.

Chapter Thirteen

Inez would have run down the stairs from the second floor if her narrow skirts had permitted. She cursed herself for taking the time to engage Mark even for those few moments. What use was it to yell, accuse, reproach, and remind? He just looked at her, those clear blue eyes patient and attentive, waiting for the torrent of words to cease, waiting for her to wind down so that he could take advantage of her exhaustion and defeat. Well, not this time. This time she had turned away.

Inez stopped at the Harrison Street end of the bar, where Sol was assiduously washing a troop of shot glasses in a small tin tub, dipping them in the soapy water and then again in rinse water, drying each one with a quick twist of a clean bar towel. "Sol, did you see Reverend Sands come down just now?"

"Oh sure," said Sol. "He came downstairs and headed out through the kitchen."

"The kitchen?" That door only led in one direction. "He went into Tiger Alley?" Disbelief colored her question.

"Oh yeah." Sol stopped mid-rinse. "After he came back, a month or so ago, most nights, he'd stop by and ask about, ah, whether we had any news of your return." Sol looked extremely uncomfortable, as if he sensed he was skating onto thin ice with this topic. He hurried forward.

"Bridgette told me that he travels Tiger and Stillborn alleys and the rows late at night, looking for orphans, folks who need doctoring, a hot meal, or a bunk at the mission. Leastways, that's what Bridgette told me. It's not like I've been of a mind to follow him out and see if it's true." Sol glanced around nervously, as if hoping that his remark would not put notions in Inez's head to order him out there.

Apparently chivalry got the better of him because he added, "Uh, do you want to take my place back here and I'll go out and look for him?"

"No! No. I'll take care of this." Inez started toward the kitchen door, grim determination marching alongside and prodding her forward. A pair of galoshes and a worn winter cloak hung by the backdoor, surety against any need to momentarily plunge out into the alley on a cold evening. Only this wasn't evening, but the darkest hour before midnight. It was most likely going to take more than a moment to track the reverend down in the nightmare dark of the alleys and their precincts of desperate and lost souls.

Gritting her teeth, Inez pulled the vulcanized boots on over her burgundy satin shoes and snugged the ankle-length cloak about her bare neck and shoulders. She cursed herself for leaving her silver skirt lifters upstairs. She had not expected to have to venture outside when the evening began. With much muttering and fussing with ribbons and bows, Inez hitched up her long skirts until the dress hems cleared the tops of her galoshes. A quick pace across the kitchen and back assured her she could lengthen her stride and protect the delicate fabric from the mud and offal that lurked on and off the alleys and the tiny crooked footpaths. She extracted her Smoot revolver from its hidden pocket, inadvertently dragging out the tangled silver and gold laces given to her by the drummer.

Emitting a huff of frustration, Inez stuffed the laces back into the satin-lined pocket of the dress. She checked that her weapon was fully loaded. With her free hand, she pulled the hood of the cloak up and over her bare head, making sure she could see to either side and still keep her face within its soft, anonymous folds.

Taking a deep breath, she opened the saloon's back door, plunged out into the biting October night air, and headed down the dark alley, her senses stretching out into the blackness, determined to find Reverend Sands before dawn stained the mountaintops.

A quick pass through Tiger Alley produced no sign of the reverend. Inez crossed State Street and pushed her way through the milling throng of carousers and curiosity-seekers toward the upper end of the block and French Row. Just short of the corner of Harrison and State, she steeled herself and turned into a dank passage between the Grand Central Theater and a law office, entering Stillborn Alley.

The warren of small, irregular and shapeless shanties were set in no regular order, the passages and footpaths between them a twisting labyrinth. Dim lights and shadows flickered behind curtains of thin muslin and ragged stained lace. Aware of shadows pulsing around corners of buildings, Inez pulled her small revolver out of her pocket, picked a path that looked as if it would lead to the center of the community, and moved forward cautiously. She tried to ignore the odd crunch and squish beneath her boots, tuning her hearing for any soft footstep from the sides or behind her and praying to catch the smooth, low tones of Reverend Sands' voice.

Instead, her ears were assaulted with a discordant orchestra of raucous laughter, angry shouts and cursing punctuated by a woman's shriek, followed by sobbing. A crash followed as if someone were thrown against the loose planks of a wall, or perhaps a floor. Inez controlled a shudder and reminded herself that, with the black cloak covering her from head to ankle, she was as invisible as the other shapes that flitted at the limit of her vision.

A group of men, voices tumbling in slurred anger, spilled out of a nearby hovel. "Let's go!" shouted one, "This way!"

They started in Inez's direction.

Catching her breath, she lurched down a barely discernable side trail, pitch-dark, squeezed between two buildings, and crashed directly into a solid form coming the opposite way.

Twin yips of surprise erupted in harmony—one from Inez, the other from the unknown party. Someone lit a candle within a nearby window and lifted the scrim to peek out at the shouts that rattled through the main pathway. In the dim light, Inez saw with shock that it was the "unmentionables drummer" standing before her. Hatless, face sweaty despite the cold rank air, shirt buttons askew, jacket hanging from one arm, he swayed, looking equally horrified to see her.

"Woods?" said Inez, not quite believing her eyes.

With a desperate *shush*, he grabbed her shoulder, then snatched his hand away when she involuntarily raised her pistol. "Madam, I'm not going to ask or even guess why you might be here," he hissed. "And I ask that you do the same for me. Let's just pretend we did not see each other under these sorry circumstances."

He glanced over his shoulder. The drunken voices seemed to be receding. He shifted past her and darted into the dark.

She stood still for a moment, readjusting, regaining her composure and slowing her speeding heart. Straining her ears, she tried to determine if immediate danger lurked from any particular compass point. All the sounds seemed to be returning to normal, if there was such a thing for that part of town. Among the many voices, high and low, she could not detect Reverend Sands'. With an internal sigh, she proceeded in the direction that the drummer had come from, moving inward and south.

Turning a corner, she found herself facing a dirty pool of light from a lantern hanging from the eves of a shack. The lantern illuminated a carefully lettered sign nailed above the door. Inez read the words on the board, feeling her skin crawl with an unnamable trepidation: FUTURES AND FORTUNES TOLD.

Somehow or other, she'd taken paths that returned her to the fortuneteller's abode where she had spotted the newsie Tony earlier in the day. Inez was certain she would not be able to retrace the path she'd taken to here, even with all her wits about her.

A diminutive rag-draped form faced the door. Small, but not Tony.

Inez shrank into the shadows, placing her back against a protective wall such that she could still observe the shanty. The thin wall at her back flexed in time with feminine cries of what sounded like patently manufactured passion. These moans were punctuated by the periodic baritone grunts of some gentleman caller working hard at the business at hand. She tried to ignore the sounds on the other side of the thin planks as the rhythm quickened in time to the groans and squeaks within.

The figure by the fortuneteller's shanty bent down, fiddled with something by the door, then still crouched, lifted a rock overhead and brought it down. Inez flinched, imagining some small animal crushed beneath the stone.

The pile of rags then stood, and Inez was close enough to see a wad of spit splat against the plank door and immediately soak into the thirsty warped wood. Apparently satisfied, the tattered shape turned. Inez stifled a gasp. Madam Labasilier stared out at the darkness, her face lifted in fierce triumph. Bathed in the dim lantern light, standing straight and tall, not bent and hobbling as she'd appeared at the Jacksons' home, the woman seemed to have magically shed decades from her slight frame.

Her dark gaze wandered the shadows, then stopped, lingering in Inez's direction. Inez's heart thumped in syncopation with the accelerated tap-tap-tap that shook her from behind the wall. A sudden duet of howls and yowls erupted. Madam Labasilier, with a dismissive shake of her shoulders, pulled a muted purple shawl over her head, and departed, blending into the night.

Inez itched to see what was beneath the rock sitting by the front door of Mrs. Gizzi's place of business, but was also loath to step into the revealing light. Reminding herself of the night's primary mission, she turned and chose a path that wound away from Madam Labasilier. Inez moved slowly to give her eyes time to adjust back to the gloom. A few more turns around dilapidated dwellings yielded a faint glimmer ahead, warning of an open door or a half-shuttered lantern. With a sudden surge of hope she detected a man's quiet murmur. Something in the tenor and flow of tone convinced her it was probably Reverend Sands.

Another voice, deeper, sonorous, responded. "He's dead. There's no doubt. No pulse, no breath."

"Any possibility of foul play, Dr. Gregorvich?" It was definitely Reverend Sands.

Inez inched closer. Two silhouetted figures knelt by a shape curled up against the wall of a lean-to. The taller thinner figure bent over the prone shadow, stovepipe hat bobbing. A slice of light appeared from a well-shuttered lantern. The narrow beam moved over the ground and the curled shape, finally pausing to illuminate a dead and open eye. "No sign of such." The lantern light traveled down over a bare torso to linger on a ghost-white length of thigh, thin as a stick. "Look at his limbs: malnutrition was foremost. If I were to guess the story behind this corpse, I'd say it began with a lack of food and a surfeit of alcohol over an extended period of time. He most likely fell into unconsciousness much earlier, perhaps even days ago, sinking ever deeper into stupor and finally succumbing. Stripped of all clothing at some point. Tucked up behind a wall like this, he is well hidden."

Both men stood.

"No papers, no name," said Sands. "If he had family, they are unknown, and most likely will never learn his fate. However, he is part of the family of man, and we shall mourn his passing as such."

Dr. Gregorvich gave a nod. He tugged something from a bag slung around a shoulder. Inez squinted. A large bag? A shroud?

He draped it over the form curled against the wall, rendering it invisible in the dark, then straightened. "I'll arrange to have the body removed as soon as possible. I should examine it for cholera before offering up exposure as cause of death to the coroner. Cholera stalks these alleys like death itself. Once we know for certain, I will contact Mr. Alexander and we will proceed per the usual arrangements between your mission, Mr. Alexander, and myself."

"Agreed. If he is unknown to you and me as well as others who with all good intent take to these places to help, then most likely he will remain anonymous. If a simple newspaper notice turns up no kin, no one to claim his earthly remains, then we shall proceed, as you say, per usual. The church will cover the expenses of a simple coffin and arrange for a resting place in the cemetery." Sands touched the brim of his hat, a simple show of respect. He added, "Thou know'st 'tis common; all that lives must die, passing through nature to eternity."

"I still find it odd that a man of God occasionally finds the need to quote the Bard instead of the Bible," Gregorvich sounded almost amused.

"Comfort and understanding of what lies beyond our last breath comes from many sources."

"Well, we have discussed this before, Reverend, often in much the same circumstances, standing over those expired and past hope. You know my position: That if it cannot be measured, cannot be seen, then most likely, it does not exist. Here again, Shakespeare is appropriate: '...to die, and go we know not where; to lie in cold obstruction and to rot.' However, I remain open-minded. If there are realms beyond this one, show me the proof, and I will consider."

Inez stepped away from her hiding place, clutching her pistol in the folds of the cloak. "Reverend?" she whispered.

Both men turned toward her. The physician's face, ghost-pale, swiveled to the reverend.

"I'll leave you to tend to your lost lambs, Sands," said Dr. Gregorvich abruptly. Without another word, he melted into the darkness.

Reverend Sands stepped in her direction. "Inez?"

She heard surprise and more in the utterance of her name: Hope? Longing? Despair?

He closed the distance between them. At the familiar pressure of his hands, first upon her shoulders, then sliding down to her back, all her explanations, intentions, and resolve dissolved. Inez wrapped her arms around his waist, one hand still holding the revolver, and pulled him in tight, seeking the warmth of his mouth to quell her hunger.

◇◇◇

After being kicked out of the Silver Queen's back door, Tony skittered aimlessly around town, trying to decide what to do next. Up to now, Mr. Brown's gun had been a source of protection and comfort to her, the gentle tug of the lanyard a constant reminder of its presence. Now, it felt dangerous, as if it could turn and bite her like one of those deadly sidewinder-rattlers Ace had told the newsies about once. "They ain't up here in Leadville. It's too cold," Ace had said after terrifying them with his yarn of ten-foot-long snakes with buzzing tails and dripping fangs that sprang over boulders to attack unwary travelers, leaving victims with swollen purple limbs, screaming their death agonies complete with blood spewing from every orifice.

Now, the cord on her neck felt as if it was trying to strangle her.

Her feet slowed, having brought her nearly to the front door of the offices of *The Independent* on East Third Street. Light poured out the front pane, indicating that the publisher and chief editor and inkslinger, Jed Elliston, was still there. Should she do as the Stannerts said, take the gun to *The Independent* office and give it to Mr. Elliston for safekeeping? She wavered in indecision.

Finally, Tony sidestepped to the front door where the light was brightest but where she could still stand unobserved by Elliston or anyone else inside. With her back to the street, she furtively pulled out the gun and held the grip up to the light, slanting it this way and that to inspect the initials. It was like some kind of trick, some magical sleight of hand. When held one way, she saw clear as day the P in the middle. When she twisted it so the light slid crosswise, a wavy curly line, which looked like a fancy doodle just seconds before, touched the belly of the P to form an R. "Maybe so, maybe no," she whispered to herself. "Pisspot or Rotten?"

Tony reminded herself that Mrs. Stannert seemed to know the hoity-toity bunch. Maybe they were even her friends, so maybe she was giving Tony the blow-off.

But still, she didn't seem like she was trying to lay a con.

Tony twisted the grip back and forth. R, P, R, P.

Maybe Mrs. Stannert didn't look closely enough. She just saw what she wanted to see. She could be wrong. The thought comforted Tony as she slid the gun back under the layer of oversized waistcoats and adjusted the leather string so it didn't chafe her nape. The safest place for the gun was probably in the cabin, buried in Mr. Brown's carpetbag and wrapped in the woolens Tony had deigned too itchy to wear.

Tony finally headed back toward French Row and home. She approached the Bon Ton Billiard Hall where she liked to enter the front and exit through the back. The proprietor William Nye always had a friendly wink to spare for her if he was there, and sometimes bought her leftover papers, if she had any. "Gives the losers something to read while they sulk," he joked with her once.

A few steps away from the entrance, she saw a strange sight. A tall, pale woman, entirely dressed in black, her upswept hair coming loose and unpinned around her face, gripped the billiard room door with one hand while a man whom Tony assumed was her husband, held fast to her other arm while also clutching a fancy black hat, its long veil trailing onto the boardwalk. "Françoise," he said desperately, "what are you doing?"

With a start, Tony recognized her as the woman she had met earlier, who had paid Maman a hundred dollars to "speak true." Who had seemed disappointed that Tony was a boy.

The woman tried to tug her arm out of the man's grasp. "I must make amends," said the woman. There was a wild look on her face, her eyes blank and staring. "I must make amends. I was wrong. Terribly wrong. I must right that wrong."

"What's done is done. There's no going back. You're lucky you weren't attacked. The alleys are dangerous!" He sounded embarrassed and frightened. "The people who live in them are animals. They have no morals, no hesitation, it matters not who you are."

The woman stopped struggling. Her hand dropped from the door and Tony saw tears course down her cheeks. "It was a gift. I meant it as a gift," she said. "Did I kill her with my kindness?" She put her face in her hands and began to weep. Her husband folded her into an embrace, glancing around as if more concerned about being seen than his wife's distress. "Come, we must go home. Now. You shouldn't be seen here. *We* shouldn't be seen here." The last was said in an emphatic whisper, which Tony, loitering in the slot between the Bon Ton Billiard Hall and the Alhambra Hall saloon, heard quite clearly. They turned and walked right past Tony, the husband's arm wrapped protectively around his wife's waist.

Tony slid into the hall and passed through its length, unseen through the haze of tobacco smoke and unnoticed among the click of billiard balls and whoops and chatter. No one took note of her as she went through the backdoor and into Stillborn Alley. Tony stopped and glanced left and right, before starting her zigzag journey through French Row.

Even in the dark, she knew the tangle of shanties and criss-crossing paths like the back of her hand. She knew the bolt-holes and hidey-holes where one could hide when brawls spilled into the maze, knew which corners the hard-looking characters, men made gaunt by poverty and despair, lurked around, waiting for the unaware and unwitting to stumble their way. She moved cautiously, keeping a straggling line of poor dwellings between her and the rear walls of the larger buildings fronting State Street. Tony listened with all her power, prepared to dodge and disappear at the first sign of anything untoward.

It didn't require a keen sense of hearing, though, for her to hear and identify the voices that snapped at each other from behind the Grand Central Theater.

"Bloody *stop* telling me what to do," slurred out Mr. Pisspot Brown. The small pinpoint of a lit cigarette winked bright, throwing a brief light on his angry pinched face with its little mustache.

"Face it, you've made a damn mess of things, Percy," said another voice, which Tony identified as belonging to the fair-haired sour-faced one with the straight-out pointy mustache. "You'll be lucky to get out of this in one piece. You heard what they said in there. That old coot took you for a song and a dance, and no doubt that reader of tea leaves was in on it. You were conned."

"Aw, stuff it, Epperley. We'll get to the truth. Blast that broken mirror in the hotel. I *knew* I should've held onto my rabbit's foot. We'll go back and pay a little visit after the dancers toss their garters into the crowd. I plan on being lucky in at least *one* venture tonight."

The ember end of the cigarette described a small arc of light as Pisspot Brown tossed it away. It made a sharp sizzle noise as it landed in a rain barrel. "Don't forget, there's that little tosser of a newsboy to deal with. That's a loose end I intend to wrap up before we leave town. He won't be hard to find, and when I do, there'll be one less newsie in Leadville." Pisspot Percy gave a nasty laugh. "He'll never be missed."

The back door of the theater swung open. Bright light spilled out, nearly blinding Tony who crouched behind a crooked and very stinky outhouse. Tony caught a glimpse inside of women dressed in bright colored dresses sprinkled with feathers and sparkly bits. They fanned themselves and laughed with their red-painted mouths, heads thrown back and showing off their dead-white necks. Sour-faced Epperley and Pisspot Brown, both togged up in frock coats and top hats, entered. The door swung shut behind them, casting the world back into darkness.

Tony retreated, a belated jolt of fear shaking her legs so she could hardly walk.

Did they know where she lived? Had they come looking for her to slit her throat?

Distress turned her feet toward home. She dodged around one corner, then another, then about four structures away, she heard: "Come back with me!"

Mrs. Stannert? What's she *doing here?* Taken by surprise, Tony dithered, uncertain what to do, hand sneaking toward her gun. She was flooded with ridiculous guilt that it was still about her person. Then, she heard another voice, lower, but filled with an urgency and despair matching Mrs. Stannert's. "And where do you propose we go, Mrs. Stannert? To your rooms, across the hall from where your husband is entertaining out-of-town gamblers? To the rectory, which is as public as a hotel? What would you have me do?"

Tony blinked, surprised twice. She knew that voice. It was Reverend Sands, one of the do-gooders who came into the rows wanting to "help." *What's he got to do with Mrs. Stannert?*

"There must be a way." Mrs. Stannert sounded almost frantic.

"Inez," the reverend's voice was gentle. "Much has happened since you've been gone. There is a movement afoot to have me replaced."

"What??"

"I had the blessings of all to accompany Grant on his tour through Colorado. And no one seemed to mind when I asked for and received permission to continue with him through Wyoming. It was only two more weeks, two added Sundays. But I returned to find talk that I was not tending my flock in a manner befitting the post."

"Who are they? Who is saying this?" Mrs. Stannert sounded as dangerous as those fops had when they were sliding out their knives to cut Tony's throat at the saloon. Tony was glad that whoever "they" were, they weren't here.

"It doesn't matter. We need to talk about the future, you and I. If it's God's will that I move on, then I accept that, as long as you come with me."

Oh…that's it. Tony knew all about these things: women and men, promises, made and broken, bonds created and destroyed. Screwing up her face in disgust, Tony retraced her steps and took a different path home.

On getting to the shack, her sigh of relief was cut short when she saw the lantern was still on over the sign. Had Maman decided to stay open late? After midnight, the only men who came to have their fortunes told were too drunk to hear and too broke to pay. Any women who came at this hour were all, every single one, crying and reeling from the latest beating or broken heart.

Tony pulled Mr. Brown's pistol out from her clothing, and after a moment's thought, removed the string from her neck so if it was grabbed from her, like in the saloon, she wouldn't strangle. The ivory pistol grip, warm from her own skin, poured courage into her heart.

She grasped the crude door handle, whispered, "Maman? It's me," and pulled the scraping plank open.

Inside was pitch-black. Tony, uncertain now, hovered, then entered, one step at a time, the gun pointed forward. "Maman?" The fortunetelling table was empty; its candle snuffed.

Tony headed toward the threadbare curtain that separated the sleeping area from the rest of the room. "Maman? I'm sorry about today. Are you awake?" Eyes readjusted to the dark within, Tony pulled back the muslin.

Drina Gizzi lay on her back, eyes staring toward Tony and the door, face dusky and still. One arm hung over the edge of the straw mattress, knuckles brushing the floor.

With a cry wrenched from the depths of her being, Tony dropped to her knees and dropped the gun. She clutched the still warm but lifeless fingers with both of her own small hands to her eyes, as if to shut out reality and the bleak future that now filled the shack and her soul.

Chapter Fourteen

"Come with you." Inez repeated the reverend's words. She squeezed her eyes shut. Behind her eyelids, it was just as dark as it was outside, just as dark as the anger and agony in her soul. "Damn him for coming back!" she whispered fiercely. "Damn him to hell!"

"This is not about your husband," said Sands. "This is about you and me." His hands tightened on her shoulders. "Leave him. Let the divorce you put into motion run its course. The grounds still stand: He was absent, without word, for over eighteen months."

"You heard him. He said he'd fight it. Mark will drag it out, as long as possible, use every trick in the book if he must. He'll goad you. He'll push and push until…" Her breath caught.

"Yes. I know." Sands sounded grim. "Next time, if there *is* a next time, I'll not let him drag me down to his level. And you need to do the same. Rise above it."

Inez bent her neck to rest her forehead against his shoulder, trying to pull strength from his words, his touch, his presence. He gathered her closer as if by molding her body to his he could shut out the rest of the world with its complications and sorrows. She turned her face so her cheek lay against the curve of his collarbone. Everything narrowed down to what she could feel and hear. The roughness of his overcoat against her cheek, the certainty of his arms about her, the steadiness of his breathing in tune with the rise and fall of his chest. She set both hands on his chest, feeling the cadence of inhalation and exhalation along with the pulse of his heartbeat. The warm scent of his sweat, intimate, musky, reminded her of tangled sheets, skin sliding on skin, and whispered words of urgency. A foreign, but oddly familiar, smoky overtone puzzled her until, with horror, she realized it was the scent of Mark's cigar, clinging to the reverend's clothes.

She almost pushed him away, but instead, grasped the lapels of his overcoat and kissed him again, with rising urgency. He responded in kind, the desperation of congress denied driving them both to disregard surroundings. The immediate world—with its filth, stink, and poverty—paled, becoming but a ghost banished by the reality they held fast between them. Inez reluctantly pulled away, breathless and dizzy, still gripping his overcoat tight, feeling the heat rush through her body. "Tonight," she said. She couldn't say more, but she didn't need to.

"The rectory." His voice was low, intense, driven. "In an hour. I need to finish here, but it won't take long. I'll give you the key." He reached inside his coat.

Her gloved hand followed his, traveling beneath his overcoat to his waistcoat pocket, stopping him there. "No. I'm staying with you."

"Inez." He spoke gently, as if seeking to restore reason in one stricken by madness. "This is no place for you, and especially not at this time of night. I'll walk you to the street. Wait for me in the rectory."

"Stillborn Alley holds no horrors I haven't seen before." She wound her fingers through his. "Don't underestimate me, Justice. I'm not one to faint when beholding the terrors of the night. I'm staying with you."

He brought her hand to his lips for a kiss. "Hold on to that fortitude, Mrs. Stannert, and there's nothing on earth or in the hereafter that we cannot face and overcome together."

"Reverend!" A child's whispered cry shattered the moment, leaving them standing once again in the dankness of the alley.

Yanking away from the reverend's embrace, Inez whirled toward the voice. Tony stood a short distance away. The whites of her eyes shone eerily in the candlelight struggling through a nearby window. curtained. With no hat, the stubbornness wiped off her face, she looked much younger than before and as terrified as if chased by the hounds of hell.

"Quick. My maman. She, she…" Tony darted forward and grabbed the reverend's sleeve. "Please!"

Tony tugged and pulled. They hastened after her.

Inez lost track of the turns and twists but recognized Mrs. Gizzi's fortunetelling hovel once they reached it. The door gaped open. Tony let go of the reverend's coat sleeve and dashed inside, followed closely by Reverend Sands and Inez. Tony was already kneeling by a single bed, tucked far into a dim corner of the room. Reverend Sands reached the bed first. Inez saw him pause, remove his hat, then go down on one knee by a still form in the bed.

Drawing closer, Inez saw the form on the bed was Drina Gizzi.

Tony, fingers working frantically at the fortuneteller's throat, sobbed, "Maman, no. No. Wake up. Wake up. Help me!" This last was directed at Reverend Sands. "She can't breathe, she needs to breathe."

Sickness grew with realization inside Inez. *Drina Gizzi, Tony's mother…she's dead.*

Stepping around to the head of the iron bedstead, Inez saw that Tony tore at a cord biting tight around Drina Gizzi's neck. Tony's frantic actions lifted the fortuneteller's neck off the thin mattress. Drina's head fell back, her crown of dark hair touching the threadbare sheet. Dead eyes—one dark, one light—stared at Inez.

Reverend Sands stilled the youngster's frantic efforts. "Tony, your mother is now beyond pain, fear, or breath."

Tony scuttled away from the reverend's touch. She curled up on the floor by the foot of the bed, fists to her face, shaking.

Reverend Sands stood and moved to the table in the center of the room. Inez heard the snick of a lucifer. Light flared as he lit the candle. The flame's brilliance flung the shadows back and made them dance about the room.

Steeling her resolve, Inez leaned over the body to get a closer look. Now aware of Tony and Drina's kinship, she could see other echoes of one in the other, aside from the eyes. The petite stature, graceful swoop of eyebrows, and no-nonsense aquiline nose, each carried them as a badge of kinship. However, Drina's blood-suffused and swollen face and protruding eyes bore little resemblance to the bird-like visage Inez recalled from the brief interval at Abe's house earlier that day.

Bile rose in her own throat as Inez focused on the thin rope wound tight around Drina's neck, savagely cutting into the flesh. The material gleamed like liquid moonlight in the wavering candlelight. Not quite believing her own eyes, Inez removed a glove, and reached out. She touched, then smoothed the silver and gold cord, cousin to the corset laces in her pocket. She picked up one end, and let its quicksilver length slither and slip through her bare fingers.

During Inez's examination, Sands had returned to the bedside. Inez rose and said in a low voice, "You must find a policeman. It won't be easy, this time of night. You'll probably have to go up State Street to Harrison or maybe over to Chestnut. It will take time. I will stay here with Tony. This," she glanced at Drina's body, "is no accident."

"It's not safe, leaving the two of you here alone," said Sands. "Perhaps whoever did this is still nearby. There's no telling what or who might be lurking around."

"Would you have me go search instead?" Inez said. "The only other option is for all three of us to leave, and I suspect Tony would not go willingly. We will wait here. And we do not wait defenseless." She showed him her revolver.

Reverend Sands seemed to turn this over in his mind, then nodded, albeit reluctantly. He then turned to Tony. "Tony." He repeated the name several times until the small body stopped shaking. "We will find who did this to your mother. They will pay. There will be justice in this world and in the hereafter. I promise you. You will not be abandoned. Mrs. Stannert and I will stand by you. Right now, I must go find the nightwatch. You understand? If the person or people who did this to your mother are to answer for their crime, I need to bring the law into the matter."

He waited.

The curled up form did not respond.

Sands continued. "Mrs. Stannert will stay here with you. I'll be back as quickly as possible. Have faith, child, in these, the worst of times. The Lord God will walk beside you to guide you through the darkness." With a final glance at Inez, he departed.

After some hesitation, Inez approached the newsie. Tony curled up tighter, as if to shut out the rest of the world.

"Tony," said Inez. Corralling her petticoats, the awkward hooked-up hem of her evening dress, and the yards of cloak, Inez eventually managed to lower herself to the floor by the child. Tony didn't respond. Inez sighed, and looked around the room. She spied the "Worthless Rotten Brown" pistol abandoned on the dusty floor, half under the bed, and decided not to delve any deeper into the shadows. That would be taken care of by the proper authorities. But who would take care of the child?

Inez tentatively put a hand on Tony's shoulder. The shoulder tensed. "Tony," she began, "I'm so sorry for your loss. To lose a mother is one of the hardest trials life can offer, aside from the loss of a child." That last just slipped out. Inez winced, realizing the ache she identified in her own heart was not only in sympathy with Tony but also tied to the "loss" of her own young William. Mothers and their children. It was an unbreakable bond, for better or worse, through birth, life, separation, and death. *William is not dead, but it often feels as if he is dead to me. He will never view me as his "maman." That role is Harmony's.*

Swallowing the lump in her own throat, Inez continued. "I wish I could offer the saloon to you as a place to stay. I myself have living quarters on the second floor. However, it would not be wise while those men you antagonized are in town. However, there are other options." She took a deep breath. "There is the mission that Reverend Sands and the brethren of the church built. It would be a safe place for you, for now."

Muffled words emerged from the ball on the floor. "I'm not going to no poorhouse or orphanage."

"The mission is a refuge, for those in need. And it's just for a little while, until we can find you a home."

"I can take care of myself." Stronger, more stubborn.

Inez shook her head in frustration. "It isn't safe for you here or on the streets. You can't live rough, under the boardwalks, like those boys that, that…Tony, I know your secret. Your name, it's Antoinette? Or Antonia?"

Tony convulsed, then sprang to her feet, staring at Inez. "What did you call me?"

"I know you are a girl. Not everyone would see through your disguise. I don't believe Reverend Sands knows, but Mr. Stannert and I, we saw."

Tony seized her red cap and pulled it down so tight it almost covered her eyes and ears. "Stop!" she shouted.

Inez began to rise, her narrow skirts and rigid corset complicating the motion. "The mission is the best, safest place for you right now until we can figure out who killed your mother and why. Perhaps you are in danger yourself, don't you see? This may sound strange, but I understand, and I want to help you."

Without another word, Tony shot across the floor and out the door.

Inez cried, "Tony, wait!" She finally made it to her feet, hurried after the girl, and unpocketed her small revolver, cognizant of the dangers that lurked in the shadows and the light. A small shadow topped with a cap ran up a small footpath that twisted to the left. Inez followed as fast as she could on the ice-skimmed paths. The makeshift lifts for her skirts had come undone, and the hems were tangling around her ungainly galoshes while she cursed her clumsy attempt at reaching out. Another sharp turn yielded a fleeting glimpse of a shadow flitting around a cistern. Inez followed, only to have three gentlemen—if such term could be applied to them—stumble out from the left to block her progress.

"Who's the pretty lady out taking the evening air?" bellowed one.

"No one you want to mess with," Inez snarled back, breath puffing into the frigid air.

The three started forward, then beat a hasty retreat after Inez sent a bullet into the crusty dirt at their leader's feet, spitting icy shards of frozen dust upon his boots.

Once they had gone, Inez stopped to catch her breath and get her bearings. She had no idea where she was in Stillborn Alley and whether she faced north, south, east, or west. She doubted she'd be able to retrace her steps to the shack. The best course of action was to head toward one of the main streets and search for the reverend.

Tony, she was sure, had any number of hidey-holes and places to go to ground. Inez hoped she had not put the girl into an untenable situation.

"I was only trying to help," she said to the night air. Her breath curled out with a sigh, the warmth rising and dissipating to leave only the icy pinpricks of stars overhead.

With that, she gripped her pistol with a firmer hand and headed toward the jagged dark line of silhouetted buildings that marked the direction of either State or Chestnut.

Chapter Fifteen

Fury fueled by grief added speed to Tony's mad dash. *Who did this to Maman? It's my fault. I left her. I said I wasn't coming back. If I'd been here, this wouldn't have happened. We should have left, today, with the gold. Now it's too late. Now I'm all alone.*

She ran, panting out tears and sorrow, gasping in a storm of contrary emotions. Why had she asked the reverend for help? What could he do? He was getting the coppers. What would they do?

Nothing.

They didn't care what happened in these alleys, not to people like her and Maman. Well, they wouldn't catch her. None of them knew the alleys the way she did. Tony's mind twisted along with the small footpaths that led her farther west, toward Coon Row. Where, where could she go? Where would she be safe, at least for a while?

The answer came to her, almost as if Maman had whispered it into her ear.

The newsie shed.

Tony doubted Mrs. Stannert, the reverend, or any of the rest knew of it. Mr. Elliston was good about keeping mum about that arrangement. "When you kids need someplace to bunk, use the shed," he'd said. "Just don't set fire to the paper stock or knock over the ink barrels." He left burlap sacks aplenty for the newsies to burrow into and even brought bread and cheese for those whose stomachs were empty in the morning.

Tony heard Mrs. Stannert shout her name and used the sound to move farther away.

Since *The Independent* office was up on East Third Street on the other side of Harrison, Tony decided the best thing to do was cross West Chestnut and use the alley on the other side to work her way up to Harrison and across, then make her way behind the buildings on the east side of town. That way, she could avoid the lights and being recognized or remembered by anyone. At least, by anyone standing up and sober. And if she ran into trouble, well, she had her gun.

Tony skidded to a stop, panting out a soft "Damn!"

She *didn't* have her gun.

It was back there. With Maman. Right by the bed, or maybe under it.

Tony swiped at tears of frustration.

She had to go back. Now. Before the reverend showed up with the coppers. Before Mrs. Stannert went back to the shack, if she did.

Tony inhaled with a shuddering gasp. The icy air felt as if it froze her from the inside out. She turned and doubled back, careful to keep close to, but not in, the deep shadows that might hold dangers that couldn't be handled without her gun.

Closing in on the place she and Maman had called home for the past two months, she slowed, then stopped, toes clenching inside the threadbare woolen socks. Cold from the ground below leaked into the thin soles of her too large shoes.

There were voices, male voices, near by.

Her fingernails dug into the rough edge of the brittle plank of the neighbor's wall as she leaned forward, venturing a one-eyed peek around the corner. Pisspot Brown lounged under the fortunetelling sign, leaning against the doorframe. The door hung open, a traitor to her and Maman, allowing any and all access. Brown was smoking, the end of his cigarette glowing red. He leaned into the shack and Tony heard him say, "She couldn't have gone far. Not this time of night."

The slam of a cupboard door and muffled curses told Tony that at least one other was inside, searching. *Are they looking for me? How do they know where I live? How do they know about me, about Maman??*

The thought of her poor Maman, lying cold and dead on the bed while those nasty nobs tossed the place looking for…what? Her fingers curled uselessly at her chest, searching for the missing pistol handle, and finally tightened into a fist. If only she had her gun. Right now. She'd kill them all. A sob ripped free from her throat. Pisspot Brown's head swiveled in her direction. She shrank back, away from the corner.

"Someone there?" he called out. She heard the scrunch of ice beneath a boot heel as he stepped in her direction. "Show yourself or bugger off!"

She faded into the embracing darkness, silent as a ghost. No use waiting now. To linger was to invite discovery and disaster.

She'd come back early morning and hope that the nobs or the coppers or whoever else showed up didn't spot her gun first and take it with them.

Wiping away tears before they froze to her face, Tony slunk away. She dashed across Harrison, small and low, trying to be invisible, and made her way over to and up East Third. Squatting in frontier splendor next to an assay office, *The Independent* had a couple of storage shacks in back, looking anonymous and no different from the storage shacks all higgledy-piggledy behind the assay office. Tony went to the rear of the shed, where empty barrels and broken pieces of equipment, and splintered crates were leaning and stacked against the plank wall. She found the barrel lying on its side, and rolled it away to reveal a hole cut in the back of the shed.

She crouched down to the opening and said in a low voice, "Ace? It's me. Tony."

A couple barrels, side-by-side, provided a sort of inner wall she'd have to crawl around to reach the interior. A weak snip of light slipped around the barrels, wavering on the dirt floor.

A small shuffle, then Ace said, "Well, c'mon in, Tony. Close it up so that wind doesn't sneak in. It's cold enough as is."

She scuttled in, and then turned and set a hand on the inside of the barrel, rolling it back in place to block the entrance. The barrel settled into a hollowed out spot, keeping it in place. She moved around the stacked barrels and spied the candle, flickering fitfully from a tin plate on the floor.

"Mr. Elliston won't like that," said Tony, aware that the candle was breaking one of the newsman's primary rules: No fire around the paper.

Ace said, "We're bein' careful. Freddy, he's scared of the dark and he's new, so hey, we're gonna just wait 'til he's asleep."

A lump of burlap sacks by the candle moved slightly, and a small hand slipped out and pushed the sacks back. A face peered out at Tony, a whopper of a shiner on the left side of his face. She moved closer, curiosity about another's misfortune dimming the darkness of her own. "What happened to him? Hey, he's just a little guy."

"Yeah, well, Freddy's pa works the smelter, like my pa."

Tony stared. None of them ever talked family. This was the first Tony'd heard that Ace wasn't a loner.

Ace continued, looping an arm over the small boy. "Lie down, Freddy. That there's Tony Deuce. Wait 'til morning and you get a gander of his eyes and you'll see why we call him Deuce. Tony sells more sheets than any of us. Tony's okay." The pride and affection in Ace's voice surprised Tony. Ace never delivered praise to the other newsies, preferring to toot his own horn or say, "Well, just had an off day, that's all" when Tony bested him in the daily sales.

The little bruised face disappeared and the burlap pile wiggled around as Freddy burrowed back in.

"His pa got tight tonight and…" Ace made a fist and punched the air. "Not for the first time, neither. So I told Freddy here I knew a nice warm place to bunk for the night, a place where he'd get a breakfast that'd fill his belly. He can help me sell the sheets for a while and I'll split my five dollars with him. That's two-fifty a week, damn good money, hey, Freddy? Right up there with old Tabor hisself. Bet he wasn't making two-fifty a week when he was four years old! That way, Freddy don't need to go back to that old mule never again if he don't want to. Let that mule go kick someone his own size, right, Freddy?" Ace nudged the pile of sacks, which shifted in response."

"Hung-y now," said a small voice from under the burlap.

With a start, Tony remembered the biscuits that Mr. Stannert had given her. She dug into both pockets and pulled out the pieces that hadn't been crushed to crumbs and crumbles. "Ace, Freddy, they gave me these at the Silver Queen tonight. Some of Mrs. O'Malley's biscuits. Take 'em."

Tony dumped the biscuit bits into Ace's cupped hands and an especially large piece into the small dirty hand that crept out beneath the sacks.

Ace ate greedily, seeming to swallow his portions whole. But he must've at least tasted them before they disappeared down his gullet, because a strange expression crossed his face and he said, "Cheese? Mrs. O'Malley put cheese in her biscuits?"

Tony shrugged. "Dunno. Didn't eat them."

Ace stared. Tony realized that passing up available food was beyond his understanding, so hurried on. "S'okay. I wasn't hungry. I had to light out in a hurry."

A way around her predicament popped into Tony's head. She sat on the other side of Ace and said low, "Listen, I can't hawk for a while, so why don't you and Freddy take my share for now? Pair up and split the money. That way, you still get to keep your five dollars and, heck, you'll even make more, 'cause I make eight a week."

"Yeah, rub it in, newsie," grumbled Ace, but Tony thought he brightened at the prospect of additional coin in his pocket. Then a shadow of worry disturbed the cheer. "You skipping *The Independent*, Tony? You get a better offer from the *Chronicle?* Elliston won't like that, skipping to the competition."

"I wouldn't go work with those spit 'n polishers," scoffed Tony. "All brass buttons and uniforms, plus I'd have to give up this cap I paid you too much for." Realization dawned again.

"Oh damn. I can't wear the cap neither," she blurted out, overwhelmed all over again with sadness. She felt the tears start to come. She swiped fiercely at them adding, "That smelter up on Chestnut sure sends up a stink. Makes my eyes hurt." She took the cap off and handed it to Ace. "Can you keep this for me? Just don't wear it or anything. And don't give it to Freddy! If anyone asks about me, just play dumb, okay?" She ran a hand over her short greasy curls.

Ace looked wary. "Why? You in trouble?"

"I, I gotta find another job," she stuttered. "Just for a while. Yeah, I'm in trouble, but not because of anything here. I just gotta lie low for a while."

Ace's close examination continued. Tony shifted on the cold dirt floor, remembering what Mrs. Stannert said: *Not everyone would see through your disguise, but we did.*

Was Ace starting to suspect that she wasn't who he thought she was?

"What about the Silver Queen?" Ace prodded. "You gonna keep working there?"

"No. I gotta stay away from there too. For a while." She looked away, watched the shadows and light from the candle leap up on the log walls of the shed, looking like they were trying to find cracks to crawl out of and escape into the night. "I made a right fool of myself," she said miserably, "and now I've got a pack of really nasty foreigner swells I have to steer clear of. That's all. But they'll probably recognize the cap, so that's why I'm saying don't wear it. I don't want you or anyone to get in a mess because of me."

Ace was silent for a moment, then cleared his throat, "You need work? Something where you're not out on the streets and seen and such?"

Tony nodded.

"Well, I heard that someone's lookin' for a boy to help a bit. Sweep floors and clean up stuff. But," he lowered his voice, "nobody's raisin' a hand or steppin' forward. If you want the job, ain't no one going to be jumping your claim, I guarantee." He took a deep breath. "There's lots of gab about ghosts and spirit lights, and there's stiffs."

Tony thought of her mother's interactions with the afterworld, her regular talk of spirits, and how the ones who paid would often look pale and shaken when her maman started talking in voices, like a ghost or spirit was something that could jump up and suck the life out of them. Tony always snickered at their frights. How scary could the "other side" be? Besides, her maman was there now.

A vision of her maman rose up before Tony—her eyes alight from a fire within, her slender hands dancing through the air, weaving folks' dreams and wishes into futures that seemed real. Tony could hear her say, as if she was right beside her: *I have seen it.*

She swallowed around the sudden lump in her throat. "That don't scare me. What's the job? At the cemetery or something? They want help digging graves, maybe?"

Ace shook his head. "Worse. It's for Mr. Alexander's coffin-shop on Harrison."

Chapter Sixteen

Realizing that shouting into the dark would gain her nothing but trouble in the alley, Inez stopped calling for Tony and focused on making her way out of the warren of sin and sorrow. She happened upon the spot where she'd first seen Sands and Dr. Gregorvich, recognizable not by the sorry framed hovels, which all looked the same to her, but by the unknown male corpse curled up by the wall. Inez realized she had to keep her eyes on the taller buildings and trust her feet to not skid on slicked-over mud or stumble into half-frozen puddles.

As soon as Inez emerged onto the boardwalk, she could feel the tension in her shoulders and neck ease. These were crowds she understood and could defend herself against, if needed.

Lights from saloons, gaming halls, and dance halls spilled out, flickering over those hurrying or lingering on the walkways. Men pushed past with hats pulled low over brows, coat collars turned up, breath misting, the occasional face lit with liquor, lust, or both.

Pocketing her pistol and wrapping her arms tight within her cloak, she crossed the rutted road, and walked up to the corner, passing the State Street entrance to the Silver Queen and proceeding to the corner abutting Harrison. Here she stopped, anonymous in her hooded shroud of wool, undecided. She could go inside. The warmth of the saloon, and her rooms upstairs called and pulled with invisible strings, strong as the cords that cut off Drina Gizzi's last breath. Inez shook off the longing with a determined shrug, and turned to stare down the length of State to where the mountain peaks lay shrouded in the dark.

Which way?

She'd be more likely to find the reverend on Harrison, where the nightwatch kept an eye on the shuttered businesses so they would remain untouched during the early Saturday morning revelry that regularly bedeviled State. Or possibly on West Chestnut, which would be replete with a better quality of foot traffic than State Street, with many coming and going from the saloons, restaurants, and billiard halls that lined this east–west thoroughfare. Chestnut once held the shining title of "business district," a crown that had been snatched by the usurper of Harrison Avenue.

If she didn't find the reverend, she could return to the saloon, or perhaps the rectory, and explain to him what happened. Or look for a policeman herself.

She hated the thought of leading a weary, impatient night watchman to the Gizzis' shack, when he'd probably rather be gathering a hot toddy "on the house" from Pop Wyman's or her own Silver Queen. Too, locating the shanty again would be by guess and by golly. Weary, Inez turned and, head bowed against a wintery gust of wind, began to cross the rutted road again, determined to try Chestnut first.

A sudden clatter of hooves accompanied by a drunken shout alerted her. She glanced up in time to see a figure on horseback careening around the corner, on course to knock her down. As the rider hauled on the reins in an attempt to stop his mount, she leapt forward to avoid the collision.

Her galoshes slammed onto a patch of uneven mud-ice and she skidded, off balance. A hand grasped her windmilling arm and pulled her hard out of harm's way. The yank sent her flying into the torso of her savior, where she instinctively gripped the lapels of a heavy overcoat. Horse and rider danced by, the rider showering epithets down on her head as he whipped his mount back into a full-tilt gallop and disappeared down the center of State Street.

"Mrs. Stannert, is that you?"

She recognized the deep voice of Sands' compatriot, Dr. Gregorvich. He still gripped her arm hard with one hand, hard enough, she suspected, to leave a bruise the next morning. Looking up from his lapels she saw that he held the end of a canvas bag, cinched closed by a leather strap. A large lump filled the bag slung over his back. A shiver sharp as a shard of ice scratched down her back, and she flashed on the curled-up naked body of the unknown in Stillborn Alley. She pulled away from his grasp, and said, voice still trembling from the close brush with death on the streets, "Thank you, Dr. Gregorvich. I'm certain that you saved me from becoming one of your clients just now."

He peered down from his considerable height. "That would be a great tragedy. It is fortunate that I was crossing the street from the opposite direction and reached you in time."

Mind still upon his appearance and profession, Inez said faintly, "I suspect your services, or that of your colleague, Mr. Alexander, will be required for another poor unfortunate from Stillborn Alley. A fortuneteller, Mrs. Gizzi, has been brutally murdered."

His eyes glinted in the reflected lights from the Silver Queen behind her as he shifted his burden and said, "Come, let us leave the middle of the road before we both are trampled by another out-of-control horse and rider." Without preamble, he gripped her again. Inez winced as he unerringly closed around the same spot on her arm as he did before. He steered her to the sidewalk in front of the Silver Queen. "Now, tell me about this unfortunate, as you call this person," he said.

"She has a small shack in the alley. I'm not certain I could find it again, but it has a sign that reads FUTURES AND FORTUNES TOLD."

"How did you come by this sad state of affairs?"

"Her child discovered the body." Inez's mind whirled to find a reason for Inez's being in that disreputable section of town at such a disreputable hour. She opted for simple. "The child came rushing to find help and then, took off." Inez shook her head in frustration. "Reverend Sands offered to go look for the police."

"Well then," his solemn voice smoothed into a comforting note, "it sounds as if all proceeds as it should. I must get this unnamed soul back to my offices, or rather to Mr. Alexander, since there is no hope of revival." He lifted one massive shoulder. The bag jiggled limply, as if it held a figure no heavier than a child. "None care about the lost and unknown dead," he said, almost as if to himself. His dark eyes turned back to Inez, sharpening. "The child, however, lives and should be the concern of all. If the child reappears, contact me or Mr. Alexander. We have, by virtue of our work, many interactions with orphans. In conjunction with Reverend Sands, I'm certain we can offer succor and shelter until a more permanent solution can be found."

"Thank you," she said faintly.

Dr. Gregorvich's penetrating gaze seemed to give her a sharp onceover, stripping her bare without lust or desire, a quick medical evaluation. "You should return inside. You are trembling, pale, and your teeth are chattering. You are exhibiting many of the symptoms of extreme exposure."

Not until I know that Mrs. Gizzi has been taken care of. Rather than argue, Inez turned to the State Street door of the Silver Queen and made as if to prepare to enter. "That I will do. Thank you again, Doctor, for the quick response that saved my life."

He tipped his hat and turned his back, vanishing around the corner to Harrison.

Inez's hand dropped from the engraved wood panel of the door, and with a quick glance to left and right, she re-crossed the street and began to head down Harrison again. No sooner had she turned the corner onto Chestnut than she spied the welcome form of Reverend Sands, accompanied by three other men, hurrying in her direction. One of the men was a policeman, his cap and the badge on his thick wool uniform jacket a dead giveaway. The second was Doc Cramer, quickly identified by his limp, his silver-headed cane, and the top hat perching atop his lumbering form. He tipped his hat back, and Inez's heart warmed at the sight of his kind, lined visage. The third man, hurrying alongside, had his hat pulled low. Inez identified him not by his lanky, bundled form, but by the pencil tapping impatiently upon a notebook: Jed Elliston—publisher, primary inkslinger, and occasional typesetter of *The Independent* newspaper.

"Reverend! Mr. Elliston! Doc!" She hurried toward them, pushing through a clutch of inebriated merrymakers, one of who stumbled off the boardwalk and swore as his boot cracked through a smear of ice and plunged into the ankle-high muck below.

Inez came up to the four men and clutched Doc's sleeve.

"Mrs. Stannert? What are you doing here?" Doc sounded alarmed and concerned.

"Where is the boy?" asked Reverend Sands.

It took Inez a moment to realize he was referring to Tony. *He doesn't know about Tony's disguise.* "It all happened so fast," she said. "Shortly after you left, he bolted. I tried to follow, but it proved impossible. I was hoping to find you, Reverend. I'm worried about the child." She added, "And I knew I couldn't find my way back to Mrs. Gizzi's shack."

The impatient tapping on the notebook increased. "Mrs. Gizzi? The fortuneteller?" The newspaperman turned to the reverend. "You didn't say that this involved her. I've heard some claim she has 'the sight.' She has a child?" Jed's sharp-faced features shone with eagerness. "I can see the headline—Murder in French Row leaves Second-Sight Child Homeless."

"Jed, you are impossible!" snapped Inez.

"Enough," Sands said. "I know the way. Once Doc and Officer Kilkenny here perform their legal duties, we can decide on the next steps."

"Which should involve a shot of something warm and potent," grumbled Officer Kilkenny as he gave his muffler an extra tug to tighten it about his neck.

"I'm coming," said Inez. "If the boy returns, a woman's presence may be calming." It seemed a weak enough reason, but between the cold and the late hour, she figured none would protest. None did.

As the reverend led the way toward French Row, Jed Elliston picked up what had apparently been an ongoing argument between him and Doc Cramer. "But Doc, you've heard the stories. The *Chronicle* printed up that piece just a few weeks ago."

"Complete balderdash," grumbled Doc. His swinging cane just missed banging Elliston in the shins. "That so-called reporter Orth Stein has a fevered imagination."

"Who?" asked Inez, from Doc's other side, far from the irritated cane.

"Orth Stein," supplied Elliston. "New *Chronicle* reporter. While you were gone, he blew into town, and interviewed all the local sawbones about these supposed underground anatomy classes. One of the medicos he interviewed as good as said that it was *de rigueur* to snatch cadavers from the Evergreen Cemetery for illegal dissecting purposes."

"I told you before, Jed, and I'll say it again. This fable is complete balderdash and is causing unnecessary panic amongst those who are most vulnerable," said Doc. "When your young Mr. Stein came to talk to me, I sniffed out a ruse right away. He said he'd graduated from The Rush in Chicago, so I quizzed him as to his anatomical knowledge. When asked how he'd reduce a dislocation of the clavicle, he completly caved and admitted that he wouldn't know a spinal vertebrae from a soda cocktail. No one with an ounce of sense would believe a word printed under his name."

"But that man back there," Jed jabbed his pencil toward Chestnut, "the one spilling his blood in the Odeon Dance Hall. He begged you to be sure, if he dies, that his corpse is sent back home to his family. He averred that he'd not want his corporeal body snatched and laid open for a carving class."

"Mr. Elliston!" barked Doc. "Please, we have a lady amongst us." Doc offered Inez his arm as they entered the narrow passage to the alley. "Mrs. Stannert, I apologize for Mr. Elliston's fourth-estate zeal in pursuing this most unnatural and immodest subject. He has been dogging my nightly rounds for weeks now, hoping to find a shred of truth to this preposterous tale."

"I have no knowledge of this particular development," said Inez, taking Doc's arm. At the other end of the passage, Sands and the officer waited for the three to catch up.

"It all occurred while you were down in the Springs," said Jed from behind them. "Stein dropped the topic quick enough, and is now more interested in pursuing the proliferation of bogus medical diplomas in town. But I feel the dead deserve as much respect as the living. It's a subject that I'm not about to lay to rest, until I know what's what."

And you can't stand to have not been the first to uncover the story. Inez knew Jed well. They had worked together as well as at cross-purposes in the past, and he was one of her regulars at the Saturday night high-stakes poker game at the Silver Queen. Luckily, his fortunes had improved over the summer, so he was once again throwing money onto the table with a free and easy air of bonhomie, as if *The Independent* were spinning straw into gold. That thought led to the next: *Tony is a newsie for Jed's paper. I wonder...*

As they emerged from the narrow egress into Stillborn Alley, Inez inquired, "Jed, you have a newsie named Tony working for you, yes?"

Now that there was room for three abreast, Jed pulled up next to her on the other side, far away from Doc's swinging cane. "Oh yeah, Tony, sure. He's one of my best. Can sell a newspaper to a blind man. Natural born newsie."

She took a deep breath and twisted so she could view Jed more clearly. "The murdered woman, Drina Gizzi, is Tony's mother."

Jed halted mid-step. Inez hauled on Doc's arm to stop him in his forward progression. Even in the murky half-light spilling from the second-story windows, Inez could see the shock on Jed's face. "You're kidding! I didn't know Tony had any kin at all. Thought he was one of those kids that was on his own."

"Well, he is now," said Inez. "He was the one who found Mrs. Gizzi, his mother."

"Poor kid," said Jed grimly.

The three moved forward again as Sands and the officer disappeared around the corner of a dilapidated abode.

"Do you have any idea where Tony might run to ground? I was with him in the shack, but then he bolted." *No need to explain why.*

There was a pregnant pause, then Jed said, "Sorry to say, I don't. Those kids, they have bolt-holes all over town. Lots of them don't want anything to do with the law or the establishment once they're done selling for the day. Some go under the boardwalks, I know that. No idea where else they might hide."

Inez had known Jed long enough, across the poker table and the bar, to tell simply from the pauses and tone of voice when he was lying or prevaricating. She resolved to wring the truth from him next time she could talk to him alone.

"Ah!" Doc sounded relieved to catch up to Reverend Sands and the policeman. "We must be near?"

The reverend pointed. "Just to the left, here."

They rounded another corner and Inez saw the shadowed shape of the fortuneteller's sign.

The reverend entered first, followed by the policeman, Doc, and Inez. Jed brought up the rear. A snick of a match, and the room was momentarily illuminated. Inez caught a glimpse of a neat table, stub of candle still centered. Cupboard doors hung open, but otherwise, the front part of the one-room shack looked much as she left it. She could see the curtain pulled back from the sleeping area as before. The reverend and the officer blocked any view of the bed beyond. However, their faces held the same grim, tight-lipped expression. The lucifer's tiny flame guttered and died, and the reverend's voice pierced the dark: "She's gone."

Chapter Seventeen

Inez broke the cold, dark silence. "That's impossible!"

Officer Kilkenny grumbled, "I knew I shouldn't've left my lantern in the Odeon." Some quiet scuffling about, the skritch and pop of a match, and another tiny pool of illumination burst into being. The matchlight, appearing disembodied in the crowded dimness of the shack, moved ghostlike to the candle stub. The wick sputtered and burst into flame. The officer shook out the match as he held the short taper aloft. "Let's take a look around," he said. The words were reasonable, but the tone said *fat lot of good this'll do.*

"She was here!" blurted out Inez. "On the bed. She was garroted. The cord was tight around her neck. Reverend Sands and I, we saw her."

"Mrs. Stannert speaks true," said Sands. "She was lying over there," he indicated the area behind the curtain, "on the bed."

The officer glanced at Reverend Sands, then Inez. She knew exactly what was racing through his mind: Reverend Sands and Mrs. Stannert? What were they doing here, together, in French Row?

Kilkenny's calculating expression vanished, leaving only a bored, professional demeanor. He moved to the stained mattress on the minimal iron bedstead and held the candle higher, causing shadows and light, deep and bright, to bounce around the cramped quarters.

"Well, no one's here now. Reverend, if I may say, you're a minister, not a medical man, and probably not as familiar with these quarters as I am. We find women all the time who seem to have expired, cold, stiff, sure as we're standing here. Between the laudanum, the liquor, and what-all they take, we come across these, uh, ladies, who seem completely corpselike. Next thing you know, they're sitting up and wanting to know what the hell—pardon, Mrs. Stannert—what the blazes they're doing in the undertaker's basement. I suspect that might be the case here. Was she warm to the touch?"

Inez said, "Yes, but that simply means she had been killed shortly before being found." said Inez.

Kilkenny shook his head. "Well, there you go. I'll bet you a dollar to a dime that after you left, she came around and took off to sober up or get more of whatever it was she'd been drinking. She'll probably turn up in a day or two."

"Officer. She. Was. Dead," said Inez through gritted teeth.

Kilkenny gave his muffler a tug. "It's colder 'n a witch's, uh, it's cold. No fire's been kindled in here for a while. Could send anyone into a stupor. Now, Mr. Elliston and Mrs. Stannert, please step outside for a moment so I can confer with Doc and the reverend."

"I'm a member of the press," blustered Jed. "I'm here on behalf of the public. They deserve to know."

Inez wound her hand through Jed's arm and pulled him toward the door. "Mr. Elliston, come." Once outside she said in an undertone, "If you put your ear to the door I daresay you will hear discussion that will be much freer and more open than if we'd stayed inside as unwelcome interlopers."

"Good idea, Mrs. Stannert!" He removed his hat and pressed one side of his face to the gap in the door, pencil and pad poised. "Dang it," he grumbled. "I think they moved away from the door. Can't hear a thing." She suspected he was sorely tempted to move around to the backside of the small hut, but hesitated to leave her alone outside.

"Go ahead," urged Inez in a whisper. "I appreciate your chivalric impulses, but they are not necessary. No one will dare bother me here with members of the press, law enforcement, medical fraternity, and clergy in such close proximity."

With a grateful grin, Jed moved around the corner of the building.

Inez waited a few seconds to be sure he wouldn't pop back out. Inside, the muffled back-and-forth between Doc, Sands, and Kilkenny sounded ongoing with no tonal hints of an imminent conclusion. Satisfied, she stepped to the far side of the door where, earlier that evening, she had seen Madam Labasilier smash and bury something beneath a rock.

Inez knelt, using the hem of her cloak to cushion her finery from the ground. As she fumbled in the blackness by the intersection of exterior wall and cold ground, she wondered: could Labasilier have had something to do with Drina's death? Maybe even pulled the cords tight around the fortuneteller's neck? Both were small women, but obviously Labasilier had strength in those arms, the way she'd slung that iron kettle around at the Jacksons' house.

Inez's gloved knuckles knocked against a good-sized stone. She shifted it aside. Holding her breath and needlessly scrunching her eyes against the night, she reached into the depression left beneath. Her hand brushed against a soft object. An exploratory touch revealed what felt like a clump of threads, seemingly secured to one end of the object. Inez gripped the threads and rose, moving closer to the faint light leaking from the curtained window of the fortuneteller's shack. She raised the dangling shape high to see what it was. The object, flattened by the rock, revealing itself to be a small fabric doll, complete with stubby arms and legs and tiny button eyes that captured the barest hint of reflection. With a chill, Inez saw several gold threads glinting around the waist, and that the dark strands pinched gingerly between her gloved fingertips formed a long, miniature braid of hair.

The voices inside rose on a sudden note of resolve and stopped. Inez hastily shoved the doll into her cloak pocket, where it bumped gently against her hip. Its sinister similarities to Mrs. Gizzi and the circumstances of its placement caused her stomach to twist in a decidedly unpleasant knot. She stepped away from the window just as the ghostly shape of Jed Elliston appeared around the corner of the shack and moved next to her. "What did you hear?" she whispered. Before he could answer, the door swung open. Reverend Sands, Doc Cramer, and the officer spilled out into the dark.

"Any clues as to the perpetrator?" asked Inez. "I would hope that, even though this murder occurred in an area where crimes are more commonplace than not, that the death of an innocent woman and mother would merit immediate attention and investigation from those who took a vow to uphold the law."

The officer shifted on his feet. "Ma'am, it's like I explained to the reverend and Doc. There's nothing to investigate. You and Reverend Sands here say you saw the fortuneteller, apparently deceased. However, there is no deceased here now, in fact no one at all. No body, no sign of a struggle, nothing to point to foul play of any kind. It's like whoever lives here just decided to step out for a while."

"But that's not possible! I know she was dead!" protested Inez.

"In any case, I can't do anything about it. She's got a boy, you said?" He turned to Reverend Sands for confirmation.

Inez bit her tongue.

At the reverend's nod, Kilkenny continued, "If the boy decides to come around and tell someone that his mother's missing, well, maybe then we can take a look around a little. In the meanwhile, there's accommodations, if the boy finds hisself in a fix. The reverend's mission, for instance, or the Sisters of Mercy at the hospital, both take in orphans. But as for an investigation," his shrug was clear in his voice, "there's nothing to investigate."

Inez crossed her arms, as much against the cold as from frustration. "This makes no sense," she said. "Reverend, you saw her. She was dead."

"She was," said Sands. "Much as we talk about 'the dead will rise and walk on Judgment Day,' that day is not here yet. I don't see how she could have vanished into thin air like this, or why."

"Corpse-snatcher!" exclaimed Jed.

Inez heard the rustle of his notebook, the scratching of pencil on paper. She tried to imagine what sort of illegible scrawl he was composing in the dark.

He continued, "The illegal anatomists have become bolder than even Orth Stein surmised, and are now snatching the dead from their beds as they breathe their last, before the blood even cools in their veins. Perhaps they have even taken to murdering those weak and unable to defend themselves in order to have fresh specimens for their devious and evil-inspired examinations!"

"Now hold on, Mr. Elliston." Doc sounded alarmed. "You will do nothing but incite panic amongst the populace with such unverified and untrue statements. We'll have the grievously ill, who are most in need of a proper physician's attention, afraid to call on such, for fear of being robbed of life before their time, or unearthed from their final resting places once their time comes."

"Great quote, Doc!" The scribbling intensified. "And Rev, I like the bit you said about the dead rising even though it's not Judgment Day. Could you repeat that for me?"

"Jed, I don't think it's a good idea to go down this road," said the reverend. "Doc is right. You'll only terrify those most in need of aid."

"Mr. Elliston, I wouldn't put it past the judge or the marshal to clap you behind bars for printing inflammatory material, if such leads to widespread panic," said Kilkenny darkly.

The scratching of pencil stopped. Inez sensed that Jed's declarations of "freedom of the press" were about to intensify, leading to perhaps endless discussion and argument in the cold and icy mud of French Row, or, even worse, that the sulking would begin.

Jed, in a sulk, was well nigh unbearable to be around, and his sulks tended to make him even more obstinate and determined to proceed despite all reason to the contrary.

He may be a valuable ally in helping to untangle this knot, but not if he's in jail.

Inez abandoned all fantasies of engaging in further intimacies with the Reverend Justice Sands in what was left of the night and interjected, "Gentlemen, I hardly know what to say. Reverend Sands and I saw what we saw. Drina Gizzi had been strangled, that was clear. She was not moving nor breathing, but dead. Absolutely and completely. The child led us to her. Now, both have vanished. I suspect nothing more can be done tonight. I doubt the child will show up again while we are hovering about in such numbers. Perhaps he will return after sunrise. I would like to suggest that we all repair to the Silver Queen where I can offer hot toddies to those who imbibe, and coffee to those who would prefer a warm, but less potent libation. But we must go now. I believe 'last call' is fast approaching."

Kilkenny said in a much improved frame of mind, "Well, now, that sounds like a sensible course of action."

Doc began stumping away from the hovel. Reverend Sands said, "Wrong way, Doc."

Doc Cramer reversed direction. "Nighttime makes this entire area absolutely unnavigable. One can't believe anything one sees or thinks. It's a nightmare."

With the lump of the doll pressing through her pocket as a cold reminder of death and the shadows beyond death itself, Inez could only silently agree with Doc's assessment.

Chapter Eighteen

Tony stirred, drifting in and out of an unformed dream, as her mother's voice floated through the gray mist. "Tony, wake up."

Maman shook her arm urgently. "Sun's up. Elliston will be here soon."

Elliston?

The floating warm sleepiness faded as Ace said close to her ear, "Hey, Tony!"

A rude poke to the ribs shocked her to wakefulness. Reality closed in, and Tony crashed to earth with a thud. *Maman is dead. I'm with the newsies.* She thrashed around in the burlap, finally sitting up and rubbing her eyes with the palms of her hands. "Sun's up?"

"Take a look," said Ace.

Even behind her hands she could sense the shed was no longer pitch dark.

Ace continued, "You said you wanted to be out of here before Elliston showed up, so you'd better get moving."

Tony groaned, dropped her hands to her lap, and looked around. Ace was crouching by her, but the lump that was Freddy wasn't stirring yet.

"The other newsies'll be here soon. When it comes to a free breakfast, no one's ever late. Hey, I had an idea." He shed his checked jacket without a break in his patter. "Give me your coat and I'll give you mine."

Tony stared at him, befuddled.

"You don't want those swells to recognize you on the streets, right? You can stay low, but if you run into one of them, it'd be better if you looked different. So, you wear my coat and I'll wear yours. Yours is extra big, so's it oughta fit me. C'mon, there's not much time."

Tony shed the gray wool jacket, gave it to Ace, and put on his distinctive checkered worsted.

"This is really fine," said Ace as he slid an arm into the sleeve. "Even lined! I could get used to this."

"Well, don't. It's only a trade 'til the swells leave town," said Tony.

"Just kidding. Oh, one more thing." Ace stood and rummaged in a nearby sack, finally extracting a rust-colored bowler hat and a none-the-worse-for-wear black muffler. He sailed the hat toward Tony. "A flannel mouth got hisself in a pickle in the wrong part of town. He took off running and his hat couldn't keep up, so I grabbed it. Put it on."

Tony gingerly set the bowler on her head. It settled low on her ears.

Ace stepped forward and looped the anonymous length of fabric around the lower half of her face. Scratchy, it reeked of cheap tobacco and stables. He stepped back and gave her the once-over. "Perfect," said Ace. "Hides your eyes and everything. The swells won't recognize you, I guarantee."

Tony tugged the muffler down from her mouth so she could breathe and talk. "Thanks." She stood and shook the cold out of her bones. "Sorry about being so testy."

Ace shrugged. "Thanks for letting Freddy and me take over for you 'til you get things sorted. And I was thinkin'," he looked out of the corner of his eyes at Tony, unsure, "maybe I could fill in for you at the Silver Queen, until you can go back. No sense letting someone else grab the job."

She cast her eyes down, working the buttons closed on the jacket. "Sure. I usually show up right after I'm done with the papers. After suppertime, thereabouts. Just talk to the Stannerts or Mr. Jackson, tell 'em I sent you, but don't let them know I sleep here." Then she looked up. "Ace, what do you know about Mrs. Stannert?"

At the name, Ace puffed out his cheeks and blew out a quick whoosh of breath, which formed a visible cloud in the early light. His eyes darted from side to side, as if he was checking that no one else was around to hear what he was going to say. Or maybe trying to decide what to say and what to stay mum about.

"Mrs. Stannert, she's a queer one. I mean, she dresses to the nines and all, when you see her walking around, you'd think she was one of the proper society ladies from Capitol Hill. But, she's not. But she's not like the whores and madams and such either. Maybe you don't know this, 'cause you showed up a couple months ago when she wasn't around, but she runs the Silver Queen and, no mistake, she's the boss. At least, she was afore Mr. Stannert came back. He was gone a long time." Ace's shifting gaze finally came to rest, and he looked Tony straight in the eyes. "I've heard stories about her, though."

Tony thought of the previous night, of catching Mrs. Stannert in a clinch with the preacher. "What kind of stories?"

"She's not someone to cross. Folks say," Ace actually bit his lip, and Tony realized that all usual bravado he brought to his "folks say" tall tales was absent. "I've heard folks say she killed a man. Killed him stone cold dead. Some say she plugged him from a mile away with a sharpshooter's rifle. Others say she used a knife to cut out his eye and then she shot him up close and personal with this pocket pistol she carries everywhere. Whichever which way it was, she sent the gent to Old Mr. Grim. Everyone's afeared of her, so no one dares do a thing about it."

"Yeah?" An idea began to form in Tony's mind.

"Yeah." Ace drew out the one syllable until it became two. "You asked, so I told ya. I guess the only thing I'd add is, should you run crosswise of her, best to mind your p's and q's." He added, "Remember what I said about Mr. Alexander. His coffin-shop is up on Harrison, and I'll bet he'll take you on, at least part-time. See you tonight?"

Tony nodded and crawled out the back of the newsie shed. Ace's jacket wasn't as warm as the one she'd pulled from Brown's carpetbag and traded to Ace, but, along with the hat and stinky but warm neck-warmer, it'd do. Especially if she could get inside work. Tony hurried through a gray dawn on the main streets, not bothering with the alleys. It was the time of morning when those who had caroused all night were asleep on sawdust floors of saloons that rented out floor space for a dime or in feather beds in the high-class hotels. Others bunked down on straw-stuffed mattresses in boardinghouses or, if unlucky, slumped against a wall in one of the alleys or under the boardwalks. Saturday's day shifts in the smelters and the mines were yet to clock in. Leadville was as silent as it would ever get.

Grateful for the lingering shadows and the comparative emptiness of the streets, Tony made her way home. She still thought of the shack as such, even though, without Maman, no place would ever be home again.

The door to the shack was closed. Tony approached, heart hammering. With a quick glance around, she opened the door and slid inside. She pulled the door shut after her, wincing at the familiar scrape of warped wood on the sill, and listened, trying to slow her breath and her pulse. Inside was as cold as outside. The gray of an overcast sky leaked in through the purple netting on the window, shedding a light that only made the place feel colder. Not sure what she would find behind the curtain, she screwed up her courage and went forward, tweaking the thin material aside.

No Maman.

Although she didn't expect the coppers and the reverend to leave her mother lying there, the emptiness of the bed only enlarged the hollow she felt deep inside. Tony approached the bed and put one bare hand on the mattress where she and her maman had slept together, huddled for warmth under the blankets they had bought and scavenged.

Gone. Where?

She'd have to ask the reverend, or Mrs. Stannert maybe, where her maman went. Where she was buried. The thought of her mother lying under the snow and dirt in a grave was unbearable. Her mind slammed down on that thought, so painful it felt like someone was digging a grave in her heart, and instead grabbed hold of a more bearable goal: the gun.

Tony scanned the area by the bed, knelt, and threw a desperate hand underneath the bedstead. Her fingers groped for the familiar leather lanyard, the cold silver barrel, the textured ivory grip.

Nothing.

She finally threw herself on her stomach so she could reach all the way to the wall. Her arm knocked into Pisspot Brown's empty carpetbag. She pulled it out in the wild hope that the gun would magically be lying inside, waiting for her.

Nothing.

"No, *no!*" It was almost like finding Maman gone all over again. "It has to be here," she hissed to herself. "It *has* to be!"

She jumped up and began manically searching every one of the meager cupboards and hiding-spots in the small living space. Not in the ash-bucket. Not in the drawer of the rickety washstand. Not behind the three cans of beans and one tin of oysters in their larder. In desperation, she approached the last place she wanted to look, but now had to.

Her mother's small traveling chest of clothes sat wedged and almost invisible between the foot of the bed and the wall. Holding her breath and her tears, Tony pulled the chest out and threw back the lid. Maman's colorful tops and sashes were neatly folded, undisturbed. Tony, sobbing between muted gulps of air, plunged her hands into the silky soft fabrics, searching against all odds for the hard and deadly object of her desire.

One hand brushed something unexpectedly dense. Her heart leapt with impossible hope, then plummeted as she pulled out a small rectangular tin box, dented and undistinguished, swathed inside a sheer purple roll of lace. She pulled off the lace and opened the box to reveal her maman's fortunetelling cards, cradled in a soothing yellow scrap of silk. She could hear her maman's voice from when they first came to Leadville and were staying in the hotel, see her wrapping the box and securing it deep within the chest: "The people here in Leadville, I do not need the cards for them. They wear their wishes, their deepest pains and desires, their craziness for riches and happiness, always on them." After she'd set the cards deep and sleeping within the chest, Maman had turned to her, taken her small hands in her warm ones and said, "My mother gave me the cards. When it is your time, when you are become a woman, I will give them to you and they will be yours."

Tony closed the tin and shut away the memories, then gripped its sharp edges tight. *She can't give them to me now. I can only take them.*

She tucked the box into the inside pocket of Ace's voluminous gaudy jacket. Taking another deep breath, as if preparing to jump into the nearby headwaters of the ice-cold Arkansas River, she plunged a hand back into the trunk. Her fingers banged into the canvas-covered bottom of the container. Scooting them along the bottom, she searched blindly, the cheap silks and satins sliding over her hand, rippling like currents of woven threads. Her fingertips touched, then recognized cold ivory and steel. Her fingers curled around the slim object and pulled it to the surface. Sashes of maroon, purple, and copper slid and slithered from her arm as she brought her hand up to examine the object, heart gladdened through the tears. Still here. Maman's knife. Delicate little flowers were carved into the ivory at the top of the handle where the blade folded; a small inlaid figure of a fox gazed over its shoulder where her palm would naturally curl around the grip.

A screech of wood ripping away from wood outside caused Tony to shoot to her feet. Her first thought: *Pisspot Brown!* Had they been watching, and now they were going to kill her too? She broke into a sweat, feeling like a mouse trapped in a corner by a savage cat. The knife in her fist whispered to her in Maman's comforting voice: *Not a mouse, my Antonia. A fox, with sharp teeth.*

The knife.

She didn't know how to use it. In the past, she'd seen Maman snap the blade open and slash, most recently just those two months ago when that man had grabbed Tony and she'd run. Tony couldn't bear the thought of using the knife, and then losing it, or having it turned against her. The distinctive sound of the door scraping open told her that, whoever was outside, they were entering the place she had once called home.

There had to be something else she could use as a weapon. She grabbed the heavy ceramic chamberpot, thinking that if they all entered in a bunch, she might be able to throw it at their heads and shove her way past them.

A light step inside, and Tony burst from behind the curtain, ready to fling and run.

"Ha!" a woman's voice surprised, greeted Tony's appearance. Tony stopped, nonplussed.

The figure, definitely female, retreated to the entry. Well-covered against the cold with many layers of shawls and skirts, the dark-skinned woman with the lined face and angry eyes was no stranger.

Tony quailed.

The voodoo lady from Coon Row, Madam Labasilier, advanced, the fortunetelling sign that used to hang over the door now swinging from her dusky hand. The bangles on her wrist jangled with a sinister edge. "Where is she, boy? Where is the pretender?"

Tony's legs trembled and would hardly hold her upright. "W-who?" she croaked out.

"That Gypsy who pretends to see the future and read hearts. Gizzi. Where is she?"

Tony couldn't say the words, couldn't make her tongue pronounce the truth. "She's, she's gone."

"Gone!" Madam Labasilier sounded triumphant. "Of course she is gone. I sent her away. So, if you are looking for an answer, you will not find such here. This place is cursed. Tell anyone, everyone. This place should be burned to the ground to destroy the evil within. Now, go!" Labasilier shifted to one side, opening a clear path to the door.

Tony didn't wait for another command. She dropped the porcelain pot and flew out the door, her maman's cards in the hidden pocket knocking against her knees as she ran.

Tony now had two places she desperately needed to go. Mr. Alexander's coffin-shop was first, because she needed a job, something to pay for bread and cheese, something to take the place of the coins she would not be able to earn from the newspapers and the Silver Queen.

The second place was the saloon. She had decided that, between the reverend and the saloon lady, it seemed more likely Mrs. Stannert would have recognized and picked up her gun.

Now, more than ever, she needed that revolver with her, its comforting weight tugging at the lanyard about her neck.

Was it too early for the coffin-shop? People died all the time, so maybe not. Maybe she could go around and see if there was a back door to knock on. There must be. They sure didn't carry the stiffs and the coffins in and out on Harrison! Maybe someone would answer. If not, she'd find a safe place to wait back there until regular business hours.

As for the saloon, Tony remembered Mr. Jackson saying Mrs. Stannert didn't hold with the Silver Queen being open all night or on Sundays, unlike most of the other whiskey mills in town. So, it was too early to go there now. After the coffin-shop, she'd go around to the back of the saloon and ask for Mrs. Stannert. She risked maybe running into the swells again, but the chances weren't high they'd be hanging around Tiger Alley before noon. She felt sure that Mrs. Stannert would've picked up the gun. Heck, she'd practically sat on it right there in the cabin, when she'd been talking to Tony. And once she had her gun, Tony felt that the world, which seemed to be wildly spinning out of control, would sit straight upon its axis once more.

Chapter Nineteen

The sun struggled through a gap between the heavy curtains. Weakened by a scrim of clouds, it was still too bright, merciless, and early for Inez. As soon as it woke her, the sun vanished, defeated by an advancing army of clouds. Inez sat up slowly in her narrow bed. Her head swam, even though she'd taken care to not move quickly. She leaned her back against the tall wood headboard, which gave out a protesting squeak, and surveyed the confines of her small sleeping room up in the second story of the Silver Queen. Daylight was too much for her pounding hangover. She pressed the heels of her palms to her eyes, blocking out the sight. The pressure caused sparks to shoot across the inside of her eyelids, providing an unwelcome light show.

Goosebumps rose on the back of her exposed neck. It was far too cold in the room as well.

With a sigh, Inez dropped her hands and reached for a heavy wool wrap that she'd thrown over her Eastlake-style bed last night for added warmth, shortly before her mind had become too fuzzy from exhaustion and brandy to think straight. She draped the wrap over her shoulders and got up, trying to keep her movements slow and deliberate. After adjusting her nightcap, she advanced on the pert, silver-shiny warming stove in the corner of the room, scraped the ashes out, revealing the sleeping coals beneath, and restarted the fire. Straightening up, she rubbed her cold hands together, anticipating the warmth that should soon begin to fill the room, and glanced around.

Her gaze first fell on her expensive, and once-exquisite maroon evening dress, crumpled on the floor where she'd kicked it aside in a fit of pique when she'd undressed, sometime before dawn. Unnamable muck, mud, and slime stained the ruffled hem and traveled up the front where it had splashed up under the cloak. Now, that muck was probably insinuating its way into the folds of fabric throughout. It would take an expert to clean it. Her mood, already dark, darkened.

Her gaze then traveled over to the small, marble-topped corner cabinet tucked neatly into the dark area below the foot of her bed. The little cabinet had magically appeared during her absence. Sporting inlaid mahogany and cherry strips, thin delicate legs, and the bevels and curves of Louis XVI-style furniture, the beautiful little cabinet looked fussy and out of place, almost as if it were sulking in the corner. Inez thought it would have felt far more at home in her parents' Gramercy Park brownstone "palace" in New York than in the second-story slap-and-dash Western boomtown saloon. She also wondered where it came from, and rather suspected it might have been salvaged from the fire at Frisco Flo's brothel earlier that summer.

Frisco Flo.

Inez covered her eyes again, trying to focus.

Yet another thing I must do today. I arranged that meeting with Flo in advance, before all this happened. I must talk to her, come hell or high water…

The thought of hell conjured another image—that of the doll she'd unearthed in front of the Gizzis' residence last night. The doll's likeness to Mrs. Gizzi, and what Madam Labasilier had done to it, gave her the heebie-jeebies. Inez was not given to faints and shivers over talk of ghosts and "haints" and stories of the spirits of murdered victims returning to drive their killers mad. Such talk and tales were the common fodder of the men who loitered at the Silver Queen, when they weren't talking investments, shares, assays, and yields-per-tonnage. Still, that doll seemed to emanate malignity. As soon as Inez had made her way up to her room, shortly before the dawn light crept over the Mosquito Range, she'd ripped it from her pocket. Holding it with the most tentative of two-fingered pinches, she tossed it into the little corner cabinet and locked the ornately stamped brass lock with the small brass key.

Now, the doll's inner darkness was jailed in the more worldly darkness of the cabinet.

The stove was doing its job, cheerfully pouring heat into the room. Inez abandoned her wrap, pulled off her nightcap, and ran her fingers through her hair as she slowly paced the floor, willing her limbs to move at her command. Twelve determined steps took her to the window, where she looped back the dark green window hangings, allowing the overcast gray light to seep in through the sheer lace. Twelve return paces brought her to the door that led into the second-story hallway. She could detect murmurings up through the planks. Mark, no doubt, in the kitchen with Bridgette and Abe. How he managed to stay up all night playing poker and present a cheerful countenance before the noon hour was completely beyond her.

When she'd dragged herself to the upper story of the saloon after the events of the night, all she wanted to do was retrieve the bottle of fine brandy secured in the office and retreat to her sleeping quarters. Mark must have been keeping an ear out for her return, because he popped out of the gaming room as she emerged from the office, took in her appearance, and said, "Darlin', you look like somethin' the cat dragged in. Are you all right? What happened?"

"Not now."

He must have gotten the message, because he held his tongue and refrained from further comment as she continued to her room at the end of the hall, holding her bedraggled and ruined hems immodestly up and away from her evening shoes with one hand and the bottle and empty glass with the other.

Now, he was no doubt waiting to hear some explanation from her as to what had transpired after she'd stormed out of the room last night.

We stepped off the train less than a day ago, but it feels like the distant past.

In that brief interim, she had met Drina Gizzi and her daughter, only to have the mother brutally murdered hours later and her corpse vanish. As for the daughter, Inez admitted to herself that the elusive Tony, with her disguise, her fierce independence, and intense, yet still childlike manner, had inadvertently unleashed maternal feelings inside Inez. And here she thought she had securely sealed all those vulnerable emotions away in Colorado Springs after kissing the top of her two-year-old son's head and saying goodbye. From there, Inez's sister had whisked him into the train and back to the bosom of Inez's decidedly complicated family on the East Coast.

All the people and events of the past day whirled about, creating a dizzy storm in her mind as she paced: Drina, Tony, Madam Labasilier and that damn poppet, the oddly disturbing and disturbed Mrs. Alexander and her undertaker husband and his solemn companion, the medical practitioner Dr. Gregorvich. On top of them all poured the Lads from London, their quarrel with Tony, and the "unmentionables" drummer, Woods.

So, what was Woods doing in that unmentionable section of town at that unholy hour? Could he have been in the area when Drina Gizzi was killed? Could he have seen or heard something that would help lead to the murderer? Elliston's tales of corpse-stealing elbowed into her thoughts. Could that have been the fate of Mrs. Gizzi? But her corpse had disappeared so quickly, almost as if someone was watching and waiting.

And Justice Sands. Was it true that he might be forced to leave Leadville? Where did the apparently sudden impetus to replace him come from? *So help me God, if Mark has been busy behind the scenes on this…*

Inez rubbed her forehead, trying to stop her spinning thoughts and the rising feeling of frustration and impotence.

The nausea that had wound through her upon waking now gripped her with a fiercer, insistent hand. No surprise there. The glass, well used, perched on the night table by her bedstead. The empty bottle, which had emptied much too quickly, it seemed, was nowhere in sight. She was fairly certain it had rolled under the bedstead when, nearly insensate, she'd dropped it, after the warmth of the brandy had cradled her and lulled her into a deep, but unrestful sleep.

Suddenly much too warm, she stopped at the window and leaned her forehead against the lace undercurtain. The icy touch of glass bleeding through the sheer fabric was shocking, but welcome.

As the sensations of hot and cold mixed within her, the interrupted passion of last night's moments flared in her memory. *Justice. Me. Minister. Minister's wife.*

The empty brandy glass, the besmirched expensive clothing, mocked her thoughts.

Despair ratcheted around, playing havoc with her insides. She placed a palm flat against the pane, watching the steady march of pedestrians on Harrison. Somber all-business black coats and hats mixed with the drab browns and rust of working men. A few women moved among them, muffled in long winter coats, bonnets, mufflers on a morning that heralded the quick approach of a long winter.

As minister's wife, my life will devolve into chit-chat with church ladies, sewing circles, visits with the sick and needy, keeping hearth and home, staying above reproach. The closest she had come to living such a life recently was her two months in Manitou Springs visiting her very proper young sister and husband. There, they had mingled with the Springs' polite society, as well as with the wealthy consumptive émigrés from the East Coast and elsewhere who had come to Colorado in desperate hope of improving their health.

She would need to be like the women she had known while growing up, before Mark had "rescued" her from their fate. Women who were quiet. Reserved. Polite. Laced up right tight and proper. Who knew what lurked behind those carefully erected "false fronts?" Despair? Contentment? Happiness? A desire to escape it all in a bottle of laudanum or sherry? Or an acceptance of women's roles and "God's will" as set forth by men?

Inez closed her eyes and took in a deep and shuddering breath. *I can't. I can't do it. I haven't the strength for that kind of life. But I don't want to lose him. And I can't ask him to give up his calling for me. Just as he can't ask me to give up who I am for him.*

She opened her eyes, and did what she did best: Pushed it away to focus on the present. First things first.

She had to perform her ablutions, dress, and go downstairs. Face Mark, Abe, and most likely Bridgette as well, and offer some slimmed down explanation of the night's events to Mark, which meant to Abe and Bridgette as well.

Then, she had to prepare herself to meet Mrs. Sweet, otherwise known as Frisco Flo, and do what needed to be done. She told herself sternly that there was no backing down now. She'd made her decision: that train was running down the tracks, full speed ahead.

Also on the list was to meet briefly with her lawyer, Mr. Casey.

Much later that night, she had to be prepared to meet, greet, and play hostess to her usual coterie of card players. She wondered how many of the "usuals" would be there and if the Lads from London would make an appearance. Only time would tell.

Between the morning's undertakings and the requisite evening's activities, other tasks demanded to be addressed.

She was determined to track down Tony. The sooner the better. And work out a plan for keeping the youngster safe until the Lads were on the train and returning to the Springs. And then, to help Tony work out a plan for her future. Did she have any other family? Inez realized she knew next to nothing about Tony's background, aside from her "maman" and some dastardly fellow named Brown. Finally…

She removed her wrap and then her nightdress, picked up the now-steaming kettle of water atop the stove, poured it slowly into her washbasin, mixed in a little cold, and tested the warmth. Picking up a washcloth and a towel, she spared a glance at the corner cabinet.

…I must ascertain where Madam Labasilier lives, arrange a visit, and extract answers to my questions, poppet in hand.

Chapter Twenty

Clean and sober by virtue of a vigorous scrubbing with the rough washcloth and a splash of ice water from the nearby pitcher, Inez donned an equally sober dark walking outfit after making sure the back laces of her corset were adjusted such that she could take a deep breath, which was a great relief after last night's tighter-by-necessity support that the evening gown required. She pocketed her Smoot revolver, then checked the tight neat knot of hair at the nape of her neck using the mirror on the wall and the heavy silver hand mirror. Satisfied that she exuded an air of serious intent and purpose, Inez retrieved a simple winter hat and her walking coat and gloves, before marching downstairs and into the kitchen, resolve as firm and bolstered as her spine by the steel stays.

The smell of frying bacon and coffee hit her full force, inducing an unexpected wave of nausea. Mark, Abe, and Bridgette looked up when she entered. Conversation halted.

Bridgette resumed first. "It's a good morning today, ma'am, although the sky looks like we shall have more snow before the day is out. Last night's flurry is all mud now, although how it could be mud as cold as it is, is a mystery to me! Now, you sit down and I'll bring you some coffee."

"Thank you, Bridgette," said Inez primly, hanging her hat and coat on a nearby hook.

Mark jumped up and pulled out her chair for her. "Here you go, darlin'." Just as she'd predicted, he looked as if he'd just come in from a full night's sleep, hair brushed to gleaming, mustache waxed and neat. He wore a waistcoat she had given him as a gift before he disappeared more than a year and half previous. Or more accurately, he wore a replica, since the original had gone up in flames when the house had burned to the ground earlier that summer.

"Thank you, Mr. Stannert."

Abe, who sat across the table from Mark, was eyeing her as if somehow divining from her somber appearance all the ghastly events of the previous evening. One arm slung over the ladder-back chair, he toyed with the knife he'd been using to cut a slice of ham.

"Any news from home, Mr. Jackson?" she asked

He unwound from the back of the chair and returned to his ham. "Nope. Angel's not sleepin' much. Lots of pacing and belly-achin'. Not that I blame her. Mrs. Buford's there when I'm not. Told me she's never seen a woman so late in her delivery." His knuckles showed white beneath the taut brown skin. He set the knife down. "Sorry, Bridgette. Just can't get much of an appetite goin' right now."

"Well, now, Mr. Jackson, that's quite understandable." Bridgette opened the maw of the hulking iron stove and pulled out a pan of biscuits. The warm smell, redolent of comfort and cheese, wafted over them all. "Just try one of these. You need to keep your strength up! I know, first-time fathers, why, they need as much care and feeding as the mothers, but so often folks don't see that."

"More cheese biscuits?" Abe eyed the baked puck of dough as Bridgette deposited it on his plate. "We close to the end of all that cheese yet?"

"Now you recall, Mr. Jackson, it was you who brought it in, such a deal, you said. In answer to your question, I've used up just over half."

Abe sighed and picked up the biscuit.

Mark, who had been watching Inez since she came in, said, "Now that you've got your coffee, any chance you'll fill us in on last night?"

Inez took a deep breath, picked up her cup, and noted with satisfaction that her hand was steady. "Abe, do you remember that little fortunetelling woman, Mrs. Gizzi, who was with Mrs. Alexander yesterday?"

Abe leaned back in his chair, and put the biscuit, untouched, onto his plate. "Yeah."

"Well, Drina Gizzi is Tony's mother. She was killed last night." The two men leaned forward, intent. Inez could almost swear that Bridgette, busy at the stovetop, also leaned backward the better to hear.

"I ran into Tony." Inez resolved to go along with Tony's dissembling while Bridgette and Abe were about, and to avoid any mention of Reverend Sands, if possible. She had no stomach for sparring with Mark after the previous night's events. "Tony was the one who found Drina's body."

"Damn," said Mark softly.

"Mr. Stannert!" said Bridgette sharply, then with a quick change of tone, "Poor little mite! He's one of Mr. Elliston's newsboys, isn't that right? Wears a red cap?"

"That's right," Inez saw that the cup in her hand was now trembling. The motion had set up tiny waves in the surface of the coffee, which looked darker than night and stronger than sin. She set the cup on the scarred wood table with a clack.

"Somehow," Inez continued, "between the time I saw Drina's body and found a representative of the law, the corpse disappeared."

Abe leaned forward. Mark's eyebrows shot up. "What?"

"She's gone." Inez shook her head. "I don't know who, why, or even how. Officer Kilkenny thinks she 'came to' and walked out. But she was definitely dead. Even if I were to give credence to Kilkenny's supposition, I cannot imagine she would leave her shack in French Row in the dead of night to go wandering about. She was a fortuneteller, not a—" Inez stopped, aware of Bridgette. The cook had given up the pretense of cooking and was standing there, a slab of raw bacon hanging from her long-tined fork, listening avidly. Inez discarded the word "whore" and continued, "She was not a lady of the evening, as it were. And I cannot see her leaving her child behind."

The sight of that raw bacon, pink meat and glistening fat impaled on the sharp end of Bridgette's fork, caused Inez's stomach to roil. She pushed herself away from the table, leaving her breakfast untouched. "I have some errands to run. If Tony should come to the back door, please let him know it is important I talk to him. I should return by noon."

Mark rose and, too late to help her out of her chair, helped her into her coat instead. Holding the passdoor to the saloon's main room for her, he said in an undertone, "You were in French Row last night? Inez, what the hell happened? What were you doing there?"

She brushed his concern away as she swept through the dim and silent room, the click of her walking boots echoing off the wood floor and walls. "I am fine, Mark. I was not dressed appropriately for the weather, but short of ruined skirts, I survived."

"Was Reverend Sands with you?"

She faced him, raising a warning hand and speaking deliberately. "Mr. Stannert, our agreement stipulates that we lead separate lives. You do not interfere with my private life nor I with yours."

He captured her hand and held it so she couldn't move. His expression, tight with frustration, held her equally still. "Yet you continue to wear the rings I gave you, rings that signify our marriage, *Mrs.* Stannert. I am still your husband by the laws of God and man. I do believe that affords me some leeway in asking after your whereabouts."

Unable to lower her arm, Inez clenched her hand into a fist, feeling the double bands of silver and gold bite into her fingers.

He let her go and stepped back. "Darlin', I'm not looking to argufy. Don't get on your high horse just because I was concerned for your wellbeing. Look at it from my perspective. You traipse off into the night in high dudgeon, then trail in hours later, all disarranged." He smoothed his mustache, as if pondering his next words. "If you were with the reverend, that means you weren't swannin' around in a bad part of town in the middle of the night by yourself. That's all." His voice softened. "Also, I want to show you something today, this morning, if possible, before you do anything else."

She'd begun bristling for a fight and his unexpected retreat left her off-balance. She responded, "Not this morning, Mark. I have an appointment with Miss Carothers. You should stay here, in case Tony comes around."

Mark seemed to consider, then nodded. "All right, Inez. I'll wait for you."

Inez departed, feeling a little guilty. She pushed that feeling aside, telling herself that what she was doing was all for the best. After all, it was Mark who had first introduced her to the technique she'd just employed on him: *When lying by omission, be sure to wrap the empty space with a thin layer of the truth.*

Inez hastened to her friend Susan Carothers' photographic studio on Chestnut. Susan had accompanied Inez to Colorado Springs and had become entangled in the events that had transpired, much to her ultimate sorrow, so Inez's words to Mark were true: She wanted to see how Susan was holding up, after her trials in the shadow of Pike's Peak. However, that wasn't the only reason Inez was anxious to be at Susan's studio that morning.

Ignoring the CLOSED sign in the window, Inez twisted the brass doorknob, gratified to find it unlocked. She entered to the clink of the tiny bell above the door. Feminine squeaks and muffled laughter floated from the back punctuated by Susan's calm admonitions: "Miss April, Miss June, please don't make faces at Miss May. She needs to hold absolutely still if I am to get a decent exposure."

Inez walked toward the voices, calling, "Susan, it's Inez."

Skirts rustled, and Susan came out of the room, pushing back the curly fringe of dark hair across her forehead. She smiled. "Inez! How good to see you. When did you return?"

"Late yesterday." Inez walked forward and put both hands on Susan's shoulders, searching her countenance. "I came as soon as I was able to catch my breath. How are you?"

The question was laden with genuine concern.

Susan's smile wavered, sorrow lingering at the corners of her mouth. "Work is the great healer, and I have been busy since my return from the Springs. Although this latest commission," she rolled her eyes toward the portrait room in back, "is proving to be more vexing and to take longer than I thought it would."

"I would imagine Mrs. Sweet is recompensing you handsomely for your efforts?" Assured by Susan's nod, Inez said, "I saw your sign is turned to CLOSED. Still, you might consider locking your front door as well."

"Good idea." Susan unhooked a key from the chatelaine at her waist and did as Inez suggested.

"I also have a favor to ask of you," Inez continued. "There is a young girl of my acquaintance, the daughter of a woman recently come to town who has just died under mysterious circumstances, most likely murdered."

Susan turned to her, brown eyes wide. Inez hastened, "It is a sad situation. The girl has no other relatives that I know of, and, for reasons I won't go into now, I need to keep her relationship to the murdered woman confidential. I would claim her as a distant relative, but I cannot, with the way things are. My question is this. Would it be all right with you if I pass her off as a distant relative of yours, a niece, who is visiting Leadville?"

"Of course! I'm so sorry to hear of this." Susan touched the signboard and set it swinging on its chain in the window. She then drew the curtain to block sight into her anteroom. "Poor child. If there's anything else I can do, if she needs a place to stay, just ask."

"I will let you know. I would like to introduce her to you, I hope later today. Thank you, dear friend, yet again." There was a thump from the sitting room and a freshet of giggles. "Meanwhile, it sounds as if you have your hands full. I will have a word with Mrs. Sweet and be on my way."

Susan pointed down the tiny hall in the opposite direction of the portrait room. "She's waiting in my parlor. Help yourself to tea, and please tell Mrs. Sweet I am working with Miss May, and still have Miss June to go."

Susan returned to her camera and clients. Clutching her handbag tight in both hands, Inez took as deep a breath as her stays would allow and walked into the parlor.

Frisco Flo sat in the red plush overstuffed armchair, idly perusing an issue of *Godey's Lady's Book*, delicate china teacup and saucer on a nearby occasional table. She had crossed her legs in an unfeminine fashion at the knee, and one stockinged ankle, fully displayed, circled idly. A fleur-de-lys pattern, picked out in salmon-tinted embroidery on ivory silk, marched up the half visible calf and disappeared under a layer of frothy red lace petticoats beneath the knife-sharp folds of her proper gray skirt. Flo lifted her baby-doll blue eyes from the page.

"Mrs. Stannert, welcome! I told my girls to deliberately drag their feet and be silly during their sittings so we'd have time to conduct our business." Flo patted her blond curls, checking that her pert dove-gray hat stayed at its rakish angle. "Please, sit and let's get started. Tea?" She gestured with the periodical to a cozy-covered teapot and second cup and saucer on the table.

"No thank you, Mrs. Sweet." Inez perched on the edge of a matching loveseat.

Flo set aside the magazine. "I hope your extended holiday in the Springs was pleasant?" Her red-painted mouth twitched.

"As pleasant as could be expected. I saw my son, my sister." Inez's fingers played restlessly along the edge of the handbag as if picking out a random tune on the piano. "Mr. Stannert belatedly joined us, as I think you know."

"Oh, yes. His absence was noted with some sorrow, just as his earlier return caused quite a stir in certain circles." Flo lifted her eyes to the ceiling, as if to indicate the angels themselves had descended to warble hosannas at his coming. The blue gaze returned to Inez. "In fact, after you left for the Springs but while he was still in town, he stopped by our new house on Fifth Street. Strictly on business, I assure you." Her mouth quirked again. "He looked around, made all the right admiring noises about the décor and the new girls, and congratulated me on making an astute and well-timed move to the 'better part of town.' Then he asked, oh so casually, whether my building on State might possibly be for sale."

Inez raised her eyebrows. "He did?"

"Oh, yes. We had a merry little waltz around that topic. Such a charmer, that husband of yours. He can talk the paint off the walls. However, your secret is still safe with me." She uncrossed her legs, and the embroidered ankle disappeared from view. "So, you are still moving forward with your plans? I heard no different from you. But there is probably time if you want to change your mind."

Inez shook her head. "I am proceeding as planned. Did you have any problems from your end?"

"Oh, heavens, no. All I needed to do was drop a hint of the whereabouts, the payment involved, a *guarantee* of success, and," Flo snapped her fingers through lace gloves, "done."

"When? The timing is critical, as I explained in my letter."

"Most likely this coming weekend. Certainly no later than the end of the month. That's what you wanted, correct?"

"Correct." Inez reached into her handbag, pulled out an envelope, and slid it across the table to Flo. "Thank you. You will let me know when arrival is imminent? I want to be prepared."

Flo smiled lazily and, with one delicate, lace-covered fingertip, slid the envelope back. "No hurry. I'd rather we wait until we know that everything works out to your satisfaction, *partner*."

"Ah, we must discuss that next. Complex circumstances, you understand at least in part what they are, have made it necessary for me to withdraw from our partnership on the State Street building."

Flo's gaze narrowed.

"I am sorry," Inez added.

Flo sat back and regarded Inez. "Our deal was once I had completed the move to the Fifth Street residence, which I have done, you would pay me the balance for the State Street building. You gave me a down payment and we signed an agreement. I've had many offers for the building since then, which I turned away as a result of that agreement. This is most unfortunate. I'm doing well, but the girls and I aren't exactly awash in gold and silver. I was counting on the balance from that sale."

Inez leaned forward. "I believe I can find a suitable buyer quickly, one who will pay as much, or perhaps even more, than I was prepared to. If so, and you are satisfied, you could then return my down payment, holding back a portion for yourself, say, ten percent, for my reneging on our deal."

Flo tipped her head, considering. Inez watched as Flo's gaze traveled to the far corner of the room and lingered there. Inez swore she could almost see the wheels turning in the madam's brain. Money was a big motivator for Flo. However she and Inez were bound by more than a mutual desire to ensure the health of their individual bank accounts. Inez was counting on Flo's desire for a compromise that would keep their relationship on an even keel and assure secrets on both sides would be kept.

Flo's gaze returned to Inez. The frown lines between her eyebrows had smoothed away and the storm clouds had cleared from her blue eyes. Before she even spoke, Inez knew that Flo would agree, at least in concept.

"Who do you have in mind for this quick and lucrative sale?"

Inez relaxed infinitesimally into the loveseat. "Isn't it obvious? Mr. Stannert."

Flo laughed, a sharp note. "Excuse me, *Mrs.* Stannert, but isn't that a bit like robbing Peter to pay Paul?"

"You will have a buyer for the building *and* your money. Do you really care whose pocket that money comes from?"

"Mmmmmm."

Inez kept her expression neutral. Flo's perceptive blue-eyed gaze seemed to pierce the deliberate veil of indifference, revealing all that Inez sought to keep to herself.

Flo finally said, "And you shall be free. Of your obligation to me, in any case." She then shrugged. "Oh, what the hell. Agreed. I shall await a visit from Mr. Stannert with hat in hand and the words I long to hear on his lips. Words that indicate he is willing to pay a considerable sum of money for that pile of bricks at the corner of State and Pine." Flo picked up the teapot, swirled its contents. "Still warm." She poured a portion into the second teacup, adding, "Shall we have a drink to seal the deal?"

Inez wanted to demur, not being a particular fan of tea, but Flo, with a sly grin, extracted a small sterling silver flask, exquisitely embossed with butterflies and flowers, from her red-lined black silk reticule. "A little something extra to smooth it out, perhaps?"

Inez smiled back. "In that case, Mrs. Sweet, I believe I shall join you."

Chapter Twenty-one

Stiff from crouching in the alley behind Alexander's Undertaking, Tony stood, stretched, and shook out her hands. She figured an hour or two must have passed while she lurked around some empty crates to the side of the coffin-shop, waiting for a decent hour to call on Mr. Alexander. She'd spent the time practicing with Maman's knife, trying to see how fast she could pull it from her pocket and unfold the blade without stabbing herself or snagging it on her coat. The handle had a ring that, when pulled, folded the blade back into its slot. Her maman could open the blade, slash, fold, and make the knife disappear in a blink. Maman hadn't used it often, but when she did...

A wave of sorrow rolled over her. Swallowing around the ache, Tony tried once again to imitate the fluid motions of her maman. The blade made a satisfying little clickety-click sound when opening, which emboldened, but also worried her. If she used the knife to defend herself against someone—Worthless Pisspot Brown and his gang came to mind—wouldn't that little sound give her away? Ace sometimes flashed a knife around. Nothing as fancy as Maman's, but he seemed to know how to use it, if his skill at mumblety-peg was proof. Maybe she could ask him for some pointers, just in case she got in a dust-up. She could imagine Ace teasing, "Think the stiffs'll come to life at night and chase ya while you're sweeping?"

For now, she had to prepare herself to go knock on the back door of Alexander's, doff her cap, duck her head, ask if the coffin-shop still was looking for a boy, and offer politenesses like "Yes sir," "No sir," "Thank you, sir." Tony glanced at the sky, trying to gauge the time. The clouds pretty much hid the sun, but she thought normal business hours were probably underway. Not that coffin-shops would keep regular hours. Folks died any time of day or night.

Tony took a deep breath for courage, polished the toes of her worn shoes on the backs of her trouser legs, then knocked on the whitewashed rear door. She was thinking that white was an odd color for a coffin-shop door when she heard the tread of masculine footsteps approach. She whipped off the oversized rust-colored derby just as the door opened.

With a shock, she recognized the bespectacled square-faced man she'd seen the previous night. The one who had had to peel the posh woman all in black away from the door of the Bon Ton Billiard Hall. The same woman who had paid Maman a hundred dollars in gold, who had seemed half mad with grief. What had she said with her crazy words? "It was a gift." Tony was struck with a thought that had the force of a thunderclap. Had she been talking about the payment to Maman? She'd also said something about killing with kindness, about making amends.

The figure of the woman in black rose up in her mind's eye: Tall, taller than Maman and strong. She'd held tight to that doorknob and her husband'd had a real struggle pulling her away. Didn't crazy people have a crazy strength sometimes? Tony pictured a tall, black-clad shape overpowering her maman in the shack, Maman falling, grabbing at the air with empty hands as cords cut off her breath, not expecting this attack from so proper a woman.

A shiver grabbed her legs.

"Yes?"

The husband of the madwoman was looking at her curiously. "Can I help you?" he asked.

A somber voice to match the somber suit. Yet, Tony detected a teeny note of eagerness. Maybe he thought she was there because someone had died and needed a coffin-box.

She finally stammered out, "M-Mr. Alexander, sir?"

"Yes?" He adjusted his spectacles. Tony noticed that the thick glass made his eyes look bigger, sadder.

"I, I heard that you were looking for help. A boy to sweep up. That kind of thing. I was wondering if the job was still open."

Mr. Alexander's magnified eyes widened. "Yes, it is." He looked Tony over, top to toes. "I was thinking of someone a little older. How old are you? And your name?"

"Tony—" It occurred to Tony that using her own last name might not be a good idea. "Tony D—" She almost said Tony Deuce, but quickly changed her mind. "Donatello. And I'm—" More quick improvisation. "Fourteen, sir. Just small for my age. But I'm strong. I can sweep right well, and probably do almost anything else you need."

"Tony." Mr. Alexander seemed to ponder. "I'm certainly well aware that size and strength do not necessarily correspond."

Tony thought of the woman in black again.

The undertaker opened the door a little farther, saying, "You *do* know what my business is? That I am an undertaker and embalmer?"

Emboldened by the wider entrance, Tony took a tentative step forward. "Yes, sir. I know."

Mr. Alexander stepped back, allowing Tony to enter. "I'm going to ask you some questions, and I want honest answers, no dissembling. By that, I mean no falsehoods. Have you ever been around a corpse?"

Tony nodded, her throat tightening.

"And what do you make of them, the dead?" he inquired gently.

Tony struggled to form an answer. She wasn't sure what he was looking for. Then, the answer popped out. "They're just... dead. Nothing there anymore."

"Nothing." He repeated encouragingly. "What about spirits, ghosts, the afterlife?"

Tony shook her head. She knew where she stood on this question. She couldn't lie, even if she wished she could, even though Maman had insisted there was more, that she had seen it.

Maybe Maman had, but Tony never had. And when she'd seen and touched Maman, so dead and empty..."I don't believe in spirits and such," she said finally. "I know other people believe different. But, what I've seen, Mr. Alexander, sir, is that when somebody dies, they're gone." She searched for a different word but couldn't find one. "They're just gone."

Mr. Alexander nodded. "It's important to be respectful of the beliefs of the bereaved who must carry on in this corporeal world. We do so despite all logic and science to the contrary, which has never managed to find conclusive proof of life beyond the grave. Now, suppose you were sweeping downstairs, where we store the caskets and where we sometimes store a corpse waiting for an inquest, or for transport to family. If you were down there by yourself and heard a thump, a scratching, some little noise, or sensed a presence, what would you think of that?"

Tony shrugged. "Someone dropped something upstairs? Or maybe there's rats? But I'm fast with a broom. If it's a rat, it won't be scratching or thumping for long."

Mr. Alexander smiled, and Tony sensed she'd passed some kind of test. "I need someone to clean and tidy upstairs and down, who is punctual, and who can follow instructions to the letter, six days a week, three hours in the evenings, after closing. This schedule makes allowance for a person to take other employment during regular business hours, if desired. For this part-time employment, I am willing to pay two dollars a day, a grown man's wage. But I need someone responsible, with a grown man's rational perspective and logic. All that said, if you are still interested in working at Alexander's Undertaking, Mr. Donatello, you have a job."

Chapter Twenty-two

After downing a satisfying cup of heavily laced black tea, Inez managed to steer the conversation between herself and Flo to local conjurors and fortunetellers, specifically, Madam Labasilier and Mrs. Gizzi. At the mention of Madam Labasilier, Flo wrinkled her nose in distaste.

"Another reason I'm glad to be shut of the house on State Street. It's too close to the rowdy element, Kate Armstead, Madam Labasilier, and the rest. We needed a more 'elevated' neighborhood for our high-end clientele."

Inez raised her eyebrows. "I thought Madam Labasilier was a hoodoo woman."

Flo heaved an irritated sigh. "When we were on State, my girls were always sneaking across the street to her for love potions, spells, curses. It's a waste of money. That's what I told them. Oh, they moan and weep about being working girls, and I tell them, straight out, if you weren't spending what you make on tonics and talismans, you could save up enough to leave the sporting life, if that's what you really want to do. Of course, they don't listen." Flo pursed her lips, then brightened. "Now that we've moved to Fifth Street, they don't traipse down there nearly so often. As I've told them repeatedly, I *do* have a certain image to maintain, now that we've moved uptown. If they don't see fit to live up to my standards, well, there are bright new faces coming in on the train every day. It's not like I'd be a Hard-luck Lucy when it comes to finding replacements."

Inez reflected that nearly every corner of society, including the whoring business, had its pecking order. Inez could well imagine Flo, being at the top of the trade on Fifth, would frown on her women paying visits to Coon Row. "I understand a few of your 'boarders' brought Madam Labasilier to the Jacksons' home with the idea of speeding Angel Jackson's delivery. I walked in just as Doc Cramer unceremoniously showed her the door."

Flo simply rolled her eyes. "I won't ask which girls were involved. I know some are betting on the date when Angel drops. Perhaps a few, seeing their chosen date approach, hoped to hurry things along."

Inez cocked her head, thinking. "Do you think Madam Labasilier would resort to physical violence?"

Flo gave an unladylike snort. "She's a little, shriveled-up hag. Not that violence is unheard of in Coon Row." Flo leaned forward, almost slopping the remainder of her tea onto her lap. "Did you hear about the dust-up that occurred while you were gone?" She didn't wait for Inez to respond. "One of Kate Armstead's girls moved to another house and Kate snuck to the window one night and threw a bucket of lye over her. Then, about a week later, Kate attacked her beau with a razor. I *knew* it was time to leave State Street." Flo sat back, vindicated in her decision.

"So, do you think it possible that Labasilier might attack someone, if provoked?"

"I'd say she relies on intimidation of a different sort, using her reputation and preying on the fears of others, waving gris-gris in the face of her enemies, spouting nonsense to scare them witless."

Inez thought that Flo was starting to sound a lot like Doc on the subject, but persisted. "What with your move, it sounds like she might have lost clients. Suppose there was a rival for her business? Do you think she might resort to physical weaponry?"

"What kind of weaponry?"

"A garrote, for instance."

"Goodness, I can't imagine she has enough strength in those skinny arms to strangle a chicken."

Thinking back to Madam Labasilier swinging her cast-iron kettle in front of the Jacksons' home, Inez was inclined to disagree with this assessment of the woman's physical strength. In addition, when Inez had spied her hours later outside Gizzi's shack, Labasilier's entire posture was different—she stood straight and seemed to have shed years in the bargain. Could the crooked frame and shuffling gait be an illusion to make herself look older and frailer than she was?

Inez's musings on that point were interrupted when Flo asked, "You say Labasilier has a rival? If there's a new spellcaster in town, please tell me. That way, if my girls start talking, I'll be able to cut them off at the pass."

Inez focused on the painted pink flowers on the side of the teacup, and decided it might be advantageous to share more information with Flo than she'd originally intended. If anyone knew about the goings-on in the netherworld of State Street, it would be Flo. Despite Flo's assertions that she had "left it all behind" in her recent move, Inez was willing to bet that the whorehouse madam paid close attention to State Street's denizens and their doings, if only to keep a finger on the pulse of Leadville's preferred vices.

Inez lifted the teapot and added another measure into her cup. Flo tipped a generous amount from her flask into Inez's tea without prompting.

"Drina Gizzi," Inez said.

"Gizzi?" Flo looked blank.

"She lived in the French Row area. I believe she had only been there a couple of months. A sign above her door reads FUTURES AND FORTUNES TOLD."

Comprehension dawned. "Oh! The Gypsy?"

"She's a Gypsy?"

"Well, she reads tea leaves, palms, cards, that sort of thing. So, she's a Gypsy. A traveler. What have you." Flo lifted a shoulder in dismissal. "Unlike most of her ilk, she seems to be operating alone. I haven't heard much about her." She paused. "Well, that's not entirely true."

Inez gestured with her cup: *go on.*

Flo obliged. "Some of my girls went to her once, but I gather she didn't really tell them what they wanted to hear, you know, the 'you will meet and marry and tall handsome man and, oh yes, he'll be immensely wealthy' type of future they like to imagine. In any case, I can't imagine Madam Labasilier would see her as a threat. Labasilier rules State Street as far as that kind of business goes."

"I am on State Street myself, but I can't say that I recall hearing about her before," Inez pointed out, draining her lukewarm tea.

Flo's mouth quirked. "I guess you move in different circles than waiter girls and whores, Mrs. Stannert."

Inez thought on Drina Gizzi, accompanied to the Jacksons by the dignified Mrs. Alexander. "Maybe 'moving in different circles' is the key here."

"Key to what?" asked Flo, adding, "Why so many questions, Mrs. Stannert?"

Inez sighed. "Drina Gizzi was murdered last night, garroted. When the law arrived, her body had vanished. Poof!"

Flo looked intrigued. "Maybe she wasn't dead. Maybe it was a ruse. Maybe she got on the wrong side of someone or owed money—'taxes' to the nightwatch to look the other way, that sort of thing—so decided to fake her own death and vamoosed, with no one the wiser."

"She was definitely dead. I found her. I saw her face. The garrote was a silver and gold cord." Inez paused. "Speaking of, have you had a 'merchant of unmentionables' selling his wares on Fifth lately?"

"Russet hair? Sly face? Oh, yes. He knocked on our door a few days ago. Had some lovely stockings, unusual patterns. And beautiful corset covers. Hmmm. It just occurred to me, he's a traveler and a loner as well. Maybe the two of them were in cahoots or…" Her voice drifted off. An odd shadow crossed her face.

"A traveler? Well, he sells door to door, so of course he travels." Comprehension dawned. "Oh, you mean he's a Gypsy?"

"He looks like one."

"And by 'in cahoots' are you saying he and Mrs. Gizzi might know each other and...what?"

Flo opened and closed her mouth, then lifted her empty cup, taking a pretend sip, pinkie finger delicately extended. Inez squinted suspiciously at her. Inez had seen Flo display many moods, including white-hot rage, heart-breaking despair, full-on flirtation, and all-business calculation. But this was the first time she'd seen her so hesitant.

"Mrs. Sweet?" she prodded.

Flo leaned forward to set the cup back on its china saucer. "A moment, Mrs. Stannert. I'm trying to figure out how to say this to you." She straightened back in the chair, recrossed her legs, and commenced tapping the arms of her chair with restless fingertips. "You mentioned this fortuneteller was strangled with a silver and gold cord."

"Two of them, actually, wound into a thin rope."

"Well, this drummer. He had some beautiful silver corset laces, although I didn't see any like those, silver and gold. We bought lots of the silver. Leadville, silver barons, you understand."

"And?"

Flo took a deep breath. Her military-style gray wool bodice, relieved by a white fichu that spilled lace down the front of her bosom, puffed up like a pigeon's breast, then subsided as she exhaled. "And he came back for a *visit* last night. He had quite a bit of money. Spent pretty freely buying champagne for the girls and was free with his pretty compliments. But when it came down to business, I asked him to leave."

Inez kept her astonishment in check. "Really? Why? Spent too much on the champagne and didn't save enough for services?"

"Oh, he had plenty more gold in that purse of his. No, it wasn't that. He was looking to satisfy unusual appetites."

Curiosity piqued, Inez said, "Unusual?"

Flo clamped her lips shut.

"Flo, I'm not exactly an innocent, for heaven's sake. What are we talking about here? Whips? Boys? Girls? Goats? Spit it out."

She shook her hair, blond curls springing left and right. "Let's just say if he were involved with the death of the fortuneteller, the act of strangling her might have excited passions quite out of the ordinary, and leave it at that."

Inez emitted a weak "Oh."

Flo continued. "I told him he was not likely to find any who would help or oblige him, no matter how much money he offered." She winced. "I actually said he'd have better luck satisfying his degenerate urges by prowling Stillborn Alley. Plenty of near-dead women to be found there. Not my exact words, but close."

"I see." Despite the warming stove, Inez felt cold, right down to the end of her fingertips.

Flo seemed repelled by the memory. "Imagine. The nerve. What kind of house does he think I run?"

"The nerve, indeed," said Inez faintly. She recalled Woods' nervousness in Stillborn Alley, his staring eyes, fixed expression, and hissed invocation to her that it would be best if they "forgot they ever saw each other." Had he found what he craved in Stillborn Alley? In Drina Gizzi's hovel? The silver and gold cords he had presented to Inez after his successful afternoon of selling at the Silver Queen, did they "tie" into his obsessions? Inez's skin crawled. She resolved to never wear those laces, and indeed to throw them away as soon as possible.

Inez felt certain from the set on Flo's face that she'd get no more information about the drummer. Since the madam seemed inclined to chat otherwise, Inez decided to test the waters on other locals of interest who seemed to have a connection to Drina either directly or tangentially.

"What about the Alexanders? He's an undertaker. Have you heard much of them? They are new to me."

Flo's indignation subsided and she fluffed her hair absently. "Well, you know Mr. Alexander is a coffin-man. Goodness, Mrs. Stannert, what is this current obsession you have with death and the afterlife? Fortunetellers, coffin-men, spiritualists."

"Spiritualists?"

"That would be Mrs. Alexander. The mister handles the stiffs while the missus talks with the spirits." Flo laughed, a surprisingly nasty sound, then covered her mouth with her fingers. "Oh, pardon. I should be more sympathetic. Talk is the Alexanders lost a girl child before they moved to Leadville. In fact, I've heard the mister hoped the move would make a new start for him and his wife. Well, that didn't quite work out."

"What do you mean?"

"I gather she's obsessed with their dead child. Since they arrived, in addition to regularly attending church, she holds séances to which she invites a select few. Seems she's determined to find a medium, a channel to reach the other world and communicate with her child. It's sad, really."

Inez nodded, thinking this explained the connection between Mrs. Alexander and Drina Gizzi. "What about this physician who seems to be allied with Mr. Alexander, Gregorvich. Is he new to town as well?"

"Oh Dr. G. He's one of the self-proclaimed 'saints of Stillborn Alley.'" At Inez's confusion, Flo elaborated. "Because of all the bad press about State Street and particularly Stillborn Alley, a group of do-gooders have taken it upon themselves to lift up the downtrodden and clean up the rows, but with Christian kindness and charity instead of just riding the unfortunates out of town on rails. Doc Cramer brought along Dr. G one night, and he's been there ever since. There are others trying to help as well, for all the good it does them or State Street, for that matter." Flo eyed Inez, as if expecting her to respond.

Inez ran a mental finger down the list of people she knew who had connections to Drina: Labasilier, the Alexanders, possibly the drummer, and maybe Doc Cramer and Dr. Gregorvich. "Thank you, Mrs. Sweet. It sounds as if I have missed a great deal in my absence."

"That you have." The three words were laden with portent.

Inez frowned. "There's more?"

"You haven't asked about the one person I assumed would be the first name on your lips after our business was completed."

Inez shuffled through her thoughts like a well-worn deck of cards and came up with nothing. "And that would be?"

"Reverend Sands, of course!"

Guilt stabbed deep. "Well, I know he's back from his own travels. That he's very busy."

"So you don't know about the brouhaha at the church?" pressed Flo.

Inez steeled herself. "I had heard rumors, but only rumors, that he might be taking another position elsewhere, farther west, away from Leadville."

"You acted so unconcerned during our little chat. I was betting all this"—Flo gestured around the parlor in a vague way—"plotting meant you knew."

Alarm grew, crowding out other thoughts. "Knew what?"

"Well, I didn't think I would be the one to tell you this." Flo set down the cup and clasped her hands tight in her lap. "A little birdy told me Reverend Sands received a telegram this morning. His new post has been confirmed. He's going to announce it tomorrow at the service. The church will be gaining a new minister and the good reverend will be leaving within the week."

Chapter Twenty-three

Inez set the teacup down gently. It felt that if she didn't take care, the delicate china cup would shatter from the sheer force of her emotion. Loss raced through her like the ferocious winds that tore in over the Rockies from the north. "And who, may I ask, was this little birdy?"

"Telegraph office messenger." Flo's gaze was tinged with sympathy. "I won't say he peeked at the message, exactly, but—"

Inez waved her hand in dismissal. She didn't want to hear another word. Not now.

Flo, apparently ignoring or misinterpreting her gesture, continued, "I thought you must have your bags still packed. What with the schedule you've given me, I was certain that you and Reverend Sands had made plans."

Inez stood up abruptly, cutting off further conversation. "Thank you, Mrs. Sweet. I have much to think on and much more to do. I'm certain you understand."

"Of course." Flo seemed at a loss for words. She finally shook her head. "Men. Always running off at the worst times and leaving us and our broken hearts behind. After Mr. Sweet left for greener pastures, I just told myself, Florence, the only one you can count on is yourself and you just damn well better keep that in mind. And I have." She stood as well. "You and me, we make our own way in the world, and that's all for the best, don't you think? No palm-reading or card scrying to pin our hopes on, or moaning after some big strong man to save us from the big bad world. We build our own fortunes, forge our own futures."

Inez was about to respond when a babble of women's voices came floating into the waiting room, accompanied by the clatter of footsteps. "I do believe Miss Carothers has finished," she said instead.

No sooner were the words spoken than Susan popped her head around the door. "Done, Mrs. Sweet. Individual portraits of each and I posed them as a group as well."

"Thank you, sooooo much," Flo gushed. "I'll arrange for July, August, and September's sittings once I have a chance to see the results. I know the photographs will be lovely. We'll hang them in the new drawing room. Won't that be nice, girls?"

The girls chorused their approvals.

Flo continued to Susan, "And I apologize for them being such a handful. I will pay you extra for the general nuisance and for any damages. Didn't I hear a vase hit the floor earlier? I promise the next group will be more sedate." Flo shook a mock finger at the three young women. "In the future, save the high-jinks for the boudoirs, yes, ladies? Now, on with your coats and let's go. We've taken enough of Miss Carothers' time."

While Susan left to unlock the front door, the three portrait-sitters squeezed into the room and converged on the coat tree which sprouted a number of small fashionable black walking hats and black, ankle-length good-quality wool cloaks. They busied themselves wrapping up, covering bright-colored outfits that were more appropriate for the drawing room than the street.

With a nod to Flo, who was extracting gold pieces from her coin purse, Inez moved out the parlor door to escape the welter of excited chit-chat and flutter of coats, hats, and gloves as the women all donned their outerwear at the same time.

When she reached the front door, Susan, who was hovering beside it, stopped Inez, asking, "Do you feel ill? You're pale all of a sudden."

Inez forced a wan smile. "Much to think on, that's all. Will you be here at your studio the rest of today?" At Susan's nod, she added, "If your 'niece' comes around, I will bring her by. In any case, I shall see you at church tomorrow. Perhaps we can talk after the service." Inez pulled the door open and hurried out, desperate for the sting of cold air to freeze the shock and dismay in her soul.

A familiar figure in an impeccable peacock blue frock coat with matching soft-crowned derby hat stood with his back to the building, apparently surveying the street, walking stick held loosely behind him.

"Mark!" Inez clutched her purse with its secrets to her waist. "What are you doing here?"

Mark Stannert swung around. "Well, Mrs. Stannert, I decided the only way I'd get to see you anytime soon was to—" He stopped and his eyes widened as Flo and her women spilled out of Susan's studio, around Inez, and onto the boardwalk.

With choruses of "Helloooo!" and "Good day, Mr. Stannert!" the cluster of black-cloaked women flowed past Mark with small finger waves and wide inviting smiles. Flo, who was last, said demurely, "Why, Mr. Stannert, what a *surprise*."

Mark who had nodded automatically at each of the spring months as they sashayed past, recovered himself enough to tip his hat to Flo. "Mrs. Sweet."

Flo fluttered her eyelashes at him. "Mrs. Stannert and I just had the most interesting chat about the State Street building. I'll let her tell you all about it." With that, Flo moved on past, clucking after at her brood like a hen after its chicks.

Mark regarded Inez with some surprise and not a small amount of alarm. "You and Mrs. Sweet were confabulating? That sounds like a dangerous combination, akin to settin' the fuse to a keg of giant powder."

"I'll explain, but first, *you* need to explain," she countered. "Why are you here? Are you following me?" The idea that Mark might be dogging her every move was disturbing. Inez started to brush past him toward Harrison.

"Wait." Mark grasped her elbow. "You said you were going to Miss Carothers' studio, so I decided to wait and…Let's walk a bit. Are you going back to the saloon or…? I know, don't say it. I have no right to ask, but I have something I want to show you, and…let's walk up Pine, shall we? It's a bit more private than promenading up the main street of town."

I have to deal with the here and now. And right now, the cards I have in hand involve 'selling' Flo's State Street house, seeing what more I can discover about Drina Gizzi's life and death, and doing what I can for her daughter. Inez's swirling thoughts settled, and she allowed Mark to guide her to the corner of Chestnut and thence up Pine. It was then she realized he was talking a mile a minute, a sure sign he was nervous or afraid she might bolt or turn on him. "I don't mean to spring anything on you," he said, "but I want you to see this sooner rather than later. I don't think I'm negating our agreement by sayin' I hope I can find a way to convince you that there can be a new beginning for us. We've always worked well together, darlin', a good team, in business and in life. We'd be fools to turn our backs and kick all that away."

They had crossed State and now stood at the corner of the two-story brick edifice that used to house Flo and her women. Judging the time was right, Inez pulled Mark to a stop. "And I have something to tell you, Mark," she said, then felt slightly ashamed at the hope that sprang into his face.

She hurried on. "When I came to Susan's studio, she was finishing up a sitting for Flo's women. Susan asked we not mention this around town, I'm sure you understand how that could impact her business. Anyhow, Flo said given her move to Fifth, this building," Inez inclined her head toward the stolid two-story structure looming over them, "is for sale to the right buyer. She as much as said that buyer could be you. Or, rather, us," Inez amended hastily, thinking an inclusive statement would arouse less suspicion.

"She did?" Mark swiveled to take in the imposing façade. "Interesting. Not so long ago, I made inquiries to Flo about this very building and was told there was already a buyer in place."

Inez shrugged. "She did mention a deal falling through. In any case, it's solidly built and in a prime location, so any offer would need to be generous, I suspect."

Mark pushed his hat back a bit to get a better look at the building. "With this, we'd own both ends of the block. It would make a fine gentlemen's club, limited to highrollers and uptown visitors. It could be right profitable. I'll arrange to talk to Flo about it."

"Abe should be in on the deal, if he's interested," Inez said, determined that the Jacksons share some of the windfall.

"Goes without saying, darlin'. After all, it's always been the three of us together, through thick and thin." Mark looped Inez's hand tighter into the crook of his elbow, and they continued walking. "I know some of those times were mighty thin for the two of you while I was gone. I'm going to make amends for that."

"We'll see," Inez said under her breath.

"Ye of little faith," he replied.

They continued walking. Mark finally said, "I know you get tired of me spinning words, and need hard evidence that I've changed my ways." They neared the corner of West Fourth Street. "Perhaps what I have to show you will restore some of that broken faith," added Mark as he turned up Fourth.

Inez balked, not wanting to walk up the street where their home had once been. Since their house had burned down earlier that summer, she'd avoided going anywhere near the blackened plot of ground that held little but ghosts of memories, a timber or two that hadn't been consumed to ash, and a few hardy weeds that had taken root in the thin red soil. "Oh no. I'm not going this way."

"Keep walking, Mrs. Stannert," he urged. He moved his hand to her back, encouraging her forward. Partway up the block, a man, dressed for business, came out of one of the buildings, and started toward them. Inez recognized him as Mr. Robitaille, a near-neighbor and well-known Leadville architect and builder. Stopping short, he removed his hat and beamed. "Mr. Stannert, Mrs. Stannert. Good to see you returned from your holiday."

Just how many people knew we were away together? The whole town? Inez mustered a polite rejoinder. "Mr. Robitaille. Good to see you as well. How is the missus? And business?"

"Both are well." His bright eyes fixed on Mark. "Has she seen—?"

"Heading there right now."

"Good. Good. Don't let me stop you. Madam," he addressed Inez, "I hope you are satisfied with the results of our endeavors. If there are any changes you wish, we shall comply."

"Satisfied with—?"

"We shall certainly let you know, and thank you again," Mark said. With a firm pressure at her back, he set walking again.

"Mark, what is going on?" She stopped, catching sight of something she never thought to see. On the burned-out lot were not the expected weeds and crumbling rubble, but a proper two-story clapboard house, freshly painted a vibrant blue with light gold trim. A small, covered front porch sported turned posts and a spool and spindle porch frieze. Drapes pulled across windows to either side of the porch and on the floor above made the house appear asleep as if waiting for the magic words to call it awake.

Inez managed to say, "How? When?"

"I commissioned Robitaille shortly after I returned, and he came up with a set of plans. I wanted to confer with you first, but you weren't exactly in a conferrin' frame of mind. Then, when you made plans to visit the Springs, Robitaille said he could have it all done, down to the spit and polish, by the time you came back." He turned to Inez. "It's a dandy little home, Inez. And it's yours." He fumbled in his waistcoat pocket, pulled out a shiny brass key, and presented it to her. "For the front door. And I'd be a liar and a thief if I didn't say that, although I built it for you, I'm hoping there will come a time when it'll be ours."

She was still staring at the house. Only when she turned to him did she realize the blue of his suit matched the blue paint of the house, almost as if the man and the abode were one. Looking down at the key, she had the awful premonition that, if she took the key from his gloved hand, at some level, she'd be making him a promise that she would later have to break.

"Mark." She covered her eyes, trying to arrange her thoughts. "Why now?"

Just then, a small determined voice said, "Where's Maman?"

She looked up to see Tony standing just beyond Mark. She almost didn't recognize the youngster—gone was the red cap, the oversized wool suit jacket. Taking their place was a derby and a checked sack coat. The mismatched eyes, tousled hair, and thin, pointed face were the same, although the eyes looked red and puffy, the face tighter, as if holding in overwhelming sorrow. Tony added, "Where's my gun?"

Inez glanced around. The street was quiet, with no nearby foot or street traffic. She grabbed the house key from Mark then said to Tony, "We best go inside to talk. You should be keeping a low profile until the Britishers leave town."

"I have a new job. I got different clothes. They won't recognize me." said Tony. "Where's Maman?"

"I'll tell you what I know when we are inside." Inez turned to Mark. "Go to Evan's Mercantile. Pick out readywear for a girl, from knickers and undervest to a warm dress, coat, shoes, stockings, gloves, the works. And a bonnet with as large a brim as you can find. If you get any questions, say it's for Miss Carothers' niece, who is visiting but didn't bring proper clothes for the weather."

"I don't need girl clothes," interrupted Tony. "I need my gun. Do you have it? And where'd they take Maman?"

Mark said, "If you want a decent fit, it'd help if we went inside and she shed that jacket. And the shoes, so I don't get shoes four sizes too large."

"Guess large if you must," said Inez, exasperated. "I'm sure it won't be the first time you've picked out an ensemble for a woman you just met." He jerked his head back as if she'd slapped him, and she regretted her sharp words the moment they were out. "I apologize. That was uncalled for. I need to get Tony inside and explain things and," she took a deep breath and told the truth, "I trust you, Mark, to do this. I know you'll do it right. Please."

He smoothed his mustache. "This is hardly goin' the way I planned, but very well. I'll run the errand, you two skedaddle inside." He leaned in toward Inez and added, "There's something special inside I'd hoped to show you myself. Look in the parlor, darlin'." With that, he began walking toward Harrison, swinging the walking stick in time to his stride.

Inez hurried Tony to the porch, and, as she fussed with the key in the gleaming new lock, Tony said in wonder, "Is this *your* house?"

"That remains to be seen," muttered Inez, as she struggled to turn the key in the stiff lock.

"What does *that* mean? If it's your house, why aren't you living here? Why are you living in the bar?"

"Long story, Tony. What we should focus on is your story right now. There." The door latch retracted with a shiny clack. Inez went in, footsteps echoing in the empty vestibule. Tony followed. Inez closed the door then turned, asking, "Did you go back to your home?"

Tony nodded.

"When?"

A longish pause. "Early this morning. After dawn. "

Inez tried to hold on to her patience. "When else? Did you circle back after I went chasing after you last night?"

An even longer pause, then "Someone told me you killed a man once."

Inez almost said *only once?* but curbed her tongue in time. "Who told you that?"

Tony scrutinized her. "Did you?"

Inez opted for blunt honesty. "Yes. I did. In self-defense."

Tony nodded. The set of her small mouth was grim. "You said you want to help me? Then kill the person who killed Maman."

Inez wanted to sink to her knees right there in the cold empty hallway and give Tony a fierce hug, tell her it would be all right, justice would be done. But Inez knew from bitter experience that life didn't always deliver justice to those who most deserved it. "Tony, I will do everything I can to find who did this."

"I know who did it."

A thrill of shock raced through her gut. "You do? Who?"

Tony took a deep breath. "I did go back last night, for my gun. And those…bad hats, the nobs. They were there." A sob caught in her throat. "They'd killed Maman, and they came back for me!"

"The nobs?" Inez quieted the urge to argue. "How do you know it was them?"

"I saw them on my way home, before I found her. They were behind the theater, and talking about it. They said no one would think it was them. That they were free and clear." Tony circled her wrists, holding onto her cuffs, looking lost. "They said they were gonna find me and finish me off before they left. Then, when I came back later, after you'd gone, they were inside, looking around." Her voice rose in pitch. "They were saying, 'She couldn't have gotten far.' They were looking for me! They want to kill me too!"

At that, Inez did reach out. She gripped Tony's shoulders. She could feel the girl shaking through the thin jacket, and vowed silently she would be sure Tony was properly clothed and warm, whether in jacket and trousers or dress and stockings. Inez crouched, bringing herself eye-level with Tony and said, "Tony. Listen to me."

Tony's eyes, glazed with terror, slowly came into focus.

"Are you sure they said she couldn't have gotten far? *She?*"

Tony nodded.

"Then, they weren't talking about you. They think you are a newsboy. A boy, not a girl." Inez felt the tension in the shoulders ease a fraction.

Inez continued. "I'm guessing they were looking for your mother. I believe that was the reference to 'she.'" The wheels in her mind turned, and gears clicked into place as she recalled the partial quarrel she'd overheard between Percy and Epperley, and the earlier conversation with Chet Donnelly.

"If I were to hazard a guess, I think one of them—who recently came into a great deal of money—might have taken your mother's fortunetelling a little too seriously and made an impulsive investment that dismayed his colleagues and perhaps didn't turn out so well for him. I'm guessing they came back to reckon with your mother, only to find the place empty. As we did."

She looked deep into Tony's eyes. "That is what I wanted to tell you. When we came back with the officer of the law, your mother's body was gone." Her fingers kneaded Tony's shoulders while Tony stayed silent, apparently trying to absorb what Inez had said. Inez continued, "As to who did this to your mother, I saw any number of shady characters in the vicinity last night. People who might have had reason to wish your mother harm. If I could track their movements, it would help. Did you see or talk to anyone else?"

Tony opened and shut her mouth, then said, "The voodoo lady from Coon Row. She was there."

The poppet in the cabinet popped to mind. Inez suppressed a shiver. "When?"

"This morning," said Tony. "She thought I was there to get my fortune told. She said," Tony wiped an eye, "Maman was gone. That she'd sent her away."

It looks like I shall be paying a visit to Madam Labasilier sooner rather than later.

"Anyone else?" asked Inez, trying to tamp down the urgency in her voice.

"Just before I found Maman, I saw..." Tony hesitated.

Inez, watching her closely, saw her eyes flicker from side to side, and suspected Tony was seesawing between prevaricating and wanting to confide. "I want to find who killed your mother, Tony," she said. "I want to see whoever did it punished. If you saw anything, even the least bit odd, I must know."

Tony's shoulders slumped, conceding, beneath Inez's hands. "I saw the coffin-maker, Mr. Alexander, and his wife. She was wanting to go into the row and he was trying to stop her. She's crazy."

The Alexanders? How peculiar. Mrs. Alexander shows up with Drina Gizzi at the Jacksons, the mister comes to the saloon, all of a sudden they are showing up everywhere. "And?" Inez prompted.

"I'd seen her before," said Tony. "I saw her coming out of our home just yesterday. She'd paid Maman a lot of money, a hundred dollars, to tell someone's fortune. Maman didn't like it. She told me," Tony squeezed her eyes shut, as if trying to call up the conversation, "that the missus was testing her and that Maman had to speak true. I guess Maman did it, because she was real unhappy. She told me what she did was wrong, that some things should not be said." Tony opened her eyes. "The missus thought I was a boy. She was disappointed, said she thought Maman had a daughter, not a son."

"Hmmm." The connections were growing more complex. Inez was growing concerned about Tony's role in it all, whether the girl wasn't getting herself firmly ensnarled in a spider's web of lies and hidden truths. Inez decided that sharing a little information might encourage further confidences. "I have heard from others that the Alexanders had a girl-child who died," said Inez gently. "I suspect Mrs. Alexander may be searching for proof of 'life beyond the veil,' perhaps for a way to communicate with those who are gone. It is not an uncommon practice. Leadville is rife with spiritualists, tableknockers, and so on."

Inez pondered a moment. "Mrs. Alexander attends my church. Tomorrow is Sunday, and I will be there." It would be Justice Sands' last service, a thought too painful to contemplate, so Inez mentally turned her back on it. "I will find a way to talk with her, see if I can bring the conversation around to your mother and her 'gifts.' Perhaps Mrs. Alexander saw your mother as someone who could be a channel to her own deceased daughter." Inez detected a flicker of a shadow cross Tony's face. "What?"

Tony slid out of Inez's grasp. "The new job I took. It's with Mr. Alexander's coffin-shop."

Inez rocked back on her heels, stunned.

"I didn't know it was him when I went to the door. But I'm glad it is. I can learn more about them. Maybe the missus killed Maman? She's tall. She's crazy. Maman wouldn't expect such a fine-dressed lady to hurt her." Tony suddenly looked older than her years.

"That seems highly unlikely," said Inez, then retreated at Tony's stubborn expression. "Not impossible, just unlikely. Mr. Alexander? Perhaps. But why? To what purpose?"

Tony shook her head. "The mister, he's too nice. He's paying me good money to sweep up and clean. He's not crazy, like her. He's kind of a mollycoddle."

"Sometimes the meek ones surprise you," said Inez, standing up.

She mentally scanned her list of those with known connections to Drina or who were nearby at the time, considering those who seemed to have an active grudge against the fortuneteller first. Madam Labasilier was top of her personal list. The specialty corset laces gave Inez pause, but it was possible such laces could have been obtained at another time and in another venue.

Then, the Lads from London. She couldn't discount them entirely. It was possible their innate propensity for violence when inebriated had taken a nasty turn in the early hours before dawn. They had been eager purveyors of the drummer's wares, although Inez couldn't recall if a set of silver and gold corset laces were among the items paid for.

Now, with what Tony had told her, she felt she should include the Alexanders, although she couldn't see either Françoise or Burton as the murderous type. He was, as Tony noted, too "meek and mild" a man to kill anyone, particularly in that manner. A rash bullet, perhaps, as anyone might have a sudden tightening of the trigger finger in a moment of desperation or anger, but to strangle someone required a killer so blind with fury that they could ignore the inevitable thrashing and desperation of the victim. Or someone so cold-blooded and dispassionate that the victim's agonies made no impression.

Dr. Gregorvich and his burlap sack materialized in her musings. However, he had no motive she could discern. He certainly didn't seem the kind of man to engage with fortunetelling and spiritualist goings-on. As far as she knew, Dr. Gregorvich was, like Doc and Reverend Sands, one of the "saints" who went into the rows to heal and help when possible, and lay the dead to rest when it was too late.

Finally, there was the drummer, the stranger passing through town: Woods. As the seller of the silver and gold laces, he had a ready hand to an ample supply. He said he had only two pair, but was that true? And according to Flo, he had unhealthy appetites. Had bumping into him the previous night truly been just a "wrong place wrong time" coincidence? Inez recalled his wild-eyed stare, his sweating in the frigid night air.

Pondering the odd collection of possible perpetrators, Inez had to concede there was always the possibility the killer was someone completely unknown. Someone whose fortune went awry, someone too full of alcohol to think straight, someone who had heard of the hundred-dollar payment and wanted the money for themselves. The possibilities, including random chance, were overwhelming.

As she mused over the shrinking chances of finding Drina's killer, much less her missing corpse, Inez watched Tony. The girl ran a tentative hand over the fancy woodwork in the wainscoting of the entryway and examined the turned balusters and newel of the nearby staircase to the second story with unabashed interest. Tony tipped her head back to look at the upstairs landing, and Inez suddenly realized where she had last seen Tony's "new" rust-colored derby. "Where did you get the new headgear?"

Tony pivoted, clamping the hat to her head with a protective hand. "One of the newsies gave it to me. T' help with my disguise."

"I would like to know how he came by it," said Inez.

Tony shrugged. "He said it came from a drummer who took a scarper in the wrong part of town and left it behind. We find all kinds of stuff in the alleys."

It looks like I shall have many questions for Woods when he shows up at the Silver Queen tonight to sell his wares.

Inez said, "Mr. Stannert will be back soon with clothes that will be a far better disguise."

"A dress."

Inez ignored Tony's scornful tone. "Anyone looking for you is looking for a boy. Dressing in women's clothes is probably the best way for you to 'hide in plain sight.' I have a good friend, Miss Carothers, who is a photographer here in Leadville. She has agreed that we can present you as her 'niece.' As soon as you've changed clothes, we will go to her studio so you can meet her."

"What about my job at the coffin-shop?"

Inez's brow furrowed. "Under the circumstances, it seems unwise, even dangerous, for you to be there until we know how the Alexanders fit into your mother's death. If they fit at all."

"If I'm there, I can find out. And maybe," her voice became almost a whisper, "maybe whoever took Maman will bring her there."

"If she is there, you must tell me. I will ensure she is given a proper burial," said Inez gently. "That is the least I can do, along with making sure no harm comes to you, her beloved daughter."

The cold from the entryway had begun to seep under her woolen coat and the vapor from their breath misted the air. Realizing that Tony's arms were now crossed tight against the chill indoors, Inez added, "Let's find out what Mr. Stannert was so anxious we see in the parlor and see if a stove is in there as well."

Chapter Twenty-four

Tony sure as shooting hoped there was a stove in the parlor. While standing in the entryway, she had become uncomfortably aware that the jacket Ace had given her "for disguise" wasn't going to keep the cold out once the temperatures fell. She looked around the Stannerts' house, thinking she'd have to find some warmer woolen drawers for nighttimes and for working at the coffin-maker's. *Undertaker,* she reminded herself. *He calls his place Alexander's Undertaking. Sounds more high-toned, I guess. Better'n coffin-shop.*

She was glad she'd told Mrs. Stannert everything, about who she'd seen, what they'd said, and even that she was working for the undertaker now. She couldn't see Mr. Alexander as a bad guy, but it couldn't hurt to have someone besides Ace know where she'd be in the evenings.

When Mrs. Stannert went to open the door to the parlor, Tony crowded up behind her, anxious to get inside the room and the promise of possible warmth. Mrs. Stannert walked in first, and Tony heard her gasp.

Tony stepped in, and then stopped, feeling maybe she should've left her dusty, worn shoes outside such a fine room. Not only was there a parlor stove at one end and a fireplace at the other, there were two fancy upholstered chairs, a cozy-looking rocker with a footstool, and a loveseat all in soft brown patterned fabric. Little tables sat here and there and at the far end, close to the fireplace, was a piano. It was beautiful, long and low, polished, made of fine dark wood that gleamed. It was as different from the honky-tonk keyboards as Mrs. Sweet's shiny uptown girls were from the shabby whores working on the rows.

Mrs. Stannert walked toward the instrument all dream-like, pulling off her gloves as she went. Tony took a few tentative steps into the room, then stopped and looked down. Covering most of the floor was a carpet, just like the one she'd seen in the windows of Owen & Chittenden on Harrison. Like the one she'd wanted to buy for Maman. It was a carpet, she realized, that she'd never have been able to afford, no matter how many pennies and nickels she would've managed to save. Something like this could only be bought with gold, and plenty of it. Just like the piano. Or the house, come to that.

Tony stepped carefully off the carpet and onto the smooth plank floor, and skirted around the edge to where Mrs. Stannert stood by the piano, running a hand over the keyboard cover.

Spying one hopper full of wood and another of charcoal by the fireplace, Tony asked, "Can I lay a fire?"

Mrs. Stannert turned to face her. "Absolutely! Let's warm this room up."

While Mrs. Stannert prepared the stove, Tony worked on the fireplace, marveling how new and unused everything looked. There weren't even ashes in the hearth. Done with the stove, which popped and pinged as it heated up, Mrs. Stannert came over and put a light to the fire using the box of lucifers on the mantel. As the fire leapt upward, Tony held one hand out, grateful for the increasing warmth. It was then that she heard the first soft notes from the piano. The liquid music took her by surprise, infusing her with a glow that started somewhere deep inside and spread out, warming her from inside like the fire warmed her from without.

Turning, she saw Mrs. Stannert sitting at the piano, her head bent forward, intent, her fingers prancing over the white-and-black keyboard. The music that poured forth beneath Mrs. Stannert's touch was unlike anything Tony had heard before. It was magic. *Real* magic.

Unable to resist, Tony moved closer, away from the fire. The music flowed from note to note, low on the left, high on the right, as if the two hands were talking to each other in a language all their own. From slow, sad, and dark, to lighter and faster, then sad again, then fast again, but different from before, then spiraling down, down. Mrs. Stannert's hands slowed. The music slowed as well, sounding of mourning, loneliness, and loss before falling into silence.

Tony said, "What's that?"

Mrs. Stannert started, as if she'd been in a trance.

"It's so," Tony couldn't think of a word, "happy, sad, lonely, and...everything."

The missus glanced at Tony with a small smile that seemed close to sadness itself, then said, "It's a short piece written by Ludwig van Beethoven, one of the greatest composers who ever lived. It's the *Bagatelle No. 25 in A Minor*, sometimes called *Für Elise*. As with most music, what it tells you has a great deal to do with what is inside of you at the time you hear it." Mrs. Stannert looked down at the keyboard, and said, "*Sehnsucht* would sum it up for me." She ran a light fingertip over the ivory keys and said, "He even had it tuned."

Tony squinched up her nose. "*Sin*...what?"

Mrs. Stannert rose and guided Tony back to the fireplace. "*Sehnsucht*. It's a German word meaning, well, a lot of things. Yearning. Life's longings. Aspiring after what is impossible, or nearly so. Sometimes it means 'love lost or unattainable,' a search for happiness," her words slowed, "in a life where happiness is hard to find. It is a word used for a complicated emotion that is hard to explain. The Germans are experts at coming up with such words. *Schadenfreude, sehnsucht*. When I was playing the bagatelle, I thought of that word and all it means to me. Particularly now."

Love lost. Tony looked down at the carpet. "Made me think of maman," she said.

Mrs. Stannert's hand tightened on her shoulder. "Yes," she said. "*Sehnsucht*, Antonia. I believe you know the feeling, whether or not you know the word."

The front door opened, and leather soles on wood echoed in the entry. Mr. Stannert appeared at the parlor doorway, a carpetbag under one arm and a large, brown-paper-wrapped bundle under the other. "I went you one better on the 'Miss Carothers' niece needs clothes for the weather' story, Mrs. Stannert, and told Evan's shopgirl that the train lost the girl's luggage." He walked in and placed the carpetbag and parcel on the loveseat. Tony noticed him glance at the piano and then at Mrs. Stannert. "So did you christen her properly?"

"A little Beethoven," said Mrs. Stannert. She went back to the piano and closed the keyboard cover with a decided click. "I won't ask how you managed to accomplish all this," she indicated the furnished room, the house, "in such a short time and without my suspecting a thing." Her hand rested on the keyboard cover. "It's a beautiful parlor grand, Mr. Stannert, with a wonderful sound. And a beautiful house."

He beamed. For a minute, Tony thought Mrs. Stannert might run into his arms and there would be some embarrassing hugging and canoodling. Instead, the missus leaned against the piano and gave him a look, like the look folks used to give maman when she gave them a reading they didn't quite believe. Like they suspected it was all made up, not real, and were wondering what the angle was. But all Mrs. Stannert said was "And thank you for getting the ensemble for Tony."

At that, she and Tony both looked at the brown parcel. "Let's take things out and set them on the divan," said Mrs. Stannert. "Make sure you have everything you need."

"I'm changing now?" Tony wasn't sure she liked that idea.

"I want to introduce you to your 'aunt.'" said the missus.

"I have to start my new job at five," said Tony. "And I need t' get something to eat." She didn't want to say that she hadn't eaten all day, but her empty stomach wasn't going to let her forget that she'd missed breaking fast with the other newsies in the morning and it was now past noon.

"Ah-ha!" Mr. Stannert pulled another, smaller parcel from the carpetbag's interior. "I stopped by the saloon on my way back and let drop to Bridgette that Miss Carothers has a niece in town." He turned to Tony. "Before long, everyone will know who you are and you'll be safe in your disguise. By the way, your 'new' name is Annabelle Carothers. Close enough to Antonia that it'll be easy to remember." He moved toward one of the small tables and began unwrapping the smaller package. "Mrs. O'Malley gave me this, figurin' y'all might be hungry after your long train ride to Leadville."

The scent of still-warm bread and cheese wafted to her, mixed with something meaty. Tony's mouth watered in anticipation.

"Mrs. O'Malley is still chopping away at that cheese wheel," Mr. Stannert continued. "She also added ham to this batch of biscuits. An all-in-one meal." He stepped back so Tony could help herself.

Mrs. Stannert finally moved away from the piano. She headed out of the parlor, saying, "You've been busy, Mr. Stannert. Thank you for your foresight and finesse. Is there a kettle in the kitchen to heat water for tea?"

"Darlin', the house has all the comforts of home," said her husband.

She swept out of the room, heading toward the back.

Mr. Stannert watched her go, then turned to Tony. "Mrs. Stannert can be hard-headed and stubborn, but there's no denyin' she cuts a fine figure of a woman. And smart as a whip. Can't pull the wool over her eyes, Miss Annabelle, so don't you even try." He winked at her.

She didn't know quite what to say to that, but her mouth was full of a half-biscuit's worth of warm bread, melted cheese, and salty ham, so she didn't try. It was starting to get warm in the room, what with the fireplace and the parlor stove, so she shed the jacket. The sleeves got all tangled in the process, and the coat went inside out and sideways. Maman's knife and cards spilled onto the rug.

Mr. Stannert's eyebrows popped up just as the missus returned with a small cast iron kettle and a tray of tea things. She paused at the doorway, eyed the items on the rug, then went on to the parlor stove with kettle and the tray, her long skirts making a soft swishing sound on the rug. "We'll see if there's time to warm the water for the tea I found in the pantry." She set the kettle on the stove. "And what are those on the floor?"

Tony stuffed the other half biscuit in her mouth and picked up the knife and tin, setting the tin down on the chair behind her.

Mr. Stannert looked with interest at the weapon in her hand. "Looks like you had backup to the pistol. A wise move."

Tony swallowed with difficulty. The bread stuck in her throat, and it took some coughing before she could say, "It was Maman's. I couldn't find my gun when I went back, so I took her knife."

"A folding knife?" Mr. Stannert smoothed his mustache, looking interested.

Tony demonstrated how to ratchet the blade out of the prettily engraved handle, the quick, little sounds the steel made as it emerged from its hiding place sounding loud in the parlor. She found the tiny clickety-click-tickety noise comforting. It made the innocuous object sound dangerous, like a small animal that without warning displays sharp claws and teeth.

She'd been working on her speed in getting the blade out and locked, so she felt a small twinge of pride when Mr. Stannert whistled and said, "Looks like you're pretty fast on the draw too. It locks?"

Tony nodded. "Maman calls...called it a *caracas*. That's the sound it makes when you open it. She also called it a *salvavirgo*." Tony stumbled over the pronunciation.

The Stannerts looked at each other. "Spanish, or Italian?" Mrs. Stannert asked.

Mr. Stannert shrugged. "Sounds like to me."

"But Maman is French for mother," said the missus. She looked at Tony. "Where was your mother from?"

Tony shrugged. The whole "where are you and your kin from?" question always made her uncomfortable, because she had no real answer. Maman would just say, "We came from over the sea. If people ask, just say the town we left behind, that is where we came from. And wherever the two of us are, that is our home." None of it really answered the question as to where Maman was born, or if she had any family, or even who Tony's father was, but it was all the information she had.

Mrs. Stannert, perhaps sensing Tony's discomfort, turned to the chair and picked up the tin. "And what is this, may I ask?"

"Maman's cards," said Tony. Then, because the Stannerts were looking at her expectantly and she wasn't sure what else to do, she opened the tin and pulled out the cards. She fanned them, face up, for the Stannerts to see.

"Looks like a regular deck of cards," said Mr. Stannert.

"Not quite," said Mrs. Stannert. "It's not complete."

The mister held out his hand. "May I?"

Tony hesitated, then gave him the deck. It felt strange give them over, but after all, they were her cards now. She told herself it didn't make any difference who touched them. She wasn't going to tell any fortunes or "read" them. They were a part of Maman. Having them made her feel as if Maman was with her, close by.

Mr. Stannert fanned them out into a near circle, looked at the fronts and the backs. "Is this a piquet deck?" He pronounced it just like Maman: *PEA-kay* Tony nodded. He handed them back to Tony and looked at his wife. "French again. I'm putting my money on France."

Mrs. Stannert frowned. "I heard Drina speak. I did not catch much in the way of French intonation. But then, does it matter? Everyone in Leadville is from somewhere else." She looked at Tony. "So, do you know how to use them, these cards?"

Tony shrugged. "She taught me a little. The face cards, mostly." They were at one end of the fan. She ran her gaze over the familiar illustrations and then up at Mr. Stannert. "It's not really fortunetelling. You start with what a person looks like, the color of their eyes and hair, and go from there." She put the cards away. Mrs. Stannert pulled the steaming kettle off the stovetop, prepared a cup of tea, and handed it to her.

"I'll be blunt," said the missus. "I don't believe in fortune-telling. To me, it's all folderol and a confidence game, and I'm well acquainted with confidence games. I don't mean to impugn your mother's memory or her occupation, but I think it's best I let you know where I stand." Her voice was brisk, but not mean.

Relieved, Tony said, "I don't believe it either, all the 'seeing' stuff she always talked about. But I know she believed it, in her powers. Still, it felt sometimes like she was lying, just making things up to tell people."

Mrs. Stannert handed a cup to the mister and said, "Please leave the room so Tony can dress."

"Yes, ma'am," he said. "You're the boss." He winked at Tony and left, shutting the door behind him.

The missus pulled the string off the packet, saying, "A little fabrication, telling people what they want to hear or maybe what they are afraid of hearing, can be useful. When running a confidence game, being able to discern a mark's deepest fears and desires can be a powerful tool. Time for a bit of a confidence game now, on your part. Put on these clothes and…Presto! Change! We'll show people what they expect to see, and they won't look any deeper for the truth."

On the one hand, Tony loved how warm the new clothes were. The soft undergarments, the woolen flannels, the incredibly thick, luxurious coat that came down to her ankles, the shoes that almost fit. "Better a bit too big than a bit too small," Mrs. Stannert had said, stuffing a little of the packing paper into the toes.

On the other hand, Tony hated the petticoats, which felt like they twisted around her limbs along with the long skirt, and she especially hated the corset, which Mrs. Stannert insisted she put on. "A girl your age would have started wearing stays several years ago, so don't whine about it now. How old are you?"

"Twelve?" said Tony, a little uncertainly. "At least, that's what Maman told me."

"Twelve. Ah. You would be young for this but have you started your courses yet?" From the way she asked it, Tony had a feeling that this question had something to do with female things, but she had no idea what.

"My what?"

The frown lines between Mrs. Stannert's eyebrows deepened. "Did your mother ever talk to you about a woman's monthly flow?"

Tony suddenly realized what Mrs. Stannert was talking about. "Oh, ugh! The curse?" She clapped hands to her ears. "No! I don't do that!"

"Well, eventually, you will," said Mrs. Stannert. "Most likely years from now. But I must tell you—now take your hands down and listen, because it would be a disservice on my part if I didn't warn you—the best thing to keep in mind when it happens is don't panic. You're not dying, even though it can be uncomfortable and messy. Just find some rags to use for padding under your clothes. I'm telling you this now, because in your guise as a boy, it would be most unfortunate if you started to bleed." She said the word forcefully and bluntly, as if to push past the unfortunate need to have the discussion at all. "Especially in the company of others. So, there you go."

To Tony's relief, that ended the conversation. Mrs. Stannert walked to the parlor door, saying, "Drink your tea, if you want it, and put on your bonnet and gloves. We must leave soon to meet Miss Carothers."

Tony gulped down her sweet, lukewarm tea, which had been cooling while she wrestled with her new clothes. She set the cup down and picked up her knife and cards. "What do I do with my things? I don't have any pockets."

"Use the reticule on the table," said the missus, pulling open the door and calling out, "Mr. Stannert! Come see the miracle thou hast wrought."

Tony put knife and cards into the small embroidered bag and pulled the bonnet on over her head. The brim, generously ruffled, hung low over her eyes, making it hard to see. Mr. Stannert came in and made approving noises. Mrs. Stannert handed Tony the wool gloves, stuffed Tony's "men's wear" and worn shoes into the waiting carpetbag, and snapped the latch shut.

"I'll need to change before I go to my job," said Tony.

"What job?" Mr. Stannert asked.

"I'll explain later," Mrs. Stannert said. She turned to Tony. "Changing is a problem. I'd give you the key to this house, but there are too many eyes around. This neighborhood is full of busybodies and looky-loos who like to gossip. If they see a girl go in and a boy come out it would not bode well for you." She tapped her foot. "Probably the best place to effect your transformation would be at Miss Carothers' studio. You could stay there for a bit, then change and leave by the back door. Or even the front door. Chestnut is a busy street, no one will take notice." Mrs. Stannert looked at Tony, all worried again. "You'll need a place to spend the night."

"No! I got a place," Tony assured her, thinking of the newsies' shed.

"Under the boardwalks?" Mr. Stannert asked. "That's not the best place to retire, if so. And you can't go back to the alleys."

"No, I got a place. An inside place. And it's safe," Tony said. She figured the newsie shed was probably the safest place in town to sleep, surrounded by all the boys. And, she could catch up with Ace and the others on goings-on in town. Once the nobs left, she wouldn't need to hide anymore, so maybe she could just be plain "Tony" again and not do all the switching back and forth. No more corsets.

She hoped she could keep the warm wool stockings. After all, no one would see them under the baggy trousers. And keep the thick socks that went over them. And maybe the shoes? They were nice and sturdy, just boots, no bows or fancy doodahs on them. The only really fancy parts of her outfit were the starched lace ruffles on the dress that poked her neck and wrists. She wondered if she could also keep the coat, and pass it off to the newsies as something she was given by one of the do-gooder ladies in town or even Mrs. Stannert.

The Stannerts looked like they were about to gang up on her about her sleeping quarters, so she quickly changed the subject. "When will the nobs leave town?" she asked.

Mrs. Stannert grimaced and a long pause ensued. She finally said, "In the past, they've lingered around until mid-week, being too hungover to make the late Sunday or Monday trains. But usually, Mr. Epperley isn't with them. He owns a hotel in Manitou Springs and has responsibilities, so I assume he would be anxious to leave Monday midday at the latest. Balcombe, Tipton, and Quick are layabouts, living from remittance check to remittance check. Now that Lord Percy has his seemingly bottomless inheritance in hand—"

"What Mrs. Stannert is saying in her circumloquacious way is that she doesn't know. And not knowin' is something she doesn't like to own up to," said Mr. Stannert. The slight edge in his tone reminded Tony of her maman's little knife with its hidden blade.

"Mr. Stannert, thank you for your help. Don't you have someplace to be?" said the missus. Clickety-click-tickety: *that* edge was out in the open.

"The hour for serious imbibing draws near," said the mister. He tipped his hat at both of them. "Ladies. If assistance is required, you can find me at the best-appointed watering-hole in town. Don't hesitate to holler for help, Tony. Mr. Jackson, all of us, we're ready, willing, and able to give you a hand."

After Mr. Stannert left, Mrs. Stannert and Tony quickly extinguished the fires in the stove and fireplace. Before they left the room, Tony touched the keyboard cover on the piano with one bare finger. The wood seemed to glow from within and felt warm, almost alive.

"Someday I'd like to be able to play a piano," said Tony, pulling on her gloves, "like you do, Mrs. Stannert."

The missus held the parlor door open for her. "It may look easy, but it takes years of lessons, ready access to an instrument, and much practice. Hours and hours a day." She must have seen Tony's disappointment, because her voice softened. "But who knows? It could happen, if you want it enough. In such cases, you focus on the desired outcome, plan your moves and make the right decisions at the right times. Of course, there are the wild cards—luck, chance, serendipity, things beyond your control—which can play the devil with your plans. That is when mettle and quick thinking come to the fore. I believe you have both of those qualities and determination as well."

They left the house and Mrs. Stannert locked the door behind them, saying, "Remember, your name is Annabelle Carothers. On our walk, keep your eyes on the ground if anyone should stop us. If you are asked a question, let me handle it. Best we take the 'children should be seen and not heard' approach."

With that, Mrs. Stannert gave Tony the carpetbag, took her other hand, and they started up the street to Harrison. Tony slowed. "Do we hafta go down Harrison? How about Pine?"

"Recall, Annabelle, you're new to Leadville, just off the train. It makes sense I take you down the main street of town rather than lurk on a side street," said Mrs. Stannert. "Don't worry. Everything will be fine."

They turned onto Harrison. Tony kept her eyes fixed on the weathered boardwalk planks. She couldn't make herself look around. She was afraid she'd see someone she knew. A newsie, or maybe one of her regular customers. Or maybe Mr. Alexander, or—

A door banged open, narrowly missing Tony. A hurried stampede of footsteps erupted, and a half circle of boots formed in front, blocking their path.

"Good day, Messeurs Percy, Epperley, Balcombe, Tipton, and Quick," the missus said politely. Her hand tightened on Tony's, a warning. "Conducting a little business at the Board of Trade Saloon to start your day on the right foot?"

"Not a bloody good day at all," grumbled a voice that Tony recognized as belonging to the tall pale man called Epperley. Fear streaked through her limbs.

"Oh now, Epperley." Worthless Pisspot Brown sounded positively cheery. "Ignore him, Mrs. Stannert. He didn't get his beauty rest last night and is just all at sixes and sevens and spreading doom and gloom today. I say, the usual poker game tonight, then? Usual time?"

"Absolutely, Lord Percy. You'll be there?"

"With bells on, m'lady! I hope you have some high rollers attending, because I'll be taking them to the bank!"

"If you've got anything left to put on the table," growled Epperley.

"Oh stuff it," said one of the others. "Percy's treating, so buck up, boy-o. Where next, then? The Tontine for some proper food and to ogle the proper young matrons dining with their spouses? Hyman's for the next round?"

"Hyman and his bloody Bible by the door, no thanks," said Epperley.

"I don't see you offering to buy the next round," commented another unknown. "Let's leave the decision to old moneybags over here, shall we?"

"Oh, very well," Worthless Pisspot Brown said. "Food then. A little ogling won't hurt either. Then, I'm off to my silver mine to confer with the experts. I say, who's this urchin with you, Mrs. Stannert?"

Tony squeezed her eyes shut and leaned against Mrs. Stannert.

"This is Miss Annabelle Carothers, niece of Miss Carothers, the woman photographer on Chestnut." Mrs. Stannert's voice became stern. "She's from the Midwest, brought up a proper young lady. I'm afraid you all have probably scared her speechless and witless with your rowdy behavior."

"Oooooh, so sorry, miss." A different voice, apologetic. "We're visitors as well. From over the pond originally, but not any more. Proper misfits, we are. Enjoy your stay in Cloud City, missy, and don't go adventuring down State Street. Toodle-oo, Mrs. Stannert! Hide the good wine and brandy for us for this evening's fun and games, and keep the coffee hot!"

The boots turned in a confused mass and stampeded away.

Mrs. Stannert blew out a breath. "Well, that was unexpected. You did well, 'Annabelle.' Kept your wits about you." She wiggled her entrapped gloved fingers and said, "You can ease up a bit. My fingers are going numb."

They walked quicker now. Mrs. Stannert seemed anxious that they complete their journey, and Tony was no less anxious to be off the streets, where she felt as if everyone was staring at her.

It wasn't until they turned the corner onto Chestnut and Mrs. Stannert said, "Not far now," that Tony began to relax a bit. She hoped that this Miss Carothers was nice, would understand, wouldn't mind if she used her place to change for the job at Alexander's.

"Good afternoon, Mrs. Stannert."

Startled by the deep, familiar voice, Tony looked up and then quickly looked down again. It was Dr. G, the sawbones who came to the row with the others to "do good deeds" when all anyone in the row wanted was to be left alone.

"Good afternoon, Dr. Gregorvich," Mrs. Stannert tried to steer past Dr. G. Tony kept her face turned to the boardwalk. The doctor's polished black boots, splattered with dried spots of…something…shifted to block them.

"And who might this be with you?" his gentle voice prodded.

"Annabelle. Niece of a friend. Just visiting." Mrs. Stannert sounded polite, but firm. "Annabelle is quite tired, just got off the train this morning. I think the journey was a bit much for her, what with lost luggage and all the excitement on the streets, so if you'll excuse us."

"Of course, of course. Just a moment. Miss Annabelle?"

She didn't want to look up. She didn't want to see his eyes, or have him see hers. A black-gloved hand appeared and, gripping her chin, forced her face up.

His long, drawn face, distant and clinical, came into view. Eyes the color of gunmetal bored into hers. His gaze felt like a knife, slicing through her disguise to reveal who she really was beneath. She started shaking. "Yes," he said quietly. "I see." He released her chin. She quickly lowered her head.

"Symptoms include pale skin, sheened with perspiration, dilated pupils, pale lips, trembling. I confirm your astute diagnosis of exhaustion, Mrs. Stannert. Possibly exacerbated by altitude. Not unusual, when journeying to ten thousand feet. All that aside, train journeys can be wearying, particularly for the young. Miss Annabelle needs rest."

"Thank you, Doctor." Mrs. Stannert took a step to the right, nudging Tony closer to the buildings. "We are on our way to be sure she does just that."

"I understand you have a card game on Saturday evenings? I am most interested." His voice persisted, even as his boots stepped to the side.

Mrs. Stannert paused mid-step and turned toward him, pulling Tony behind her. "Yes, that is true. You are, of course, welcome, but I warn you, it is peopled primarily with high rollers who don't mind throwing their gold and silver around rather freely and don't mind losing. Although, of course, everyone would rather win."

He gave a laugh that sounded like it came from a chest as deep and hollow as a mine shaft. "That is no problem for me. You see, I am a student of the workings of the mind and brain, and I believe I could learn much by observing and participating in your game."

"Certainly, just no dissections upon the felt," she said.

There was a long pause. Tony felt Mrs. Stannert shift. "Apologies," she said, finally. "I was talking to a newsman recently about the rumors of—"

"Anatomists in town." His voice wasn't so gentle now. "Yes, Mrs. Stannert. I, too, have heard the rumors, and was one of the unfortunates interviewed by Mr. Stein of the *Chronicle*, under false pretenses, I should point out. He was followed in short order by Mr. Elliston of *The Independent*, who at least didn't try to pass himself off as someone he is not. I tell you what I told them both: all medical physicians are students of anatomy. Every time we probe a mysterious ache, test a fever, set a broken limb, address a gunshot wound, we bring to the fore what we know about human anatomy, and through our diagnoses and actions, we shed light on what we have yet to learn."

"Apologies again," Mrs. Stannert sounded more meek than Tony had ever heard her.

"Accepted. Looking forward to this evening, Mrs. Stannert." The footsteps receded, blending into the general bedlam of the street.

"*That* was interesting," said Mrs. Stannert. They started walking again. "I do believe we shall get you a pair of tinted glasses, nothing too dark, to mask those eyes of yours. Lovely as they are, they are also distinctive." Tony thought she sounded worried, even though the words were casual.

"The anatomists, are they bodysnatchers?" Tony tried to recall what Ace had told the newsies about the article he'd seen in the *Chronicle*. "Do they steal bodies from the graveyard and cut them up?" A horrible possibility rose in her mind: her Maman, pulled from a pauper's grave, cut up like a sheep under the butcher's knife.

"Rumors only. No one has found evidence that such happens. However, I will say that I regretted that so-called witticism as soon as it left my lips. Goodness, it's been a long time since someone has looked at me that way. Highly unpleasant. Ah, here we are. It's safe to look up now," she added.

Tony looked up just as Mrs. Stannert pushed a door open. A small bell tinkled overhead. A woman came out of the back, not as tall as Mrs. Stannert and younger too, with black shiny hair done up in back and a fringe of curly hair across her forehead. Her solemn face broke into a welcoming smile. "Inez! You are here, and at a good time. It is quiet and I was thinking of turning the sign to CLOSED and perhaps doing some work in the darkroom." She looked at Tony with warm brown eyes. "So this is my niece! Welcome to Leadville, ah, what is to be your name?"

"Annabelle Carothers," said Tony quickly.

"Annabelle. Lovely name. May I?" Miss Carothers came forward and gave Tony a quick hug. The gesture almost put Tony in tears. The last real hug she'd had was from Maman. She'd tried to hug her during their last, awful argument. At the memory, tears did spill over. Tony turned her back to dry her eyes on a sleeve.

Miss Carothers patted her shoulder and said, "Why don't you go down to the room on the left? It's a showroom, displaying examples of my photography. You can look around while Mrs. Stannert and I talk."

Tony headed in the direction indicated. The two women's voices floated soft and low, like the murmur of a river. Once in the showroom, Tony dropped the carpetbag on the small rug and looked around. Big pictures, little pictures, pictures of people, even pictures of the mountains and of waterfalls. They all looked so real she felt if she touched them her fingers would encounter real skin, cold water.

Footsteps came up behind her, and Mrs. Stannert's hand landed on Tony's shoulder. "I must be on my way. You are safe with Miss Carothers. You can come to her, to me, if you have any trouble. I'm not happy about you spending the night wherever it is you plan to go, but we can talk about that further tomorrow, Sunday. Miss Carothers and I attend the same church, so we shall come by the studio after the service. She is going to give you a key to the back door. You are responsible for keeping track of it. She said you can come in and stay at any time. You can trust her," Mrs. Stannert said again and gave Tony's shoulder a little squeeze. "Be safe, Tony. Particularly tonight, at Mr. Alexander's and after."

For a moment, Tony was tempted to turn around and give the saloonwoman a fierce hug. Tony turned, but Mrs. Stannert was already moving away. Tony said, "Thank you. I don't know why you're doing all this for me, you and Mr. Stannert and everyone, but...thank you."

Mrs. Stannert just smiled and left.

Miss Carothers came in and said, "Well, since we are relatives, Annabelle, you must call me Aunt Susan. Can you do that?"

Tony nodded, examining a picture of a dead woman in a casket, surrounded by flowers. She looked asleep, not dead at all. Next to that was a picture of a baby, eyes closed, sitting on a woman's lap.

"Are you hungry?" Susan asked.

Tony shook her head, then asked, "You take pictures of dead people?"

Susan picked up the photo of mother and baby. "Yes, I do, when asked. These are special kinds of photographs, called *memento mori*. They are remembrances of loved ones, and meant as a comfort to those who are grieving and must go on."

Tony swallowed hard and heard herself say, "My maman is dead. She's gone, and I don't have a picture of her. Not one."

Susan looked at Tony as if she might cry too. Finally, she said, "You carry a picture of her here." She touched Tony's forehead. "In your mind, in your memories, you can remember her in many ways, not just in death. Pick the picture you love most, and then you can pull it out any time, day or night. Good memories are the most precious *memento mori* anyone can have." She put the picture down and said, "I was about to develop some photographic plates in my darkroom. It's almost magical, how the images rise out of the glass plates, like ghosts made real. Would you like me to show you how it's done?"

Tony nodded.

Chapter Twenty-five

"Ma'am, a hot Scotch whisky sling?" The stranger on the other side of the bar had a sprinkling of snow decorating the shoulders of his heavy ulster. He tapped a fifty-cent piece on the counter and removed his hat on which the dusting was beginning to melt and soak into the felt. "I asked the first two people I met off the train where to get a proper whisky sling. They both pointed me to the Silver Queen."

Inez smiled automatically. "Lovely. And welcome to Leadville. Your first time here?" She hardly registered his polite "Yes ma'am, it is," as she turned to pull the kettle of hot water, still steaming from the big stove in the kitchen, and a hot water glass off the back bar. She scanned the better brand of liquor on the top shelf and selected one. Into the glass went a portion of water from the kettle, a lump sugar, a piece of lemon peel, and a proper quantity of Scotch whisky. Round and round it all went with a spoon, with Inez's thoughts equally awhirl.

It was well past the hour that the drummer Woods had agreed to arrive and set up shop. There was a disgruntled crush of customers milling about where he was supposed to be, nursing their drinks and asking, "When's he comin' back?" with irritating regularity, as if asking would change the promised arrival time. Inez had changed her response from "Soon, no doubt," to "Perhaps he's been held up, what with this wet snow and his heavy trunk." She was running out of excuses, assurances, and patience. Although she smiled and nodded at each inquiry, inside she was just as disgruntled as the would-be-purveyors of delicate ladies' goods. In her mind, the certainty grew stronger and stronger that he wouldn't show at all.

To Inez, it was inconceivable that the drummer would turn his back on such a lucrative proposition as selling his stock of sought-after unmentionables inside the warm and inviting saloon…unless he had a damn good reason.

Earlier, in preparation for the drummer's arrival, Inez had paged through his receipts, which she'd secured in the saloon's safe until his promised return. A quick mental calculation of the totals at the bottom of each verified that the monies he'd given her the previous evening were indeed five percent of his total take. Woods had not cheated her of a penny.

Was it really just last evening?

So much had happened in the past twenty-four hours that Inez felt she was no more in control of events than the bit of lemon peel gyrating in the hot drink.

She placed the savagely mixed sling before the waiting customer, who prodded, "Nutmeg?"

"Ah!" She hunted the cluttered backbar until she found the grater and the small, pit-sized nut. She grated furiously, the spicy warm, fragrant tones of nutmeg conjuring memories of winter holidays long past and the uncertainties of winter yet to come.

Where will this winter find me?

Despite the warmth of the room, her fingertips went cold.

"Uh, ma'am, that's plenty."

She returned to the present with a shake of the head and sprinkled the proper amount of ground spice on top of his drink. "If you want a refill, we now have more than enough ground nutmeg. In fact, I feel a chill coming on, so I do believe I'll join you." She pulled a second hot water glass off the bar and proceeded to mix herself a sling with a generous portion of Scotch.

He nodded. "Winter's coming on." He dropped two silver Seated Liberties on the counter to make an even dollar and tipped his cup to her. "To your health, ma'am."

"And to yours," she replied, touching her glass to his with a small clink. She took a sip, savoring the warmth of the water, the fire of the Scotch, the sweetness of sugar warring with the bitterness of nutmeg. With a sigh, she set the drink down, letting her cold hands linger on the warm glass as her insides slowly unclenched. Chet Donnelly took that moment to wedge his girth up to the bar in front of Inez, nearly causing the traveler to spill his drink.

"He ain't comin', is he?" rumbled Chet. "And here I brought these fellas." He jerked a thumb in the direction of his two companions. "Told them all about them lacy things. More customers." He squinted at Inez. "So, where's the drummer man?"

Inez lifted a shoulder in a shrug. "I'm not his keeper. Maybe he found greener pastures elsewhere."

"Or mebbe browner ones in Coon Row," sniggered one of his cohorts.

"Enough of that talk." snapped Inez and glanced toward Abe, halfway down the bar. Had he heard, he would have bestowed more than a frown on the clutch of men. Her gaze switched back to the speaker as the meaning of his comment sunk in. "You saw the drummer in Stillborn Alley? When?"

"Ooooh, lessee, we'd finished a few rounds of billiards. Wandered down State a ways, and that's when you pointed him out to us, right, Chet?

He was missing his hat. Cold night for no hat. He's got a sneaky kind of gait, so I remembered that too. Anywhoo, he was a-slippin' past Kate Armstead's crib," he stopped, apologetic. "Sorry, Miz Stannert, you bein' a proper married woman and all. Mrs. Armstead's 'bood-or,' I guess you'd say."

"Boudoir," Inez corrected the mangled French. "But when, exactly?"

"Late last night." He affirmed, then paused. "Well, mebbe early this mornin' is more accurate."

Inez drummed her fingers against her whisky sling glass, thinking. The imprecise timing didn't help determine whether the drummer was responsible for Drina Gizzi's death. Assuming he was the murderer, he might have vamoosed after realizing Inez could place him at the scene. Although that didn't explain where Drina's earthly remains had gone or who had taken them.

Chet's companion turned to the third, younger man, who by the look of his clothes and fingernails had spent a long day underground, although his face was clean enough and his dark hair combed neat.

The younger miner spoke up. "Yep. It was long past the midnight hour. That was about when we decided to turn in, since me and my partner had to be up and in the district in the morning." He glanced at Inez. "You gotta forgive Chet his sour state of mind, Mrs. Stannert. He got a shock today. The fancy-pants dude he sold his last get-rich-quick claim to might get rich after all."

Chet hunched his shoulders as if to ward off bad news. "Ain't necessarily the case," he grumbled.

"Looks likely, though," retorted the younger and added to Inez, "Chet sold that salted claim yesterday. The buyer wanted to work it further, so he hired one of those geologists and a few of us," he indicated his older partner. "The geologist had a looksee around, and we did a little blasting in the drift. That claim might just be worth something."

Inez finished her hot drink, intrigued. *Could Lord Percy have struck it rich in Leadville? Maybe, with the inheritance, his luck has turned.* "Any assay results?" she asked.

"Not yet," grumbled Chet. "It'll come up snake eyes, you'll see. There's nothin' there. Area's all played out and what's worth anything is all tied up by the consolidateds."

"Could be like Chicken Bill and Haw Tabor," said the younger. "Bill sold the Chrysolite claim for ten thou to Tabor, and it's made Tabor how much? A million and a half?"

Chet hunkered further, saying, "If that drummer's not comin' then I'm goin'." He turned and left.

The two miners looked at each other and shrugged.

"After selling worthless claims for so long, his luck was bound to turn," said the younger philosophically. "Lady Luck is fickle."

He flicked a coin onto the counter. "A shot of your house for me and my partner here, if you please, Mrs. Stannert."

After Inez dispensed the drinks, a glance at her lapel watch told her it was time to repair upstairs and prepare for her Saturday night poker game. She was dreading it a bit, wondering what kind of player Dr. Gregorvich would be. Her Saturday night regulars, she knew them well and their quirks and tells. The Lads from London, the same. But this physician was an unknown quantity and tonight, in particular, she didn't want any "unknown quantities" in the mix, what with so much else on her mind. And then, there was Reverend Sands. In the past, he had always been there at the end of the night's gatherings to walk her home.

But now?

Everything had changed.

She hoped she would see him, somehow, before the service Sunday morning, before he made the announcement of his official leaving. He wouldn't leave town without talking to her, would he?

Unknown. It was all unknown.

As for the drummer's whereabouts…

She untied her apron, hung it on the hook by the backbar, caught Abe's eye, and gave him a shrug. He pulled out his pocketwatch, glanced at the time, looked at her, and returned her shrug.

…another unknown.

Inez tapped a finger on the muted gloss surface of the round mahogany table, waiting for Dr. Gregorvich to cut the cards. No one seemed in a particular hurry for the game to progress. This, the first Saturday night poker game she had hosted at the Silver Queen in some time, seemed to have evolved into a social event for her regular players, the Lads from London, and the guests to chat, gossip, argue politics, and smoke their cigars, cigarettes, and pipes.

And draw down her liquor supply.

The windowpanes, hidden behind heavy moreen wool curtains, shivered in the gusts of wind that slapped the glass, while the walls creaked under the heavy hand of sudden weather. The flickering gaslights behind the etched glass lamp fixtures of the chandelier caused the moire pattern in the curtains to dance. She resigned herself to waiting while Dr. Gregorvich expounded on some finer point of medical theory to Doc Cramer, who was nodding then shaking his head. Looking around, Inez took in the waxed and polished wood floors and paneling, the green and gold wallpaper, framed prints and paintings of hunts and battles past, the carpets of Axminster and Moquette velvet. All touches she had engineered and designed when she'd first breathed life into the exclusive, second-floor "gaming room" of the Silver Queen earlier that summer.

The sideboard was well stocked, although the levels were falling rapidly in the decanters and bottles, and the crystalware had been appropriated by the room's inhabitants. The coffee service remained, for the moment, untouched, except by Inez, who increased the potency of her cup of the "devil's dark brew" with a tot of brandy. *I must remember to tell Sol he did well today.* She knew that he probably had spent the better part of the afternoon preparing the room for the evening, and was even now helping Abe downstairs behind the bar, while Mark was heaven-knows-where-hell-and-gone.

There was no question. She was in charge tonight. And that suited her just fine. More than fine. Easing back in her upholstered chair, Inez felt like a queen, if only for the evening.

She brushed the skirt of her narrow, dark green velvet dress with the back of her hand, letting the smooth warm fabric comfort her. The silver and pearl bracelet on her wrist caught briefly on a bit of fringe and she shook her wrist to release the hold. If all went according to plan, her time in Leadville was ticking down like a watch abandoned by its wearer. This secret knowledge tasted bittersweet and pulled her away on a drift of past memories and future hopes. She took a firm hold of her mental wanderings, as a mother would of a toddler's hand, and pulled herself back to the present. *I cannot afford to get maudlin and wistful, particularly with so much at stake and with events still so uncertain.*

She finally turned to Dr. Gregorvich, cutting his conversation short. "If you please, cut the cards?"

He did so. She said, "Ante, gentlemen." Quarter eagles flew to the center of the table. Doc Cramer examined the meager pile before him, remarking, "This will probably be my last hand tonight, m'dear, unless Lady Luck should deign to smile upon me."

"Ah, you might as well say good night and bar the door, Doc, because that lady, she's all mine tonight," crowed Lord Percy. She had marked his extremely genial mood, his wind-burned countenance, and an unprecedented jaunty bounce to his step when he had entered the room earlier with his mates. She knew something was up when she had offered him his rabbit's foot, which had been in careful concealment in the Silver Queen safe, protected from inadvertent theft or loss. "You may secure the rabbity-rabbit back in the safe," he announced. "Dame fortune has been casting come-hither looks my way all day."

In contrast, Epperley looked like a pale, wrathful shade following in Percy's wake. Tipton, Balcombe, and Quick seemed much as usual, falling upon the free liquor with their customary alacrity. They joshed and chatted up the others, including Bob Evan, a successful mercantiler who was one of Inez's regulars and David Cooper, a lawyer whose riches rested on interpreting mining law for his well-to-do clients. The only regular missing was Jed Elliston of *The Independent.*

Inez had ascertained early in the evening's activities that Dr. Gregorvich wasn't there for the poker. Since he came as Doc Cramer's guest—and she was inordinately fond of Doc and owed him much—she had offered Gregorvich the seat on her right so he could get a "feel" for the game and players on each betting round. She'd hoped he'd be generous in his betting, but instead, he played weak, folding early and often. At first, he seemed quite content to simply watch the players with an odd, almost clinical gleam as each round unfolded. She got the uncomfortable feeling that his gimlet gaze was fixed a large percentage of that time on her. After a few hands, he turned his attention to his host, Dr. Cramer. Inez felt sorry for the beleaguered old-time physician, who seemed hard put to focus simultaneously on his cards, his beloved brandy, and his loquacious guest.

Gregorvich was saying, "Why sir, in the recent volume of the *Transactions of the American Medical Association,* Dr. Hibberd notes the climbing interest in investigations to determine whether certain parts of the brain give rise to certain attributes of the mind or if the brain, as a whole, is the organ of the mind as a whole."

Doc harrumphed politely. "I admit, I've been too busy tending to the medical needs of an overpopulated mining town, what with rheumatism, broken limbs, pneumonia, consumption, erysipelas, catarrh, inflammation of the bowels, cholera infantum being but a few of the crises in any given day."

"Ah, but sir, we must stay on top of the profession and its advances. The brain and the mind are unknown territory. As inhabitants of the storied West, we should appreciate that, as physicians, we are also on the frontier of modern medicine. We must advance with courage, observe the strange wonders presented by the confluence of the human physical and mental conditions, and make our maps."

If things had been different, Inez would have tried to redirect the flow of medi-babble at her right elbow, but she had her hands full keeping the game moving smoothly forward. There was an odd buzz of energy in the room that made it hard to concentrate. She wasn't sure whether it was because it had been nearly two months since the Saturday night regulars had gathered around the table or because of Percy's increasingly reckless and loud behavior. He didn't seem to care if he won or lost and was betting extravagantly and bluffing outrageously. Then again, perhaps it was simply her present cup of coffee-brandy was not mixing well with the earlier hot whisky sling.

"Great advances are at hand regarding the histology, physiology, and pathology of the brain," Gregorvich droned. Doc continued nodding.

The tide of medical mumbo-jumbo emanating from Gregorvich didn't help as she tried to focus on her own hand and take in any tells from the other players.

Evan, sitting to Inez's left, shook his head, his steel-rimmed glasses flashing with the motion. "Pass." Inez knew him as a cautious player, so his "wait and see" attitude was to be expected. Even when his hand was a good one, he gave little away on the first round of betting.

Cooper cocked his head and frowned a little, so small a grimace that if Inez had not been watching intently she probably would have missed it beneath the silver of his neat, short-cropped beard. A careful and astute interpreter of mining law, Cooper had a subtle set of tells. The cocked head indicated something interesting was held in his well-manicured grip. The frown could mean many things. Inez decided whatever he held intrigued him, but he wasn't entirely sure at this point what to do about it. However, the lawyer did tend to be impulsive when it came to cards, so Inez was not surprised when he sent a half eagle sailing into the nest. "Five dollars, just to keep things interesting."

"Oh, let's make it more interesting than that," drawled Percy. "Five and raise you ten."

So soon, Percy? Inez kept her thoughts to herself and worked to keep her expression pleasantly neutral, her gaze steady and her eyebrows relaxed.

Epperley wasn't nearly so subtle. "You're going to run through that inheritance in all of a weekend, aren't you?" he said with a nasty edge.

Percy shrugged. "Don't have an aromatic faint, old boy. There's more where this came from."

"But for how long?" Epperley countered. He swirled the golden liquid in his brandy goblet with increasing agitation. "You have financial *obligations*."

Percy gave an exaggerated sigh and twisted around to look at Epperley. "Do I now?" he said with heavy sarcasm, "My mind is a little foggy on that point. Too much brandy, too many cigars, too many lovely women. Oh, of course, you're referring to the *mine!*"

He swiveled back to the table. "Mrs. Stannert, did I tell you I am in possession of the next silver bonanza?" His face shone with excitement. "I struck up a conversation with an engineer late last night, a fine chap, working with the estimable Samuel F. Emmons on a monograph of the Leadville mining region. Anyhow this engineer, good fellow that he is, was initially dubious of my claim, but agreed for a modest sum to take a look this morning and give me his opinion. Upshot is, he told me things look a right go. I guess I didn't need to worry about that broken mirror after all! No seven years' bad luck for me. With the help of some mining chappies of his acquaintance who were agreeable to making some Saturday pocket change, we now have samples out for initial assay."

That caught Cooper's attention and he looked up from his cards. "Is that so? I thought all the promising claims in the mining district had long been staked, sold, re-sold, and subsumed by the consolidated concerns. If your property assays well, Lord Percy, you'll need a crack lawyer to help you navigate the arcana of mining law and statutes." He reached into his waistcoat and withdrew a silver card case. "Allow me."

Evan shifted in his chair. "Doc? What'd you say? Fold, raise, call?"

Doc stared at his cards with intense concentration. Inez suspected he was on the fence between call and fold. *He did say this would be his last hand of the evening unless he was lucky. I'll wager he'll stay put to at least see if he can improve what he has.*

"...of course, it's been established that the brain is composed of bundles of minute fibers..."

"Call," said Doc, and slid three half eagles into the pot.

"Dr. Erasmus Wilson counted the number of fibers in a very minute surface section, reported that a square inch of brain is composed of no less than one hundred millions of fibers!" Gregorvich continued. "Is it not probable, then that each fiber has a distinct office?"

Doc Cramer finished his brandy before remarking, "Interesting. But truly, sir, unless this can provide practical insights into medical aid I can offer the unfortunate man who happens to be in an iron bucket when the brake of a whim fails and sends its human cargo hurtling two hundred feet to the bottom of a shaft—"

"Well, sir, think of the unfortunates who dwell on the surface, some in total misery, as we have seen firsthand in the alleys, suffering and indeed dying from the effects of alcohol, insanity, and other diseases of the mind. Intemperance is well known to be transmissible. Those who become victims of this disease through hereditary tendencies are seldom, if ever, cured, and they transmit to their children not only a tendency to drink but to crime and insanity as well."

Growing impatient, Inez leaned toward Gregorvich to invite him to take his turn at the table. He held his cards so carelessly that, in turning, she inadvertently saw his hand in full. With a shock, she realized he held a very good hand indeed: three kings conferred, accompanied by a ten and an ace.

The physician continued, barreling straight ahead with his argument like a train on a straightaway with no curves in sight. "What if a predisposition to a specific mental aberration of the *mind* could be determined by reading the physical organization, the convolved regions of the cerebrum, indeed the very fibers themselves?"

A new voice from the door said, "Then I take it, Dr. Gregorvich, you've no objection to carving and dissecting the brain fibers of poor unfortunates who have no more use for them, being dead and all?"

Inez twisted around to glare at Jed Elliston, who was, in turn, glaring at Gregorvich with an expression close to triumph. "Sounds to me like you might have some insights into these illegal anatomy classes that I've heard whispers about."

Inez interjected, "Doctor, it's your turn."

Without even glancing at his cards, Gregorvich said, "Fold." He tossed his hand facedown on the table by Inez's elbow, adding, "The study of anatomy is not illegal, Mr. Elliston, and neither are private anatomy lessons provided by a proper physician.

However, as I have patiently tried to explain to you several times, I am in no way involved in such activities."

The abandoned cards lay ignored, but the image of their worth sizzled in Inez's memory. Inez set her jaw hard. This casual discard of what was probably a winning hand was enough to convince her that Dr. Gregorvich was most definitely not there for the poker, but for something else entirely. *Perhaps he intends to bore us all to death with his erudite medical knowledge and then pick our brains apart.*

However, with Dr. Gregorvich and his three kings and singular ace out of the game, her own two aces twinkled with an encouraging light. "Call." She contributed fifteen dollars to the cause.

"Call," said Evan quickly, perhaps sensing that if there was a moment's hesitation the momentum might dissolve. The rest followed suit.

Once everyone was square with the pot, discards were offered up and replacements dealt. Inez tried to keep track of who discarded what and reactions—obvious or subtle—upon viewing replacement cards.

Evan discarded two and refilled his hand. *He looked pleased just then. A decent three of a kind, perhaps?*

"Mr. Elliston, have you heard the saying, 'He must mangle the living if he has not operated on the dead.'? I wager you have not, so I will tell you who said such: Renowned English surgeon and anatomist, Sir Astley Paston Cooper—"

"No relation!" the silver-haired lawyer said hastily as he picked up the singular replacement for his discard and grimaced.

Ah! Cooper trying for a flush or a straight, I should guess. He should know better. He'll probably fold this time around.

"—Sir Astley made historical contributions to otology, vascular surgery, and, apropos of our discussion here, cerebral circulation."

Percy stayed pat, looking more jolly by the moment. Inez experienced a twinge of suspicion.

"Yeah, yeah." Jed had pulled out his notebook and was tapping it with his pencil. "This Astley fellow, he gets all the glory, and who's getting the short end of this deal, or maybe I should say the sharp end of the scalpel? The dead and their families, right? Probably the poor, come to think of it, because who misses the unknown wretches who die and are dumped into the potters' fields?"

Percy took that moment to say cheerfully, "I say, I shall have to think of a good name for the mine. Perhaps I'll call her the Silver Queen. How about that, Mrs. Stannert? An homage to you and your hospitality?" His gaze roved to the ceiling, fixing on the chandelier. "Why, I might just move to Leadville so I can keep a close weather eye on my investments here and hobnob with Tabor and the other silver barons."

"Move?" inquired Inez.

Doc picked up his three replacement cards and sighed, making no attempt to hide his disappointment.

"Investments?" said Epperley incredulously. "Plural? As in more than one? In Leadville?"

"Why, yes. I bumped into Mr. Stannert earlier, and he mentioned the possibility of opening up a gentlemen's club not far from here, semi-exclusive and all that. I imagine he heard of my good fortune on the hill and was looking for backers." Percy's teeth flashed.

Tipton, Balcombe, and Quick stirred from their posts by the sideboard. Quick squinted at the empty brandy decanter while Tipton pulled out his pocketwatch, announcing, "Don't want to miss the show at the Grand Central. You coming, Epperley? How about you, Percy? Remember that little redhead from last night? I'm certain she'd love to rekindle her acquaintance with you, especially now that you're a silver baron."

"After this hand," said Percy. "Save us a box seat."

Quick said, "Right-o, we'll put the champagne, on your tab, Percy."

The three squeezed past Elliston, who repositioned himself by the sideboard and helped himself to a whisky, neat.

Inez discarded a lowly trio comprising a deuce, three, and six, and studied her replacements, keeping her face and hands still even as her heart did a joyous little caper. Not only had chance graced her with the last vagrant ace in the deck, but with two queens as well. She turned to Evan.

"Twenty," said Evan.

Cooper shook his head. "I'm out."

He tossed his cards toward the center of the table, as if waving goodbye to the pot in the center.

Inez switched her attention to Percy.

"Let's liven things up a bit, what say you, Evan, old son? See your twenty and raise you one hundred." Percy pushed a portion of his remaining coinage into the center of the table.

Doc rubbed his jaw as if deep in thought, the jowls beneath the muttonchops quivering. Inez knew it was all for show. For as long as she'd been playing poker with Doc, he never stayed in for the high stakes. Being a patron of the Saturday night game and being able to drink a quantity of brandy in the company of the regulars had always seemed enough for him. In fact, sometimes he didn't play at all, preferring to take his brandy, sit by the parlor stove, and chat with other nonplayers who happened in, such as Reverend Sands.

Sands.

She thrust his name away from her thoughts, keeping her gaze steady on Doc for his pronouncement.

"Ah well. This is where I bow out." Doc threw in his cards and gathered his meager stash of currency.

Gregorvich had pointedly turned his back on Elliston and was now watching the remaining players as if they displayed some intriguing symptom of a mysterious disease he was determined to diagnose.

Inez pushed in the requisite one hundred-twenty, then turned to Evan. He added a hundred and said, "Call."

They revealed their hands. Evan had a decent flush, all clubs. With a triumphant flourish, Percy presented three jacks and two queens. "Sorry, Evan, better luck next time," he said with a grin.

"Indeed, gentlemen," said Inez, setting out her aces-high full house. "Better luck next time."

There was a moment of silence, then Percy exploded in laughter. "Well played, Mrs. Stannert, I've been comb-cut most expertly! And here I thought the lovely owner of the Silver Queen was simply here to grace the table with her presence and provide the feminine touch. I was so addled I forgot that she has as keen a mind as any highly trained Inner Temple barrister." He gave her a sly wink to show he was not holding any kind of grudge.

Inez addressed both Evan and Percy. "Thank you, gentlemen, for being such good sports. I will confess that my good fortune is all due to Lady Chance." She slid the winnings into the moneybox she kept near at hand. "Surely you will all stay and allow the lady an opportunity to smile on you as well. The night is still young."

Evan and Cooper nodded.

Percy shrugged. "Apologies, dear lady. Places to go. Redheads to see. You understand." He pushed back his chair and stood, looking relaxed and happy. "Ah well, it's a come-day, go-day for me. Jolly good fun all around."

Epperley however was scowling as if it was his money, not Percy's, that was sliding into the Silver Queen's moneybox.

Percy caught his expression and said, "Oh, buck up, Epperley. You're as bad as the paterfamilias, scolding me to 'save for a rainy day' et cetera. Let's go on down to the Grand Central and you can wash your neck with some of their imported champagne."

Without a word, Epperley disappeared out the door. Clapping hat to head, Percy followed, pausing with one hand on the crystal doorknob. "You must forgive Epperley. He's been working much too hard at that resort hotel of his in Manitou. Fellow'd be a lot happier if he let that money-losing property go and loosen up a bit. Ah well. Cheerio!" He departed, and they could hear him whistling a jaunty tune as he descended the stairs.

Inez stood. "Gentlemen, shall we take a short break and then resume? Jed, will you be joining us?"

"Of course." Jed drained what was left of his whisky. "Seems like a good time to pull up a chair, now that Evan and Cooper have been properly humbled."

Inez tucked the moneybox under her arm and began heading toward the office, with the idea of depositing a portion of the winnings in the safe. Too much available was too much temptation to take chances.

A quick tread behind her warned her that she was being followed. She pivoted, moneybox in one hand, the other sliding into her hidden silk-lined pocket for her revolver.

Dr. Gregorvich stood in the hallway, too close for comfort. Inez retreated a step. "Doctor, can I help you?"

He said, "I want to apologize, Mrs. Stannert. I was made aware by my colleague Dr. Cramer I may have been overbearing in my enthusiasm for my chosen field of medical passion." He smiled, and the lingering threat in the air dispelled.

She, however, kept her hand in her pocket. "Apologies accepted. All of us have our passions, and sometimes they can overtake us."

"Yes, indeed. The brain or the mind, if you wish, is such a fascinating subject. Our knowledge is yet imperfect, but compared with the obscurity which surrounded it for years, we are rich in material and in observational results." He held up a hand as if to forestall her shifting yet another step toward the office. "But I don't want to overstate the position of our profession. We are not yet able to demonstrate that particular lesions in the nerve cells are found only in connection with, for instance, the hypertrophied caudate cell which has been found in general paresis, melancholia, and brain atrophy. Ah, but I wanted to ask a question regarding that young charge of yours from the afternoon."

The abrupt change of subject put her on guard. "Yes?" she said cautiously.

"The niece of your friend. I should pay a professional visit so I can check on her symptoms and progress. The vagaries of high altitude and exhaustion, particularly in children and women, can be most damaging."

"Yes, well," Inez thought quickly. "I should ask my friend. You understand. The young girl was not my charge. I was merely bringing her to her proper family."

"Of course." He paused. "I have particular interest in the mind and brain's connections to vision, the eye, and the optic nerve. How does vision work? Are hallucinations created in the brain proper or through aberration in the optic nerve? It is an area of fascination to me. I noticed your young traveler had *heterochromia iridum*—eyes of different colored irises. Very unusual. I would like to see her again, to ascertain she has recovered from her travels and also perhaps run a simple examination regarding her sight."

His gentle manner aside, the doctor's words and looming presence set off alarms for Inez. She decided to parry with regret. "You are most kind and I appreciate your concern. I shall pass your request along to my friend. I can assure you that the young girl in question was made to rest and, by all accounts, is doing well. As for her eyes, you are far more observant than I, for I didn't notice."

His own eyes narrowed, and she feared she had perhaps overplayed her hand.

"Will you be staying for the second half of our evening?" she asked. "Lady Luck may smile upon you yet."

"I'm afraid not," he said. "Other duties await. Our presence on State Street and in the alleys is particularly needed on the weekends, so I shall be on my way to provide medical aid to those who need it and prayers to those who are past need." He inclined his head. "Thank you for a most educational evening, Mrs. Stannert. I have not had the pleasure before of meeting a woman who can 'think like a man' in the rather demanding game of chance. Oh yes, I watched, and saw you watching as well."

He stepped forward, and she involuntarily stepped back. "Do you know," he continued, "the weight of the average female brain is an estimated five to six ounces less than that of the average male brain? That general inferiority in size exists at every period of life, from newborn to old age, even taking into account body weight." His gaze lingered in the vicinity of her forehead, and Inez could imagine that he was attempting to weigh her brain by virtue of his gaze. "It is accepted in medical and scientific circles that a woman's body and mind are inferior in vigor and power to those of the man. Accordingly, if pitted against one another in a physical or mental race, she, to use a sporting phrase, would be heavily handicapped."

Inez blinked, thinking of all the women she knew who spent their lives in hard physical labor—cooking, washing, cleaning, birthing and raising children. Those same women and others as well used their "inferior brains" to keep household accounts, negotiate in the buying and selling of daily goods, and run family- or self-owned businesses, all while negotiating the minefield of what was "right" and "expected" of the so-called weaker sex.

She responded with cold asperity, "I would suggest, *Doctor*, that you look not to the size of the brain nor its weight but to the use an individual puts that particular organ. I would further suggest that, if we were to be pitted in a mental race, the winner would entirely depend on what the race was about. If it were about anatomy of the brain and medical matters, well, sir, you would certainly finish the easy winner. But if the race involves dissecting Chopin's Waltz Number Seven or Milton's *Paradise Lost*, or the practicum of running a business successfully—balancing the books, weighing the investment options of the myriad opportunities in a mining boomtown—I do believe I would leave you spinning in the dust."

With that, she turned on her heel and went into the office, closing the door with a firm click behind her.

Chapter Twenty-six

Tony knocked on the back door of Alexander's Undertaking, glancing around as she did so. Crumpled papers skittered in the ice-cold breeze that skirled through the alley. Back in the clothes borrowed from Ace, Tony shivered. She found herself longing for all the fancy girl's clothes and layers that she'd left folded neatly at Miss Carothers' studio. The key to the back door of the studio was fastened to a simple piece of string around her neck.

"You can come and go as you please," Miss Carothers had said. After a worried pause, she'd looked at Tony with those soft brown eyes and said, "You could just stay here. Do you really need to take this job at the undertaker's?"

Tony was tempted, but shook her head. "If I'm going to find out what happened to Maman, I need to know more about Mr. Alexander and his missus."

Although she hadn't said so to Miss Carothers, Tony also figured that she was less likely to run into anyone who might recognize her at the coffin-man's place than at the studio. Turns out, the woman photographer knew the nobs, or at least they'd been her customers. Tony had recognized one of them, the one with the pale hair who always looked so angry, in a photograph in the studio showroom.

Tony shivered again at the recollection, but then reminded herself where she was. If any of the nobs showed up here, well, they'd probably need measuring for a pine overcoat, so no worries there. She knocked again, a little louder. A wavering light leaked through the dusty window in the back door, growing stronger, until she heard the unmistakable grind of a door latch being withdrawn. The door opened, revealing Mr. Alexander on the other side, holding a lamp. The sharp scent of kerosene wafted out with the warmer air. He said, "Right on time. Excellent. Come in, Mr. Donatello."

For the briefest moment, Tony wondered who "Mr. Donatello" was. Then, she remembered. Here, she was Tony Donatello. She was wearing so many different names for so many different places and people that it was hard to keep track.

Alexander ushered her inside, saying, "No need to come to the back. Feel free to use the front door. If it's locked, there's a bell to ring. If I leave it open, it has a bell above the door to let me know someone has entered. I happened to be coming up the stairs just now, otherwise I might not have heard your knock."

He locked the door behind her and led the way down a dark, wide hall toward the front of the building, the lamp hissing venomously. He continued, "I don't often leave the front door unlocked, however. This isn't the kind of business, where people come in off the street for a look-around. Most of my clients make appointments."

For one wild moment, Tony thought he meant the corpses. How could the dead make appointments? But then she realized he had to mean the living.

The light from the lamp threw dancing shadows around the dark hall. As they emerged into a large, gaslit room the light from the lamp shrank and disappeared, overwhelmed by the intense brightness. Tony looked around, bedazzled by an array of hulking, oblong wood and metal coffins.

"These are some of the more expensive 'eternity boxes' we have to offer," Alexander said matter-of-factly. "Tonight, you're to dust and polish these, inside and out. That will take you some hours, if done correctly. But first, I'll just tell you a bit about them. I find some people are uncomfortable around these wares. Throwing the light of knowledge upon them lessens the fear and makes them what they are—resting places for the dead, not objects for holding sorrow, fear, and distrust."

He extinguished the lamp and moved to the first. "To begin with, most of these are properly called 'caskets,' not coffins. We have bronze," he laid a hand atop a gold-colored container, "copper, various woods such as oak and mahogany." He moved on. "And here is a metallic burial case."

Tony gulped. "It's kinda shaped like a body."

Alexander lay a hand on the case. "This was designed with Egyptian mummy cases in mind. When sealed, it is airtight, slowing the decomposition of the remains to a remarkable degree, making it the perfect choice for long distance transport. But this kind of burial case is expensive, so mostly of interest to the well-to-do."

Tony ventured closer. "Why's it got a window?"

"For one, it allows those who receive the coffin to identify the one who lies within. We line the interior with fabric in the head and shoulders area. My wife takes care of the fabrics we use here and in the shrouds and so on."

Tony thought of the pale sad-eyed Mrs. Alexander, all in black, standing outside her maman's shack and looking her over with her disturbing gaze, and then later that night, hanging onto the billiard-hall door with a grip of pure death. No wonder she's so death-crazy, having to always be sewing shrouds and things for corpses.

"So, the bodies—"

"The remains," Mr. Alexander corrected.

"The remains aren't up here?"

"That's right. When someone dies at home, I go to the house and take care of the arrangements and do the embalming on the premises. I also hire the help and transport necessary to bring the casket or coffin to the home and arrange bringing the remains to their final resting place."

"Embalming?" She wasn't sure what that word meant, but it didn't sound pleasant.

He nodded, and she detected a touch of pride in his voice as he answered, "Embalming replaces the blood and fluids in the body with a special mix of chemicals, including alcohol, creosote, zinc chloride, sugar of lead, turpentine, and so on. It is the modern, medical way to preserve a body after death from further decomposition."

"How'd you learn all this?" His business obviously went far beyond just knocking together pieces of wood to throw the dead corpses into.

Alexander retreated to a countertop at the back of the room, which reminded Tony of a shortened version of the bar at the Silver Queen. Minus the drinkers and the drink. "I started as a furniture maker. Making furniture and coffins went hand-in-hand, back in the day. Eventually, I moved into the undertaking business and all that entailed. As for embalming, it's been an area of interest to me since the Great War, when I worked with the embalming surgeons. After the War, I aligned myself with physicians who offered such services so I could learn more about it."

He stopped rummaging under the counter to nod at the far wall. "Dr. Gregorvich next door and I have such a relationship, to our mutual benefit. He knows much of the field and has made it possible for me to offer embalming along with customary undertaking services. I will say, however, I find Leadville, progressive though it is, to be reluctant to embrace the idea of an undertaker providing embalming as well." Alexander pulled out a can of polish, several rags, a stack of newspaper, and a feather duster, lining them up on the counter. "But times change, so I must be patient," he said, frowning down at the cleaning supplies.

"What happens to the bodies of folks who don't have family or nobody?" asked Tony. It was the question that had been burning in her heart and on her lips, and now, out it came.

Alexander looked up from his brown study. "The indigent, you mean? And those who are not readily identifiable? For the truly indigent with no family, we—by that, I mean the undertakers in town—have contracted with the city to handle the disposition of the remains. We take turns, switching monthly, so it does not prove too burdensome for any one business. Right now, October, is my month. Most of the local churches here have collections to defray the cost of simple boxes. Sometimes, we provide them at no cost. We also hold those remains awaiting identification and in need of preparation. Or, if there has been a crime and a postmortem is required, we store those bodies as well."

"Do you," Tony's voice stuck in her throat, "have anyone here now? A body, I mean. Waiting."

The square lenses of Alexander's glasses flashed as he adjusted them. "Why yes, I do. I have a poor unfortunate recently brought in from Stillborn Alley. I am waiting to hear whether a postmortem will be performed. It appears to be a matter of foul play, but whether the city decides to pursue the case or not, I cannot say."

"Can I...?" she couldn't say it, and begged him silently to finish her sentence.

He looked at her curiously. "Mr. Donatello, do you want to see the remains?"

Mute, Tony nodded.

"Very well, downstairs for a moment and then you need to get busy on your tasks. Perhaps tomorrow I can give you a more complete tour of the basement." He picked up the kerosene lamp, relit it, and retraced his steps to the back.

He stopped at the head of the stairs, and pointed to a staircase heading up to the second floor. "My wife and I live up there. I hope to eventually buy a home for us, but property has proven expensive in Leadville. Until then, we make our home above the business."

Tony wondered what the missus thought about living above all the coffin-boxes and dead corpses, much less being married to a man who rubbed elbows with Old Mr. Grim himself. As they descended the stairs to the underlevel, Tony hugged herself, partly from the cold, partly to steel herself for what might be waiting.

Alexander said, "This is an unfortunate case. Well, they are all unfortunate, of course. I suspect eventually one of the churches will provide for a pine box, and we will lay the remains to rest in the free section of the cemetery, what folks commonly call the pauper's field."

Downstairs were more gaslights, thankfully. Tony wasn't sure if she could have stood that cavernous ice-box of a room, dank low ceilings, brick walls and wood joists, smelling of death, dirt, and stinging chemicals, if not for the gas lamps pegged to the walls. A set of livery-sized doors were along one side at the bottom of the stairs. He saw her looking at them.

"That is where I take deliveries, the caskets and coffins, the supplies. Also, any remains. It wouldn't do to have them carried into the front door, you know."

Sharp tools, tubings, and odd-shaped dark metal objects were lined up on a far table and hanging on the walls nearby. There was another door, smaller, just beyond that table, with a bright shiny lock. Tony realized it must go into the building next door. "Where's that go?"

Mr. Alexander looked to where her finger pointed. "Ah, just another door. Not used, really. I keep it locked up tight."

Off to one side was a table with the unmistakable shape of feet pushing upwards under a gray sheet. An odd box clamped down around the body, from the legs up. A metallic drip-drip echoed as water dripped slowly from two spigots mounted on either side of the box.

"Is that?" Tony couldn't say more.

Alexander smiled. "What you see here is a corpse cooler and a cooling board. It is only necessary to freeze the trunk and the chest to halt the worst of decomposition." He continued talking, walking to the head of the box. "Am I correct in guessing you are an urchin of the streets, Mr. Donatello? If so, it occurs to me that you might have light to shed on this poor soul. But if nothing else, you can perhaps rest easy as you work this evening, knowing that the deceased are nothing to be afraid of. They are, after all, simply dead."

With that, he took hold of the handle on the lid of the box, lifted it, and beckoned Tony forward. "Come lad. Have a look."

Arms wrapped tight around Ace's loud checkered jacket to keep her heart from leaping from her chest, Tony ventured forward. She could feel the hard shape of Miss Carothers' key bite into her ribs. Her eyes stung. *Maman? Is it you?*

No voice answered in her mind.

She stepped up to the head of the box, summoned all her courage, and peered in.

The face of the drummer, Woods, peered back—eyes open and flat, lips stretched back in a frozen grimace, mocking her fear.

Chapter Twenty-seven

For the rest of the evening, Inez had to endure Jed Elliston muttering about the difficulties he was having unearthing leads on the "underground anatomy classes" that he was certain were lurking in Leadville.

"Did you see Gregorvich's face?" Jed said, tossing his losing cards in with the rest at the end of a stubborn betting round between himself and Cooper.

She almost hated to ask, but she did. "When?"

"Earlier this evening, when I accused him of grave-robbing from the paupers' section of the cemetery."

Doc, who had taken up a post by the warming stove, harrumphed. "Good lord, Jed, he is a respected physician! Yes, he is a tad overexuberant on matters of modern medical research as regards to cerebellum and particularly cerebrum, but that doesn't make him a criminal in any sense of the word." Then, to Inez and the others, "My apologies. I had no idea when I invited him to join us that he would hold forth at such volume and length."

Evan said, "No matter, Doc. We all have our obsessions not necessarily shared by others outside our professions. You should have heard Richard Oliver and me the other day as we dissected the costs and profit margins for stoves and tinware."

"Or when those of us in the legal profession gather to dissect the rulings and decisions of the court," said Cooper.

The door opened and Inez looked up. Reverend Justice Sands lingered on the threshold as if to take her in and lock her image in his mind. For Inez, that moment of seeing him in the doorway took her back nearly a year ago, to the first time she saw him. At first glance, he didn't seem particularly extraordinary. He was a man of mid-height, mid-thirties, light brown hair, clean-shaven, someone who appeared well acquainted and at ease with hard weather and hard times.

Then, she heard him speak. She, who loved music, who felt the melody, harmony, pulse and purpose of a piano composition down to the core of her being.

Inez had to admit she was initially seduced by the warm timbre and sensuality of his voice. The rest inevitably followed.

Much of what was then was now, only more so. He was, if anything, a little leaner, with a few more lines around the blue-gray eyes and a touch of sorrow shadowing his face.

That, and the way he was looking at her now caused her heart to sink.

She now knew it was true.

He was leaving.

The moment between them broke when Sands removed his flat-brimmed black hat and Doc exclaimed, "Reverend! Come in. How are Stillborn and Tiger alleys this evening? More of the destitute and unlucky seem to pour into the city daily, and with the coming of winter, I fear we shall lose the battle to help them all. And given tonight's snow and wind, it's going to be a difficult night for those without shelter or sustenance."

Sands moved inside, removed his heavy winter coat, a dense black wool, and hung his hat and coat on the cherrywood and brass coat rack off to one side, where they proceeded to discreetly drip onto the small rug placed beneath. He nodded to Doc and the players before heading toward the sideboard and the coffee.

"Gentlemen, Mrs. Stannert," he said by way of greeting, then added, "You're right about that, Doc. I spent some time with your colleague as we tried to convince the most desperate to seek out the mission or, if they can make the trek all the way to Tenth, to Saint Vincent's Hospital." He poured coffee into a cup, saying, "It's the children who suffer most."

Evan glanced at Elliston, whose turn it was to deal, and said, "I understand from one of the newsies that you take good care of those boys of yours, give them a place out of the storm. And not just your boys, but some of the others who don't have a place to go."

Inez watched as Elliston flubbed mid-shuffle.

Doc sat up straighter. "Is that so? Well, who says that newsmen are hard of heart and cold of temperament? Glad to hear that, Elliston!"

Elliston gathered up the scattered cards, saying, "It's only good business sense. I do what I can to keep them hale and hearty. My boys may not have brass-button uniforms like the *Chronicle* gives to theirs, but at least they have a belly-full in the morning to help them get through their day."

Now, more than ever, Inez was convinced that Tony must be one of the "boys" that burrowed away with the rest, benefitting from Elliston's largesse.

They all played one more hand, Inez aware of Justice Sands standing by the stove, talking with Doc, watching the game unwind.

Inez was about to propose calling it an early night when Cooper, who won the modest pot, beat her to it. "Last call for me," he said, gathering the coins before him. "It's been a long day for me, and tomorrow I'm afraid it's back to the office. Not the way I intended to spend my Sunday, but needs must when the devil drives."

Doc stood up and leaned on his silver-headed cane, saying what Inez and no doubt others had been wanting to ask. "Now, Reverend, is there any truth behind the rumors I've been hearing that you are leaving town?"

Inez, who had gathered the cards, paused and watched as he turned to Doc and said, "You hear right, Doc, although I'd ask you to keep the fact under your hat until I inform the congregation tomorrow morning."

He surveyed the room, finally settling his attention on Inez. "As you all may recall, the position was initially an interim one.

When the offer to make the post permanent arose, I stepped forward. However, there appears to be a greater need for me in churches other than the one in Leadville. Leaving is difficult, but I hope I will have occasion to return." His words were polite, regretful, studied. But Inez heard what really lay behind them.

She read him, just as she read the unspoken message that only surfaced when the left hand and right hand made a marriage of harmony and melody, pulling a perfect marriage from white and black keys of the piano keyboard.

The others murmured sympathetic noises of shock and regret. Evan said, "If you were a drinking man, Reverend, I'd buy you a drink." He came over, clasped Reverend Sands' hand and said, "I'm not a church-goer, but in this instance I wish you Godspeed in all your future travels. I know, wherever you go, the folks will be lucky to have you there."

He nodded. "Thank you, Bob."

The others took their leave one by one. Elliston paused and said, "Promise you'll drop by *The Independent* before you leave. I'd like to write a story up about you and all the good you've done for Leadville."

Sands said, "There's no need for that, Jed. My works speak for themselves."

Jed shook his head. "That's not good enough, Reverend. Surely you've heard the other side of the gossip floating around. There are those who said you weren't focused enough on the congregants, that your extended leave while you traveled with Ulysses S. Grant on his recent trip West just showed how your allegiances were elsewhere."

Doc interrupted. "Lord in Heaven, man. We should identify those who spread these unfounded rumors and suppositions and show them up for the liars they truly are and—"

"No, Doc." Sands cut him off. "It doesn't matter who blew upon the embers, fanned them into a flame. The fact is, the congregation feels I have completed my work here. When the people lose faith in their chosen leader, it's time for someone else to lead them." He smiled slightly. "In my work as an interim minister over the past few years, I stepped in often enough to fill the breach in such cases, so I know. True, I never expected to find myself on the other side of the situation, but life and God's will can be strange that way."

He addressed Jed. "We can discuss the good the church as a whole has done this past year, but only on the condition that we don't lend credence to any of what you just said by repeating it in print. By repeating and denying the rumors, we only breathe life into what I would prefer to see die."

Elliston's mouth opened, closed, then opened again. Obviously he was loath to let it go. "But the *truth*," he sputtered.

"We tell the truth, give the facts. We don't repeat lies and half-truths that would cause harm to the church or draw suspicions onto any of its congregants."

Elliston glanced from Inez to Sands and back again. The light finally dawned, and he actually had the grace to flush a little. "Well, yeah. Of course not. I mean, of course. See you Monday, then? Monday would be good. I can get it into the mid-week edition. Good night Rev, Mrs. Stannert." He pulled on a coat, wrapped a scarf tight around his neck, and grabbed his hat.

Inez said, "Jed, stop by the bar and tell Sol or Abe to load up any leftover biscuits, ham, and beans into a couple of large tin lunch buckets we have back in the kitchen. Take them for your newsies and bring back the buckets when you can."

"Thanks, much appreciated," he said gruffly, and left.

Inez and Sands were alone in the room. He took a step, whether toward her or his coat, she didn't wait to find out. She held up a hand. "Wait."

He looked at her, questioning.

She repeated. "Wait. Give me twenty minutes."

After a moment, his expression softened, and he nodded.

She hurried to the office, did a quick count of the night's take from the game and shoved the moneybox into the safe. From thence to her chambers. Her past life on the road with Mark and Abe came to the fore, the times when they had to pack light and move fast. Those nights, while terrifying, were also exhilarating as they sped away from the consequences of whatever deeds caused them to race away by the light of the moon and stars.

It took less than ten minutes for her to pack a carpetbag with clothes and shoes appropriate for church the next morning. She pulled her Sunday winter cloak from the wardrobe, where it had waited, unused, all through the glorious summer months and all through the early months of autumn, when she'd been down in the shadow of Pikes Peak in Manitou Springs. The poignant smell of cedar wreathing the heavy smooth weight was a reminder, a whisper of the long, cold winter months ahead.

She wound a thick cashmere scarf around her neck and head, tucked a fur muff under one arm, and turned, last, to her nightstand. A brass key glinted, still, solitary, on the marble top. She picked up the key to the blue-sky house on Fourth Street. *Her* house. Extinguishing the light in her chambers, she walked out, secured the door, and headed to the waiting Reverend Sands without a backward glance or a shadow of regret.

"Inez, where are we going?" His voice was close, pitched low, for her hearing only.

They walked the Harrison Street boardwalk, both bundled into unrecognizable forms in scarves and outwear, just like the other late night revelers and workers hurrying by in this, the first deep snow of the season. Inez, with her hood pulled low over her head and her voice muffled by the scarf, only said, "Wait."

She withdrew one hand from her fur muff, entwined her fingers with his, and drew their clasped hands into his overcoat pocket, hidden deep between them. He tightened his grip on her fingers and she responded in kind. Warmth enveloped her. Their clasp was a haven from the never-ending clatter of wagons, carriages, the shouts of drivers and riders, the snorting and huffing of beasts of burden, all sharp-edged sounds now muffled in the falling snow.

She nudged him to turn onto West Fourth.

He obliged and tried again, gently, "Inez?"

"Wait."

They walked toward the west, the snowcapped peaks of Elbert and Massive showing like ghosts between the whirling dancing snow that swirled around them, obscuring, then parting.

She stopped him before the new-built home, its blue hue unseeable. Inez felt his body tighten beside hers. Leaning toward him, she pulled down the scarf that covered her lips and whispered, sending her warm breath into his ear. "Did you know this was here?"

"No. I'd not been down this street since I returned."

"It's mine," she said in response to the unspoken question. "Mine alone. I have the only key." Inez had thought carefully about this, about bringing him here, but had concluded there was no other place they could be together and away from prying eyes: not her saloon chambers, not his rectory, not a hotel. This was the space that chance and serendipity had offered, so she took it.

They went inside. She led him to the parlor and lit two small hand lamps waiting on an end table. "Will you set a fire going?" she asked. "There should be some embers still in the stove."

He nodded and shed his outer coat.

She took one of the lamps and carried it upstairs. There was a bedroom, already heaped with quilts, with its own small stove.

She prepared the fire in the room and returned to the parlor.

Reverend Sands was walking around the room, hands clasped behind his back. She noticed, with an ache that reached deep inside, how he moved with an easy, physical, almost animal grace, with an assuredness that seemed to command the room and all within it.

Handy for a preacher pounding the pulpit.

Handy for a killer who wouldn't hesitate to draw first.

Handy for a man who aims to seduce a woman and walk away.

Inez shook her head to silence the murmurs. Months ago, she had laid to rest her suspicions about Sands and his past and finally come to accept and trust him. Now, with him preparing to leave, all those old suspicions and doubts were rising to taunt her.

He turned, saw her, and smiled, with a smile tinged with regret that sent a pain scorching through her even as it warmed from within. She held out her hands. He walked forward, took her hands, and gently drew her to him.

This time, there was no savage despair in their embrace, not like the fierce clutches and kisses in Stillborn Alley. The moment of deep peace and yearning between them ended too soon. She pulled back, without letting him go, and asked, "Would you like me to play something for you? One last time?"

The fire in his eyes softened. "Not for the last time, Inez. Never that. Until the next time, yes. I will hold your music and your image with me, no matter where I am. Always."

She nodded, a lump in her throat, then moved to the piano, her green satin and velvet skirts whispering as she pulled off her gloves and flexed her fingers. She laid the gloves on the piano top and opened the keyboard cover. "Do you remember the first time?"

He pulled one of the overstuffed chairs around so he could sit to her side. "Of course, Inez." Every word was a caress. "Mendelssohn. No words."

Lieder ohne Worte.

It was a piece she had learned by heart as a child, and her heart would help her play it now. She positioned herself properly, arms relaxed from the shoulders, wrists level with the piano, palm of the hand curved, bridge of the hand round, fingertips lightly touching the keys. Her mother's words from long ago echoing in her mind: "Power comes from *behind* the fingers… not *from* the fingers." That patient, beloved voice—one she had not heard for over a decade—sounded so real and immediate that Inez almost turned around to see if she were there and if she approved. She held the silence for three beats, then released the liquid music. Peace enveloped her, and an unexpected sense of gratitude. Gratitude for having music to guide her life, gratitude for having found a love that allowed her to be who she was, without censure, with complete acceptance, gratitude for having the strength and power to help her friends and those in need.

As with all that she wanted to hold onto, the simple piece ended too soon, the shimmer of notes fading into silence. Inez closed her eyes, waiting. The warmth of his hand upon her neck made her sigh with pleasure and anticipation. She tipped her head back until his lips came down and met hers with a passion that promised to never let her go.

Then, for a while, time stood still, as they retreated from the world into a private place.

But only for a while.

Afterwards, buried under quilts, her cheek upon his chest, and his arm looped warm and safe around her, holding her close, she willed the clocks to stop ticking and the moon to stay its course. Neither happened.

After listening to the play of snow and wind upon the pane of the bedroom upstairs, she stirred. He slowly pulled his arm from under her, his words rising in the dark. "I can't stay."

"I know."

He kissed her, first on the forehead, then again, more lingering, on the mouth, and extracted himself from the piles of quilts and the flannel sheets. She watched him dress, a silhouette in the gloom, then sat up and pulled one of the smaller quilts around her shoulders.

"Where will you be going?"

His head turned toward her. "I've decided to stay, Inez. To help you with what's ahead and be here for you. At this morning's service, I'll announce I am leaving the ministry, but remaining in town. Once your divorce is final, I'll see about returning to the Lord's work."

"No!" She tried to soften her alarm, to explain. "I cannot do that to you. And also, there is this." She took a deep breath. "If you stay, I very much fear either you or Mark will end up dead."

"I assure you, it won't be me." His voice darkened, shaded with anger and a promise of violence.

After a moment's silence, she saw him shake his head, rueful.

"You see?" she said gently. "That is why you need to leave. Your remaining in Leadville puts everything at risk. Mark will be looking for anything, anyone he can exploit to derail the dissolution. He will not succeed, I promise you, but I can only guarantee this if you are not here. You must leave. For my sake and for yours. So, tell me, where are you going?"

He sat on the edge of the bed and touched her cheek. "Wyoming, first. After that, wherever they send me."

"How can I reach you?"

He reached for a boot. "Will you be staying in Leadville afterwards?"

"Probably not. I will go away, for a time."

He paused, boot in hand. "Where should I send letters? Correspondence?"

Inez bit her lip. Not to general mail, that would not do. Any more than sending to the saloon directly. Finally she said, "Send letters to me in care of Susan. I'll be sure she knows where I am."

She almost expected him to press her further on her plans. Instead he nodded again, pulled on his boots and reached for the waistcoat that was slung over a post on the bedstead. "All you need to do is send word you need me. A letter, a telegram. I'll come, no matter where I am or what I'm doing."

"I know you will, Justice." She watched him with a lump in her throat.

He stood, shrugged into his waistcoat. The black frockcoat turned him into a shadow. He gathered his pocket watch, his keys, his hat. She slipped out of bed and wrapped the quilt tighter around herself, trailing it after her as she followed him down the stairs.

As he reached for the door, she grabbed his hand. "Say you'll wait for me!" The desperation in her voice was clear, even to her, and she shrank inside. She had sworn to herself she would not do this. Not be the kind of woman, who, hanging onto her lover as he prepared to leave, begged him for promises that, when broken, would break her heart.

Rather than shake her off or make light of her words, he turned to her, eyes wide with surprise. He released the doorknob, gathered her to him, and said, his warm voice wrapping her in a blanket more soft and secure than any quilt could be, "There is no question I will wait for you, Inez. I've waited for you all my life, without knowing it. To wait from this point will almost be easier, because now I know you exist." He kissed her again, and said, "We'll be together, I promise. Your courage and will, our love, God's grace and redemption, will see us through."

"We will get through," she whispered back.

With that, she took one last kiss, one she tried to burn into her mind and all her senses so that, later on, when the hard times came, when circumstances felt nigh impossible to overcome, she would be able to call up his touch, his scent, his voice, his love.

Then, she let him go.

Chapter Twenty-eight

Inez planned her walk so that she would arrive early, but not too early, to the Sunday service. The snow had stopped sometime around dawn. When she stepped off the porch of the blue house, her boots scuffed up a fluff of white snow crystals. Any footprints Reverend Sands had made in his leaving were filled in, vanished without a trace, as if she'd only dreamt their time together.

As she walked to the little white church, its steeple standing out sharp like a needle against a clear winter-blue sky, she wondered how many of those coming to hear Reverend Sands preach knew what he planned to announce that morning.

She dreaded to hear it said in public, but knew, given the rumors that swirled around her and Reverend Sands, she couldn't *not* come to church. It was important, for his sake and hers, to put in an appearance and keep a calm demeanor when he talked about his leaving. Heads would swivel in her direction, and she had to be ready for the stares and the speculation. She had armored herself for the service, dressing in her good, no-nonsense Sunday gray and adding an ivory lace jabot to provide a touch of feminine softness.

As she had brushed her dark hair, taming it for a chignon, she realized that strands of silver shot through the near black. *When did that happen?* Her hair now reached far below her shoulders. Was it really just last December she had cut it all off? Was it all so long ago, now?

Twist, hairpins, haircombs made her hair prim and proper. Add a small dark gray hat, gloves, cloak, and she was ready. She looked around at the tumbled bed, the gaping carpetbag, her dark green dress from the night before laid out on a nearby chair, and remembered Justice Sands' warm touch as he had slowly, patiently worked her out of the dress's many fastenings.

Pulling herself back from the memory, Inez mounted the steps to the church doors and entered, taking her customary seat. She surveyed the church as it filled. There was Doc, looking glum, sitting at the right end of a back pew, ready to slip out unobtrusively if a medical emergency required his attention elsewhere. Mrs. Alexander, head held high, dressed all in black, walked in and took a seat at the other end of Doc's pew.

Shortly after that, there was a tiny murmur and stir as Mark slid into Inez's pew and sat on her left. She turned to him. "What are you doing here?" she said with a harsh whisper.

He glanced at her, face bland, impassive, but she caught a slight tightening of his mouth under the mustache. "Just here for a little religion, Mrs. Stannert. It's been a while since I've had a chance to partake, what with us bein' down south and all."

She wanted to hiss at him to go away, but Susan Carothers appeared and slid in to Inez's right. "Good morning," she said, pulling her prayer book from her reticule. "I wonder what the sermon will be today?"

Inez shifted so she could scrutinize Susan. Could it be she didn't know about Sands' imminent departure? Inez detected nothing but a small tremor in Susan's hands as she bent studiously over the prayer book. "I think I heard something…" she murmured.

Inez held her breath. She didn't know what would be worse, that her dearest friend in Leadville was ignorant of what was coming or that she knew and hadn't shared that information with Inez.

"…Something about today's topic. Grace? Grace and mercy?"

She couldn't stand that Susan might not know. She leaned toward her, saying, "Susan, have you heard—"

"Good morning."

Reverend Sands stood behind the pulpit. Somehow, he had made the journey without Inez seeing him pass by.

He studied the congregation as the murmurs settled on an uprising note of anticipation. His eyes locked onto hers, for the briefest of moments. An odd sense of peace and comfort settled over her, completely at odds with what she has expected to feel at this time. His last words to her reflected through that fleeting visual touch. *We will get through this.*

Mark stirred at her side, and Reverend Sands' gaze moved on.

"We shall dispense with the opening hymn today as I have much I want to cover."

Another anticipatory murmur. Many of the congregants leaned forward in their seats.

"To open," he continued, "I would like to offer you a restatement of a portion of our covenant, as set forth by another minister of our faith: we should set the bond of human brotherhood high above that of creed or church."

He paused. Silence filled the church, interrupted only by the ticking of water dripping from the outside eaves.

"I had a different sermon planned," said Sands, "but under the circumstances, I believe our gathering is best served by asking you to meditate upon those words and their meaning."

From that point, Reverend Sands without admonishment nor heavy handedness took his congregation to task for paying lip service to "service" for those most needful and for turning a blind eye on the straits of the poor, the indigent, the lost and anonymous souls of Leadville, instead demanding more, more, more, for themselves.

Knowing what she did of the misery that lurked in the mud behind State Street and Chestnut Avenue, Inez felt his broad castigation was well deserved. She, in turn, felt chastened by her obsession with her own woes and troubles. After all, it was the powerless and vulnerable who had real cause to despair. She had options, plans for the future, which could be eased by her relative wealth and her power, limited though it was, to maneuver circumstances.

The Drinas, Tonys, and Aces of the world did not.

Even the self-centered, competitive, need-to-break-the-story-first-obsessed newspaper man Jed Elliston, was doing more to "help and service" the abandoned of Leadville by sheltering and feeding his newsies than she was.

At the end of the sermon, or religious rebuke, Reverend Sands closed his bible with finality and said, "I have one announcement to make."

Then he made it.

Susan gasped and turned to Inez, eyes round.

He concluded, "I look forward to hearing of great things from this congregation from your next minister, who will be arriving later this week. I know you will all step forward to make him feel welcome, as you did for me when I first came as your interim minister. Leadville is a city of great promise, and her religious community is strong and wealthy. May that strength and wealth be used to further the Lord's work, with His grace and mercy. Please turn and greet your neighbor."

Susan seized Inez's hand. "I, I didn't know," she stammered.

Mark smiled slightly. "I think you spend a little too much time with your darkroom and your cameras, Miss Carothers."

Susan released her grasp. "This is awful. I hardly know what to say."

The congregation stood, and the low murmur rose to a loud buzz. Reverend Sands came down from the pulpit and was swarmed by churchgoers.

Susan rose, saying, "I must go talk to him, if I can make my way through all the others. Are you coming to say your good-byes?" This last was addressed to both Stannerts, although Inez suspected it was mostly meant for her.

Mr. Stannert said, "Well, now, I do believe Mrs. Stannert has already had opportunity to wish him well with his future endeavors." There was no innuendo in his tone, but Inez didn't let that fool her.

She said, "Mr. Stannert, why don't you say our formal good-byes for us both? I need to talk to someone." Turning to Susan, she added, "May I walk to your studio with you when you are ready to go? I know Mr. Stannert has much he needs to do, and a stroll will give us time to catch up."

"Of course." Susan seemed confused, but taking Inez's cue, she didn't inquire further, and instead moved off to join the line patiently waiting to wish Reverend Sands adieu.

"And just what are all these to-dos that require my immediate attention on the Lord's day of rest?" inquired Mark.

She looked at the waiting line for the reverend. Mrs. Alexander, obvious in her funeral black, was talking with Sands. He clasped her hands in both of his, nodded encouragingly, then released her. Head bowed, she began to move away, heading toward the door and on target to pass Inez.

"Oh, you'll think of something, I'm sure," said Inez. "Excuse me."

She moved to the end of the pew and fell in step beside the tall pale woman, who was holding a black-hemmed handkerchief to her mouth, apparently deep in thought. "Mrs. Alexander, may I walk with you a bit?"

She looked up startled, then said, "Mrs. Stannert, of course." She shook her head. "So unexpected, his leaving. I found his counsel a comfort, true to the heart. I cannot believe this."

"Yes, it is a shock to us all," said Inez.

Mrs. Alexander drew Inez's arm into hers, as if they were the best of friends. "It has been difficult times for me in Leadville. I found comfort from this church, although my husband is a nonbeliever, a rationalist." She faltered.

"Yes, Reverend Sands has an openness toward those who are seeking understanding through beliefs and means not universally accepted," said Inez, looking for an entry that might lead to a discussion of Drina Gizzi, "such as Spiritualism," she added in hopes that her gambit for connection would not be too obvious a ploy.

Mrs. Alexander's face lightened. "*Exactement!* He listened. Even if not a believer, there was room in his thinking for acceptance. I have found acceptance is not so with others," she finished bitterly, nodding her thanks as a gentleman opened the door for them.

Encouraged by her openness, Inez slowed her pace on the steps. "Others such as your husband, perhaps?"

"Oh him, certainly." She brought her handkerchief back up to her mouth. "I know he loves me. But perhaps he loves me too much. He cannot bear my pain, and wishes to erase it, and all the beloved memories that I hold so dear. Spiritualism gives me hope that death in this world is but birth and awakening into the spirit world. It helps me rise above sorrow, this belief. No. I was referring to Dr. Gregorvich. Do you know him?"

Inez halted in astonishment. "Why, yes, I do."

"Well then, you know he is even more a rationalist. A man obsessed with the mechanical workings of brain and body. Not a physician to 'heal the heart.' He has convinced my husband through sharing of his medical journals and his overwhelming talk, talk, talk that Spiritualism is the cause of women's diseases and that I suffer from many such diseases as a result of my beliefs."

She looked at Inez, pleading in her eyes. "Are you a believer too?"

The hope in her voice almost caused Inez to backpedal. How could she lie to a woman who was so desperate for friendship and connection? "I am…a seeker," Inez temporized.

"I thought I saw an aura about you!" exclaimed Mrs. Alexander.

Aura? Inez wasn't sure what she meant.

Glancing around as if concerned someone would overhear, Mrs. Alexander lowered her voice. "I am hosting a séance this coming Friday. Please come. I have few friends." It was such a basic admission of loneliness that Inez felt a compulsion to either flee or give her a hug.

"Of course." Inez said. "When and where?"

Mrs. Alexander extracted a silver card case and gave Inez her calling card. "My home, above my husband's business. He is an undertaker, embalmer too."

Inez accepted the card and said, "It is well to find kindred spirits, is it not?"

Mrs. Alexander nodded vigorously. "Oh yes!"

"Fancy, we only just met at the Jacksons' a few days ago. It must be Fate."

Inez could tell she liked that, so continued, "You were with that amazing medium. Mrs. Gizzi, wasn't it? I was quite impressed. Will she be at your séance?"

Inez had been angling to speak Drina's name, if only to observe Mrs. Alexander's response.

She broke eye contact with Inez, looking down at her coat and adjusting one of the jet buttons. "I, I had hoped so. She has a true gift. But, she has disappeared. I have no idea where she is, where she went." Mrs. Alexander looked at Inez, distressed. "I even went to where she lives, which is not a nice part of town. Her sign is gone, no one is there, it looks abandoned." Bewilderment touched her voice. "I do not understand what happened. However, I have found someone else who claims to communicate with those who have awakened into the inner sphere of life. We shall see. Drina had such sensitivity and second sight, it was remarkable, it was…"

She trailed off. Her face went a little slack, as if a light within had winked out.

"Mrs. Alexander, are you feeling unwell?" Inez asked in concern.

The undertaker's wife started, then began digging through her reticule with jerky movements. "Let, let me give you my card."

Inez held it up between two fingers. "You already did. What time would you like me to come by on Friday?"

She gave a tiny "Oh," and touched her forehead. "I probably need to go home and rest," she whispered. "Too much excitement, my husband would say."

"What time is the séance on Friday?" Inez prompted again.

"We begin at midnight, when the veil between this world and the next is thinnest, when we will have the best chance of reaching beyond." Subdued, she said, "I must go rest." Without further courtesies or farewells, she walked away.

Inez watched her go, thinking that, if Mrs. Alexander had anything to do with Drina's death, she was a far finer dissembler than any sharp or con artist of her acquaintance. Sighing, she tucked the calling card into her pocket and retraced her path up the church steps to find Susan.

She had one hand upon the slightly open door, ready to push it open, when a sharp feminine voice on the other side said, "Well, Mr. Stannert, you were right in every way about Reverend Sands. What a blessing you spoke with my husband and the board in August and pointed them in the right direction. How such a man could have been called to the ministry is completely beyond me. And his total disregard for the health of our little congregation, his mockery of our faith and outright flaunting of his pastoral responsibilities. Well! We certainly found out what he thought of us today, didn't we?"

Inez held her breath, her hand flat on the door panel, and listened.

Sure enough, Mark responded, that charming Southern drawl laid on extra-thick, like a heaping helping of too-sweet marmalade. "Well, now, Mrs. Terrence. I was glad to help. I've been gone a spell, so perhaps it just needed someone unbiased, with eyes wide open, to suss out who this Justice B. Sands was, and is. It was my bounden duty as a concerned congregant to talk to your husband and the other fine, upstanding gentlemen of the board."

"So true. So, so true. You weren't here this past year, but I wish you had been, because we might have been able to act sooner and avoid the current unpleasantness. I expressed my doubts to Mr. Terrence all along, told him what I saw, such as the incident with Miss Snow in July, and your wife…" Her voice trailed away as if she realized she might be straying into dangerous territory. She recovered with "Well, he was too charming by half with *all* the women."

Not you, thought Inez snidely, *and maybe that's what has you in such a huff.* But Mrs. Terrence's appalling self-righteousness was a small sin. What stunned her, but did not surprise her, was the undeniable and unadulterated proof of Mark's machinations. It was clear, now, exactly what he'd been up to once he returned, and it wasn't just talking with Mr. Robitaille about building her a new home.

He builds me a house and tears down my life. Anger sparked inside her, like the flicker of far-off lightning, distant, accompanied by a soft rumble of thunder, warning of more to come.

"My husband is such a busy man," the sharp, self-satisfied nasal whine continued. "Not that church matters are unimportant to him, but it takes someone of equal stature to get his attention. Someone such as yourself, another concerned businessman, who knows how important it is that we put our best foot forward as a church and congregation. As a mining broker, he has so many things on his mind, so thank you for being so—"

Someone inside pulled the door open, and Mr. Johnson, a male member of the church board, reared back in consternation at finding Inez standing on the other side. She glared at him, recalling the time she'd seen him exiting from Frisco Flo's State Street boardinghouse at an hour better suited for sleeping in his proper home with his proper wife than rising from a brothel. Another incident, even more damning, rose to her mind, overheard at the Silver Queen. Mr. Johnson had boasted to his colleagues within her hearing how he had "cleaned up" the area in front of his business by rolling a sleeping vagrant off the elevated sideway into the deep mud of the street. He continued, describing how he had proceeded to wash the filthy boards with cold water, "flushing out" two waifs sheltering beneath the walkway. Then, he and his cronies had laughed and ordered another round.

"Peace be with you, Mr. Johnson," she said, making it clear by tone that peace was the last thing she wished upon him.

He responded, "And with you, Mrs. Stannert." He could not have known what she was thinking, exactly, but a quick, guilty glance from him told her that he sensed her contempt. With a flush building from collar to cheeks, he maneuvered past her and hurried down the stairs.

Mr. Johnson's guilty reaction, however, was nothing compared to Mark's.

With a savage satisfaction, Inez watched as he whirled around to face her. She saw the knowledge dawn that she had heard everything, *everything* that had just transpired in the conversation. And that there was no denying it.

"Why, Mrs. Stannert," he said, Southern drawl suddenly absent. "You're still here."

"As are you, Mr. Stannert," she said, adding with a smile of poisonous sweetness, "I'm on my way to find Miss Carothers. I understand you have *important* church matters to discuss, unless everything is settled? I imagine there are things you still have to do, so I will not keep you now."

Mrs. Terrence, who was facing the door, had lifted a suede-gloved hand to her lips as if to recall the words that she had released into the air just moments ago. Inez headed into the church interior, brushing by her and Mark with a cold "Peace be with you." She reflected that, if it were up to her, it would be an ice-locked day in hell—with the demons screaming in frostbit agony and Satan himself begging for a stick of firewood to stave off the eternal freeze—before Mark, Mrs. Terrence, or any of the church board felt peace again.

Chapter Twenty-nine

Susan shielded her eyes as they crossed the street on the way to her studio. The late morning sunlight shattered and broke off the frozen heaves and ruts in the street dazzling the eyes and making it difficult to see. When she spoke, she sounded calm, but sad. "I will miss Reverend Sands."

She was, Inez thought, a true "Christian soldier," one who had faith, but didn't trumpet it about or display it like a gold medal of her "worth." Inez reflected that Susan had been through much the past year, and even before, all while trudging at Inez's side, guiding her through, being there for her. From the dark times after Mark's disappearance and through the horrifying death of the husband of their mutual friend Emma Rose. Later, there was all that business with the railroads, when Susan had been lucky to escape with her life. Finally, most recently, were the events that had transpired in Manitou Springs when Susan had accompanied her on what was supposed to be a simple reunion for Inez with her son and sister. Inez's throat constricted. The jaunt to the Springs had brought Susan deep sorrows and the loss of someone who had become near and dear to her. All this she had, for the most part, borne alone in silence.

What kind of friend am I, that I did not follow her back to Lead-ville, to help her through that most difficult personal loss? Instead I stayed in the Springs, dallying about with Mark. But no, it wasn't just Mark. She had stayed because her son was there with her sister, who was his guardian in all but name.

Inez took Susan's unoccupied hand and squeezed it. Together they steadied each other across the treacherous street.

"Inez, what will you do?"

Inez squeezed her hand again. As always, Susan's concerns were for others, not herself. "I will have to deal with matters here in Leadville before I can do anything else. Reverend Sands and I talked yesterday. He understands. I wanted to tell you about his leaving yesterday, but I was bound to silence." She paused, then said, "Whatever Mark and I once had, it is gone now. We cannot go back to what we were." Bitterness burned her throat.

"What a difficult situation for you, Inez. If there's anything I can do to help, just ask."

"You do plenty. More than enough. You accept me for who I am and do not censure me, despite my many faults and failings. For that, I'm eternally grateful, Susan. It seems I am always running to you, asking for help, for this and for that. You never ask for anything in return."

"Only for your friendship, and a chance to share a cup of tea and confide about the doings of our lives."

They reached the relative safety of the boards on the other side of the street. Susan released Inez's hand and spoke with a forced lightness. "Your life is so much more exciting than mine. It's like reading one of those adventurous dime novels. One never knows how the hero, or in your case, the heroine, will overcome the trials and challenges. But just as with the dime novels, I have faith that, in the end, you will make things right and justice will prevail."

Inez smiled in return. "Ah, if only I had some of the abilities of your dime novel heroes, Susan. To plug a black-hearted villain in the eye from a mile away with a pistol, to lurk around incognito behind a false mustache while seeking out clues in illegal opium dens, to mount a horse at a gallop…from behind."

"Oh, you do make fun of me!" Susan seemed to be regaining heart. "But they are a harmless pleasure, after all."

At her studio, Susan extracted her key, saying, "Speaking of a cup of tea, would you like to join me? We might finally have a chance to chat, uninterrupted by my little ringing doorbell and your many adventures."

"That sounds most excellent."

Susan opened the door, the bell tinkled, and a small shadow popped up from the rear hallway. "Miss Carothers?" Tony's timorous voice floated out of the unlit interior.

"Tony?" Inez stepped past Susan into the interior.

"Mrs. Stannert!" Tony's voice flooded with relief. "The drummer man, the one with all the ladies' stuff. He's at Mr. Alexander's, and he's dead!"

◇◇◇

It took a couple servings of tea heaped with sugar to get a coherent account from Tony of what she'd seen.

"Mr. Alexander said he gets all the dead bodies that nobody knows or cares about," Tony said, looking down at her cup. She'd bypassed the dainty handle and was cradling the china bowl in hands that looked as if she'd been working as a bootblack. "I was polishing coffins," was her short reply when Susan exclaimed over their appearance.

"What on earth possessed him to show you the remains?" Susan was obviously horrified that Tony had been subjected to the sight.

Tony shrugged. "I asked to see. I thought, 'cause of what he said, that maybe Maman was down there. No one cared about her but me." Tony's mouth trembled, then set into a determined line. "But it wasn't her. Mr. Alexander said all the bodies no one cares about go to the Free Cemetery. I want to go there and look for her."

Susan put a hand to her forehead and slid a sideways glance at Inez. "Tony, ah, Annabelle, oh dear. Please, what is your real name?"

"Antonia," she muttered.

"Antonia, perhaps it's best not to go back to Mr. Alexander's."

Inez said, "Susan is right. What if you run into Mrs. Alexander? You said she saw you in French Row and recognized your kin to your mother. Or, God forbid, what if Dr. Gregorvich shows up? I don't trust him as far as I can throw him. Or, more likely, what if Mr. Alexander recalls you from somewhere? Your 'disguise' from your newsie friend is hardly foolproof. Surely you've sold papers to Mr. Alexander in the past."

Tony shook her head. "He's a *Chronicle* man. Got their paper all over the place, behind the counter and downstairs. Mr. Elliston sure wouldn't like that. Anyway," she took another sip of tea, "I figure if, like he says, all the unwanted bodies this month go to him for putting below ground, then Maman probably ended up there. I want to find out what happened. I'm going to stay until I know."

Susan compressed her lips and looked at Inez. Inez shook her head, then addressed Tony. "If you must, you must. But promise us, at the first sign that someone sees you for who you really are, and *especially* if they recognize you as your mother's child or as the boy who almost shot Lord Percy in my saloon, you will run. You will not linger and try to offer truths or invent lies. You. Will. *RUN.*" She said the last word as if to brand it into Tony's stubborn brain. "Run to me. Run to Susan. Run to Mr. Elliston or even Mr. Stannert. You have to trust enough to come to us. Agreed?"

Tony stayed silent.

Inez crouched, insisting by sheer will that Tony look up. Finally those unnerving, extraordinary eyes met hers. "I need this promise from you," said Inez. "Promise me and Miss Carothers that you will not go into danger. You will run for help. Say 'I promise.'"

"I promise."

Inez and Susan's cherished chat was deferred yet again. Tony insisted she had to go back to Alexander's right away. "He has lots for me to do, and he pays really good," she said. "Plus, I got to find out what happened to my maman. I'll be careful." She then added, "I promise."

Inez doubted Tony's definition of "being careful" corresponded with what Susan and she herself had in mind, but for now, it would have to do.

Glancing at the clock, Susan remarked that no sooner would Tony go out the rear door than clients would be coming in the front. "My sitting appointments fill up Sunday afternoons, when people are normally dressed in their Sunday best," she told Tony. She'd tried one more time. "You could change into your Annabelle clothes and help me. I'll show you my camera, you could look through it and I could explain how the process works."

Tony shook her head again. "Can't. But," she held out her cup, "can I have one more before I leave, please?"

Inez returned to the saloon, intending to lose herself in paperwork. She was concerned about the direction things were heading with Drina's death, Tony's situation, and the constellation of characters that swirled around them. It was difficult to see ahead clearly, to ascertain the next step. Woods was dead. So what did that prove? Couldn't he still have been the murderer? Inez had seen him on her way to Drina's, which would have been after she had been strangled. Inez decided she needed to focus on the others on her list since the drummer was past answering her questions. Top of that list was Madam Labasilier.

The saloon doors were open for an airing, and Sol was sweeping out the clumpings of dried mud and dirt that had accumulated the night before. With surprise, Inez saw Epperley and the other Lads from London, *sans* Percy, lounging about the door, looking hangdog and hungover.

"You're all up early for a Sunday," she said. "We aren't open today, but I suppose I could make an exception in your case."

"We've come to collect our ticket money and things," said Epperley.

"Too much wine, women, and song," said Tipton. "Poor Epperley hasn't got the stamina for it. Needs more practice, obviously. From now on, we insist, old chap, you must come up with us on our monthly Leadville romps. You are becoming much too much the old man, always fussing about that hotel of yours and muttering about the bills. Hang the bills. Hang the hotel. You need to give that all up, like Percy said, settle in with us, and just enjoy the good life with your remittance."

Epperley didn't seem in the mood for a lecture. "Let's talk later when my head's stopped pounding. Don't know what happened to Percy, but he knew we were leaving today. Just give us our money and whatever he left with you, his confounded rabbit's foot and so on, and we'll take it with us. Serves him right for abandoning us like that. Tell him we're at the depot, if he shows up."

Quick said, "Oh, he'll show up all right. Probably still cavorting with that redhead he was so keen about yesterday. Although I do say, it's not like him to abandon his mates without a word."

Inez tuned out their bickering and watched as one of Leadville's deputy marshals approached, grim purpose written in his face. He stopped, tipped his hat to Inez with a short, "Mrs. Stannert," before addressing the Lads. "Am I right to assume you gentlemen are associated with a Mr. W. P. Brown?"

Epperley blinked. Tipton frowned. "What's this about?" said Quick. "We have a train to catch."

"I'll get to the point. Your *compadre* was found in a bad part of town, not healthy for much of anyone and definitely not healthy for him. In fact, sorry to tell you this, he's deceased. Must've really ticked someone off, because they not only shot him, but strangled him as well."

Quick stumbled backward as if punched him in the chest. Epperley looked outraged. Tipton emitted a faint, "Oh fuck me!" that earned him raised eyebrows from the deputy.

The lawman dug into his copious pocket, saying, "I have something here, found next to the body. Thought it might belong to your friend because of the initials." He pulled out a pistol, holding it by the barrel. "It's a mighty fancy piece for someone to leave behind after an attack. This look familiar to any of y'all?"

With shock and dismay, Inez took in the unmistakable ivory grips of Tony's gun, etched with the damning initials, WRB.

Chapter Thirty

She corrected the deputy marshal on the initials, pointing out the "P" was really an "R." This fine point didn't really clear up anything and just seemed to perplex him all the more. "So, it's not his firearm, eh? Mighty similar initials. Maybe belonged to the fella who shot him? But why would he throw the gun aside? It's all mighty strange," he concluded.

Inez wanted to extract more information from him, but she only had time to express her astonishment and sorrow over Percy's death and ask where and when he was found before the deputy verbally dismissed her. "Can't really discuss that right now," he said. "I need to chat with these gents, if you don't mind."

After settling the deputy and the Lads at a table in the Silver Queen for their "chat," she pulled Sol aside and asked him to keep an ear out to what transpired. Inez returned to the sky-blue house on Fourth Street, packed up her few things, washed the few teacups, and put them away. She managed to keep the memories of the previous night at bay until she turned to the piano and lowered the keyboard cover. Smooth, polished, it silently begged her to stay. Inez ran both hands over the top, recalling the feel of Reverend Sands' arms around her.

An overwhelming sorrow engulfed her in a dark wave. Sorrow for the reverend's impending departure came first, but then, as the black tide advanced, much, much more followed. Sorrow for Tony and her situation, sorrow for the snuffing out of lives known and unknown. And, despite the reverend's call to heed the desperate needs of others, an overwhelming, personal sorrow for her own mess of a life.

Fingertips resting lightly on the sweet, smooth polished wood, she wished she could go back in time. Back to the early days with Reverend Sands, when it might have been possible, just maybe, for them to have left Leadville together and go, go somewhere where she could imagine her old life had never been. *But then, what of William? What of Susan, and Emma Rose, and Abe, and Sol?*

Further back then, to the day of Mark's disappearance, to stop him from taking that fateful walk. *We were together as a family, but we weren't happy then either, not really. We were like the couples I see every day, unhappy wife at home, making the best of her lot, the husband never home, busy with work, busy with colleagues.*

Perhaps further back, to the day Mark, she, and Abe had first set foot in Leadville. What would have happened if they had not stayed, but moved on, kept moving west, to Virginia City, and eventually to San Francisco, as planned? What then? A whole different life would have unfolded.

Inez shook her head.

This self-pity was unlike her. And looking back never solved anything.

"No use crying over spilt milk," she said aloud. There was only reckoning with the present and planning for the future.

She locked the house and returned to her chambers in the saloon, wrote a note to her lawyer, enclosed her calling card, and sealed it in an envelope. The envelope went into the hand of an urchin lingering by the kitchen door and hoping for a late Sunday handout, along with a nickel and a cheese biscuit from Bridgette's dwindling supply. Inez instructed him to drop the note off at the office and residence of William V. Casey, Esquire, and promised a dime when he returned with a response.

Inez hovered in the kitchen, loath to go elsewhere until her little messenger returned. Sol showed up with the dirty crockery from last night's poker game and set it all in the sink to wash. "The Britishers are still here," he commented. "You did say it's okay for them to stay a while after the deputy left?"

Inez nodded, pulling her thoughts back to the present. "What did the deputy want to know?"

"Well, mostly he asked when did they last see Percy and where. And he wanted to know about the pistol." Sol looked at her curiously. "It belonged to a newsie, right? The one who tried to shoot Lord Percy and put a hole in the ceiling instead?"

"Yes." Inez determined not to volunteer any more information than necessary.

"Geez, so young to go so bad." Sol shook his head.

Inez pondered whether to go talk to the deputy, but what could she say that wouldn't make things worse? She'd given the gun back to Tony. There was no one to vouch that Tony had mislaid it, except for Tony herself. And Inez could just imagine how that explanation would go over with the law.

"The blond one, Epperley, he's really on the warpath," commented Sol. "Says he's got to get back to Manitou Springs, that he has a business to attend to. He told the deputy the youngster needs to be smoked out and strung up for Percy's cold-blooded murder."

Inez shuddered.

I should be sure that Tony cannot be found by those who are looking.

She asked, "What was this about Percy being strangled?"

"Yeah, strange, that." Sol leaned against the sink, which gave off a faint metallic rattle. "Seems to me, if you shoot someone, you hightail it out of there, don't stick around to squeeze his neck as well. Or, if you shoot someone once and the job's not done, why not shoot him again?"

"Did anyone hear the shots?" Inez asked. "Where did this occur?"

Sol scratched his chin. "Apparently it happened in an abandoned shack in Stillborn Alley."

A chill ran up Inez's back. She sat up straighter. "What?"

"Yeah. Used to belong to a tea leaf reader or something like that. Anyhow, she left, I guess, and the place was empty. Huh. Wonder if she might've been mixed up in this? Didn't Percy go to a soothsayer who told him to invest? Maybe it didn't work out, he went back and threatened her or demanded she return his money, and she panicked and shot him. Maybe she didn't leave after all and is still in town, hiding from the law."

Inez reflected that, as of the previous night, Percy had been cheery with the results of Drina's prognostication of future fortunes. In any case, Drina was definitely "departed," in the most permanent sense possible, although there was no way to prove it.

◇◇◇

Inez found it hard to sleep that night, and spent restless hours turning things over in her mind. Early Monday morning found her pacing in front of her lawyer's home, waiting for the appointed hour at which she could knock on the door. When her lapel watch read eight o'clock, she mounted the stairs and gave the bell a twist. The door opened immediately, almost as if Casey had been waiting for her.

He greeted her warmly. "Mrs. Stannert, I received your message yesterday evening and I see by your presence that you received my reply. You said the matter was urgent. Please come in."

Inez entered and he ushered her into his office. She glanced around the room, all was the same as when she had first begun her consultations with him in July. The neat, almost-to-a-fault, walnut desk held a collection of sharpened pencils marching in a row along one side of his leather-bordered blotter. In the exact center of the spotless blotter was a squared-off sheaf of papers. The top sheet was covered top to bottom, side to side, with neat, penciled handwriting. Inez assumed these were his notes from their previous meetings. She hoped that they were just legal notes and didn't include his private assessment of her prevarications the past summer as she had wavered to and fro over the wisdom and timing of pursuing a divorce on grounds of desertion. She also hoped that he'd kept his thoughts to himself regarding her sudden plunge forward into the process, only to have her yank back on the reins upon Mark's unexpected return.

The welcome scent of fresh coffee drew her eyes to the coffee service on the sideboard beneath the shelves of legal volumes lining one wall. "May I offer you some coffee, Mrs. Stannert?" Casey's kind voice only reinforced her feeling of being welcomed, as it were, by an old friend.

She nodded. He prepared her a cup, saying, "As I recall, you take it black," gave it to her, then moved to sit on his side of the desk, gesturing her to the chair on the other side. She took one sip allowing herself a brief moment to appreciate the rich dark flavor, then set the cup aside on its saucer.

He was watching her with a steady gaze, twirling his half-glasses idly in one hand. It was the first time she could recall seeing Casey exhibit any sign of tension. She laced her hands and placed them on the edge of his desk, preparing herself.

"How was your recent trip to the Springs?" he inquired.

She was taken aback that he even knew. "It went well," she said cautiously. "I saw my son and sister. You may recall, she and her husband have been acting as guardians for little William in all but name."

"Your husband was there as well?" The glasses swung back and forth from one temple piece, like a metronome.

"He was there," she said tersely, then gathered her courage. "I want to proceed with the divorce. Now. Right away."

The glasses ceased swinging. He folded them, and set them on top of his neat stack of notes. "Right away as in?"

She talked fast, hoping that the information that she recalled from their previous visits and that she had pieced together from here and there was correct. "The next county court session begins the first Monday in November with Judge Updegraf, am I correct?" Without waiting for him to respond, she rushed on. "I want to be there, that day, with suit in hand, asking for a dissolution of the marriage on grounds of desertion. The fact that he has returned does not negate the time he was gone, correct? I have been a resident in Colorado for three years, far more than the one-year minimum. We published a summons in the newspapers. I stopped the procedure when he returned. Well, now I am certain. I *want* that divorce."

Casey leaned back in his chair, which squeaked as if wanting to flee from her intensity. However he responded calmly, as if it was a normal occurrence for a woman to march into his office and demand that he effect a dissolution of marriage *right now.* "The timing of this does not look good, Mrs. Stannert."

"What do you mean?"

"I will speak frankly. It is common knowledge since yesterday that the reverend from your church is leaving. It is, perhaps, only somewhat less common knowledge that you and he…" His eyes flickered to one side and she could almost see his mind at work, busy picking up and discarding words, looking for the right ones. "You had a 'relationship' that, whatever its true nature, has the unfortunate appearance of being improper, even illegal. So, your haste has the appearance of being suspect."

"You are saying that I am painted as an adulterer in the public eye and that there is the expectation that I am eager to get a quick divorce so I can jump on the next train out of town to join him," said Inez bluntly.

After a slight pause, Casey continued, "Judge Updegraf is an honest judge. There are still cities and towns in the Western 'frontier,' even in Denver, I understand, where you might find a judge who will wink and nod as he delivers a speedy divorce decree in favor of an attractive woman." He held up a hand. "I'm speaking hyperbolically, but not by much. The point is Judge Updegraf is not one of those. When we come before him—you, I, your husband, his lawyer—you need to be aware of the possible adverse consequences."

She unlaced fingers and gripped the edge of the desk, leaning forward. "Mr. Stannert will not be there. He will send no lawyer. He will accede to whatever requests I have. I guarantee it."

Now Casey looked surprised. "Did he say this to you?"

"I can promise you he will." Inez used her considerable force of will to project her assurance. "I need to pick the right moment to discuss it with him. When he and I talk, there will be no argument from him." She pushed forward. "What are the legal limitations to having the divorce go smoothly through the court? Assume Mr. Stannert is not there, he offers no resistance, the charge of desertion stands, and I can produce witnesses of impeccable reputation who will aver that he has been gone for the stated period of time. What other barriers might arise?"

Casey broke eye contact to gaze out his window. He seemed to be addressing the curtains as he said, "If there is any hint of collusion, the judge will take issue. For instance, if it appears the two parties have manufactured a charge of cruelty, simply to obtain a divorce, the judge will throw out the divorce request. Similarly, if both parties have been guilty of adultery, when adultery is the grounds for the complaint, no divorce will be decreed." He swiveled back to face her. "There is also the matter of alimony. If it rises above the amount of two-thousand dollars, the case becomes the jurisdiction of the district court."

"No alimony," she said. "I only want the divorce."

He put on his half-glasses, chose a sharp pencil from the parallel row alongside his blotter, pulled out a fresh sheet of paper from a desk drawer, and began making notes. "What of your son?"

She told him her plan. He shook his head but kept writing. "It may be enough," he acknowledged, adding, "perhaps. And you say Mr. Stannert agrees to this?"

"He will." Inez gripped the edge of the desk even harder, feeling that she was in the midst of the most important poker game of her life, and despite her careful preparation, she was counting on Lady Luck and bluffing to see her through.

Casey asked her a few more pointed questions, to which she responded as best she could. He finally sighed and set down his pencil. "If you want this suit to be in the first day of the November calendar, I must prepare the summons paperwork immediately and have it served on Mr. Stannert today. The newspaper summons we placed in July is no longer valid, so as you correctly surmised, he needs to be served again. The law requires that he have a minimum ten-day window to respond. Although, you are saying he will not respond, and he will not appear in court."

"He will not."

They stared at each other for a long time, across the wide walnut expanse. Casey finally said, "It's a long shot, Mrs. Stannert. I would not be honest if I didn't state so in the bluntest possible terms. I can see but small chance for the outcome you wish, and a great possibility of failure of the most catastrophic kind. The case could very likely proceed to a higher court, but that's not the worst of it. You might not receive your divorce at all, at any court level. It may be that, no matter how much you—and even Mr. Stannert—want the divorce, no matter how estranged the two of you are, it may not happen. To me, that is the greatest injustice of all, but it is the law."

Inez gripped her right wrist with her left hand, trying to steady the shaking that threatened to envelope her. The two rings, one silver, the other gold, pressed unyielding against her flesh.

He tapped a finger restlessly. "I must admit I have some reservations with moving forward on this, at this time. Don't misunderstand me, Mrs. Stannert. I am not obsessed with my professional win-to-loss ratio as some lawyers are. I am concerned about what this may mean for you personally, if we lose the suit for *any* reason, including whether Judge Updegraf remains unconvinced that the suit has merit or whether his breakfast eggs were undercooked and he is having an 'off' day. However, I will do my best. I can see you have decided and are not to be swayed from your course. Just keep in mind: once you throw the dice, to use a gaming analogy, you cannot call it back for another throw, you can only leave the game."

"I understand. Thank you." Inez couldn't look him in the eye any longer. Instead, she focused on his desktop, the blotter, the square stack of papers, his tapping finger. It was then she noticed that he had placed his pencil aslant, the only item on his desk not at perfect perpendicular and parallel.

◇◇◇

A little shaken, Inez retraced her steps to the saloon. She wondered when Mark would receive the summons. According to the agreement they drew up in Colorado Springs, Monday was his day to tend bar with Abe and Sol, and her day "off." Sol was already present and accounted for, polishing the bar with sweet-oil and a piece of old soft silk. Inez could hear Bridgette rattling around in the kitchen, humming to herself. If Abe had been back there with her, Bridgette would be exclaiming, clucking, and commenting, not humming.

"Where's Abe?" Inez inquired.

Sol adjusted a sleeve garter and looked up, a strand of copper-colored hair hanging loose over his forehead. "He sent word that he's at home, probably be there all day. Things are finally… moving?" Sol seemed unsure about his phraseology, "With Mrs. Jackson?"

"At last!" Inez reversed direction, heading to the State Street doors. "I better see what I can do to help."

"No!" Sol hurried out from behind the bar and then flapped his cloth at her like a white flag of surrender when she turned on him. "I mean, wait! That's what Mr. Jackson said. His message had instructions for you and Mrs. O'Malley. He asked you both *wait and not come down to help*. I guess he has his hands full, and people keep coming by, asking how are…things going. He said he's got Doc and Mrs. Buford, and can't handle any more folks. As soon as everything's…done," again he seemed at a loss for words, "he'll send word. He said Doc thinks nothing will happen for a while, maybe until the end of the day or tonight." He looked sheepish. "Mrs. O'Malley wasn't happy either, but hey, I'm just the messenger."

"Did Bridgette come at you with a frying pan?"

"Nearly." He went back behind the bar again. "I'm afraid to go in and ask for a cup of coffee. Hear her humming back there? That's not a happy hum."

Now that he'd mentioned it, Inez thought the humming did have the buzz of an angry bee.

"I'll respect his wishes, then. No Mr. Stannert yet?"

"Not yet."

She wondered if he might be busy trying to cover his tracks with the church board members regarding his role in Reverend

Sands' departure. As far as she was concerned, there was no magic rabbit he could pull out of his hat that could change the content of his damning conversation with Mrs. Terrence. "Rabbit" made her think of the next visit on her list for the day. She slipped up to the saloon office and opened the safe. There, tucked inside the moneybox from last night, was Percy's lucky rabbit's foot.

Lifting it free by its silver chain, she addressed the furry bit as if it were Percy by proxy. "Maybe you should have taken your good luck piece with you last night after all. Although I doubt it could have stopped a bullet or a garrote." With a sigh, she counted out a few smaller-denomination gold and silver coins, closed the safe, and repaired to her chambers to prepare for a visit to Madam Labasilier.

For this expedition, she changed from her sober gray outfit to a well-worn walking suit which was more sensible for venturing into the lower end of Stillborn Alley. No reticule. Such little handbags were open enticements to cutpurses. Plenty of pockets were to be had in her faded brown flannel skirt and more still were available in the worn cloak hanging by the kitchen door.

She approached the genteel little marble-topped corner cabinet by her bed and extracted the poppet from deep within, pinching its threaded braid between two fingertips. *Perhaps the rabbit foot and this nasty bit of work will cancel each other out.* Such foolishness was not part of her usual thinking, but still.

She lowered the poppet on top of the rabbit's foot in her pocket and gave the tiny doll a deliberate pat to demonstrate she meant no malice, before adding her few coins to the opposite pocket. The Smoot revolver would go in the cloak, where she could pull it out in a hurry if need be.

The cloak, however, was in the kitchen.

It required quick maneuvering on Inez's part to avoid a lengthy session with Bridgette, who was positively bristling with injury that she was banned from the Jackson residence at this critical juncture. "Why, it's not as if I haven't been present and attending at many a lie-in over the years," she announced the minute the passway door swung open. "And I made all these lovely biscuits, sausages, and gravy this morning—Mr. Jackson's favorites! A basket of these, well-wrapped, would no doubt be a blessing to both Mr. Jackson and Dr. Cramer. They will want a spot of nourishment and goodness knows Mrs. Jackson is in no condition to cook for them! And I thought, well, since I'd be there, I could just take a wee peek and see how things were going, offer a little advice from someone who has had five boys, and none of them small, mind you. I always say, walking around as long as possible is a necessity. So many doctors insist on the poor mother spending her travail in a lie-down on her back, which is not helpful at all."

Inez grabbed the cloak and escaped, assuring Bridgette she would return and, when word came, they would go together to see the new "baby Jackson" and congratulate the parents.

Once outside, she silently thanked her foresight in having her sturdy walking boots dry and ready. The snow from Saturday's overnight storm had thawed, hardened, and thawed again, leaving an indescribable mess of sludge where there were no boardwalks. She pulled the shabby cloak's hood up for anonymity, and headed down State to Pine Street, approaching Stillborn Alley for the quickest access to the rear of the buildings and Coon Row. It was still early Monday morning, so everything was quiet. Only a few people were out and about, no revelers to speak of, everyone most likely sleeping off the weekend's debaucheries.

Madam Labasillier's lean-to, in the rear of a larger dwelling, was easily identifiable by a door on which was painted a jaunty-looking skull with a top hat. A wide plank, serving as a stoop, was thoroughly coated with the red dirt so prevalent in the mining districts around Leadville. Inez took a deep breath and rapped on the skull's eye-socket. The thin panel shivered under her knuckles. Although she heard no movement inside, the door opened almost immediately. Madam Labasilier was wrapped so thoroughly in layers and layers of shawls and skirts, it was hard to tell her size. She craned her head up to view Inez from her crook-backed stance.

"Aaaaaah, Mrs. Stannert." The "s" in Stannert escaped in a long sibilant hiss. "*Bonjou.* It is early in the day, eh?" She turned and shuffled inside. "Come," she threw over her shoulder.

Inez took two cautious steps inside. Her gaze first fell, as no doubt intended, on what looked like a shrine that took up nearly all of the opposite wall. A yellow candle burned, and religious cards of the Catholic variety were propped up and about on the velvet-covered board, surrounding a statue of the Virgin Mary. A large painting of who she guessed to be Saint Peter, holding a set of keys, leaned against the wall close to the statue. Little oddities also populated the altar, including small baskets holding what-not, little wrapped candies, a child's toy top, and what appeared to be a real skull complete with a real top hat and a stub of cigar clenched between its teeth.

Inez had been expecting…Well, what had she been expecting, exactly? She wasn't certain. Perhaps black-feathered chickens squawking and running about, a cauldron of foul-smelling suspicious liquids. More of those little poppets, with pins stabbed through their eyes or hearts. The only faintly ominous thing she saw, besides the unnerving hatted skull, was a black cat, crouched under the skirt of the altar and eyeing her with deep yellow eyes.

Madam Labasilier stood by a small table covered with another red velvet cloth that looked the same vintage as the one on the altar. Her arms were crossed and, most surprising of all to Inez, she was smiling.

"Eh, not what you expect, yes? I see that look all the time from nonbelievers. But here you are. *Asi vou.* Sit." She gestured to the rickety chair on the other side of the table. "So, you come about that man of yours, yes? You want him, what? To stay or go?"

Surprised, and stifling a desire to laugh out loud, Inez moved to the chair and sat as commanded. *As long as she is being courteous, so will I. More flies with honey than vinegar.*

"That is not why I am here, but I commend you on an astute assumption," she said, arranging her cloak and skirts so that all items were near to hand, including the pistol in the cloak's right-hand pocket. "So, is that what brings most of your female clients here? A request regarding a man?"

"With women, it is always the men. Or sometimes it is the children." Labasilier shrugged and adjusted one of the shawls that had fallen off her shoulder. "Whatever breaks a heart is why they come." She placed both hands, gnarled and knobby, on the table.

"My query is different." She pulled the poppet out and placed it on the table between them. "Perhaps you can explain this to me."

Madam Labasilier didn't move her head, but instead looked down the length of her nose at the dirt-encrusted doll on the velvet cloth. She slid her hands into her lap.

Inez slid her right hand into her cloak pocket and tried to look blandly attentive and nonthreatening.

"So you took it."

It was not a question, but Inez answered as if it was. "Yes. After I saw you smash it with a rock, bury it by Mrs. Gizzi's shanty, and spit upon the door."

There was a long silence. At last Madam Labasilier said conversationally, "For each answer I require payment."

Inez noticed that the woman's diction had slid into a slightly higher vocabulary, although still with that Creole, near-but-not-quite French tonality. Inez reached into her left pocket, pulled out a silver dollar, and placed it on the table. "Is this enough for the truth?"

"Truth? Of course. So much easier than lies." She didn't touch the money. "It was business. The rows, these alleys, they have always been mine. Then she, that Mrs.-Gizzi-fortuneteller-of-futures, comes and starts with her 'seeing' and 'foretelling.' She had to leave. So," another shrug, "I help her leave with just a little, what do you say, inducement?"

Inez regarded her calm, lined face. "Yes, I think inducement will do."

"It worked," said Labasilier. "She left, no? All is back as it was, as it should be. She has found another place, somewhere else."

"She is dead," said Inez.

There could be no mistaking the sudden jump of eyebrows, although the rest of her face stayed immobile. After another pause, she said, "I had nothing to do with that. The doll was to make her go away."

"And exactly how was this poppet to induce her to leave?" Inez wanted to keep her talking, see if she said anything that would point to a more active role in Drina's "permanent" removal.

"Oh, is only cloth, with a bit of her hair." One arthritic finger emerged from her lap and pointed at the braid, "and a thread from the sash she always wore. Inside," the finger moved to prod the doll, "dust from her footprints, dried *gato krot*...cat shit." At this, the black cat emerged beneath the altar and began to prowl the perimeter of the room, tail held high as if proud of its contribution. "Red pepper, and sulfur." The hand retreated back under the table. "How did she die?"

"You don't know?" Inez asked, all innocence. "I thought you heard everything that happens here."

She shook her head. "No. How?"

"She was strangled. Then her body," Inez waved her free hand, "vanished."

Madam Labasilier sucked in her breath. "Where was she killed?"

"She was found in her shack. I saw her body. Soon thereafter, she vanished."

"That is an evil place," the old woman said.

Inez noticed that the hunched-over curve of her back had disappeared. Madam Labasilier was sitting up as straight as any woman in a tight-laced corset.

"That woman, Mrs. Gizzi, she opened doors that should stay closed. She knew not what she did. Her place. It should be burned down, and the ground cleansed. And you," the finger jabbed again, at Inez this time, "you should not have touched it. It was to make her leave, to send her away. Now, the spell may be attached to you."

The conversation was beginning to wander into territory from which any useful information was unlikely to emerge, so

Inez steered things back to a more fruitful direction. "You were there that night, then, at the time of her death or close to it. That doesn't look good, you know." She left the incipient threat hanging in the air. "Can you prove that you didn't strangle her, then put the poppet outside?"

Labasilier actually laughed, a sharp bark. "Why I do that? And how? Look, these hands." She held them up for Inez to see, the fingers gnarled with age. "No strength for strangling. Besides I have other ways, should I have wished to do her harm. I wished her no harm. Only to go away."

Inez leaned back in the chair. The rails and spindles made small snapping sounds. Inez quickly straightened up. "Prove it to me. Where were you before that?"

"I was with the women of a woman you know, Miss Flo."

"Flo Sweet?" Inez shook her head, trying to clear it. Flo had said she forbade her boarders to continue their consultations with Madam Labasilier and the like. "I don't believe you."

"Is true. As I say, truth easy. Lies lead to roads of much trouble and difficulty. You know that, eh, Mrs. Stannert?" She continued conversationally, "You want proof, talk to those silly girls with the silly names of the months."

Inez thought back to her visit at the Jacksons' home and even more recently to Susan Carothers' studio. "You mean April, May, and June?"

A nod. "I was with them. And then, I went and set the spell for leaving. And then, here. I did not set foot in her place. Why would I want to go into a place so evil? Death walks there."

Inez tried to switch the subject. "You may be right about that. Last night, someone else died in that shack."

The watery brown eyes narrowed. "Who?"

"A gentleman visitor to the city. Someone well-bred, someone who was probably much out of his element."

"The one with the rabbit's foot?"

"You know him?" Inez asked, intrigued.

"He came to me, in the past. Every time to town, he comes and tells me about his rabbit foot and then asks what his luck will be with the women and the cards. That is what men mostly want. Charms to bring luck for the cards, the dice, the faro. Well, if they pay, I give. But this time, no rabbit-foot man. So, he went to that cursed place? And died?" She paused, thinking. "Ah yes! Last night I saw…" She stopped, and a calculating expression crossed her face. "To tell you what I saw, you must pay first."

Inez found the end of the silver chain in her pocket and slowly pulled it out, allowing the rabbit's foot to emerge. She held the object up, spinning at the end of the chain, then gently lowered it to the table.

"His?" A note of suspicion.

"He gave it to me for safekeeping. Perhaps he should have kept it." Inez added softly, "We were friends." She continued, "You know about this talisman, do you not? He told everyone about it, all the time. Let's see if I can recall his words. It's from New Orleans, I know that. As for the rest," Inez rattled it off like a catechism. "It's the left hind foot of a rabbit killed in a country churchyard at midnight, during the dark of the moon, on Friday the thirteenth of the month, by a cross-eyed, left-handed, redheaded, bowlegged Negro riding a white horse."

The weathered hands leapt to the tabletop, gripped into loose fists. She leaned forward over the amulet. "*We*," she said, which sounded close enough to *oui* for Inez to get her drift.

Inez nodded. "That's right. Tell me what you saw and it is yours."

"It is powerful," said the old woman, looking at her narrowly. "Why you give up such a power?"

"As you said, I'm a nonbeliever. It means nothing to me, but I can see it means something to you. So, let's do a little horse-trading. The lucky foot for information." She leaned forward. "What did you see last night?"

The hand crept forward and covered the furred object. "I saw the Devil. Tall, in a top hat and smoking a cigar. Talking with rabbit-foot man. The tall one is like Baron Kriminel, the Ghede, but with pale skin. He was not a Ghede, not one of ours. He was one of *yours*." The last word was expelled vehemently as if she was tossing something repulsive to Inez. "An evil man, and they went into that evil place. Together."

Inez tried to gather the essence. "Top hat? Cigar? Tall? Anything else? Mustache, beard, glasses, a cane?"

"One of yours. Pale," she answered stubbornly. The rabbit foot was gone, already secreted beneath the shawls.

Inez sighed, thinking that the description could fit many men of Leadville, including three-quarters of those who had been at the Grand Central Theater the previous night. "Would you let me know if you see him again? I want justice for my friend."

Madam Labasilier nodded. She stood, as if preparing to escort Inez out the door. But Inez had one more question. The description the voodoo woman had provided certainly fit all the Lads, as well as Doctor Gregorvich, and Mr. Alexander, if he had a top hat. Which he probably did. About the only male of interest who was left out of that description was the drummer, Woods.

"One more question," said Inez, not moving from her chair. "And I think the rabbit's foot should cover payment for this as well."

Madam Labasilier looked at her. Waiting.

Inez said, "There has been a man around the rows, a drummer of women's goods. Small, russet hair. His name is Woods. He also died recently, but not in the 'cursed house,' as you call it. Do you have any knowledge as to when or how he met his end?"

The bent posture had returned, the head cocked up, peering thoughtfully at something above Inez's head. She said, "For an answer, you must ask the neighbor." She took up an ornately carved wooden stick, which had been leaning against a three-legged washstand, and banged on the wall behind the statuary. Almost immediately, there was the heavy thud of feet crossing a wood floor on the other side of the wall, the crash of a door opening, more rumbling down a short set of stairs, and a loud voice outside the door said, "You all right?"

Without waiting for an answer, the speaker heaved Madam Labasilier's door back so violently that Inez feared it would fly off its rickety hinges. The black cat escaped between the feet of the giantess now blocking the exit. With apprehension, Inez realized she was staring at someone who could only be Kate Armstead. Tall, taller than Inez by far, Kate was regularly vilified in the Leadville papers when the reporter wanted to describe the horrors of Coon Row and the plight of its denizens and those who ventured there. A woman of strong arm and strong features, Kate was imposing and, Inez had to admit, highly unnerving in appearance despite the fact that she wore a frilly cotton houseshift sprinkled with tiny blue flowers.

She turned to the old woman. "Is she giving you trouble?"

"*Non non*," Madam Labasilier assured her. "This is Mrs. Stannert. She has question for you."

"Mrs. Stannert?" Kate looked down at Inez. "So, you're that uppity woman runs the Silver Queen."

Madam poked Inez with her stick. "Pay her and ask," she hissed.

Inez gulped and pulled out another silver dollar. "I'm trying to find out what happened to a drummer who, I gather, was in the neighborhood a couple nights ago. Name was Woods. Sold women's undergarments."

"Undergarments." Kate folded her arms. Her biceps bulged impressively. "Why do you want to know?"

"Tell her," Labasilier urged Kate. "It will be secret." She looked at Inez. "You will not tell others."

Inez nodded fervently.

A long moment passed. Then Kate took the dollar. "He was here." She clenched the coin in a fist. "He was hurtin' my girls. No one hurts my girls."

Inez imagined the silver warping in her powerful grip.

"So," Kate said in a reasonable tone. "I gave him a glass of whiskey to calm him down and sent him away."

"You. Tell her," urged Labasilier.

Kate's eyes gleamed. "I might've slipped a little tobaccy juice in that whiskey. To make sure he learnt his lesson. It can make a body feel mighty sick. And he was such a little feller. Maybe I slipped him a little too much."

Chapter Thirty-one

Inez assured both Kate Armstead and Madam Labasilier that their secrets were safe with her. She may have been an unbeliever, still, she didn't want to find a disfigured poppet sporting her hair at the back alley door of the Silver Queen. As she hustled to Pine Street, intending to go to *The Independent* newspaper offices where she hoped to find some of Jed's newsies hanging about and perhaps Jed as well, her pockets were considerably lighter, but her thoughts heavier. Was it possible the three deaths were entirely unrelated? The only role that the drummer appeared to have played was to provide the laces that robbed Drina of her breath.

Inez's feet slowed.

According to the deputy, in addition to being shot Percy had been strangled. Could it have been with a set of corset laces? Would a simple string of silk link the two deaths? Unbidden, a strange vision rose in her mind of poppets dangling on a corded lace—the Drina poppet at one end, the lace knotted around her neck, a Percy poppet at the other with neck similarly captured, and a tiny russet-brown poppet of Woods midway between the two. The whole ensemble danced at the whim of invisible hands.

Inez shivered, but not from the mild gust that wrapped her skirts around her limbs. *I see how the world of the unseeable and unknowable can affect the gullible. Just a little exposure to all this mumbo-jumbo and talk of the hereafter, spells, auras, and visions, and my own imagination is conjuring up its own set of impossible phantasms.* She reached the corner of Harrison and Third Street. Looking across the wide main street to plot her way through the rolling traffic, she spotted Dr. Gregorvich, on the opposite corner, bent over, in deep conversation with a tiny newsboy who didn't look older than four. The little fellow handed him what appeared to be his last paper. The physician tucked it under his arm, gave him a coin, then stayed him with a hand to the shoulder. He must have asked a question, because the tot began nodding vigorously and said something in return, pointing up East Third, the direction Inez was heading. Dr. Gregorvich straightened to his considerable height, fished in his pocket, and handed another coin, a quick flash of silver, to the newsie, whose little face lit up. The physician gave the boy's oversized cap an affectionate tug before turning away and continuing on his way up Harrison.

Viewing the brief interaction, Inez's estimation of the physician rose a bit. He's one of those "who cares," she told herself. One of those she would strive to be more like, as Reverend Sands had admonished them all on Sunday. Gregorvich was a constant in the alleys, offering his medical services and so what if he was obsessed with the workings of the human mind? The mind, as she well knew, was a mystery.

She navigated her way across the street without turning an ankle and strode up the worn footpath—no boardwalks yet, on East Third—to *The Independent.* The building, which, dated back a couple of years, was a large no-nonsense log edifice with a canvas half-wall above the door, without a false front or fancy architectural embellishment in sight. What was in sight, however, was a small covey of newsies. Inez counted four, including the smallest one she'd seen with Dr. Gregorvich and the tall skinny one that she'd seen with Tony when they'd first met in front of the Silver Saloon the previous week. They appeared to be waiting, perhaps for more papers to sell. One was smoking the stub of a cigarette, while the tall, skinny one was playing mumblety-peg with another. The little one was watching and picking his nose.

"Excuse me, boys," she said, walking up to them. They all peered at her from under their visors or hat brims. "I'm looking for one of *The Independent* newsies, Tony."

"Tony Deuce?" piped up the smoker. "Yeah, sure. What about him?"

"Has he been about at all today?"

"Nope," said the eldest boy shortly and went back to focusing on his knife throw, resting it on his left fist, point uppermost, and then throwing it sideways. It stuck into the soft ground without a quiver.

The smallest one looked up at her, curious.

Inez pushed on. "It's important I get a message to him. I'm Mrs. Stannert and I'm a friend. Any chance that any of you might see him later?"

"He sleeps here," said the tyke. "In the back building, with us."

The tall one rounded on him. "Freddy! You weren't supposed to say anything about that. It's a secret!"

"Secret?" said the tyke faintly. His mouth formed an "O" and he glanced nervously around, as if someone else might have heard.

"Cat's out of the bag now, Ace," said the smoker. "Elliston ain't gonna be happy about you and Freddy flapping your gums about our arrangement."

Freddy looked crestfallen.

"I'm a friend of Mr. Elliston's as well," she assured them.

The tall skinny one, Ace, grumbled. "Aw, lookit whatcha made me do, Freddy, tellin' what Tony told us not to say."

He pulled his knife from the ground, flipped it once, and stashed it away in the top of his well-worn boot. "Oh well. I heard Tony talk about you, Mrs. Stannert, so's I guess it's okay. Just don't tell Mr. Elliston we let out about the shed. He's been really great about letting us all sleep there. With winter coming," he shrugged, "lots of us, we don't have much else place to go."

"If he wants you to keep it as a secret, then it will remain a secret with me as well," she said. Then asked, "So Tony comes by at night? Sleeps with you all in the back?" She glanced at the hulking building before her.

"Yeah, in the shed where he keeps his ink, paper, and all that." Ace scratched his chin. Inez thought he couldn't be more than thirteen, or maybe fourteen, but assumed the role as spokesman with an easy air. "Tony shows up late, leaves early."

"Well, when he comes tonight, please let him know that I must speak to him. Tomorrow morning. As soon as possible." She fished out a small collection of nickels and dimes from her dwindling pocket. "Deal? And don't tell anyone else about this. Consider it a secret as well. Can you do that?"

Ace looked at her as if she was crazy. "Of course we can." She nodded and gave each of the four a dime. "Easiest money I've made all day," said the second mumblety-peg player cheerfully. He took off his unseasonable straw hat and wedged the dime into the sweatband.

The door to the building flew open and Jed Elliston appeared, looking more like a printer's devil than a publisher or reporter with his ink-stained hands and leather apron. "Hey, Mrs. Stannert! Just the person I wanted to see! Come in a sec." He turned around and vanished inside without waiting to see if she would follow.

Inez winked at Ace and the other boys and mimed locking her mouth with a key and tossing the key over her shoulder. Even the littlest got the message. "Hey guys," said Ace. "Let's go see if we can rustle up a couple bowls of stew from Mrs. O'Malley. She makes the best. I'll buy and we can all share."

That seemed to cheer everyone up, and off they went.

Inez trailed Jed to the entrance of the building, where he was busy inside giving some instructions to his typesetter, who was nodding automatically as if he was used to Jed hovering and was just going along. "And don't forget we got that last-minute advert from the Clairmont Hotel to insert on the second page," Jed finished.

He turned to Mrs. Stannert, said, "Let's talk over here," and headed to his desk, absently rubbing his face. When he turned to face Inez he had a smear of black ink down the side of his long, aristocratic nose and another along his forehead. "You're just the woman who can help me out," he said, crossing his arms.

Inez eyed him suspiciously. Usually it was she who wheedled favors from Jed, not the other way around.

"What do you have in mind?" she asked.

"Well, you see, I'm in a bit of a spot, editorially speaking." He picked up a copy of the rival *Chronicle* newspaper, lying on his desk. "This Orth Stein is staying one jump ahead of me on every story. This one, for instance." He proceeded to read in loud ringing tones, "'The country was startled only a few weeks ago by the discovery that a fellow named Buchanan had scattered some eleven thousand bogus medical diplomas throughout the country…' and so on and so forth and, ah! Here! '…if there should be any possibility of driving any medical imposters from our midst through the cooperation of our legitimate practitioners, THE CHRONICLE pledges itself to stop at no hazard and leave no stone unturned in the prosecution of that laudable object.' Bah!"

He tossed the paper to one side. "I need something to top this. Something to *strike* at the hearts of readers, make them sit up and take notice. I need to uncover proof of those underground anatomy sessions! I have to break that story!" His face was reddening with enthusiasm, or maybe aggression. With those streaks of ink like war-paint on his face, he looked like a fourth-estate warrior, preparing to do battle with a mortal enemy. Inez almost expected him to give a bloodcurdling whoop and gallop into the street, pen held aloft like a deadly lance, going in for the attack on the *Chronicle*'s Harrison Avenue offices.

"Jed, I sympathize with your journalistic dilemma, but how on earth can I help? You've talked with Doc, I understand. He's well connected with the medical community here. If there were underhanded doings, I'd think he'd know."

"Doc is too trusting by half," said Jed dismissively. "When it comes to any in his medical fraternity, he rises to the defense, and won't hear a word against them until the evidence is overwhelming."

"You mean he believes a man is innocent until proven guilty?"

Jed frowned, wounded. "I thought you were on my side."

She sighed. "What is it you want me to do?"

"This Dr. Gregorvich…" he began.

Inez groaned.

"I thought you didn't trust him either."

"No, well, I'm not sure."

"Look, I know he's hiding something. Call it a sixth sense. The fellow's shady." His narrow nose actually twitched. "Why don't you go to his office and talk to him?"

"Me? Why?"

"The way he was looking at you last night over the poker game, he admires the way you think."

Inez winced.

"Just make an appointment. Complain of the vapors or something. I'm betting he'll jump at the chance to talk with you. And once he gets started talking, just listen, ask some leading questions, and look around."

"Look around for what? Body parts in jars and bones on the bookshelves?"

"Oh, anything! Anything unusual! You're a perceptive woman!" He made as if to grip her shoulder, but she pulled away saying warningly, "Ink."

Startled, he looked down at his hands, then laughed self-consciously. "You see? Perceptive. That's what I was talking about."

Inez thought about her upcoming séance with Mrs. Alexander and how she was not happy about being Dr. Gregorvich's patient. What was it she had said, exactly, after the Sunday service? He's obsessed with the mechanical workings of brain and body. Doesn't look to "heal the heart." And Mrs. Alexander seemed to be looking for an ally, as her husband was apparently convinced that she suffered from whatever ills and conditions the physician had offered in his diagnosis.

"I might have a way to find out more about him and his practice," she said cautiously.

"Thatta girl!" Jed leaned back against his desk, his greasy hands now carelessly hitched into his trouser pockets. "I knew I could count on you."

"Not right away," she added. "Toward the end of the week."

He nodded. "Fine, fine."

The typesetter came up and said, "I finished that piece about Reverend Sands, if you want to take a look." He then wandered back to his station.

Jed's face sobered, and he threw a glance at Inez that was half embarrassment, half condolence. "The reverend, he got the bum's rush. I'm really sorry about that. I wish I knew who the instigator was, because I'd see him strung up for slander, if I could."

Inez gave him a tight smile. "My sentiments are in line with yours, but I do believe Reverend Sands wanted to do what he thought best for the church."

"Yeah, well," Jed seemed at a loss. He finally blurted out, "Look, if I can ever do anything for you, Mrs. Stannert...I think you got a bit of the bum's rush too. None of my business, but you've always come through for me and, well, just want to let you know you have a friend in the press, if you ever need one."

Touched, she said, "Thank you, Jed. That's very kind."

He reddened and scratched his neck, leaving another greasy mark. "Well, back to work. And thanks for helping me out with the Dr. Gregorvich business. I'll bet that, once you get inside his lair, you'll find something that'll show him for what he is. He can't stay hidden forever. I believe, I have to believe, that wrongs will always, eventually, come to light, sooner or later. And I want to be there, shining the light, when it does."

Chapter Thirty-two

Inez walked back to the saloon, slowly, thinking of what Jed had said. The fact he had offered to be "in her corner" had set her musing about Casey's dire warning that her petition for divorce could devolve into a public circus. She was determined that would not happen, had taken secret steps to prevent it, but there were still so many factors outside her control.

If push came to shove, who could she count on to be on her side? Susan Carothers would, without a doubt. But in a court of law, just as in the rough-and-tumble world of commerce, Inez knew it was the testimony of men which carried the most weight and respect.

Jed had as much as raised his hand on her behalf. Doc Cramer, she felt, would take a stand for her, even if it meant standing "against" Mark. He had seen all she'd been through the past year and a half and offered his veiled and not-so-veiled sympathy and support throughout. Too, there was this: Doc and Sands had both fought for the Union. They had a shared connection, an important one for Doc, if one were to give weight to his many rambling stories of "back in the War" and his more oblique references to less-talked-about aspects of those uncivil times. Inez had had many opportunities to observe how the War had wounded all who lived through it—physically, mentally. Even now, fifteen years after, some of those wounds remained on the surface, festering, open. Others may have scarred over, disappeared deep beneath, but they were still there.

And Mark had fought for the South.

A small point, but one that could encourage Doc to step to her side, should she need to square off against her husband. It could also work in her favor for hammering out a legally binding agreement for ensuring a secure future for her little William, no matter what the outcome.

She returned to the saloon and pushed open the Harrison Street door. A sprinkling of customers occupied the tables, some filling up on Bridgette's stew and biscuits, others apparently preferring to drink their afternoon meal. Sol was behind the bar. Mark was nowhere to be seen.

Sol saw her, did a double-take, and walked to where she stood by the counter, next to the gallon jar of pickles. Clutching the bar rag to his chest, he said, "Mr. Stannert's in the gaming room upstairs. Waiting for you."

"For me? Really."

He nodded and glanced toward the staircase, then back at her. He ran a hand over his hair, neat to begin with, now less so. "Yeah. The undersheriff was just here."

She waited, in case he had more to say.

He licked his lips. "He's, uh, not happy."

She nodded. "Thank you, Sol."

The stairs rose to meet her, then the dark second-story hallway unrolled beneath her feet. The door to the left, leading to the gaming room, was closed. She knew her footsteps would be audible from inside. He would know she was coming.

She braced herself, gripped the crystal doorknob, turned it, and walked in.

Mark was waiting for her, standing on the far side of the round gaming table, thunder in his face.

He raised a packet of thick papers, seal broken. The silence stretched taut between them until he broke it with, "What's this about, Inez?"

Leaving the door ajar, just in case, she squared her shoulders and moved to face him across the table. She curled her fingers around the top rail of one the chairs, keeping close watch on his expression and his hands.

He was angry. Angrier than she could recall ever seeing him. That, more than anything told her: she'd caught him unawares. He had not believed she would really file for divorce, once he'd returned. Moreover, it was apparently dawning on him that not only had she stoked the engine and set this train in motion, it was picking up speed. Perhaps he was even starting to see his options for stopping it were slim to none, not even if he were to throw himself in front of it and allow the engine to grind him to shreds of bone and blood.

She responded, "That's an empty question, Mark. You opened it. You know. It's a summons for our divorce."

The upheld papers shivered, a mute warning of the depth of his rage. She caught herself being glad he didn't have a gun at that moment.

He began to circle the table toward her. Her instinct was to circle away, keeping the circumference of the table between them. However, doing so would place her farther from the door. So, instead, she stood her ground, one hand on the back of the chair, the other resting on her hip, only inches from the Smoot in her pocket. When she didn't move, he finally halted, arm's length from her. He shook the papers in her face, his blue eyes burning through her. "We made a deal in the Springs, Inez. You signed and agreed not to press forward with a divorce for a year."

"You *broke* our deal," she retorted. "We were to lead separate lives for that year. Those were your exact words. Our agreement was you would not meddle, not interfere. Well, you didn't stick to your side of the bargain, rendering our agreement null and void. Your maneuverings did nothing but free me to do what I always intended to do at the end of the year—obtain a divorce."

His expression tightened. For a minute, she was afraid he was going to hit her across the face with the papers. Instead he flung them violently onto the poker table. They skittered and slid across the top to fall off the other side. "You will not do this, Inez. I will not let you. I will bury you."

"You bury me, then you bury yourself and you cast our son into an uncertain future. Is that really what you want to do?" she asked, hand on the engine throttle, easing it forward.

She watched as he visibly pulled himself together with a deep breath and tried to gather the reins of self-control. "Don't. Just...don't do this." He changed tack, the Southern intonation creeping back in. "Darlin', we need to talk."

A sudden clutch of excited voices rose up from below accompanied by a clatter of footsteps ascending the stairs. It was warning enough so that they were able to step away from each other and turn their eyes to the open door.

Doc burst in first, followed closely by Bridgette. Doc said, "Mrs. Stannert! Mr. Stannert! She's arrived at last and is as beautiful as the day is long!"

Inez pressed a hand against her bodice to slow the terrified hammering of her heart. "She? She who?"

"Why, Miss Hazel Jackson, that's who!" Doc's face was red with exertion as if he'd been the one giving birth. He took out a voluminous handkerchief and wiped his face and neck. "Arrived with a healthy set of lungs, as evidenced by a scream that brought the neighbors to the door asking who was being beaten."

"Dr. Cramer!" huffed Bridgette. "That is not the *least* bit amusing!"

"No, Mrs. O'Malley, but it is what they said." Doc leaned heavily on his cane. He looked done in, oblivious to the tension in the room and the Stannerts standing as frozen as statues in a tableau. Bridgette darted to Inez and said, "Dr. Cramer said we are to be the first outside of family to see her, but we mustn't stay longer than just for a quick peek and give our well-wishes to the parents. I'll gather up the basket I made earlier and take it with us. It has food enough for today and tomorrow, and I daresay they will need it I'm sure. I'm dying to hold the wee one, for just a minute, mind. I remember what it was like with the first, and Mrs. Jackson will not want that child apart from her for long."

Doc gave them an exhausted wave. "Go, ladies, go."

Inez said, "Doc, why don't you sit. Have a brandy or two, on the house. You look like you could use it."

"Come along, Mrs. Stannert!" Bridgette darted out and headed down the stairs, moving faster than Inez thought possible.

Inez was glad she still had her cloak and walking shoes on, as Bridgette grabbed the basket of edible offerings, her hat, and her coat almost before Inez had time to descend the stairs. Sol quizzed Inez with his eyes as the two women headed out but all he said was "Add my congratulations."

As they hurried west down State Street, Bridgette said between huffs and puffs, "He said 'not too long,' well, that's not clear at all, is it? If Mr. and Mrs. Jackson want us to stay a bit and help, that wouldn't be 'too long' for them, then, would it? I was so excited to hear, a girl! Hazel! Such a beautiful name! I'm afraid when Dr. Cramer came in and told me I insisted we find you right away. Is the mister unwell? He looked under the weather."

Inez glanced sharply at Bridgette and didn't answer, but Bridgette brightened as the Jacksons' cottage came into view. "Why look at all that!" she exclaimed.

Neighbors and others were indeed gathered along the front, standing back a bit from the walkway, murmuring amongst themselves.

Bridgette pushed her way through, saying, "Excuse me, we have permission from Doc Cramer, pardon, we have permission." She gained the little porch quickly, with Inez just a half a pace behind. Bridgette rapped on the door, a hummingbird vibrating with nervous energy. Without waiting for someone to greet them, she twisted the knob and poked her head in. "Hellooooo," she called with a lilt at the end of her salutation. "It's Mrs. O'Malley and Mrs. Stannert here."

A dark shadow loomed and Abe Jackson, looking weary, drawn, and older than his years pulled the door open and said, "C'mon in. Just for a bit, though. We've been through the wringer here, 'specially Angel."

He accepted the basket from Bridgette and led them to the back. Mrs. Buford sat outside the bedroom, knitting. She glanced sharply at Inez and Bridgette—an imposing Janus at the gate. "I tol' Doc that Mrs. Jackson needs her rest," said Mrs. Buford under her breath, needles clacking away.

"Doctor Cramer said we could take a peek at the wee one," whispered Bridgette back. "Just a quick peek."

Mrs. Buford's round face creased in a frown. "Well, I suppose if Doc said so."

"Inez? Bridgette?" Angel's voice, hoarse, exhausted, drifted out of the darkened room. "Please. Come."

Bridgette didn't need a further invitation. She hurried past Mrs. Buford who looked like she was about to offer a reprimand. Instead, she just looked at Inez, shook her head, and returned to her knitting. "Not too long, then," she said. "That was a right difficult passage, and the good Lord knows, mother and child need some sleepin' time."

Inez ventured into the dim room. Bridgette was cooing over a low-lying cradle. "She's as lovely as her mother, the wee one, look at her sleeping, I can't see her face under all the blankets. Hazel, is it? Haaaazel." Bridgette sounded like she was trying to coax the newborn awake.

Angel reached out an arm. The simple movement seemed to take all her strength. "Inez."

Inez moved over to the bed and said, "Congratulations, Angel. I know you had a hard time of it," she soothed, "but it's over now. Now you have a beautiful baby girl."

Inez heard Bridgette gasp. Inez looked up. Bridgette was holding a bundle and staring at Inez in bewilderment. "Her eyes!"

Inez felt her blood run cold. "What about her eyes?"

Bridgette seemed perplexed. "Just the biggest blue eyes I have seen on a child since, well, I can't remember when. I was surprised, that's all." A little pale fist emerged from the blankets.

Angel gripped Inez's arm. "Doc said, her eyes can get darker. Skin too."

Inez moved to Bridgette's side and took the baby gently, stroked the little hand, which opened, only to close fiercely on her finger. Hazel blinked sleepily, still holding tight to the tip of Inez's glove, and Inez saw that Hazel indeed had pale blue eyes, nothing like Angel's brown or Abe's near black. Her skin had none of Angel's warm mahogany or Abel's dark as coffee tones. Instead, Hazel had a few wisps of blonde hair, the color of summer hay, and white newborn-wrinkled skin. And eyes, lighter blue than the sky.

She will not know her father, I have seen it. Drina's pronouncement from her "session" with Angel, just the previous week, haunted Inez all the way back to the Silver Queen.

It's all stuff and nonsense, no need to have a case of the vapors, Inez told herself sternly. Anyone who knew anything of Angel and her previous life on State Street, before she married Abe, could reasonably "foresee" that Hazel's father might be anyone, anyone at all, and not the man who will be raising her as his own. So, of course, the babe is very likely to never "know" who her real father is. It was a lucky guess, that's all. Nothing more than a few vague words strung together, from which the gullible can weave the truth in retrospect.

When they walked into the saloon, Mark was at the near end, tending bar. He stopped when they entered and came toward them, wiping his hands on the bar rag. "Doc told me," he said, "about the little one, Hazel. A surprise turn of the cards, but she's got a crackerjack set of parents, so it'll work out. I hear she is perfect in every regard, with a set of lungs that could get her a job as a fire bell."

"Well now, we didn't hear her cry," said Bridgette, pulling her hatpin out, removing her small hat, and patting her gray hair distractedly. "She wanted to sleep and sleep she did. But she is a beauty, absolutely."

Mark nodded, gaze fixed on Inez. "Loud scream, good lungs, already knows when a good rest-up is needed and not about to be convinced otherwise. I'm going to go out on a limb and wager she'll grow into a lass of strong will and determination. A lucky girl, to be born to a mama and papa who will give her a good life, no matter what. Life sometimes works in strange ways, turning left when we expect it to turn right. Isn't that so, Mrs. O'Malley?" Although he addressed Bridgette, Inez knew that last was directed at her.

"My thoughts exactly, Mr. Stannert." Bridgette looked around the room, the occupied chairs and the crowded rail. "Heavens, look at how busy it is and so early in the week, not even a weekend! I'd better be getting back and put another batch of biscuits in the oven."

"A word with you, Mrs. Stannert?" He'd had time to compose himself. The anger was gone, replaced by a careful politeness.

"Only one?" Her voice was no less polite.

"I apologize for my earlier behavior, Inez. I was taken by surprise," he lowered his voice, "as I'm sure you knew I would be. We need to talk."

"So, talk." She started to strip off her gloves, heading toward the staircase.

He moved with her, careful to not bump into the backs of the men positioned along the rail. "Not here, not now. We need a neutral space. Somewhere where we can discuss this situation like the two civilized beings we are, or at least were, at one point. Somewhere I can be sure you won't tear me to shreds afore I've had a chance to say my piece."

Exactly what I thought he'd say.

"Very well," she said coolly. "Our agreement, which, I will reiterate, *you* broke, stipulated we spend one evening a week together. Shall we say dinner? In a public restaurant? Where neither of us will be likely to cause a scene? I warn you, there is little chance you can say anything to change my mind at this point."

She saw him eagerly grasp the straw she'd held out and could imagine him thinking: *a little chance is better than none.*

"The Tontine?" he offered. "Thursday? Or any place, any time you wish."

She nodded. "Tontine, Thursday. What time? If we are both gone from the saloon, do you intend Sol and Bridgette to hold down the fort during our *tête-à-tête?*"

"Abe'll be back by then," said Mark. "He and Sol, they can handle things. It's not like we're skedaddling on them on a Friday or Saturday night. How about nine o'clock? I'll make the reservation."

So eager to please now.

"Very well."

He smiled, obviously relieved.

Perhaps he thought I would turn my back and walk out.

He added, "That'll give us both more time to calm down and consider the situation, don't you agree?"

And gives you more time to prepare and for me to prepare as well.

She refrained from smiling and simply said, "Agreed, Mr. Stannert."

Chapter Thirty-three

Tony pushed open the front door of Alexander's Undertaking slowly, trying to keep the little bell from tinkling.

Yesterday, Sunday, had been no day of rest for her. When she had arrived late afternoon, Mr. Alexander had set her back to work on the main floor, saying, "Mrs. Alexander came back from church and is upstairs with one of her 'sick headaches,' so quiet as a mouse, if you please." Tony understood quiet, and proceeded to creep about on silent feet, finishing up with dusting and polishing the caskets, then sweeping and cleaning the floorboards, which involved trying to dig out the grit between the planks with a bristle bush before taking a mop and a bucket of vinegar to them. The vinegar fumes stung her nose, reminding her of the chemicals Miss Carothers used to develop her photographic plates.

Just when Tony thought she might be done, Mr. Alexander was back, exclaiming in a whisper, "Excellent job!" and "Well done!" before handing her a tin of paste wax and asking her to also clean and polish the counter. "Be sure to get the front side," he added, "since that's what people see when they first walk in."

Tony wasn't about to grumble, since he was paying her extra for the extra hours, so she set her aching muscles to work on the counter, neatening out the papers and odd bits of stuff on the shelves below as she went. Before she left, Mr. Alexander told her he wanted her help in the lower level on the morrow. Tony didn't know if she was more curious or nervous about that.

Monday afternoon, after fooling the doorbell, she tiptoed across the floor just in case the missus still had her headache. Mr. Alexander was nowhere to be seen, so she went to the back and started down the stairs to the basement. She was only two steps down, far enough to see the bottom level was lit up, when she heard Mr. Alexander talking, and not quietly either.

He said, "But the family wants him shipped as soon as possible! There's no time."

Another voice murmured.

Tony stopped and strained her ears.

Then Mr. Alexander said, "But, they aren't even close! How do you expect me—?"

More murmuring.

"All right. I'll make it work, somehow." Mr. Alexander sounded defeated.

Tony waited, but didn't hear any more.

It occurred to her it might not be good to be caught on the stairs eavesdropping. She retreated to the main level, wondering what to do when Mr. Alexander and whoever was down there came up. She finally went to the front door, opened it, shut it normally so the little bell rang, and then walked with a normal tread across the floor.

Mr. Alexander appeared from the back hallway so quickly Tony figured he must have been on his way up when she scooted out of there.

"Ah! You're here," he said. "Good. I need your help downstairs. I'm going to introduce you to some of the tools of the trade a little earlier than expected. Are you ready?" He turned and headed toward the rear of the building.

Tony followed, saying, "Is the missus feeling better?"

"What? Oh, her headaches. They usually last a couple of days. She resting now, sleeping. She has special medicine that helps her sleep through them."

He sounded distracted, like he was thinking of something else. When they got downstairs, they were alone. Tony looked around, trying to figure out where the other speaker had gone.

She would have seen or heard if someone had come upstairs with Mr. Alexander. If they'd gone out the back door, she would've heard that squeaky thing shut. The large door that led to the ramp was still closed and barred. The door with the brass lock, though, now had a key sticking out of the keyhole.

Tony was going to ask Mr. Alexander about it, but he was busy with the drummer's remains on the table. Only, Tony realized, it wasn't the drummer at all. For one thing, the body was wearing fancy duds. In fact, those duds looked kinda familiar.

Mr. Alexander spoke without turning around. "Tony, will you help me remove the clothing here? We'll be getting fresh ones to dress Mr. Winslow Percival Brown in for his final journey. He'll be heading home across the sea, once the coroner sends us the final papers."

Tony advanced, unable to look away.

It was him! Worthless Pisspot Brown!

And he had a hole the size of a dime where his heart was, and his fancy duds were soaked with blood from his collar to the top of his trousers. But his eyes, his face, something reminded her of Maman with those laces around her throat.

Tony felt her stomach turn over and rise. She dashed over to a bucket, which thankfully only held the dregs of the vinegar wash she'd used yesterday on the floor upstairs, and vomited.

"Oh dear. I'm sorry, Mr. Donatello. I should have warned you. Will you be able to help? I can do it myself. You could come back and clean the floors and tables tomorrow night."

"No!" gasped Tony, face down in the bucket. She stood up and wiped her face on the sleeve of Ace's jacket. "I, I'm okay. All the blood surprised me. What happened to him?"

To show she was fine, she went to Pisspot Brown's feet and started removing his boots.

"The coroner and physician who examined him said he was shot. Well, that's obvious, but there's more." Mr. Alexander looked at Tony, his eyes huge behind the glasses.

Tony steeled herself and moved to the other side of the table to look.

"See this?" The undertaker moved the jacket collar aside a little. "He was strangled as well."

There was a straight-line bruise on his neck.

Tony felt sick again. She'd hated Worthless Pisspot Brown, was ready to kill him herself. But now, she felt sorry for him. And she wondered. Maybe Mrs. Stannert was right. Maybe Pisspot wasn't "the" Mr. Brown.

"Why would someone do that?" Tony tried to make sense of it.

"They don't know yet. According to the examination by the physician and coroner, poor Mr. Brown here didn't die from the gunshot wound."

"Didn't he get shot in the heart?"

"No, the heart is on the other side of the chest." Alexander busied himself with the cufflinks. "He apparently was shot, lay there for a while, bleeding, then was strangled. It was the strangulation that killed him. We'll save these cufflinks for the clothes his friends will provide us. I'm sure the family will appreciate that we send them home with Mr. Brown."

Tony's blood ran cold. "They're bringing his clothes *now?*" She did not want to see the nobs here, where they might recognize her and she'd have no way to escape.

"No, no, later. The marshal wants them to stay in town until the law figures out who killed him." He pointed to a wooden box on the far table. "Bring me that. We can put his clothes in there and throw them away later. They aren't even any good to the poor, as soiled as they are." He nodded to a large, worn-looking trunk against a wall. "We put the clothes from the indigent and unknown that are in good shape in there. When the trunk is full, we give them to the missions and the churches in town to give back to the poor. But Mr. Brown doesn't have anything useful to offer."

Tony went and grabbed the small trashbox. It was then she noticed, tucked in one corner and held up off the floor by three sawhorses, a fancy casket, twin to one she'd polished upstairs. "Is Mr. Brown going to be packed in a metallic burial case?"

"Very good, you remembered the proper terminology. However, he won't be *packed* like a crate of eggs, he'll be *laid to rest* in the case."

"So his family is paying for it?"

"Oh yes, and the embalming too. They are also putting pressure on the marshal, coroner, and everyone to just be done with it. According to what I've heard about their telegrams, they view the American West as being full of gunfighters, wild animals, and savage natives. They don't care how he died, oddly enough, they just want him brought home for burial in his native England. We'll see what happens. The marshal seems intent that justice be done, but with all the violence in town, there's not a lot of time to investigate one death, particularly if the family doesn't insist. However, he has the gun and some leads, so perhaps this will be over quickly."

His voice got faraway. "I'd like to try the Lyford embalming process, but I don't have all the necessary equipment. I'll probably just use Dr. Gregorvich's recipe, since it's worked well in the past. When we're done here, Mr. Donatello, you can help me check whether I have enough of the requisite chemicals. I'll need zinc chloride, mercury chromate, creosote, and alum."

Tony focused on removing Brown's stockings. The skin on his lower limbs was cold to the touch and dead white to look at. She tried to do neither. "So they have the gun that killed… shot him? They know who did it?"

"Well, it's a fancy revolver," said Mr. Alexander. He turned to pick up a pair of scissors and began cutting away the bloody clothes. "Apparently the gun belongs to a boy who tried to shoot Mr. Brown a few days ago." Tony, who was preparing to toss the balled-up stockings into the trashbox, froze. Alexander continued, "I gather the incident happened at one of the saloons in town, the Silver Queen. I heard it caused quite a ruckus. They're looking for the boy now, and I imagine it won't be long before he's found."

"Where," she found it hard to speak, "where did they find him? I mean, the remains?"

She had a bad feeling about this, which was confirmed when Mr. Alexander said, "In an abandoned fortuneteller's shack off Stillborn Alley."

◇◇◇

When Tony slipped into the newsie shed in the dead of night, Ace was awake and waiting. "Tony," he whispered. "All kinds of people are looking for you."

"I know!" she whispered back.

"They think you killed somebody, a swell from out of town." A beat. "Did you?"

"No!"

"Mrs. Stannert asked us about you," Ace continued. "She wants to see you, says it's important, and you gotta meet her tomorrow morning. She said you'd know where."

"I know," muttered Tony. Things were getting complicated. She wanted to run and hide, but wasn't sure where to go.

"I mean, you can stay here with us still. You gotta hide somewhere and here is as good as any place. I don't think anyone knows about it except for Mrs. Stannert, and she's sworn to secrecy now."

"You *told* her?"

Even in the darkness, Tony could sense Ace's shrug. "She kinda knew already. But, that makes me think others might be guessing as well and they might come looking for you." Ace leaned toward her. "We could make you a place behind those ink drums, with a bunch of the old burlap bags. You'd want to leave afore sun-up, though."

"No, it's okay, Ace. I don't want you and the rest to get into trouble on account of me. I know a safe place I can hide. Thanks."

Clutching the key to Miss Carothers' studio through her layers of shirts, undervests, and jacket, she melted back into the night.

Chapter Thirty-four

Tuesday morning, Inez hurried to Susan's studio, arriving before she opened for business, but not by much. Tony was there. Inez wondered where the youngster had spent the night. The newsie shed, perhaps? The girl, dressed in her proper "Annabelle" clothes, was finishing a sausage roll and tea breakfast with Susan. Tony had dark circles under her eyes, and her hands were shaking.

The first thing she said when she saw Inez was, "Pisspot Brown's dead!"

Inez turned to Susan. "It might be best if I talk to Tony alone. I don't want to put you in a situation where you will feel the need to lie. The less you know about certain things, the less complicated it will be for you."

"Are you sure? You know, I'm always willing to help, any way I can."

"I know, Susan, and you do so much for me. It often seems, however, despite my best intentions, whenever I embroil you in these doings you are the one who ends up in trouble."

Susan smiled. "Well, not all the time, Inez. However, I do need to make tea. Miss Sweet is bringing in Misses July, August, and September for portraits soon, so I must get the tea going and the sitting room prepared." She added, "Tony's going to help me today. I showed her how to develop plates yesterday, and I think I can trust her to do some developing on her own while I take care of the sittings I have booked. Annabelle is a quick study."

"Excellent!" said Inez. Keeping Tony bundled in skirts and with her distinctive eyes hidden behind the tinted glasses Inez had secured seemed like a good idea. Keeping her behind the doors of Susan's darkroom sounded even better.

Once Susan had left the room, Inez said to Tony, "So you know about Mr. Brown."

"Yeah! I saw his remains at Mr. Alexander's, and then I puked," burst out Tony.

Inez winced in sympathy. "I wish I could have talked to you sooner. We have to figure out a way I can reach you if I must."

"He was killed with my gun!" wailed Tony. "Someone stole it and killed Mr. Brown with it! Now all his friends think *I* did it!"

"I know you had nothing to do with his death," soothed Inez. "And you have proof, should push come to shove, that you were nowhere near when he died. You were working at Mr. Alexander's and then you were with your newsie friends, right?"

"Yeah, but…"

"So, you must be extra careful until things are sorted out. Remember, they are looking for the newsie Tony. They are not looking for Annabelle Carothers." Inez furrowed her brow. "I believe you should stop working at Mr. Alexander's. It's too dangerous to go about as a boy now."

Tony put her head in her hands. Her glasses slid down her nose. "I can't," she whispered.

Inez tried to hold onto her patience. "Why not?"

"He has a trunk, where they put the clothes of people who die and nobody cares. I want to see if Maman's clothes are inside."

Inez leaned forward. "Tony…Annabelle…oh hell, Antonia."

Tony looked up. "If you find her clothes, what does that prove?"

"It'll prove her remains were brought there. I can ask Mr. Alexander about her, and he won't be able to lie. I thought it all out last night, while I was sleeping here at the studio." Tony took a deep breath. "Mr. Alexander, he's asking me to clean and straighten stuff. So, if I say, 'How about if I clean out the trunk, fold up the clothes for the mission?' I bet he'll say yes. And then, if I find, say, her sash or her waistcoat, I can hold it up and say something like, 'Oooh, this is nice. Where did this come from?' And he'll have to tell me and then I can ask some more questions. But if he says he doesn't know, I'll know he's lying."

Now Inez wanted to hold her head in her hands. "Tony, first of all, you'll be dressed as a boy, and I do not believe a boy would hold up a fancy gold ladies' sash and say, 'Ooooh, this is nice.' Besides, if he does have your mother's clothes, I'm not sure how you will go about probing without raising suspicions. Remember, Mrs. Alexander went to your mother at least once, probably several times. I think it's a sore point for him, his wife's interest in soothsaying, fortunetelling, and so on. What if he brings Mrs. Alexander into the discussion and she recognizes you?"

Tony's mouth set in a stubborn line. "I'll think of something. I want to know. I have to know. Besides, there's strange things going on there."

"Such as?"

"When I got there yesterday, he was talking to someone downstairs where the bodies are stored and stuff. I heard two voices, but when I went down, it was only him and Mr. Brown, and Mr. Brown, well, *he* wasn't talking, that's for sure."

Inez sat back, her scalp tingling with alarm. Her thoughts turned immediately to the upcoming séance and tableknockings, messages from beyond, disembodied voices from the dead…

She said, "Well, this Friday evening, I will be there. Mrs. Alexander is holding a séance at midnight and I'm invited."

"You?" Tony sounded incredulous.

"Yes, me. And while I am there I plan to ask a few questions and see if I can learn more about your mother's relationship to Mrs. Alexander as well as any doings she may have had with Mr. Alexander. Too, there's Dr. Gregorvich, an odd duck if ever there was one."

"I don't like him," said Tony.

The doorbell clinked, and Inez heard a bevvy of female voices. "Look, you better go. I have to talk to someone who just arrived and it's best you aren't around."

Tony vanished in the direction of the darkroom.

Frisco Flo sashayed into the little waiting room and said brightly, "Why Mrs. Stannert! Imagine meeting you here!" She turned to the three boarders lingering behind her and said, "You all know where the sitting room is. Go, and don't make trouble for Miss Carothers."

"This way, ladies," Miss Carothers' voice floated down the hall.

The women adjusted hats, tweaked their sleeves, and departed in the direction of the photographer's voice. Flo sat down and examined Tony's half-full cup of tea and the leftover crumbles of a sausage roll. "Someone was here before me? Am I your second meeting of the day? Goodness, you start early."

"It never stops," said Inez. "I have yet another appointment after this one, so I'll try to be brief. I hope you got my message last night. We are set for Thursday evening, the Tontine, nine o'clock. Will this work for all the parties involved?"

Flo waved an airy hand. Her silver bracelets chimed. "Mrs. Stannert, please, do *not* worry. I received your message and have alerted all the players. Well, the ones who were to be alerted, that is."

"Is there any possibility that at the last minute—?"

She sighed. "Honestly, you are as nervous as some sweet young thing preparing to turn out in the sisterhood. Trust me, I have my hands on the reins and all will be well. Of course, there's always a chance something unexpected will happen. People get sick, the weather turns, the restaurant burns down." She scrunched her face, then allowed it to relax, leaving not even a small crease at the corners of her baby-blue eyes. "But there are always alternatives. Bribing a judge. A little poison in the stew—"

"The judge is unbribable and I'm not turning to poison," said Inez.

Flo patted her springy blonde curls. "Well then, we'll just have to think of something else if it comes to that, won't we?"

It was Inez's day to cover the bar, so after her conversation with Flo, she hurried back to her station, trusting Tony was safely tucked out of sight for the day. Still, she couldn't focus. Wheels upon wheels whirred, everything was in motion, and all she could do was stand back and watch.

Halfway through the afternoon, Abe came in to work. "Ain't nothin' I can do at home," he informed Sol and Inez. "Miz Buford practically pushed me out the door and told me to stop actin' like an old woman, and go to work and support my family like a man. Don't know why I let her talk to me that way," he grumbled.

"And little Hazel?" she ventured to ask.

"As pretty as a new-made day," was the response. "She takes after her mother, no question."

Inez ventured, "But her eyes..."

"Miz Buford, she says sometimes eyes darken up. Angel, I can tell she's a mite upset, worried of what folks'll say and what the future might hold for Hazel and all. I figure it'll work out, and time will tell. Speakin' of time," he checked the ice box and turned to Inez, "I hear tell you gave Mark his walkin' papers and not much time for him to do his usual two-step waltz to change your mind."

She looked down at the clean apron she had put on less than an hour ago. It already had a spot. She smoothed her hand over the stain, as if she could magically make it disappear. "I have."

"So, this ain't no long con? Not just a way of makin' him come crawling to you on his knees over broken glass while offering a thousand apologies for all the bad things he's done over the years?"

"No. It's not a ploy."

Abe nodded once. "Well, then. Just know I don't be takin' sides in this fight and I'll be tellin' Mark the same. But that don't mean I don't care. I plan on bein' civil and a friend to you both. I can't just cut off this leg or that, and still be walkin'. So, no matter how it all comes down, you can count on me to be there for you, when you're in need. Me'n Angel both." He added, "I will say this, Angel sees a lot more in you than she does in Mark, and she don't mind sayin' so, loud and long."

Inez had to smile at the thought of mostly silent, low-voiced Angel saying anything "loud and long."

"But then, you and Angel been through a lot together," he continued. "Kinda like Mark and me, at the end of the War and after, afore you came along and shook things up." He leaned against the backbar. "You still plannin' on stayin' a partner in the Silver Queen?"

Inez moved to stand beside Abe and let her gaze sweep the saloon—its plank floors, the paintings on the walls, the slightly moth-eaten buffalo head mounted above the State Street door, the always slightly-out-of-tune upright tucked at the bottom of the stairs, the faces new and familiar at the tables and the bar. She said, "How could I not? The Silver Queen is as much a part of me as the air I breathe."

Abe nodded. "Good. That's what I wanted to hear."

As Inez expected, the four Lads from London, who seemed universally despondent at the loss of their fifth, came in later that day, commandeered a table, and commenced drinking. Inez offered her sympathies and worked around to solicitously inquiring whether they had any funds for their extended stay in town. Quick looked as if he might burst into tears. "Poor Percy, he was paying for our lodgings and expenses, in celebration of his, you know, newly inherited wealth and later to mark his entrance into the mining industry." All this came out a great deal slurred, which led Inez to believe this wasn't their first stop of the day. "Surely, Mrs. Stannert, you can tide us over until next month's remittances come in?"

Inez decided the loss of income was preferable to having to toss them out into the street. "Don't worry about it," she assured them, and rather than pour them the next round of drinks, simply left the bottle on the table for them. "On the house, in honor of Lord Percy's memory," she said. They raised their glasses in unison and drank. "Do you still have lodgings?" she asked.

Tipton nodded. "Tabor, fine chap that he is, offered us rooms *gratis* at his hotel until we're released by the marshal."

"Good thing or we'd be sleeping in the gutters," said Epperley sourly, adding, "I don't know why we have to linger. They know who did it. It was that *boy*." He said it was a nasty snarl. "Why don't they just smoke him out? It's an all-around muddle, is what it is."

"Now now," said Tipton. "The family said mercy is better than justice. They just want dear old Percy home so he can be buried in the family plot in native soil. They always thought he was barmy for coming to the colonies, you know. They fully expected him to have a sorry end. Well, all our families think that of us, right?" Glum nods all around. Tipton continued, "We need to stick around to make sure his mortal remains are sent properly on and without delay."

As the evening progressed, Inez kept an eye on her lapel watch. Finally, she turned to Abe and Sol. "I'm going out for a bit," she told them. "I'll be back within half an hour." She exchanged her apron for her winter cloak, a shawl, and a thick muffler and walked down Third, heading toward the mountains and stopping well short of the train tracks. She pulled the cloak and shawl tighter, closing out the wind, and waited. It wasn't long before she heard the whistle and saw the light of the train. Inez watched it approach, feeling the thunder under the soles of her shoes, the rush as it passed. The cinders flew, painting the dark sky with streaks of light. She watched the train recede, carrying Reverend Justice B. Sands away from Leadville.

She didn't need to see any more than that. They had already said their good-byes. Their lives, close for too short a while, were now like two trains departing from the same station, but traveling in different directions, the distance between them growing. Inez hoped their intentions held fast, through all that was to come, and that the necessary distance between them would eventually disappear. Wrapping the night around her shoulders, she turned and walked back toward town and the Silver Queen, feeling his presence as clearly as if he kept pace beside her.

Chapter Thirty-five

Wednesday started early and passed quickly. It was Mark's day to tend the saloon, so Inez planned for an early breakfast and a full day. Breakfast in the kitchen had a rocky start. Bridgette, who had apparently worked up her courage to talk to Inez about the impending divorce suit, had burst out, "But ma'am! Why would you and the mister—?"

One look from Inez stopped her right there.

After an uncomfortable silence, which Inez refused to break, Bridgette finally said, "Well then, will it be ham or bacon with your eggs this morning? And perhaps some cheese atop your sunny-side up?"

After breakfast, she spent a fair space of time in the saloon's office, pulling together certain papers she wanted to be sure she had at the ready to show her lawyer and Mark, when the time was right. She signed for and added three telegrams which arrived from back East and kept her mind studiously turned away from Frisco Flo and all that was going to unwind on Thursday.

Finally, when she couldn't stand being inside any longer and Mark's voice downstairs heralded his arrival for the day, she went into her rooms and changed for riding into her discreet tailor-made split riding skirt. Inez passed through the saloon with a cool nod and continued on to the stables where she kept her horse, Lucy.

"Here comes Isabella Bird," said the livery owner good-naturedly. "Haven't seen you in a coon's age, Mrs. Stannert.

Your girl here has missed ya." He saddled up the black horse and handed her off to Inez. Lucy was jumpy, shying at the crack of whips directed from drivers of wagons and carriages at their teams.

"I'm sorry, girl," Inez said, one hand tight on the reins, the other smoothing the coal-black neck. "I've neglected you sorely. I shall be sure I leave you in hands better than mine and hopefully more attentive to your needs."

She directed her equine companion to The Boulevard, the wide and smooth road leading down Third Street, across the railroad tracks, and onward to Soda Springs. Once they were out of town, traffic thinned to near nothing, and Inez let Lucy have her head. She cantered, then galloped a stretch, Inez reveling in the rush of air, the cold stinging her cheeks and making her ears and nose burn. Lucy's rhythmic chuffing sounded in time to the pounding of her hoofs on the macadam and Inez relaxed into the motion, momentarily letting go of all her worries and concerns. After a while, they pulled up, Inez turned Lucy, and they headed back to town at a trot and finally, at a walk.

It was nearing time for the final act. Inez could only hope for a future in which she and Tony were clear of their troubles and the victims received justice.

"Here we are," Mark said to Inez. "Thursday evening, nine o' clock, the Tontine, the two of us, just as planned." He stopped her at the door to the Tontine Restaurant on Chestnut Street and offered her his arm, saying, "For appearances' sake, darlin'?"

Inez had noticed "darlin'" creeping back with some regularity as the day had advanced toward the supper hour. However, she simply replied, "For appearances' sake, Mr. Stannert," and took his arm.

He smiled at her and pushed the door open so they could enter together.

It was the busy hour of the evening for Leadville society. The fashionable restaurant was filled with many familiar faces, including County Court Judge A. K. Updegraf and his wife, who were supping with church board member Mr. Johnson and his missus.

Johnson saw them first, and he paused, soup spoon hovering at chin level, horrified eyes pinned on Inez, his sallow complexion building toward a flush. His supper companions stopped chatting and turned to see who had entered, for indeed the conversation level throughout the room had dropped precipitously.

The headwaiter took Mark and Inez past the judge, who nodded to them both. Mark tipped his hat, full of gentlemanly bonhomie. No one watching would guess he was slated to appear a few days hence before the judge and stand as defense to a suit brought by the woman at his side. Updegraf returned his gesture with a courteous smile, but Inez noted his eyes narrow as he regarded them both.

The Stannerts continued to their table. Mark held out the chair for Inez, adding, "I made inquiries earlier about the menu tonight." He rounded the table and sat, smoothing one end of his meticulously waxed mustache. "And if my choices meet with your approval, we need not worry about being interrupted by waiters nor wine stewards."

Now, sitting across from him, she could see Mark had prepared himself with special care for their dinner together. His trousers and frock coat were a restrained black, well-tailored and of expensive wool, and freshly pressed. The broad-brimmed black hat had been brushed with similar care. Inez suspected he had even taken a side trip to the barber earlier that day. His thick, light brown hair, gleaming with macassar oil, looked recently cut, and his fingernails, when he removed his gloves, were squared off and buffed.

Handsome is as handsome does, Inez reminded herself, spreading the heavy linen napkin across her lap. Right now, the word "handsome" just about summed him up, although a few other descriptors vied for consideration, such as serious, successful, wealthy, honest as the day is long, and sober as a judge.

Inez folded her hands upon the spotless white tablecloth, assuming an attentive pose. "And what choices have you made, Mr. Stannert?"

"We'd start with soup, fresh oysters in chicken broth."

She nodded.

"Then, baked trout, turkey and quail pie, prairie chicken on toast, green peas. Potatoes, lobster salad, nuts, coffee, and pound cake." He shifted in his chair. "If you'll trust my judgment on the wine?"

"Certainly."

He seemed surprised at her compliance but didn't question it. Mark looked at the waiter, hovering at an unobtrusive distance, and nodded.

Mark leaned back in his chair, his gaze roving over the room. It was only through the faintest of tells—the smoothing of the mustache, a slight twitch of the free hand on the table as if he was refraining from drumming his fingers on the damask table-cloth—that Inez could discern his tension. She kept her hands clasped, her expression composed, doing her best to offer no hint of the turmoil playing havoc with her stomach.

"Busy for a Thursday night," he said. "Even the good judge and his wife are here."

"I saw," said Inez. The soup bowls appeared, redolent of the salty scent of chicken and steamed oysters. She viewed the oysters, half-submerged, determining which one would be the first.

"I have been thinking about Lord Percy," she said, picking up her spoon. "Poor fellow. I do believe he honestly thought his little rabbit's foot, knocking on wood, avoiding ladders and so on would bring him good fortune. Alas, no sooner did Lady Luck smile upon him then the Devil took it all away." She sighed. "You know, do you not, that the *revolver*," she shot him a look, and he nodded to show he understood, "was found by Percy's body? However, although Percy was shot, I heard a garrote was the ultimate means of his demise."

"I heard as well." He picked up his spoon, then put it down, uncharacteristically restless. "I also heard told he died in the same shack."

"Heard tell from whom?"

"Sol."

Inez chose an oyster, chewed slowly, and swallowed. "Have you talked to the deputy? Do you know what was used to strangle Percy?" She thought of the corset laces around Drina's neck.

Mark shook his head.

Inez added another task to her list.

"Your soup is getting cold," she pointed out.

They ate in silence, the sound of cultured conversation, subdued laughter, and cutlery on fine china washing over them.

He finally put down his spoon, soup only partially consumed. "Inez—"

The waiter glided in, picked up Inez's soup bowl, and turned to Mark. "Don't the soup meet your satisfaction, sir?" He sounded like he was trying for proper, but stumbling a bit in the process.

"It was fine," said Mark.

The soup was whipped away to be replaced by…"Baked mackinaw trout!" announced the waiter proudly, as though he'd caught, gutted, and cooked it himself. Inez made admiring noises about the presentation and the waiter departed, satisfied.

The trout lay on its bed of parsley and lemon, its mouth agape as if astonished to find itself in this predicament. One glazed fisheye glared accusingly up at Inez. She selected her fish knife and fork, and separated the head from the body with an incisive cut. Pinning the trout with the fork as if it might leap, headless, from her plate, she used the sharp knife to slit it from head to tail and opened it up. With the focused delicacy of a surgeon, she nudged the tip of the knife under the backbone, lifting the skeleton with its many small ribs with the fork, and placed it in the bone dish, then removed the skin.

Mark cleared his throat. Inez looked up from her flayed fish.

He leaned forward and Inez sensed he was gathering himself to make his case. "I'm glad we have this time together, Inez. It's been difficult for both of us for a while now to just hold a civil conversation. I hope we can take some time, talk our situation over, clear the air and let everything settle now that—" He stopped short, evidently aware of where his speech was heading.

"Now that." She set the fork on the plate, tines down, and retained the knife. "Now that…what?"

Now that Reverend Sands is gone.

The words hung between them, unsaid.

Mark sidestepped, saying, "Darlin', let's see if we can't talk reasonably. You say I broke our contract. However, it wasn't drawn up until we'd been a while in the Springs. Since we signed, I've been an angel, I swear to the good Lord above, that is the case." She could hear him maneuvering, getting ready to move forward with his argument. "But, in the interest of full disclosure, I will confess to certain behaviors of mine occurrin' before I came down to the Springs to meet you. Try to see it from my point of view, Inez. I came home, after a long time away, to find my wife besotted with a man of the cloth who is a wolf in lamb's clothing."

Her hand tightened on the wicked little fish knife.

He must have seen that, because he added quickly, "Well, let's face it, darlin', you have a soft spot for black sheep. After all, you married me. As for the reverend, I didn't do anything other than voice my concerns, as a member of the congregation. That's all."

"I doubt that was all," said Inez, and began on her trout.

Mark changed direction again. "You have to admit, darlin', while we were in the Springs, it was like old times. The *good* old times."

"Yes," she said quietly. "It was. For a short while."

"It can be that way again. I acted rashly, I know, but I did it because I love you, I didn't want to lose you. I couldn't let you just walk away. I hope you can see my thinking. We can put all that has happened behind us, darlin', and mend whatever's broken between us. You and I, I know we can. Hang the past, what happened while I was gone. We can just work at forgivin' each other and agree to move forward, as if that part of our lives never was."

He was all earnestness. Despite herself, Inez found herself leaning toward him over the table.

A sudden fervor commenced from the front of the restaurant, a rising tide of whispers that grew into a wave of audible murmurs. Inez, sitting with her back to the door, saw Mark's eyes go wide in disbelief. The glibness, the smooth talk, the warm, inviting gaze, the earnestness—it all slid away, vanquished by whatever, or whoever, was approaching.

"Mark Stannert!"

The throaty feminine voice had a commanding timbre which carried to the far corners of the dining room.

The murmurs increased, wreathed in speculation. Inez shifted around so she could see the speaker. A petite woman of impeccable posture, skin all peaches and cream, hair as bright as a new-minted gold piece, was making her way toward their table, her gaze as fixed on Mark Stannert as a sharpshooter's rifle sights on his target. Her furled parasol was a deep, shimmering violet that matched her dress and echoed the color of her eyes.

Even though they had never met, Inez knew without a doubt this must be Josephine Young, whose fame in treading the boards was legion in the West. Inez knew her best as the traveling actress who, according to Mark, had played a leading role in rescuing him, near death, from a savage back-alley beating in Leadville. According to Mark, Josephine had spirited him, unconscious, out of town with her retinue of actors and nursed him back to health from his lingering injuries.

However, it was clear to Inez and anyone else in the dining room with eyes in their head and sense to see, a lot more than just "nursing" had been going on during his lengthy recovery.

Josephine was obviously in a family way.

And, by all appearances, she had been so for some time.

The actress advanced leisurely, seeming completely unabashed about exhibiting her "delicate condition" in such a public venue. Everyone in the dining area watched, rapt, their attention fixed upon her. Everyone, that is, except for Inez, who was watching Judge Updegraf. The judge, after taking Josephine's measure, had turned his gaze on Mark. If that gaze were a knife, Inez thought, Mark would have been as filleted and deboned as the trout upon her own plate.

Mark, who at first had looked as if he wanted nothing more than to hide under the table or dash out the restaurant through the rear door, appeared to have collected his wits at last. "Miss... Miss Young," he stammered. He began to rise from his chair as Josephine came within striking range.

The brass tip of the purple parasol came up, settled on the center of his chest, and guided him back into his seat. She spared Inez one cool glance, a quick sweep that summed her up and dismissed her, all in one. Josephine returned her attention to Mark and said as sweet as a box of chocolate-covered cherry cordials and as loud as if she was saying her lines in the Tabor Opera House, "Mr. Stannert. Now that I've found you at last, you will do right by me and our unborn child. And you will do it as soon as legally possible."

Inez addressed Mark, who for once was speechless, saying, "I find I have lost my appetite for our dinner and for any further conversation with you."

She stood and, holding her handkerchief to her mouth, walked toward the entrance through the gauntlet of diners, frozen at their tables and watching her every move. A waiter hurried to her side, solicitous, offering her his arm as if he was afraid she might faint before she made it to the door. Inez leaned upon that steady support, giving the impression the kindly waiter's arm was the only thing keeping her upright and moving. She kept her eyes cast down, shoulders drooping, the very picture of a wife whose husband's erring ways have left her too shamed and embarrassed to hold her head up in public. Out of the corner of her eyes, she saw Mrs. Updegraf's expression of horror slide into sympathy, and her hand creep over to cover the hand of her husband, the county judge.

Once outside, the waiter seemed unsure what to do. "Madam, do you wish me to call someone for you? A doctor? We have a telephone connection, I know doctors Hewitt and Miller are on the exchange."

"No need," she murmured from behind her handkerchief. "I will walk from here. It is safe enough at this hour. Thank you for your kindness." She started moving up Chestnut, not giving him a chance to protest and act the gallant to a lady in distress.

With her back to him and the mountains, she started toward Harrison, blowing out a hard, deep breath. It had been more difficult than she had thought it would be, this maneuvering and game of chance. Yet, it had played out well. Better than she could have imagined. So why did she feel so empty?

Her head in a muddle, it took a moment for her to hear the faint cries of alarm ahead and to discern the distant, dreaded shout, "Fire!"

She tucked her handkerchief into her sleeve and quickened her pace. At the corner of Harrison, she stopped a harried fellow coming from the direction of the noise and asked what was happening. "It's all done now," he assured her. "A small fire of some sort up on East Third. They put it out fast. Everyone jumped on it, the minute smoke was spotted. Good thing someone sent up the alarm so quickly. I'm off to find a physician. One of the little chaps is having difficulty breathing, because of the smoke, I expect."

"Little chaps?" she asked, her own internal alarms now ringing loudly. "Where was this fire?"

"In a shed behind *The Independent* offices."

Inez didn't stay to hear another word. She raced as fast as her narrow skirts and the uneven Harrison Avenue boardwalks would allow, almost turned her ankle on the corner of Third, and puffed her way uphill, hand to her side to ease the stitch begging her to slow down. A crowd milled around in front of *The Independent* building. Smoke scented the air, thinning, but still enough to clog her throat.

A tiny symphony of coughs sounded by the door, so she set herself in that direction, pushed her way through to the front of the crowd. There was Elliston, all duded up as if he'd been called from the opera house or theater, hovering over five boys who were sitting with backs against the wall. Someone had draped what looked like horse blankets from the nearby livery over their shoulders and across their laps for warmth. She saw Dr. Gregorvich was already present. A bystander held a lantern while the physician had each boy stand up so he could look down each throat and peer into each eye. The doctor completed each examination by listening to each boy's chest and back with a stethoscope. The instrument's tin case lay to one side as Dr. Gregorvich moved methodically from boy to boy, looking and listening.

Elliston was jittering around the newsies like a nervous mother duck, almost quacking. "Are they all right, Doc? Jeez, boys, what were you doing? I've told you, no fires in there."

The one Inez recognized as Ace said, "We didn't, Mr. Elliston, honest! We had one candle in the dirt, and then, all of sudden, all this smoke kinda just poured in."

Dr. Gregorvich took the earpieces from his ears and let the scope hang from his neck. "Some minor coughs and throat irritation, smoke irritation in the eyes. Nothing serious. You are lucky boys. Is this everyone, Mr. Elliston? Is anyone missing?" He addressed Elliston but was looking at the littlest one, whom Inez recalled as Freddy.

Elliston removed his top hat and held the brim while he swept his forehead with a sleeve. "Where's Tony? Tony Deuce?"

Gregorvich's head swiveled to the newspaperman. "Tony Deuce?"

"Yeah. Newsie with the two-color eyes. Hence, Deuce."

"Tony Deuce," said Dr. Gregorvich softly. Then, more briskly, "So, one is unaccounted for? Perhaps we should send someone inside the shed to search."

Half a dozen men headed toward the back of the lot.

"Not supposed to say," whispered Freddy in a voice so soft that Inez, standing just to his side, could hardly hear him. But Ace heard him just fine because he said, "Jeez, Freddy…"

Elliston paused mid-swipe. "Tony's not here? Where is he? I thought he bunked with you guys."

Ace shrugged. "Haven't seen him in a while." He shot a warning look at Freddy, who pulled the horse blanket over his head, disappearing underneath like a turtle.

Elliston turned to Inez. "Say, Mrs. Stannert, I heard Tony got in a spot of trouble at your place last Friday. I didn't know until just this evening. Obviously I need to get out of the office to more social events. You seen him around any?"

Inez sensed the doctor's attention switch from Freddy and the other boys and settle on her. "Can't say that I have," she said, following quickly with, "Perhaps the boys should go to the church mission down on State Street. The mission would provide a bunk and a bite to eat."

Ace looked stubborn. "Bible-thumpers."

"No," Inez assured him. "Just a meal and a warm place for the night."

Elliston nodded. "Mrs. Stannert's right. They'll feed you breakfast too. I'll take you there myself after I get a look at the damage."

"I'll come with you," Inez said, and the two of them worked their way to the back.

The small group of men, who were gathered in a huddle by the front of the shed, broke apart as Jed approached. "You're lucky, Jed," said one. "There's no damage to the interior, none at all. And those boys were right. It wasn't a candle."

Jed sputtered. "Well, something must have caused it to smoke up like that."

"Yep," said another. "Take a look around the backside of the shed. You'll find the fellas from the station takin' a gander at the setup."

"The setup?" said Jed in wonderment.

He and Inez fell in step as they walked the perimeter of the storage shed. "Pays to be only one block away from the central fire station," said Jed dryly as representatives of Harrison Hook and Ladder and Tabor Hose companies left off examining one of Jed's empty ink barrels lying on its side behind the shed. "Hey, Mr. Elliston, c'mere and have a look," one called.

Jed and Inez went over. Inez noticed a small door, standing wide open at the back. "What's that?" she asked.

"I made it for the newsies so they could get in and out at night for, well, the usual necessaries and so on," he said. "Couldn't exactly give them the key to the shack, you know."

As they approached, the familiar scent of coal oil grew stronger. Coughing, Inez pulled out her handkerchief and covered her nose, and even Jed reared back.

"Yeah," said one of the firemen giving the barrel a shove with the toe of his boot. "Stuff it with rags soaked in kerosene, and then all you gotta do is…" He rolled the barrel up to the small door in the wall. "Light 'er up and stand back. The smoke goes into the shed at the back and out pop the newsies from the front, just like smoking a fox out of his hole."

Elliston looked at Inez, dumbfounded. "Someone wanted the newsies out. But why?"

"I think a better question to start with is whom," said Inez shortly. "I suspect it wasn't all the newsies, but a particular one."

She didn't say the name, but from Elliston's grim expression she could tell he was thinking about the same person she was.

Tony.

Chapter Thirty-six

Inez offered to help Jed herd the newsies to the mission down on West State Street. She hoped to talk with him about Tony and, truth be told, was in no rush to return to her four-walled chambers upstairs at the Silver Queen Saloon.

The two of them trailed the boys, keeping an eye out in case one decided to make a break for a hiding hole. However, between the coughing and the plummeting night temperatures, none of them seemed to have the desire to bolt.

"So give. Where's Tony?" said Jed under his breath as he walked beside Inez.

"I can't tell you," she said under her breath back at him.

"Ha! I figured you knew something. You know everything in this town."

"Well, here's a tidbit that has nothing to do with Tony but might make good fodder for your social column. Miss Josephine Young is back in town."

He stopped in his tracks and looked at her across the space of the narrow boardwalk, his eyes wide under the shadow cast by the brim of his opera hat. "Miss Young, the actress?" There was caution in his tone.

"The very one. Mr. Stannert and I were at the Tontine and she waltzed in demanding...well, 'satisfaction' of a sort from Mr. Stannert."

The two of them resumed walking to catch up with the stragglers.

"How'd he take it?"

"I did not stay to find out," she said coolly.

Jed shook his head. "What's that saying about sowing and reaping?" He winced. "Sorry, Mrs. Stannert. I didn't mean to be crude."

"I've heard worse."

"I'll need to be more circumspect if I add it to my society page."

"If you are looking for an urbane equivalent, you could go with Voltaire. *Chacun doit cultiver son jardin.* Each person must cultivate his own garden."

He grunted. "I like that. Might use it. Goes right back to sowing and reaping. So, I guess you aren't the heartbroken wife in this scenario?"

"If you write it up in the papers I most surely am."

They delivered the exhausted newsies to the mission and left them in the motherly care of the night guardian for the women and children's section.

Jed waited until they were walking back up State before asking, "So if I go to the Tontine for a nightcap I'm bound to get an earful? Is that what you're telling me?"

She tilted her head side to side. "Most likely. I would imagine you'd like some independent corroboration if you are going to mention this little episode. Flesh it out with details from the witnesses."

"You don't mind?"

"No."

She sensed him scrutinizing her, but kept her gaze straight ahead.

"You know," he started, "as a newspaperman, I've always got an eye on the upcoming calendar for the courts."

"Mmm-hmmm."

"I saw your suit for divorce is scheduled for this coming Monday."

"Mmm-hmmm."

"The timing of Miss Young's return is kinda fortuitous."

"It does look that way."

A long pause. Until…"*The Independent* is a progressive paper," said Jed thoughtfully. "A strong supporter of women's property rights in marriage and divorce and all."

Inez raised her eyebrows. "Since when?"

"Since, oh, lessee, when did I get a gander of the court calendar, about nine o'clock this morning."

She half-smiled. "As a shocked and shaken wife, I do believe I shall have to retire early tonight. Such a mental trauma at the Tontine. I shall have to partake of a hot toddy or two before I can sleep, I'm certain. But don't print that last part."

She turned to Elliston. "About Tony," she said more seriously. "There's no time tonight to explain everything, but Tony must take care and stay out of sight until the air clears. Somehow, his pistol ended up being used to shoot Lord Percy. You know about that row between Tony and Percy at the saloon last Friday. All in all, it does not look good. Tony didn't have the pistol at the time of Percy's death, so someone else used it on the poor fellow and left it there. If I were the skeptical type, I'd say they did it deliberately to cast suspicions upon your little newsie."

Elliston whistled softly. "I heard about a nob who died in Stillborn Alley. So that was Lord Percy? The fellow who lost big at your game on Saturday?"

"It was."

"Why hasn't there been more out and about all this? You'd think the law would be up in arms. 'British citizens not safe in the streets, we must find the perpetrators of this heinous crime and make an example of them,' and so on. Come to think about it, I haven't seen a peep about it in the papers either."

"I gather the family doesn't want a fuss. They just want him brought back as soon as possible." She sighed. "But it does put Tony in a tenuous position. So, while you're out at the Tontine and theater tonight, or wherever you intend to go, keep your ears open not only for your society column but for anything that could help Tony's case."

◇◇◇

Perhaps it was the hot toddies imbibed before retiring, her talk with Jed, or having Thursday "done and gone," but Inez slept well for the first time since returning to Leadville. After her morning ablutions, she dressed conservatively, popped downstairs to gather toast and coffee, and promptly carried them back upstairs, pursued by Bridgette's solicitous queries as to her state of mind after the events at the Tontine. *Salacious news travels fast,* thought Inez as she escaped with her slightly burnt toast and very strong coffee. Bridgette had tried to be circumspect, but finally just put the toast fork down on the iron range with a loud clang, exclaiming "I *never* thought that the mister…that is, I never thought he would be the kind…She must have used her worldly wiles on him, ma'am, otherwise he'd *never…*"

Inez did not envy Josephine's future relationship with the saloon's cook. *Well, who knows? She will soon have a child and Bridgette could never turn her heart away from a baby. They might eventually come to terms.* At the thought of Mark and Josephine's unborn child, Inez braced her arms on the blotter of the rolltop desk, shut her eyes, and allowed pent-up pain to rip through her. Thoughts of her and Mark's son, William, crowded in and threatened to tear her apart further. Josephine's condition was a development Inez had not foreseen. She had to remind herself, sternly, that it all worked to her advantage. In his own way, Mark was honorable. He would not abandon Josephine in her condition. Thus, circumstances had aligned with the end results Inez was driving toward: she wanted a divorce and a stable, secure future for her small son. Josephine wanted a marriage and a father for her child. As for Mark, it hardly mattered what he wanted at this point.

She sat at the desk and stared out the picture window. The view embraced State Street and the high peaks, bright with morning sun, dressed in virginal white of the recent snows. *I'll miss the mountains. I'll miss the town. But, there is more to the world than this. And I can always return. Someday.*

She opened the safe, pulled a bottle of bourbon that was buried in the back, and added a dollop to the coffee. With a sigh, she pulled out the stack of receipts that the drummer Woods had left with her a single week ago. *Only a week?* His words floated back to her, as plain as if he was in the room: "I note the buyer's last name and the merchandise bought. That way, when I return, I can inquire of Mr. Smith if Mrs. Smith liked the black silk stockings previously purchased. It also helps me determine what stock to bring for the next trip."

No more trips for him.

Inez paged quickly as she ate her singed, well-buttered toast and drank her fortified coffee. She recognized names here and there, some scribbled in a sort of shorthand. The types of merchandise were also recorded in abbreviated form. Still, it wasn't a complicated system. She deduced that *ss* must be silk stockings, *cs* cotton stockings, *ws* wool stockings. Corsets were *cors*. Laces had to be *ls*. Other letters eluded her until she found a receipt he'd created for the laces he'd given her gratis. The form read: *Mrs. Stnrt—s/g ls*. The *s/g* must be silver/gold, while *bl* was black, *br* was brown, *r* was red, *wh* white, and so on. Corsets had complicated notations, probably to do with sizing, colors, construction and so on, but she ignored that.

She was only interested in the laces.

The grandfather clock ticked loudly in the corner of the office breaking her concentration. She looked up.

It was time.

Inez returned the receipts to the safe, gathered the papers she planned to show her lawyer, chose a reticule large enough to hold them, then checked and pocketed her little pistol, preparing to "walk the gauntlet" through the saloon.

It all proved a little anticlimactic, however. Downstairs, Mark was already behind the bar, arms crossed, talking in a low voice to Abe. Abe faced him, mirroring his crossed-arm stance. They could have been matching pieces in a chess game, facing each other across the board: one dark, the other light. Mark swiveled toward her, his expression tense and drawn. Inez detected circles under his eyes and surmised that Josephine must have given him holy hell in public and private the previous night.

Mark said nothing to her, so she responded in kind.

Instead, she addressed Abe. "I'll be back later to help tend bar so Mr. Stannert can prepare for his game tonight."

She swept out, her cloak held tight against the cold.

First stop: her lawyer.

He was expecting her and had the door open almost before she knocked. In his office, she pulled out the papers, spread them before him, and explained her intentions. He listened carefully, without interrupting, then examined the papers closely, which took some time. He finally said, "Medical testaments from New York physicians, another from the Colorado Springs physician, and you say you will have another statement from Doctor Cramer as well? Although, it may be better if we can have Doc attend the session in person and give his testimony and opinion before the judge himself."

"Whatever you think best, Mr. Casey."

He straightened the stack, bringing the slapdash pile into order. "And letters from your brother-in-law, and your father, that is, your son's grandfather. Quite compelling, given how the world works. I didn't realize you were the daughter of Thomas Underwood, of Underwood Iron and Steel in New York. That name carries weight, even out here in the West."

Inez smiled tightly. "It is not a relationship I've cared to exploit, and would not have done so now, but since it could be an element in convincing the judge that legal guardianship of our son would be best bestowed upon my sister and her husband..."

"Just so. All in all, it is a persuasive argument for legal guardianship. However—and this is key, for the state takes the rights of the parents, particularly the father, very seriously—will Mr. Stannert agree to this arrangement?"

"He will."

They discussed a few more details.

Finally Casey set his pencil down. "Good. You have done all you can, Mrs. Stannert, and although this will not be an easy hearing, if things proceed as expected, we can expect the judge to render as fair and just a verdict as the law allows."

Casey made as if to put the papers in his desk, but she stopped him. "I will need these still. May I bring them to you tomorrow?"

"As long as I have them in hand before Monday," said Casey, returning the papers to her.

After that meeting, tracking down the deputy marshal who was "investigating" Lord Percy's murder was easy. Inez checked his favorite watering hole, but upon learning he was not at Steve's Health Office back of Harrison, she made her way to the marshal's office, where she found him idly working a toothpick on his large, wide-spaced teeth. When she entered the office, he stood quickly, pocketing the toothpick in his waistcoat watch pocket.

"Mr. Percy Brown was a good friend of the family," she explained. "We knew him in the Springs and are quite distraught about his tragic demise."

"Well, you and his friends seem the only ones who give two hoots about the circumstances," he said, offering her a chair and settling in himself.

"I am quite baffled and hope you might clarify," she said. "You indicated he was shot *and* strangled?"

"Yep. Real odd, that." He fished his toothpick out in an absent-minded manner, then most likely realizing that wielding it in the presence of a lady was impolite if not downright rude, he tucked it away again. "That gun is one fancy piece. Mr. Epperley said a newsie was carryin' around that firearm. Awfully fancy for an urchin."

"I agree," said Inez, "But is it true it was *not* the gun that killed him?"

"Right."

"Well, I wondered if I could ask how he was strangled. I have seen the revolver but not the ultimate instrument of his death."

She hoped she didn't come across as particularly ghoulish. Oddly enough, the deputy perked up. "Hey now, I haven't shown this to a female. Didn't want to upset delicate sensibilities, you know. But since you ask, Mrs. Stannert, maybe you have some ideas. It's peculiar all around."

He excused himself, went into a back room, and returned with a small box. He opened it and Inez glimpsed the gun. "Here we go." He pulled out a coiled cord and let it unfurl—corset laces of silver and gold, crusted brown with dried blood. "Poor fella, strangled with a ladies' set of laces."

A cold finger traced down her spine. Except for the blood, the cords were a twin set to those given to her by Woods. What had he said when he gave them to her? "Not my usual stock, only brought two this trip. Sold one, and this is for you."

Of course, that didn't mean similar laces couldn't have been purchased in another time and place, but still…She found her voice and said, "They were found on the deceased?"

He chuckled grimly. "The deceased. Now you're sounding like that undertaker feller. No, actually, we found 'em just inside the door. We're thinkin' whoever did this dropped them on the way out. Must've been in a hurry, I'm guessing, and didn't realize he'd missed tucking them in a pocket."

"Makes sense." Inez could not take her eyes off the gold and silver stays. The deputy was also looking at them with appreciation. "Mighty fancy. Not like something you find at Daniels and Fisher's, eh? Wife's are plain white. Bet she'd love something like this." He stopped and reddened from neck to hairline, as if just realizing what he'd said out loud.

Inez decided it was time to depart. "Thank you, Deputy." She stood. "If I think of anything that can help you, I'll let you know."

He dropped the blood-stained laces back in the box. "Good deal, Mrs. Stannert. Although, as I said, no one seems particularly interested in clearing up what happened here. Maybe because he was a toff in the wrong part of town. But I'd sure like to know, just for peace of mind, if nothing else."

Inez hurried back to the saloon, afire to re-examine the drummer's receipts. Didn't she see one that said *s/g ls*? Well, there was her receipt of course. But there should be another, since he said he'd sold the only other pair. And she hadn't gone through the entire stack, just enough to interpret his notations.

Inez swung open the Harrison Avenue door, intent upon the upcoming task. Abe and Sol were working the bar, Mark was nowhere in sight. She paused to ask Abe how Angel and Hazel were doing.

"Doin' better than fine," was the answer. He pulled out a brandy snifter without her even asking, and one of the better bottles high on a backbar shelf, adding, "I know for most women, baby arrives in the morning and it's back to washing and cooking in the evening, but I told Angel, she's gotta rest. That's why I decided to keep Mrs. Buford on for a while. What with the hours I work and all, it just makes sense." Along with the brandy, he gave her one of his rare smiles. It vanished when he said, "Mark and Miss Josephine are in the gaming room, just so's you know."

She saluted him with her glass and, cradling it in her hands, slipped upstairs to the office. As she approached the gaming room, she heard an intense, low-pitched discussion going on inside. She couldn't make out the words, not that she tried to. She closed herself in the office, then pulled out the stack of receipts and dove into them again, trying to ignore the rising crescendo of voices from the gaming room, where Mark and Josephine were apparently no longer concerned about whether the tenor of their "discussion" stayed private or not.

Shaking her head, she paged through the receipts, from first to last, without any luck. With a sigh, she started over and went through them again, slower and more carefully. She quickly discovered two receipts stuck together, apparently the victims of a sticky spill. Encouraged, she continued to look for papers that were glued together. The second such pairing yielded a lower page that was undecipherable, the pencil markings blurred and smeared from whatever liquid they'd bathed in. However, with the third such, she hit gold—or perhaps more appropriately, silver and gold. She separated the crackling thin papers with a careful hand, revealing the notation *Alxndr, s/g ls*, and in tiny letters under that: *undertaker*.

A buzz that was almost electric shivered through her body. "Well, well. Mr. Alexander," she said softly. "I didn't think you had it in you."

Strangle Drina? She could see that. Perhaps. If his wife had been circling the vortex of fortunetellers, mediums, and so on, and he became desperate. Too, didn't Tony tell her that Mrs. Alexander had paid Drina a hundred dollars for a reading, or vision, or whatever it was? That was an inordinate amount of money. Mr. Alexander seemed the cautious type, not one to toss his earnings around. But he didn't seem capable of murder either. Inez looked down at the receipt. She couldn't see him as the type to buy such expensive, flashy laces for his wife either. Maybe they had an argument, and these were to be a peace offering? There again, she couldn't imagine him arguing with her. Pleading, yes. But arguing? One never knows what happens behind the closed doors of a marriage, she reminded herself. It was then she noticed that all was silent down the hall, and perhaps had been for some time.

Tonight was the night of the séance. Inez decided she would wait and see. If Mrs. Alexander was still reaching out to "the other world," her husband had obviously not been very effective in getting her to stop. Inez couldn't imagine how she would work corset laces into a polite conversation, but perhaps during the séance, or before or after, she could posit additional queries about Drina and the day Drina died.

Percy, however, was an anomaly.

Inez could think of no connection that the undertaker might have with the Colorado Springs remittance man, nor why he'd wish him harm. Percy liked to dabble in the world of omens and fortunetelling and had apparently gone to see Drina at some point. Could that have led to his death in some way? She recalled what Madam Labasilier had said about the shack, about it being "an evil place." Inez was not superstitious, but some primitive part of her responded and she actually shivered.

So, what now?

She sat, thinking. She could take the receipt to the deputy but only had the now-dead drummer's word that he had brought two sets of silver and gold laces to Leadville. Saying so would only lead the deputy to wonder about the second set. Although Inez couldn't imagine she would be under suspicion, she suspected that bringing her so-called "evidence" to the deputy's attention would just muddy the waters. No, better to wait and see what could be gathered at the séance in the way of further information. *Perhaps Drina and Percy will deign to appear as orbs of light from the great beyond, accuse their killer, and offer up the motive for murder as well. Now that would be a fitting resolution to this unholy mess.*

Chapter Thirty-seven

It was well after sunset on Friday when Tony finally showed up to work at Mr. Alexander's. She had asked him if later would be okay, thinking once the sun went down she'd be more invisible when on the move. He had said that was fine, and then gave her a list of the tasks he wanted her to do. "I will be out," he said, "but Mrs. Alexander will be around if you have any trouble."

The tasks were mostly sweeping, dusting, and cleaning downstairs. "Be careful around the workbench and bottles," he'd admonished. He added she should take special care in polishing the metal case that would transport Mr. Brown's remains back to England.

"Will he be in there when I'm working?" she'd asked, a little nervous at the thought.

Mr. Alexander had misinterpreted her nervousness, though, and had said reassuringly, "Absolutely. I will prepare him Friday and by evening he will be in the case, closed and sealed tight. *Air* tight. She then asked if he maybe would like her to sort through the box of old clothes and fold them so they could go to the poorhouse or the mission.

He nodded. "Good idea, Mr. Donatello. They've been piling up, and I should send them on."

That, at least, lifted her spirits. Now she had permission to be digging through the box looking for anything that had belonged to Maman, just in case anyone wandered in, which didn't seem likely. If the box held anything Maman had been wearing—her layered blouses, her shawl, scarves, sash, stockings, shoes, even her underthings—Tony was sure she'd recognize it. Still, she felt jittery. She could almost hear Maman whisper: *Listen to your voices! They are trying to tell you something.*

Tony figured it was just because she'd be working downstairs with all the stiffs. That reminded her: what had happened to the drummer? Mr. Alexander hadn't said. The drummer disappeared and Pisspot Brown took his place. Maybe he'd been hauled off to the cemetery and dumped in a hole and buried already?

While the sun made its slow journey across the sky on Friday, Tony, swathed in an oversized apron, "hid" in Miss Carothers' workroom sorting plates for Miss Carothers to review later. "Take the ones that look out of focus or too light or too dark, or where the sitter's eyes are closed or they have a strange expression, and put them to one side," she said. "From the remainders, pick the ones you think are best, and put them to the other side. We will look at them together later, and talk about them. This will help develop your 'eye' for a good photograph. Being able to identify good photos from the plates saves one from wasting chemicals and materials on disappointing results."

Mrs. Stannert showed up later in the day, looking nervous too. That made Tony even *more* nervous, because Mrs. Stannert was the last person Tony'd expect to have the jitters. She came into the darkroom and shut the door so it was just the two of them with stacks of glass plates, bottles of stinky chemicals, boxes of photographic paper, and the "burnishing roller machine" that Miss Carothers used to made the prints look all nice and shiny.

"Tony, someone set fire to the storage shed behind *The Independent* last night," she began.

Tony shot up out of her chair, but Mrs. Stannert stopped her. "No one is hurt," she said quickly. "And actually, I misspoke. It was not fire, only smoke, but that was bad enough. It drove all the newsies out of the shed and brought the fire companies on the run."

"But, why?" Tony couldn't figure it. And then she did. "Me??" She stared at Mrs. Stannert. "Someone was looking for me and they did that to my *friends?*"

Mrs. Stannert tucked a strand of dark hair behind her ear. "It seems a likely motivation and did cross my mind."

She looked really tired, Tony thought. Tony felt bad that maybe she was the cause of Mrs. Stannert being so upset.

"In any case," the saloonwoman said, "I wanted to warn you: Don't go back there. I believe, somehow, someone found out that you regularly bunk with the newsies. So, where *did* you spend last night?"

"Here," said Tony, a little abashed. "I just thought after Pisspot, uhhhh, Mr. Brown was found dead, I should keep out of sight."

"Good." She took a breath. Tony noticed her lace collar was a little crooked and she was pulling on the fingertips of one glove, almost like she was thinking of taking it off, but then kept changing her mind. "Are you working at Mr. Alexander's, later?"

Tony nodded. "I have a lot to do, downstairs."

"He will be present, I expect?"

"No, he said he'll be out tonight. He's leaving me to take care of things by myself." It made her feel proud to say that. It meant he trusted her enough to leave her with a list of tasks to do and not hover around, offering tins of polish and pointing out spots she'd missed.

"Well, that's good. When you go, it would be best to stay downstairs. Don't come up to the main floor, if you can avoid it. I'll be attending a séance Mrs. Alexander is holding at midnight, so she may be out and about on the main floor today, since they live just above. Have you seen her yet? During your times there?"

Tony shook her head.

"Well, that's good too. Keep yourself small and unobtrusive. The séance isn't until midnight, so I would guess you will be long done working and back here in the studio by then. I plan to ask questions, look around." She stopped talking and chewed on her bottom lip, as if not sure about something, then looked

Tony right in the eye, like Tony was a grownup and they were having a serious grownup talk. "I am going to tell you something I found out today. I would rather not, but I think you need to know." And she told Tony about the laces—silver and gold, just like the one around Maman's neck—that had been used to kill Mr. Brown. "And Mr. Alexander bought those laces shortly before your mother died," she finished bleakly.

"*What?*" Tony couldn't believe it. "Mr. Alexander? Oh no. He couldn't."

Mrs. Stannert shook her head, obviously dismayed as well. "I thought that too. But, Tony, I've had the…opportunity, shall we say, not just once, but many times to see a side of human nature that most keep hidden. The mildest of people, the ones you least expect, everyone carries a darkness within themselves."

"Everyone? Even Miss Carothers?" Tony felt as if the world was spinning like a top. Was there anyone who was as they seemed? Did everyone wear a mask?

Mrs. Stannert's face relaxed into a smile, and she looked much younger all of a sudden. "Again, I misspoke. I do not believe Miss Carothers has anything but light to offer the world. Come to think on it, my sister is another such, and her husband is a kind soul as well. So, yes, there are good people in the world, and then there are people who are mostly good, who mean well, but struggle, and then there are those who put on a semblance." She stopped and frowned.

She'd finally taken off the glove she'd been fiddling with, and Tony noticed that she was twisting the two rings on her finger: one winked silver, the other gold.

"Never mind," the saloonwoman continued. "I've strayed far from what I came to tell you. I just wanted to warn you about Mr. Alexander and the missus as well. Let's not forget she paid your mother a lot of money to foretell the future. She doesn't seem entirely balanced to me, one foot in the here and now, another in a different realm. I can't help but feel you would be safer staying here."

More than ever, Tony felt she had to look into that box of clothes. "I'll be careful. No one will be around. Nothing's gonna happen. It's just me and the stiffs." She regretted saying that as soon as it was out, but Mrs. Stannert didn't seem taken aback.

"Well then. I can't hogtie and keep you here. All I can say is be careful. And remember what I said about danger. If you think anything is wrong, if you feel in danger, *run.*"

And now, Tony was here, back at Mr. Alexander's, having fooled the little doorbell over the front door into silence once again with her sneaky ways. She tiptoed across the dark, silent front room, through the dark hallway, and started down the stairs. She was nearly at the bottom when she heard something—a rustle—and then saw something—a wavering light. Her first thought: *spirit lights!* But she stopped herself. That's unkum-buncum. There are no spirits. And the dead wouldn't be making that soft little rustling sound. It was probably Mr. Alexander, not left yet.

But just in case, Tony pulled out Maman's little knife with the folded blade and advanced with a light step. The light was wavering around the corner, so Tony stepped out in the room to see.

There was an oil lamp, turned low, and a white shapeless form bent over the box of clothes.

For a vaporous moment, Tony thought it might be a ghost in its shroud, looking for the clothes it left behind. She must've gasped or made some kind of sound, because the white shape whirled around, and Tony saw it was Mrs. Alexander, all dressed in a long white loose-fitting dress. *Too late to run now.*

Mrs. Alexander had the lamp in one hand and the other hand clapped to her throat, looking as guilty and shocked as Tony felt. The missus came forward quickly while Tony stood there, staring, the little folding knife forgotten in her hand. Mrs. Alexander held the lamp high. Tony squinted and looked away...too late.

"You, you're Drina's child!"

Tony heard the whisper and shook her head, but a hand gripped her chin and forced her face up.

"The eyes! The face! Yes! Yes! You are!" Mrs. Alexander didn't seem angry or like she wanted to hurt her. If anything, she seemed happy, triumphant even.

Mrs. Alexander continued, "I saw you, remember? Outside your home? I was leaving." The hand on Tony's jaw squeezed tighter. "Where is she, your mother? Where did she go?"

"She's dead!" Tony burst out.

Mrs. Alexander stepped back. She didn't argue. She didn't demand to know more. All of sudden, she just looked sad and then she said, "Yes, yes. I know that now."

Tony wanted to ask her how she knew, and did she know about Mr. Alexander, but the missus didn't wait, rushing on with, "This is a sign, finding you here, now. You are the boy? The one my husband hired?"

Tony nodded.

"Then, this is meant to be. The spirits wanted me to find you. Your mother guided us, you and I, to this moment, this night." She stared hard at Tony with those nearly colorless eyes. "Your mother. Do you know what happened to her?"

"Someone killed her. Strangled her. Then," Tony could hardly say the rest, "they took her away, like she vanished and never was."

Mrs. Alexander was nodding, nodding slowly. Then, she did something Tony didn't expect. Not in a million years. She took Tony's hand. "We will find out what happened to your mother," she said gently. "And we will find out tonight. This is what we will do…"

Chapter Thirty-eight

Late that night, having finished her shift tending bar, Inez prepared to dress for the séance. Staring into her wardrobe, she was uncertain what to expect with regards to the other attendees. A clutch of women in Reform dress? A sad group of men and women clothed in deepest mourning, still grieving loved ones long gone? Not having any Reform dress options in her wardrobe, she ended up wearing simple black, an accordion-pleated underskirt that allowed easy movement paired with an overskirt notable only for its lack of flounces, shirring, bows, tucks, and folds. Keeping in mind that she would be sitting at a table and there might be fashionable Leadville ladies present, Inez opted for a striking diagonal-closing inverted V-shaped polonaise, hoping the diagonal march of buttons along the front, echoed by similar groupings of buttons along the outside of each sleeve, would at least indicate she was not a fashion outcast. The plain, rounded collar was velvet, providing a little relief from severity. Her sable cloak covered all, night over shadow. Before she left her chambers, she opened the little corner dresser and pulled out the gold and silver corset laces, gleaming like an exotic variety of snake, and dropped them into her pocket beneath her handgun.

As she passed the gaming room, she heard the masculine chatter and commentary indicating a hand in play. Mark sounded as if he had not a care in the world aside from having a good time. *He can just switch it on and off so easily. It does make one wonder where the truth lies with him.*

The scent of expensive cigars and pipe tobacco accompanied her to the head of the stairs, where it dispersed.

Friday night was in full swing in the saloon. She caught Sol's eye, raised a black-gloved hand briefly. He nodded in acknowledgment. She'd told both Sol and Abe where she would be that evening because…*well, one never knows, does one?*

Out the Harrison Avenue door and it was a brisk walk to Alexander's Undertaking, made quicker by her skirts' forgiveness of her long strides. Next to the business entrance with its glass-paned windows, a plain door displayed three brass numbers corresponding to the address on Françoise's calling card. That door, Inez surmised must lead to the Alexanders' second-floor residence.

Estimating the time at about eleven-thirty, half an hour before the séance, Inez gave the brass twist in the center of the panel an experimental half-turn. A bell gave a metallic ring on the other side of the door. She gave the twist an additional revolution, just to be sure the bell was heard, and waited.

Hurried footsteps pattered down the stairs on the other side, and the door was opened by Françoise Alexander, dressed completely in white, with a black cloak and hood over all. Inez's eyebrows shot up, and after a warm greeting passed between the two women, Inez inquired, "Have I inadvertently committed a fashion faux-pas for séances? I have not attended one before. Is white the color to wear?"

"Ah!" Her voice was light as she ushered Inez up the stairs to the second floor. "Is no matter. One wears what one wishes. I wear white, because it brings me close to my daughter, who translated to the Spirit land, now one year past. I wear the cloak because it is so cold on the staircase. You agree? It is warm inside, however." On the landing, she slid the cloak off. Inez saw the sleeves were long and full, the outfit flowing and unusual in style. It reminded Inez of the costumes worn by the aesthetes.

Mrs. Alexander continued, "Spiritualists, we wear white at funerals, for instance, for death is seen as a transforming event. The spirits communicate to us from Summerland. You know Summerland? That is our heaven, where our loved ones live happily, joyously, communicating with us through their knockings and floating orbs, using the medium's voice to deliver words of comfort, the medium's hands to deliver messages of the future."

"Ah," said Inez, who had not expected this sermon, but was grateful for the fashion reassurance. "And who is the medium tonight?"

"I have found a young man, here in Leadville, Mr. Pickering. He requests a slate and pencil, so we will receive written messages tonight." Her smile lit up her pale face. "But first, I have a special guest. We will see if he is a natural conduit. I have hopes. So much has aligned to bring him to me. I think you will be as pleased as I am, but no more. It is a surprise." She opened the door at the top of the stairs, adding, "Among us tonight is a skeptic I hope to convince. But again, we shall see."

At first, Inez only saw a young aesthetically pale man draped over the mantelpiece, who was talking earnestly to two other women dressed, like Françoise, all in white. It was only when a black shadow moved away from the window overlooking the street that Inez realized another gentleman was in the room. Her jaw dropped as he turned and she recognized Dr. Gregorvich.

"Good evening, Mrs. Stannert," he said solemnly.

She snapped her mouth shut and then, as he headed toward her, said, "Pardon me, Doctor. I am just surprised to see you here."

"As I am to see you." He sounded jovial enough.

As Françoise moved off to join the animated grouping by the fireplace, he added, "Our hostess is full of little surprises tonight." He sounded like an indulgent father discussing a small child who was not responding to parental discipline. He added, "Am I correct in my estimation that you, like me, are more of a rational thinker with regards to these spiritualist matters?"

Before she could respond, the young man, who could only have been the aforementioned Mr. Pickering, detached himself from the mantelpiece and came toward them, saying, "As a medium, I must give you fair warning, I am a mesmeric sensitive, susceptive to every dominant influence present here tonight.

If there be a positive mind filled with doubt at our circle, that mind will react upon mine own. If there be a scoffing, jeering presence, it will cut into me like a knife. If someone, *over-clever,*" Pickering drew out the word, "thinks he, or she, has detected or suspected fraud, that suspicion will bite into me and the iron enter my very soul."

"I endeavor to keep an open mind," said Gregorvich, courteous as ever. "I am a devotee who worships at the altar of science and the wonders of the mind. Indeed, there is much we do not understand of the brain and mind's workings. I am fascinated by all the various paths taken in our attempts to further the journey to understanding."

Pickering looked surprised and pleased at that. He turned to Inez. "Madam?"

She thought how this Pickering reminded her in sound, look, and stance of a certain effeminate Mississippi riverboat cardsharp of many years ago, who took her down to her bootlaces in a bloodthirsty game of vingt-et-un, much to her chagrin and Mark's delight.

The memory soured her impression of the medium standing before her. He waited, head thrown back, eyes half-lidded, for her reply.

"I am of the 'wait and see' persuasion."

He smiled, his eyes supercilious. "Then I have no doubt you will finish the evening as a convert, madam."

She smiled back, but not in a friendly way. "We shall see."

"Please, everyone, let's begin," said Françoise.

Inwardly, Inez sighed, disappointed that she didn't have the opportunity to talk privately with Françoise. *I shall endeavor to do so when this charade is over.*

The participants took seats at the round table centered in the room. Inez placed herself in the chair closest to the door leading to the staircase and the exit. Dr. Gregorvich took the seat to her right. The medium sat on the opposite side of the table; Inez wondered if he was trying to distance himself as far as possible from the "rationalist" auras emanating from the two of them.

The two other women in white sat to either side of the medium. Françoise moved about the room, her white skirt hissing softly across the carpet. She lit a single taper and extinguished all the oil lamps. Whether this deliberate interior twilight was by séance custom or medium request, Inez didn't know. The candle was placed in the center of the table. François drew the curtains. Darkness invaded, dimming all except for the meager pool of light contributed by the lone candle. The table still held two empty chairs: one to Inez's left, and the other on the physician's right. The three on the other side of the table removed their gloves and joined hands. After a moment, Inez did the same, taking the physician's proffered hand. He had, she realized, enormously large hands, almost paws. However, he held her hand gently, almost tenderly, as if he realized he had to temper his strength.

"Are we missing one?" inquired Pickering.

"Ah, Mr. Pickering, before we begin, I have another who will be trying to reach someone very close and dear. I believe this other has an innate connection to those beyond, and an inherited power."

"Mrs. Alexander, this is quite unprecedented and upsetting!" he sputtered. "I must be calm and passive to be a fit vehicle for corresponding influences, if I am to be an effective link between the circle and the spirits."

"I'm so sorry, Mr. Pickering." However, she didn't sound sorry at all but rather eager. The physician's hand tightened a little. Inez looked over at Dr. Gregorvich, who was gazing at Françoise. His long face, the lines looking almost like gashes in his skin in the uncertain light, was touched with concern.

"One moment, only," she soothed the prickly Pickering. And she left the room, her white gown floating about her.

A murmur arose on the other side of the table and Inez heard one of the women, who she'd not been introduced to, say, "Most unusual! I hope the spirits are not offended."

The door opened. Françoise entered, guiding a small figure before her.

Tony!

Inez couldn't help it. Her grip tightened on Dr. Gregorvich's fingers. He looked at her curiously.

Tony was looking at Inez with an imploring expression. Two things flashed across Inez's mind simultaneously: Tony was dressed in her boy's "disguise upon disguise" garb, and her unusual eyes were shadowed by the hat brim and leached of color by dimness of light—at least at this distance.

Inez struggled to control her alarm as Françoise guided Tony to the chair on Inez's left. "Hold hands," she said encouragingly. "It helps to focus the energy and call the spirits."

She rounded to the other side of the physician, sat, and took the doctor's hand. Instead of taking the hand of the woman on her right, she said, "Spirit is independent of matter relative to mere existence, yet dependent upon it for its manifestations. To help our little visitor call the one that has so recently left our world for blessed spiritual birth, I have an object, holding the aura of the one who has passed over, which may be used to reach the attention from the other side."

She pulled a length of diaphanous and glinting fabric from some hidden pocket, leaned past the candle, and dropped the material in front of Tony. "Hold it, child. Call your mother."

Tony dropped Inez's hand, grabbed the gleaming puddle of material and clutched it to her chest, then glared at Françoise. "Maman's sash!" Her voice rose, unmistakably feminine. "Where did you get this? Did you kill her?"

Dr. Gregorvich leaned past Inez, addressing Tony. "Antonia Gizzi?"

Tony flinched in her chair and returned his gaze, her vari-colored eyes exposed by candlelight.

He said softly. "It *is* you."

Chapter Thirty-nine

Tony couldn't move, couldn't breathe.

It wasn't supposed to happen this way. When Mrs. Alexander had explained she wanted Tony to be part of her séance, to help find out what happened to Maman, Tony's first impulse was to say no. But then, she remembered Mrs. Stannert had said she would be there.

And, she was curious. She'd do anything to find out more about Maman.

How did Mrs. Alexander think she was going to "call" Maman's spirit to the table?

Mrs. Alexander had assured Tony she would make it right with the mister that Tony didn't do her tasks for the evening. When she promised not breathe a word of Tony being at the séance to her husband, saying, *"Non, non, absolument pas. Je te promets,"* Tony wavered. Then, Mrs. Alexander asked when was the last time Tony had eaten.

The missus had taken her up to the second story, sat her in a little parlor, cozy with a popping stove, left her with lots of chicken baked with mushrooms, bread rolls not hard as rocks but soft and fresh, and a pot of tea with a little plate heaped with sugar lumps so she could add as many as she wanted. So, Tony sat in the dimness, not completely dark, because there was a window and a teeny slice of moon, and ate, and waited.

She heard people coming, arriving, but couldn't tell the voices apart. Then, things got quiet. The door opened, and Mrs.

Alexander came in. She held a finger to her lips and said softly, "I told no one who you are. We will see what happens."

"But, I, I don't know what to do," she stammered.

"You join the circle with us." She took Tony's hand in one of her soft ones. "Your Maman comes to you or not. But I think she will, if you open yourself to the spirit world."

"Open?" That sounded a little scary. "How am I supposed to do that?"

"I will give you a—how to say?—a 'key' to open the door, when we are in the circle."

When she came into the room, it was pretty dark. Everyone was dressed in black or white. She saw Mrs. Stannert, staring at her. Next to her was a tall man. Dr. G. *Why is he here?*

Tony felt sick. She wasn't sure the chicken was going to stay down. The room was creepy. Everything felt "wrong."

Then, Mrs. Alexander sat her down. Mrs. Stannert grabbed Tony's hand, and that helped, but only for a moment, because then Mrs. Alexander put Maman's sash in front of her, and Tony just had to grab it, hold it tight, and then Dr. Gregorvich called her by her real name and—

The table bucked violently, flying away from Tony, up and over in the air, smashing down onto Dr. G.

The candle flew off the table, rolled onto the carpet, and went out, plunging the room into darkness.

Hands grabbed her and slithered off.

Then…

Maman screamed.

Her voice filled Tony's head: *Run!*

Chapter Forty

Chaos. Pitch dark.

Screaming.

Françoise cried out something unintelligible in French.

Pain raged through Inez's right knee and the toes of her right foot where her vicious and desperate kick had connected with the underside of the table, which, thank goodness, wasn't of solid mahogany or walnut but something lighter. It felt as if she'd nearly bitten her tongue off when, after shouting at Tony to run, she'd thrown herself atop the overturned table. Her hope was to trap Dr. Gregorvich underneath, pinning him down long enough for Tony to escape.

She clung to the table legs to either side as the table jumped and rocked beneath her, like a horse intent on throwing a rider from its back. Under all the exclamations, the thumping and bumping as, she supposed, those not trapped tried to reach the window to pull back the curtain, she heard the quick flutter of footsteps racing down the stairs.

Good! She's running!

Inez's relief was short-lived as with a loud oath and roar from beneath, Dr. Gregorvich heaved the table up and off. The end of the table swung up, pivoting on its thick rim. Inez braced to keep it on end and from crashing back all four legs. In the process, she slid down the underside and onto the floor. The table wobbled, then balanced on its thick rim, rolling slightly.

She tried to get her feet underneath her to stand—the rug was all rucked up—then someone's flailing foot smacked her hard in the back.

"*Son esprit est ici!* Drina, Drina, we want to help you! Who did this to you? Who took your life?" cried Françoise on the other side of the wall formed by the tabletop.

Someone pulled the curtain partway back just in time for Inez to see Dr. Gregorvich rise from behind the barrier like one of the undead from the grave. Inez huddled in the deep shadow on the other side.

"You absurd, brainless, *asinine* woman!" the physician roared. "That was no spirit! The child has gone! I must find her. Where would she go? Where would she run? And *who*," he thundered, "had the brilliance to scream *run?* When I find out who that was…"

Inez fumbled at her skirts and cursed silently. Her pocket revolver was in her cloak, hanging on the landing of the staircase that led down and out.

Françoise was still crying somewhere behind the table. Inez could see the medium standing by the partially drawn curtain, off to the side. He was frozen in place, staring at the physician and most likely Françoise on the floor on the other side of the table from Inez.

Dr. Gregorvich's head disappeared from Inez's sight as he bent down behind the table, apparently pulling the weeping woman upright. Both of their profiles reappeared above the rim, above Inez's head. "Where would she go?" he roared at her. Inez saw Mrs. Alexander's head wobble back and forth, and she imagined Dr. Gregorvich was shaking her by the arm. "If you do not tell me," his voice lowered, "I shall go to the law." Inez suspected his words were not audible to anyone besides Françoise, to whom his speech was directed, and Inez, who crouched unseen on the other side of the table. "I shall tell them what I know about your husband. How he was the instrument of death for not just this *seer* of yours but for the young Englishman as well. He bought the laces used as a garrote. I was a witness to the purchase. The law has those laces as evidence, and they will tie him to the murders as surely as I stand here. No one would suspect me of such doings. Your husband will bear the burden and the consequence. So, you silly woman, tell me, and tell me now! Where has the girl gone?"

"She, she, goes to find her mother," gabbled Françoise. "To the cemetery?"

Inez put her forearms on the underside of the table, intending to push the table over and trap them again if she could.

The physician beat her to it, giving the table rim high above her head a shove. Inez curled into a ball as the table crashed over the top of her and onto its four legs, hiding her from sight.

"The cemetery," he muttered. Inez saw his legs move past her at a rapid gait. Moments later, footsteps pounded down the stairs.

Inez crawled out from under the table as soon as he left the room. She had a momentary flash of Mrs. Alexander, all in white, swaying dangerously with her hand to her breast, whispering, "*Une fille.* No. No."

Inez grabbed her cloak, the weight of the revolver steady against her side, and flew down the stairs and out into the street as fast as her throbbing knee and foot would allow. She looked up Harrison, toward the cemetery. A few late-night strollers were about, but Dr. Gregorvich's distinctive tall figure was not among them. The cemetery was up and over Capitol Hill, west of town. Tony, running fast, might be there by now. The physician, with his long stride, would close the distance in short order. Inez, with her burning knee and foot…

"Damnation!" she yelled in frustration. Two gentlemen passing on the other side of the street halted and looked her way. She stopped, feeling ridiculous, as if she were channeling Percy or one of the other Lads with her outburst. An equine snort erupted behind her. She spun to see a fine piebald horse tied to the hitching post in front of Alexander's Undertaking. No doubt Mr. Pickering's, she thought, who probably envisioned himself as a dashing prognosticator when he rode the noble steed through the streets of Leadville with his hair whipping in the wind. No matter. The piebald was saddled, and ready to go. Inez needed no further signs from the spirit world as to what to do.

She freed the reins from the post and hitched up her skirts, which thankfully weren't of the form-fitting variety, to an indecent height that would have been cause for arrest if any had seen it. Putting her good foot in the stirrup, she heaved herself astride into the saddle and tucked her cloak around her exposed limbs. The piebald didn't seem to mind a new rider and promptly pointed his nose downtown. "Not that way," she said, turning him around. "We're off to the cemetery, on the double."

She took him from a walk to a trot, heading to Poplar. Inez hoped to arrive on Twelfth by a parallel route so as to not run into Dr. Gregorvich first. Although, she was sorely tempted to simply chase him down on the horse, trample him, and be done with it.

Which brought up a troubling question.

What weapons did the physician have about him? Did he carry a sidearm? Inez could not recall. He didn't seem the kind to be bristling with hidden hardware, knives up his sleeves or derringers in his pockets. He was an imposing presence, tall and strong, so perhaps counted on that for intimidation and as weapon enough. Anyhow, she hoped to not have to face him. It would be best to reach the cemetery before he did, find Tony, and haul her out of there.

The time had arrived, Inez decided, to go to the deputy marshal with what she knew, but she needed Tony, and Mrs. Alexander as well. Would the woman agree? Be willing to step forward, if it meant damning her husband?

The road steepened. Inez scanned the empty street on the lookout for a small figure or a tall one, as she reflected further. She didn't see Mr. Alexander as the one to tighten the cord around Drina and Percy's necks. No. That had to be Gregorvich. He had the strength, the hands, the ability to overwhelm them entirely and kill them quickly. He had the nerve, she knew. And he knew about the laces. He knew they were in the hands of the law. He knew too much, and he'd tipped his hand when he spoke to Françoise.

She pulled up to the gates of the cemetery and looked around. It was quiet as, well, the grave. The new-built Union Veterans Hospital, just east of the cemetery, sat dark. No one was in sight, either coming down Twelfth or within the cemetery. The cemetery was dotted with headstones, larger monuments, even a crypt or two, and included a copse or two of trees that had somehow escaped being reduced to firewood.

She led the horse behind the hospital. "This is where I leave you for now," she said, tying the reins to a stunted pine that couldn't decide whether it was a tree or a bush. "The ground isn't safe for you to travel over, and we will be much too obvious."

The horse didn't seem to mind, shifting his weight and settling down to a quiet exploration of the withered grasses clustered about the pine.

Inez pulled her revolver out, wishing she had something with greater range and firepower, and stepped forward, knee protesting, toward the cemetery grounds.

Chapter Forty-one

It seemed like she'd been wandering forever around the graveyard, Maman's sash clasped in her folded arms.

"Where are you?" Tony whispered. "Maman, tell me! Tell
me where! Please!" The tears cooled on her cheeks, stinging
and chilling.

There was no reply.

There'd been nothing after that command to *run!* at the
séance, when Maman had made the table fly and the room go
dark. Now, Tony felt alone. Really alone.

The only whispers she heard were from the wind, coming off
the mountains and making shushing noises around the graves.
The little bit of moon danced among the clouds. It was hard to
see the potholes and dips and divots among the graves.

And there were so many graves. So many. Hundreds and
hundreds.

Some had stone markers with names and dates carved in
them, many more had wood boards jabbed into the dirt. There
were a few white-railed enclosures, and fewer still large stone
monuments.

Venturing out farther away from the gates and all the markers, she came to the area where there were no markers at all.
Nothing but corpse-sized heaps of earth. The paupers' field. Just
rows and rows of mounds, they rose and sank, up and down,
like a frozen sea of earth.

There was nothing inside her—no words, no whispers, no visions or voices that rose to guide her through that sea.

Cold, empty, sad, Tony wandered back to the part of the cemetery where the dead had names. She ended up by one of the bigger monuments, topped with a statue of an angel baby, looking over one shoulder at its tiny wing, looking as sad as Tony felt. She buried her face in the gold-threaded fabric her mother had loved to wear. Closing her eyes, she put her forehead against the stone stamped with the name and date of someone loved and mourned, and let the icy cold seep through her...

Someone grabbed her, yanked her away, and clamped an arm around her chest.

She shrieked and struggled.

A gun fired, close, loud.

Stone chips showered down on her.

"Doctor Gregorvich!" It was Mrs. Stannert's voice, strong, determined. "Let her go! Next time, I won't miss!"

Tony was hauled up and yanked around, her attacker holding her back up against his chest. Something sharp as a needle pricked her neck and she stopped struggling, afraid to breathe.

Mrs. Stannert stood a good ten feet away, the hood of her cloak blown back from her head. The moon came out for a wink of a moment, showing her face shining almost as white as the stone markers around her, with her dark hair blowing around her face. She looked grim, dangerous, wrathful, like an avenging angel who had come to rescue Tony and the little stone baby angel that looked down at all of them. Mrs. Stannert had one bare hand braced on the top of a headstone. The other held a gun pointed straight and steady at her. No, not at her, but at the doctor who was squeezing the breath out of her.

Dr. Gregorvich's voice, calm, spoke loud in her right ear, ticklish. "It doesn't matter if you miss or hit, because if you pull the trigger, this girl dies. That's not what you want, is it, Mrs. Stannert?"

Tony knew now what was going on. Dr. G. had his back against the stone tomb and was crouched low, because he was tall and Tony small, trying to hide behind her. One of his arms was wrapped around her chest and over Maman's sash. Out of the corner of her eye, she could see that one end of the gold fabric had escaped and was rippling in the gusty wind, as if waving and signaling for help. She could hear and feel Dr. G's unsteady breathing in her ear and against her back, as if he'd run a long way. She blinked hard, trying to rid her eyes of the stone dust. She wiggled her fingers, realizing that her hands were free. He held her high up, near her shoulders. She could, maybe, even reach her pocket.

The pocket with Maman's folding knife.

The free end of the sash, so colorless in the small bit of moonlight that it looked silver, not gold, curled and flapped, as if in agreement.

Tony inched her right hand over and up a bit, slowly, slowly moving it, inch by inch toward the pocket obscured under the rippling sash.

Inez knew Dr. Gregorvich was right.

There was no way she could kill him, even if she had a clear shot, before he plunged his knife into Tony's neck. She needed him to move, to come out a little farther....

"Let's be rational about this," he said in a reasonable tone.

"This does not seem to be a rational situation by any definition of the word," she responded. She tried to keep her eyes on his hands, the deadly knife, the thinnest slice of his face, not much more than the slice of the moon above, a few days from its full dark.

"Well, then, we need to decide how to resolve this most unfortunate confluence of events," he said. "I am thinking, we can stand here and talk until sunup, but I suspect, given the chill of the wind, you will start shivering and your arm will get tired. I can simply outwait you."

"And do what?" she rejoined. "What is this about anyway? You killed this girl's mother, and you killed my colleague, Percy Brown. That does not seem like the actions of a rational man."

"Oh, but they are." He seemed lighthearted, jolly. "That poor Englishman had bled out almost entirely. By putting him out of his misery I acted out of mercy. It was quick, painless, he felt nothing, I'm certain. And I put him to good use. Most specimens I obtain are diseased, old, not good subjects for my studies. To find one in the prime of life, healthy, with no syphilitic brain lesions, is as good as gold. Both he and Mrs. Gizzi, they gave their all for the future. If you want to accuse anyone, I suppose we must lay the blame for this at the feet of Mrs. Alexander."

"What?" Inez would have shaken her head, but she didn't want to lose a chance to shoot him by moving her head an inch. All she needed was for him to move his face out a little more from behind Tony.

If she could just see his eyes. Even one eye. "That's absurd."

"No, the absurdity lies in her. Or perhaps, I should say, the delusions do. She has been in the clutches of this notion that it is possible to communicate with those who have died. Total nonsense. Her husband and I, time after time, we drew her away from those who fed her obsession. Then, Drina Gizzi took her fancy. Drina, the fortuneteller who *sees*. As Mrs. Alexander's physician and her husband's colleague, I went to *see* who this charlatan was."

Tony wiggled at that, but froze as the pressure of the knife increased. Inez could see the thinnest line of blood gather and weep beneath the blade.

"Sorry my child, but that is what your mother was," soothed the physician. "So, I went and met her, this fortuneteller. I talked with her. I tried to conduct some unobtrusive experiments. Her eyes, of course, most unusual. I wondered: could this so-called 'sight' have something to do with those eyes? An unusual pathway of optic nerve to the lateral geniculate nucleus, and thence to the cortex? Could the eyes merely be an indication that something more profound was at work in the brain? I became obsessed, I suppose, in my own way. But for completely rational reasons, of course."

"Well, in that case, killing her makes no sense, because no more experiments. You have done in the goose that lays the golden egg," said Inez bluntly.

"Ah well. It was problematic, because Mrs. Alexander was spending exorbitant amounts of money upon this Drina, who in turn refused to talk with me. She told me to go away, that she didn't like the darkness she *saw* inside of me. That *seeing* business again, which was probably just an excuse. I believe she was afraid of me. Maybe she was afraid I would expose her shenanigans." He sounded regretful. "But my aim was always and has always been to find the truth. Are you getting cold, Mrs. Stannert? Your arm shaking? You should have worn gloves," he commented solicitously.

Inez gritted her teeth to keep them from chattering. "So, you killed her because Mrs. Alexander was besotted with Drina's visions?"

"Nooo, not that." He sounded affronted, as if her lack of understanding wounded him deeply. "As far as her husband was concerned, it was all about the money. When she dropped a minor fortune into Drina's lap that was the last straw. I told Mr. Alexander I would retrieve the money and arrange it so Drina no longer provided her prognostications. I looked forward to the opportunity to examine her brain more closely. But he had to help me."

"The laces." She said under her breath.

"Just so. He bought them, a very distinctive pair, and was going to give them to his wife. Instead, he gave them to me, tying him to the deed. Which was only right, as he owed his livelihood to me, given my guidance to him regarding embalming and my endorsements of his business."

He sighed slightly and said, sounding irritated, "I should have taken her corpse away as soon as the deed was done. Unfortunately others were about, including that ridiculous voodoo woman. This delay allowed you, Reverend Sands, and the child to find Drina in her deceased state. No matter. I returned, removed her, and it was as if she'd never been. No one noticed or cared she was gone, besides the three of you." He tipped his head a little as if to see Inez more clearly. "You look positively chilled, Mrs. Stannert."

Just lean over a little farther…

"Why bother with Tony? That I cannot see."

"See? Ha! A little joke. Good, Mrs. Stannert, your wits are still about you, so we shall continue our stalemate a while longer. To be blunt, I saw nothing obviously unusual in Drina's brain or visual system, but we know so little, and I was unsure. What if I were to compare what I found with a near relative? And thanks to Mrs. Alexander's natterings, I knew Drina had a child, a girl. Perfect! Same sex, and even with the same unusual eye-color variation. Obviously an inherited feature. What else might I see, were I to peer inside?"

Inez could swear that the hand holding the knife was shaking.

"I have to find out," he said. "I must *see!*"

Inez heard the deadly little clickety-click of a ratcheting blade and saw a flash of metal under the blowing end of Drina's sash. Her scream—"Tony, don't!"—was lost in the crash of gunfire.

But the shot came not from Inez's revolver.

The fragile wing of the tiny stone angel above Dr. Gregorvich and Tony shattered.

Dr. Gregorvich jerked, turning instinctively toward the sound. His knife hand wavered, and he breathed, "No!"

Tony ducked her head and plunged her mother's little *caracas* into his leg.

But Inez was only peripherally aware of this. All of her attention was focused on one thing: Dr. Gregorvich's face, which had turned away from her, now swiveled into view, gimlet eye open wide in shock and pain.

A perfect target.

She pulled the trigger.

He slumped, one-eyed and unseeing.

Tony ducked, ran to Inez, and wrapped her arms tight around her waist.

Now Inez was shaking. Shaking so hard that everything seemed to be in movement.

The gold sash started to blow away. Mrs. Alexander stepped forward, wrapped in a cloak as dark as the night around her, except for the merest of white hem that appeared and disappeared with the wind. The sash tumbled against her, writhing around her feet. She shifted her revolver clumsily to her other hand and picked up the sash. She approached Inez and Tony, holding the sash out like a peace offering.

"I am so sorry," she said, almost inaudibly.

"Sorry? You probably saved our lives," said Inez, arm wrapped around Tony's shoulders, keeping her close.

"No. I am sorry, for all this. It is my fault."

Inez shook her head. "No. It is not. Dr. Gregorvich…he was mad. Delusional."

Françoise was looking at her strangely. "You shot him. You killed him. Is that not trouble for you?"

Inez thought of her upcoming day in court and the complications of having just shot a prominent member of the community, no matter his state of mind. "It will take time to unravel things," she hedged. "We must go to the deputy marshal and tell him everything, including your husband's role in this. I will need to turn over my gun and—"

Without a word, Françoise raised her firearm awkwardly. Inez saw that, like her small Smoot, it was a Remington, but a larger, heavier, War-era revolver.

Françoise turned and walked to the physician, his head leaning against the hard stone of the monument. She said, "They all think me mad, you know. But he was the one who was mad. And a murderer. He killed all the hope and faith I ever had for a better tomorrow, for a better life after this one." She cocked the hammer, pointed the revolver at his head, and pulled the trigger. She repeated this over and over until all evidence of Inez's shot was obliterated and the doctor's face was unrecognizable, his brains splattered dark upon the stone, and the hammer clicked uselessly on an empty chamber.

Chapter Forty-two

It seemed to Inez that the racket had been enough to wake the dead, but those in their graves—named and unnamed—slept peacefully on. Even among the living, it appeared that no one heard or, if they did, they didn't care enough to come investigate the cause. The volley of shots brought no one running, no lights came bobbing down the hill from Twelfth. The only thing that stirred was the wind, the clouds limned in silver by the slice of moon, the dead flowers frozen and brown on the nearby graves.

They walked back to where the piebald horse was. At least he was waiting for them and hadn't spooked at the noise and taken off. Inez insisted that Tony climb on up. Her knee and foot were feeling better, or perhaps they were just frozen into senselessness. She held onto the bridle with one bare hand and walked back to town alongside Françoise. Both women pulled their cloaks tight around their heads and faces, while Tony wrapped her mother's ephemeral sash around her neck and head and seemed to gather comfort and warmth from the layers.

Françoise said, "I believed. When my little Sasha died so horribly and slowly, I believed she went to a better world, and that I could reach her, talk to her. I could not touch her, but she would be waiting for me. That was my comfort. But my husband, he never had my faith in a world beyond, as is said in *spiritisme*. He agreed with Dr. Gregorvich, who said my delusions were all in my mind, mere delusions. I kept looking for proof they would accept of the world beyond. Drina, she had the sight. When I paid her to see, my husband, he became angry. Then, Drina was gone. He said, she must have left, town, disappeared, like the charlatans do. But I found her clothes, in the box where my husband puts the clothes of the dead. He did not tell me. He lied. And I knew." She lifted her face to Tony, muffled up on the horse. "Then, when I saw you, child, I knew it was a sign. Drina wanted me to know the truth. To reach her. I told Dr. Gregorvich, told him I had proof, a conduit that could reach her, in the beyond. But now, I am left no hope, no faith, nothing."

Inez reached out and touched her arm. "That is when faith is most needed, when nothing else is left." They were poor words of comfort, but the best she could come up with while thoroughly chilled and exhausted.

After a space, Françoise said, "We will go to my home. We will talk to my husband. He will be home by now, and no doubt wild with concern."

Sure enough, on arriving back at the undertaker's residence, lights were blazing from the second-story windows and, as the three of them went in through the door, Inez detected a buzz of masculine voices, with Mr. Alexander's frantic words rising above them. "Look at this place! It was like this when I came home! She is nowhere, there is evidence that she held a séance. I have forbidden her to do so, these sessions unbalance her mind, which is in the most delicate of states. I fear she is in mortal danger, perhaps gone mad at last or…and my firearm. It's gone! I keep it loaded, just in case. We must find my wife's physician, Dr. Gregorvich. He will know what to do!"

"I am here, Burton," she called up the stairs, sounding far more sane than her husband.

Several men appeared up on the landing, looking down, including the deputy marshal and several policemen. Mrs. Alexander started up the stairs. Tony, who was behind her on the narrow entryway, took a step back and bumped into Inez.

Inez gripped Tony's hand. "Courage," she whispered. They began climbing the stairs together.

Mr. Alexander hastened down to his wife. "Françoise! Where have you been? What happened? I've been mad with worry."

"Burton, you will tell them everything." She lifted the empty revolver, still cocked, and pointed it at him. He stumbled backwards up the stairs, hands raised up. She continued, "Everything about Drina and what you have done to her and to that poor Englishman downstairs. Everything."

Inez slid her hand into her cloak pocket, groping with frozen fingers.

"I, I don't know what you're talking about," he sputtered. His eyes behind his spectacles looked terrified.

Françoise's finger tightened on the trigger. He screamed and covered his face with his arms. The hammer fell with a harmless click. "Tell them," she said.

Mr. Alexander looked up, face slick with sweat, confused. His gaze slid past his wife to Inez. Inez pulled her hand out of her pocket. The long silver and gold corset cords, twins to the ones he had bought for his wife and given to Dr. Gregorvich instead, twisted in her grip. "I think you'd better tell them," Inez said to the undertaker. "As your wife said, you'd better tell the law everything."

He sank to the riser, covered his face with his hands, and began to rock.

◇◇◇

And tell them everything he did. Apparently thinking Dr. Gregorvich was still among the living—and neither Inez, Françoise, nor Tony disabused him of the notion—the undertaker threw his colleague to the police, intent on saving his own skin.

What he told them compelled Inez to hustle Tony upstairs to the second floor and seat her in a chair. "This is not for you to hear," she said, and gathered a cloth, soaked it in a pitcher of water, which had somehow remained unbroken on a sideboard all through the séance frenzy, and attempted to remove Dr. Gregorvich's gore and blood that had splattered her with Inez's shot. "Y-y-you got him like Annie Oakley." It was the first words Tony had said since the cemetery. "Sh-shot him in the eye."

"I was lucky," said Inez. "Not likely I'll pull that off again in this lifetime." She dabbed some more, then found a thick shawl on the floor by an overturned chair and wrapped it around Tony. Tony still clutched her maman's sash as if it were a lifeline. Inez then returned to the doorway. Françoise was coming up, accompanied by one of the policemen. "They are all going downstairs by the back way, to the workroom," she said. "Burton will show them."

"I must see as well," said Inez.

The deputy marshal, who was carrying a coal oil lamp, glanced at Inez, but didn't voice any resistance. She followed the deputy marshal and the two policemen who held the undertaker between them in a firm grip down the back staircase, then down another set of stairs into the underlevel. Burton pointed with a shaking hand at a door in the wall. "That leads to Dr. Gregorvich's work area. We both have keys. But, you must be careful. Perhaps he is in there, working. If we surprise him, he may become dangerous. He is a strong man and will not go without a fight."

Inez thought that Dr. Gregorvich was in no position to fight anything, unless it might be whatever demons existed in whatever afterlife there might be.

By common consent, the police and the deputy stood back in the shadows and allowed Alexander to unlock the door with a key from his waistcoat. He said tentatively, "Gregorvich? Are you there?" and pushed open the door into heavy silence and complete darkness.

The police and the marshal crowded in after Alexander, their sidearms drawn. Inez followed them in, just in time to hear one of the policemen say, "Jesus, Mary, and Joseph! What *is* this?" followed by retching sounds from one of his companions. The smell of a charnel house clashed with harsh chemical fumes, and Inez clapped a hand over her nose and mouth. The lantern light danced around the room as the deputy marshal pivoted.

"Awgh," grunted the deputy marshal. "We'd better not let the papers get ahold of this. Especially that Elliston fella. He's been a bother about all the bodysnatchin' and dissectin' rumors."

The third policeman, who apparently had a stronger stomach than the rest, lit the gas lamps on the nearby wall, muttering as he did so, "Jesus on a cross. God have mercy on his soul."

What the light revealed Inez wished heartily she could soon forget: Percy. Poor Percy. Identifiable by his face, but with the top of his head and his eyes removed, his ribcage cranked open and parts of the body that were never meant to see the light of daily clearly exposed, all as neatly and cleanly as if he were a fish being prepared for plating.

Inez turned her head aside, but that, in a way, was even worse. Facing her now was a long shelf of neatly labeled glass jars, with what only could be the brains, eyes, and organs of those poor or unfortunate enough to have passed, unnoticed, from the undertaker's to the anatomist's domain. One jar was given the place of honor on a table by itself, further protected by a polished brass and glass case. It held yet another organ of thought, belief, and emotion, floating in the preserving liquid. Floating with it, and still attached by fibrous gray strands, was a pair of eyes—staring unseeing into the room— one brown, the other blue.

Inez hastily exited the underground horror chamber and beckoned the deputy out, who seemed only too willing to comply. In an undertone, she summarized what happened at the cemetery, leaving out nothing, including Dr. Gregorvich's intent to harm Tony, and Inez's own part in his death with Mrs. Alexander's finishing touches. The deputy responded gruffly, "Serves the old bastard right. Got his just deserts, that one."

"So, what do you think will happen to the three of us?" she asked cautiously.

The deputy glanced into the physician's workroom then back at Inez. "Who all was there? You, the girl, and the Missus Alexander, you say? No one else?"

Inez nodded.

"Well, hell. Let 'im rot. I'm going to just forget we ever had this conversation. See if you can't get the missus and the girl to keep their mouths shut, eh? Lots of cut-throats and footpads roaming around. I'm thinkin' the doctor was in the wrong place at the wrong time."

With that, he turned to one of the policemen, "Well, you'd better fetch the friends of this here toff and get them to identify him. The family wants him home, but I'm beginning to wonder if it might not be better to just lay him to rest here instead."

While the law was off rounding up the other "toffs," Mr. Alexander confessed that the body lying within the ornate metal case, waiting for transport to England, was not Percy—obviously, thought Inez, sourly—but none other than the drummer, Woods. Inez insisted on looking through the little glass window. She had to admit that, with his russet-colored hair and eyebrows blacked, mutton-chops trimmed, and a little moustache obtained from somewhere or other, the drummer might pass muster as Percy. Provided one didn't look too closely or hadn't seen Percy recently. Given the nature of things, that seemed a likely scenario.

"It's sealed," said Alexander miserably. "So, if they don't open it, well…"

The marshal sent Alexander upstairs under the watchful care of the remaining two officers. Moments later, still dressed in eveningwear, the Lads from London came tumbling into the undercellar, grumbling and complaining. The deputy marshal explained that he wanted identification of the remains, warned them of the graphic nature, and let them into the physician's workroom. Sharp exclamations erupted of an unsavory nature and they were back out, lickety-split. "A physician did that?" gasped Quick, hands on his knees, bent over and trying to catch his breath. "That's just bloody barbaric!"

"Yep, no argument there," said the deputy. "Now, I know his family is expectin' to receive his body and give him a proper burial. They aren't fussing about the who done it or why done it, they just want the matter buried, I guess you'd say. With that in mind…" He took them over to the metal casket. The four peered in the little window at the entombed deceased.

Epperley retreated. "Who *is* that?"

"A drummer fella what died recent in Stillborn Alley," said the deputy.

Tipton adjusted his monocle. "Well, the hair's right, his eyes are closed. It's been a long time since the family have seen dear old Percy. Too, being out West *can* change a man."

Inez decided that she had enough secrets that she had to carry and didn't need to hear how this particular situation would play out. Upstairs, she found Tony fast asleep in the little parlor across the hall from the séance room, blankets piled atop her, the gold sash gripped to her chin.

"Mr. Alexander is gone," said Françoise. "He will not be back." She glanced at the sleeping child curled up on the love-seat. "May she stay here? I will be sure no harm comes to her." She looked at Inez, hopeful. "You will stay too? We have an extra room for widows who come from out of town and prefer a private place or cannot get rooms in the hotels."

Inez wavered, thinking of her rooms in the Silver Queen. The cold sleeping chamber, dark and no fire.

"I have the fire started," Françoise continued. "And an extra dressing gown."

Inez was tempted.

"And, I think it is good for Antonia if you are here when she wakes. She trusts you, and it will comfort her to know you did not abandon her."

Inez capitulated. It sounded like a reasonable solution, given that dawn was but a few hours away.

It had been a long night.

She was tired.

Chapter Forty-three

Inez slept like, if not like the dead, then the unconscious. Sometime after sunrise, she heard the door to her room creak open and Françoise whisper, "See? She is here. Let's let her sleep." The door creaked shut.

When Inez awoke, she splashed cold water on her face to clear her mind and joined Françoise and Tony in the sunlit sitting room. Over a late breakfast, she summarized her conversation with the deputy about the fitting end of Dr. Gregorvich, finishing with, "So, we must all agree. Shall we stay silent?" None offered to do otherwise.

Inez warned Françoise newsmen would be knocking at the door once the news got out of her husband's arrest. "I will not answer," was her reply. She asked, tentatively, "I wondered, might you both come back tonight? It would be good to have company. I have no one else." She slid two keys across the table to them. "For the back door."

Inez looked at Tony, who looked back and nodded. "Very well. Thank you for your many kindnesses," said Inez. She gathered herself to go. Tony said, "Can I go to Miss Carothers'? She's expecting me today. I don't want her to worry."

So Inez walked Tony, dressed in her boy's clothes, to Miss Carothers' studio. Along the way, they heard a hello and saw Ace waving at them across Harrison. He dashed toward them, weaving expertly through the traffic, arriving hardly out of breath at all. "Hey! Tony Deuce! Long time, no see. Did you hear about the undertaker? The one you work for? He's been arrested! Mr. Elliston is going batty. He can't get anyone to talk about it."

Inez chewed her lip and then said slowly, "Ace, you might suggest to Mr. Elliston, strictly on the Q.T., that he nose around and enquire about Dr. Gregorvich. He might find something interesting up at the cemetery or down in the sublevel of the physician's business."

Ace's eyes went wide.

"Tell him you got this information from a reliable but anonymous source," she added.

"You bet!" He dashed off, clutching his hat with one hand and his papers with the other.

Tony looked at her, questioning.

"I promised the deputy I would not speak to Mr. Elliston, but Ace has no such injunction. And I owe Mr. Elliston a debt of gratitude I can never repay." Inez turned Tony to face her, adding, "You may hear upsetting things about what the doctor has done. Just remember, he is dead. That must bring justice to the matter, as we cannot pursue him over the River Styx." At Susan's front door, Inez said, "I will see you tonight at Mrs. Alexander's. She is expecting us to come in the back entrance. You know where that is?"

"I know all the ways in and out," said Tony and disappeared inside.

Back at the saloon, Inez checked at the bar. Abe and Mark tending, Sol was taking orders and running between the kitchen and tables with food and coffee and ferrying bar orders. Inez leaned on the counter and said, "Mr. Stannert?" He turned toward her. For just a second, something like hope flashed across his face before his expression settled into wariness.

"If I could have a word with you?" she asked.

He came over, wiping his hands on the barcloth, with a terse "Yes?"

She glanced around the saloon. Way too many eyes were studiously looking anywhere but at them and she could almost see the ears straining to hear. "Someplace private."

He winced, and Inez guessed that was what Josephine was wont to say. Inez could almost hear her throaty intonation: "Mr. Stannert? A word? Someplace private?" And then, fireworks.

"Where?" He tossed the rag under the counter.

"In the office."

"I'll be there in a minute."

She went upstairs and pulled the papers she'd taken back from her lawyer from the safe. Jammed to one side, she saw the packet with the money the Lads had given her when they'd arrived in Leadville. *They'll want to be heading out of town soon, no doubt.* Snugged between it and the inner wall of the safe was the thin envelope Percy had given her "on the sly" when the Lads had all disembarked from the train for their grand carouse about town.

Mark paused in the entry, hand on the doorknob. "Open or closed?" No hint of flirtation, no "darlin'," no twinkle in his eye. This was Mark as she'd seldom seen him: dead serious.

"Closed, if you please. We have personal business to discuss."

He closed it and came over to the loveseat at right angles to the desk where she sat. She scooted the swivel chair on its brass rollers closer to the low parlor table facing the loveseat.

Before she began he said, "I just want you to know, Inez, I won't be there Monday. You and your lawyer, whatever you decide, that's what it'll be. But..." She saw definable pain wash across his face. "What about our son?"

"That is exactly what we are going to discuss right now," she said. She found she was speaking more gently to him than she had intended. Inez laid out the sheaf of notarized affadavits, all the information and assurances that she had gathered and her lawyer Casey had reviewed. "I'm proposing we make my sister and brother-in-law, Harmony and Jonathan DuChamps, William's legal guardians."

Mark looked down at the papers, then selected one. "On proper Underwood Iron and Steel Incorporated letterhead," he commented. "Clever gambit. The judge will no doubt be impressed. You even got your father's signature here along with

Jonathan's," He glanced at her. "You haven't spoken to him since we married. Or did I miss something else while I was away?"

"The signature was Jonathan's doings, not mine," she said. "You know Jonathan essentially runs the company now, he told us so when we visited them in the Springs. Papa is up in years, but apparently not willing to relinquish the reins. The point is, Papa and all of them, Underwoods and DuChamps alike, dote on William. If we do this, if you do this, because the father's rights are paramount when it comes to children, William will remain in the only family he's ever really known. He will be surrounded by people who love him, people who will do everything in their considerable power to keep our son healthy, happy, and secure in his future."

She leaned forward. "Mark, we are still his parents. In name and law. They will be appointed his legal custodial guardians. They will come to the Springs regularly. You will be able to see William, be a part of his life, and so will I."

She stopped speaking and watched as Mark paged through the papers, picking them up one by one and reading them with the same care that her lawyer had taken. "These New York physicians," he finally said, "they make a persuasive case for him staying in the East for health reasons." Mark looked up. "So, Inez. Do you believe this in William's best interests?"

"I don't just believe it, I *know* it." She spoke fiercely, from the depth of her heart. "This is absolutely, without a doubt, the best for our son."

Mark let the paper in his hand drift to the table and join the rest. He put his elbows on his knees, viewed the blizzard of assurances, of evidence, of proof that their son would be protected and raised in a web of family care and love that neither he nor Inez could provide. Finally, he straightened up, his face drawn, defeat mixed with determination. "What must I do to make this happen?"

The gathering for her Saturday evening poker game was, in a word, subdued. Her usual circle seemed to have forgotten how to carry on a casual conversation. Most of the stilted talk revolved around the unsettled weather and the upcoming election, which promised to be entertaining with Evan prognosticating a landslide by Democratic candidates. Things finally loosened up when Doc arrived, late, his cane thumping out his approach down the hall. He came in, looking a little stunned, and said, "Have you heard about Dr. Gregorvich?" The game stopped right there as he treated everyone to a wild tale of the physician being found shot, most brutally, in the cemetery. "His body was found on the grave of a child!" Doc said.

"Who found him?" queried Cooper, looking from his new cards to his discards with a frown, as if he now wished he hadn't thrown them away.

"Elliston did. And there's rumor of more to come. Some unsavory doings." Doc harrumphed, uncomfortable. "I am sorry to say we welcomed the good doctor into the medical fraternity here at Leadville without any doubts or misgivings. Now, we are sorry we did."

Then Elliston burst in, all triumphant, and told the story again but with more adjectival embellishment. He stayed coy on the details of what was found in the physician's office, merely saying, "You'll have to read *The Independent* for that!"

The energy in the room picked up, and everyone seemed to be more relaxed and having a good time. When Inez sensed the night was winding down and Doc proclaimed it a long day, his cue for leaving, she said, "A moment if you please, gentlemen."

She walked to the door, shut it, and said, "I have a favor to ask of each of you, but I will not take it amiss if you decline."

Not a one of them did.

That is how it came to be that on Monday, November 1, 1880, Inez stood beside her lawyer William Casey, Esq., in county court, before County Judge A. K. Updegraf to have her suit for divorce heard and decided upon. The judge cast a sharp look about the room, said, "Mr. Stannert? Not here?"

That was clear.

"Was he served a copy of the summons?"

Upon receiving the legal proof that indeed, Mr. Stannert had, the judge nodded, pulled out his docket, picked up his pen, dipped it in the inkwell, and said, "Note that defendant, Marcus Stannert, being duly summoned has failed to appear at the appointed hour."

"Now then," the judge said looking up at Inez's circle of Saturday night players, "Mr. Casey, I understand you have a few witnesses in this matter." One by one, each man took the witness stand, and was sworn to tell the truth. Evan the merchant, Cooper the lawyer, Elliston the newspaper publisher, Doctor Cramer—all well-regarded men in the community. Each averred Mark Stannert had, to their best knowledge, been absent from Leadville and his wife's side from May 1879 to July 1880, a length of time falling well within the bounds of the definition of "abandonment." The judge nodded, again and again, and Inez thought she noted a slight impatience to this gesture, a "get on with it" air. Although she could have been wrong. The judge, she knew from hearsay, was an excellent poker player, so it was hard to tell exactly what he might be thinking.

After the last witness had testified, Casey motioned for the court's attention. "Your honor, I have a settlement proposal that sets forth how the parties have agreed to divide their marital assets. If I may approach the bench?"

Casey stepped forward and presented the terms of agreement he had hammered out with Inez. The judge spent a good long while looking through the document, written out in Casey's neat legible hand, while Inez felt her insides twist into an undissolvable knot. He asked a few questions, to which Casey quickly and clearly responded. The judge nodded and made more notes in the docket. Inez tried not to fidget.

Then, Casey said, "To the matter of the child…" and presented the signed and notarized affidavit from Mark allowing Mr. and Mrs. Jonathan DuChamps to act as William Stannert's legal custodial guardian. Inez thought she saw the judge frown, just a little. Casey followed up with the papers Inez had collected—all the carefully gathered assurances and promises, signed, sealed, delivered on letterhead, in yellow telegraphic missives, and in fulsome medical forms. The judge's eyebrows went up a little as he read through them, taking his time. Doc stepped forward to add his own medical opinion, in concurrence with the rest. Inez gave in to the urge to fidget, twisting the string of her reticule around and around one finger, nearly cutting off the circulation.

The entire process seemed to take an eternity, and at the same time, to happen in an instant. The judge carefully restacked the papers, laced his fingers on the bench and looked her straight in the eyes. Inez held her breath. It was then she detected, well-controlled and barely noticeable, a touch of sympathy. "Mrs. Stannert, you have proven to the satisfaction of the court the allegations in your complaint in this action. As I look around the courtroom, I notice that Mr. Marcus Stannert has still not made an appearance, and from what I've heard here today, he does not intend to make an appearance in this matter. Therefore Mr. Stannert is declared in default in this matter and your bill of complaint is deemed uncontested."

The judge then addressed those assembled, saying, "It is hereby ordered, adjudged, and decreed by this court that the marriage between Inez Underwood Stannert, plaintiff, and Marcus Charles Stannert, defendant, is dissolved accordingly and that Mr. and Mrs. Jonathan DuChamps be deemed the legal custodial guardian of the minor child, William Stannert."

He paused for the space of a heartbeat. "The parties, one and each of them, is freed and absolutely released from the bonds of matrimony and all the obligations thereof." He made a record of his words on his docket, then brought down the gavel, saying, "Court is adjourned to meet again tomorrow, Tuesday, November second, at ten o'clock in the morning."

Inez released her breath in a long sigh.

The judge stood and everyone relaxed. Casey turned toward Inez and said, "Congratulations, Mrs. Stannert. Will it still be Mrs. Stannert, then?"

"For now," she said weakly, feeling like her knees might give way.

The judge came down from the bench, and to Inez's utter amazement approached her, and smiled. "My legal prescription is to treat yourself to a glass of sherry, Mrs. Stannert, and to move on from there. I wish you well with your future, wherever it may lead."

Chapter Forty-four

Inez agreed to Casey's suggestion to partake of the sherry in his office. He raised his glass and said, "To you, Mrs. Stannert. You played against the odds and won what could have turned into a difficult and ugly case."

She raised her glass in return. "It would not have been without you in my corner. Thank you, Mr. Casey." They drank.

She rose to go and he escorted her to the door, saying, "If I may add…?"

Turning to him, she caught his smile. "If you decide to ever divorce again, please, pick a different lawyer."

"Once is more than enough," she assured him.

She returned to the saloon and looked around. Monday, and it was fairly quiet. Abe looked up, question plain on his face. She went up to the bar. "It's done."

He nodded, brown eyes lingering on hers, and offered her a shot glass with the best whisky they had behind the bar. "I'm thinkin' you might need this."

"I'm thinking I might." She drank and sighed. "I need to go upstairs."

"Might want to avoid the gaming room. I put Mark where I could keep an eye on him, make sure he didn't bolt for the door at the last minute and run pell-mell to the courthouse."

"Somehow, I suspect Josephine would have been there, barring the door, if he tried."

Inez was intending to head straight to her chambers to change, and thence back to Mrs. Alexander's, where she knew she was welcome to stay as long as she wished.

But she couldn't just pass by the gaming room, its door ajar, the scent of Mark's cigar curling out into the hallway. She gave the the door a little push. Mark sat in the twilight, smoking, a glass and bottle by the ashtray. She leaned against the doorframe. "It's over now. The judge went along with everything."

He nodded.

"Are you drinking to forget the past?" She meant it lightly, but was afraid it came out sounding awkward and mean. She moved to stand inside the door.

"Not possible." He poured himself another shot, pulled over an extra glass, filled it and held it out to Inez. She couldn't see his expression in the dark, but he added, "However, I fully expect Josephine will find a way to knock me senseless, drag any memories she deems not useful out into the light, and take to them with a rugbeater." She heard it then: the faintest hint of that Southern drawl.

Inez took the proffered shot glass, with no need to hide the smile easing the knot inside her stomach.

The old Mark was still there, inside, busy licking his wounds for now.

He'd be all right.

After changing into a more comfortable outfit, something for walking and breathing, Inez stopped in the saloon office for her last task of the day.

But before that, she pulled out the cabinet card photograph showing her son William sitting on the lap of her sister Harmony, now his legal guardian. She noticed the little things in the crisp image, how his eyes, which Inez had always thought of as mirrors as her own, also looked like Harmony's. How his chin echoed the Underwood determination which had stamped both Inez's and Harmony's faces. How his chubby hand curled trusting and relaxed on Harmony's wrist. Inez touched the small nose in the photograph and spoke to the paper image. "We did this for you, William. Because your father and I love you, want the best for you. Where you are, the people you are with—that is your home and family now. You are where you should be." She stopped speaking, because the longing was just too great to put into words. She set the photograph aside to pack for later.

Inez turned to the safe. She wanted to have the ticket money for the Lads available and handy, in case they came looking and she wasn't there. Her first thought was simply to leave the cash envelope with their names scrawled across it in the safe, and let Mark and Abe know it was all there. She pulled out the sleeve, dislodging Percy's thin envelope, which fell at her feet.

A sign?

Inez picked it up, tapped it thoughtfully against the palm of her hand, and then reached for the letter opener on the desk. She slit the sealed envelope open, pulled out the single sheet of folded paper, unfolded it, and read…

The next morning, Inez lingered at Mrs. Alexander's, preparing telegrams to send back East and farther West. Tony was at Susan's studio again, helping Susan set up the sittings. "I like it," Tony had said. "It's fun."

Mrs. Alexander spent the morning sewing in the kitchen, and explained her busy fingers to Inez. "It is a shroud," she'd said somberly. "I have my sewing talents to help me, for now. Later, I will return to home in France. Once I have settled things here." Inez had promptly given her the address and name of William Casey, Esq., for help with legal matters.

As she drafted her messages and made her plans, she waited, with half an ear, for the arrival of a visitor or two or three, or maybe four. She wasn't disappointed. The doorbell gave its metallic ring as someone twisted the knob on the door. "I believe it is for me," she told Françoise. "If you don't mind, I will take it in the parlor."

Sure enough, it was Epperley. And as she surmised, he'd come alone. He stepped into the entry, and looked around, suspicious and dour as always, his blond mustache at perfect horizontal, echoing the narrow line of his mouth. "I went to the Silver Queen and they said you were here."

"They were correct." She turned to go up the stairs, throwing over her shoulder, "You're here for the ticket money, I gather. So Percy or his lookalike is on his way home?"

Epperley's step was loud behind her, and very close. "We're all at sixes and sevens," he muttered. "No choice, really. Can't send Percy home without the top of his head or its contents. Even if he was always the empty-headed fool." Inez winced. Epperley's snarl was harsher than usual.

"Tipton is the worst," he continued. "Absolutely, positively insists we give the family all the bloody details. The family doesn't want all the bloody details. It's a rum do all around. I told them I couldn't wait any longer. I have to get back to the Springs and the hotel. It'll be run into the ground if I don't."

"Hmmmm. Your hotel is a monster of a mistress, isn't it?" she said, leading him into the tiny parlor where she'd been working.

"I'll make a go of it yet. I'm determined." Epperley sat without being invited and crossed one boot over his knee. "Oh, say, you have Percy's other things, right?"

"Other things? Oh! His lucky rabbit's foot?"

"No, dash it. Hang the rabbit's foot." He uncrossed his legs and leaned forward, eyes narrow. "The envelope."

"Envelope?" she echoed innocently. "I don't recall an envelope. The past two weeks have been such a muddle. But I have everything here, so, if it he gave it to me with his money, it's most likely in the cash envelope." She lifted papers, pushing them around as if searching, making a further mess.

He exploded. "Well, then, bloody well *find* it!"

She continued, ""Maybe it's in his clothes or in his hotel room?"

"It wasn't in the hotel room or his clothes because I—" He stopped.

His hand clenched into a fist, as if he wanted to grab back his words and strangle them.

Inez gave him her full attention, noting his anger, his awful dawning realization of what he had just said, or almost said.

"You know it isn't in the hotel or on his clothes, because you looked," she said quietly. "At the start of all this, on Friday, Drina read Percy's fortune. Later, you and Percy revisited her shack, probably to threaten her, demand the money back because Percy thought she had conned him with a story of untold riches to be had in the mining district. You didn't find her, but you did find Tony's handgun and you took it. Then Saturday night late, while the rest of the Lads were enjoying a toot at the Grand Central Theater, you and Percy returned to the shack, and you argued. About the money he promised you. The money he agreed to *give* you, no strings attached, from his inheritance, good friend that he was. You couldn't stand to see him spending it all and having a good time, am I right? So you shot him. With Tony Gizzi's fancy handgun. And you looked for the envelope so you'd have proof of his generous gift, when you couldn't find it in his pockets, you ran away, and left him—your friend—dying."

Epperley said nothing. She sensed something coil up inside him, preparing to strike. Her hand went to her empty reticule on the table and pushed it aside, revealing her pocket pistol beneath. She touched the grip, not doing any more, and said, "Don't."

He finally muttered, "I didn't kill him."

"Ah, but the intent was there." She bore down, relentless. "And what would have happened if, instead of drawing the attention of Dr. Gregorvich, it had been someone like Doc Cramer who had stumbled upon Percy? Doc would've done his best to save him, stop the bleeding. What a mess you'd have been in then, hmm?"

His eyes slid away from hers.

"So," she prodded, "what are you going to do about this, Epperley?"

"Where's the envelope?" He sounded glum now, but determined. "He wanted me to have the money, he said so. I admit it, I lost my blasted temper. It was a row that got out of hand."

"A row. That got out of hand. And poor Percy pays the price." Inez shook her head. "It seems your temper gets the best of you at the worst times. Hold it in check, now, because I need to tell

you I'm afraid the envelope and its contents got out of hand as
well and sailed right into the…" she let her gaze meander to the
parlor stove. The stove popped a merry reply.

Epperley actually gaped. "You *burned* it?"

She crossed her arms, revolver in one hand. "I guess I lost
my blasted temper. So, again, what are you going to do to make
this right?"

"*Do*? What do you mean, *do*?" He stood. "Turn myself into
what passes for the law here in Leadville? That'll be the day.
Nobody cares what happened to Percy but his mates. The physician killed him, that's what everyone says. If Percy hadn't pushed
me, changed his mind, none of this would've happened. And
now, 'Percy' is heading home. What a charade!" He sneered.
"You can't prove anything, in any case. What I will *do* is go back
to the Springs, to my hotel, and raise the money elsewhere so I
can save my business."

"It will not end well for you," she said.

"Do your worst, Mrs. Stannert!" he snarled and banged out
the door and down the stairs, cashless.

"Oh, I won't need to, you'll do it to yourself," she said into
empty air. With a sigh, she set her Smoot back on the table.

Mrs. Alexander came to the parlor. Inez was surprised to see
that, instead of a needle, she held her husband's old, and most
likely still empty, revolver.

"I heard noise. An argument?" she asked. "You are okay?"

"Quite," said Inez.

Mrs. Alexander returned to her sewing, and Inez returned to
her sorting and planning.

"Miss April, please!" Inez could hear Susan down the hall, in
the posing room, getting more frustrated. "Antonia, will you
please tip the light reflector just a bit more? Perfect! Now, Miss
April, hold still."

Inez and Mrs. Sweet, aka Frisco Flo, sat in Susan's little
parlor, teapot steaming between them amongst the periodicals.
Flo seemed pleased with herself. "So it went even better than

we planned?" She clasped her hands like a young girl. "I wish I could have been there to see!"

"Oh, yes, Miss Josephine made quite the entrance to a full house at the Tontine," said Inez. "And I spotted Mr. Johnson right away. He looked like he wanted to crawl under the table."

"It certainly was handy the Johnsons are such good friends of the judge and his wife," said Flo complacently. "And Mrs. Johnson, there's much she doesn't know and Mr. Johnson wants it to stay that way."

"Oh, I bet she suspects." Inez leaned back in the chair and dug through the reticule. "Wives always do," she added, sliding the envelope of paper money toward Flo across the table.

Flo picked up the envelope and let her fingers tiptoe through the aligned bills. "Perfect." She tucked the envelope into her reticule.

"Covers all the expenses?" Inez asked. "Helping Josephine get here, telegrams, hotel room, whatever was needed? Plus what I owe you for 'services rendered?'"

Flo laughed, a tinkly sound. "Oh, we are square, Mrs. Stannert. I think I would've done it even if you hadn't paid me. I do like to see a charming con man get his comeuppance. Not that I would've dreamed of doing so without your consent," she added hastily.

Inez sighed and relaxed into the chair. "Well, it was a bit of a walk through fire, but I made it to the other side."

"Welcome to the land of grass widows," said Flo.

"Did you know Miss Josephine was…" Inez raised her eyebrows.

"No! I had no idea at all. But I must say, it certainly added to her persuasive powers when it came to convincing your husband, excuse me, *former* husband, to agree to a divorce."

"That it did."

"Are you going to keep your name, Stannert? I didn't realize you were an *Underwood*. My heavens. I think I would snap back that name toot sweet. Oh, the doors of opportunity the name Underwood would open."

Inez made a face. "Some of us prefer to make our own way, without the burden—or the privileges, which mark my words, can also be a burden—of the past. The present and the future is all that matters."

"Well, I certainly agree. I always said, Mrs. Stannert, you and I are cut from the same bolt of cloth. We were just fashioned into different suits, that's all." Flo wound a blond ringlet around her finger, staring at Inez expectantly. "So, what's next? A trip to Laramie, Wyoming? Rumors are there's a good-looking interim reverend who just took up residence there."

"Not right away," said Inez. "I have plans to go West. As for the rest, well, time will tell."

Inez gathered her gloves, preparing to leave. "Mrs. Sweet, it has been a pleasure. I am glad we will continue to be business partners, quietly, at a distance, and under the table. So sorry I had to withdraw from the sale of your State Street brick building, but I understand Mr. Stannert and Mr. Jackson have tendered an offer to you. I am sure Mr. Stannert and the soon-to-be second Mrs. Stannert will jump on the opportunity to expand their sphere of influence. I will look forward to your missives telling me how our fortunes continue to grow in Leadville."

Flo's gaze rose to the corner where the walls met ceiling, and she said, "That's it? So, when are you planning to tell me, or are you going to let me puzzle it out for myself?"

"Tell you what?"

Flo huffed, exasperated. Her eyes snapped back to Inez. "Honestly. I am a madam. I run a boardinghouse for women of a certain sort. I *know* these things. Sooooo, were you going to let me in on your little secret about your…*condition?*" A small smile playing mischievously about her mouth.

"I have no idea what you are talking about," said Inez.

They stared at each other for another long moment, then Flo threw back her head and laughed. "You win, Mrs. Stannert," she said. "As you say, time will tell."

Chapter Forty-five

Antonia tugged on her blue bonnet. The knot bit into the spot under her chin where Dr. G's knife had jabbed her. It had pretty much healed, but was still sore. "So, where are we going again?"

Mrs. Stannert was watching the baggage men as they loaded their trunks, luggage, and boxes onto the train. "Sacramento first, and from there, to San Francisco," she said. Antonia heard her say under her breath, "There was a day when I traveled with whatever I could fit in a carpetbag, but no more."

"So, is Mr. Jackson going to ride your horse while we're gone?" Antonia asked. She had only met Lucy the previous week and had fallen in love with the horse right away.

Antoina had begged Mrs. Stannert to bring Lucy with them, but Mrs. Stannert had said, "We must decide where to settle first. Then, we'll see." She had added, "Too, it's not such a long train trip from San Francisco to Leadville. We will come back. Actually, you are nearly old enough to take the trip by yourself, if you wish. Miss Carothers said she would love for you to come visit and assist in her studio."

Antonia liked that idea. She was ready to leave, more than ready. But to come back, for a visit, maybe next summer? Well, that might be nice.

Mrs. Stannert had spent a lot of time talking about the future as she was making all the arrangements for what was to go with them and what was to stay. It was mostly Mrs. Stannert's stuff being loaded into the baggage cars. Antonia didn't have much besides her two dress outfits, and her maman's sash, cards, and knife. And her newsie clothes, of course, which she had refused to part with.

She danced on her toes on the platform, anxious to get on the train, yet reluctant to leave. She looked in the direction of the mountains, toward the cemetery. Mrs. Stannert, Mr. Stannert, Mr. Elliston, and a whole bunch of them had pitched in and bought a plot for Maman and a fancy casket all rosewood with silver swirls along the top and sides, but no viewing window. When Antonia had finally worked up the nerve to ask Mrs. Stannert whether Maman's remains had been in Dr. G's workshop, the saloonwoman had looked long and hard at her and didn't answer right away. She finally laid a hand atop Antonia's head. "This is where your mother is. Here, in your memories of her, and here," she touched a spot above Antonia's beating heart, "where your love for her will never die."

So, inside the fancy case were the other little bits of Maman's clothing and whatever they'd found of her in Dr. G's but weren't telling her about. Then, they bought a headstone. It wasn't a big fancy one, like where Dr. G had been all shot to pieces. But it did have an angel carved on it, along with her maman's name, Drina Gizzi, and the words "Death is only an horizon, and an horizon is nothing save the limit of our sight." Carved below that was "She now sees."

Antonia was glad there was a place where her maman would always be and where she could come visit. A lump rose in her throat.

Mrs. Stannert glanced at her. "Your maman?" she asked.

Antonia nodded, unable to speak. Mrs. Stannert always seemed to know what was going on inside her, almost as if she had "the sight" herself.

Then, from behind, Antonia heard a shout:

"Tony! Tony Deuce!"

She turned just in time to brace herself as Freddy tackled her around the waist. Ace drew up short, panting, still with a good armful of papers left to sell. Embarrassed, she really didn't know what to say to them. She'd hoped to say goodbye to the newsies, but everything had been so busy and then she never seemed to have time to go up to the newspaper office or anything and she wasn't sure what she'd say anyway, so…

She pointed at the stack under Ace's arm. "You better get busy. Mr. Elliston won't like that unsold stack of sheets. He'll want to see you with empty hands and full pockets."

"Well, these are mostly Freddy's. He's still working on getting his patter down and his volume up, so I help out." He looked at her curiously. "I didn't know you were a girl. Mr. Elliston told us, and wow, crimany, you could've knocked us all over with a feather. You're the best newsie that ever was, Tony. I'm gonna miss you."

"I'm gonna miss you too, Ace." She dug at the platform with the toe of her fancy girl's boot and had a sudden yearning to be back in her ragtag newsie clothes, walking the streets and shouting, "Extra! Read all about it! News from St. Louis, New York, and Bostonnnn."

"Little guy here wants to apologize." Ace yanked on Freddy's cap. "Go on. Say it."

"I'm sorry," he whispered. "I wasn't supposed to tell anyone about you sleepin' in the newsie shed. But the tall doctor, he gave me a quarter. He was nice."

"Yeah, and did ya see what happened? He almost burned the place down around our ears! Goes to show, Freddy, next time I say something's a secret and to tell nobody, that means *nobody*." Ace looked at Antonia. "Don't know if you know, but we're gettin' a bunkhouse built on the back property. Mrs. Stannert talked to Mr. Elliston, and they got some fancy-pants guy to build it. Name's Robitaille?" He wrinkled his nose. "Not sure I said it right."

"I got my own bed!" said Freddy, tugging on her coat. "And blankets! And we have a stove!"

"All the comforts of home," agreed Ace. Then, to Antonia, "Wish you coulda seen it before going. We just moved in there two days ago. Crimany, I'm glad to be out of the mission. So, you coming back? Soon?"

"Maybe." Antonia wavered. "Summer?" She looked around for Mrs. Stannert, but she was talking to one of the baggage handlers, giving him heck about something. "We're going to California for a while, where the streets are paved with gold."

"Gold, huh? Gold ain't got nothin' on silver, Tony. Just remember that, okay?" And he actually nudged her arm with his elbow. She felt a weird little shiver pass from her arm to her neck. And then her maman's voice whispered in her head: *I have seen it.*

"I gotta go, Ace. See you in the summer, if I come visit? Miss Carothers wants me back to work in her studio, I think."

"You bet." Ace grinned. "And if Miss Carothers can't use you, well, Mr. Elliston will. A girl newsie, you'd sell a hecka lot of sheets."

He grabbed Freddy around the waist and hauled him off of Antonia. "Hey, you're gonna get that pretty blue dress of hers all smudged up with your inky hands. C'mon, we gotta get to work. See ya, Tony!" And they wandered down the platform, with Ace yelling, "Extra! Get *The Independent*, right here! All the latest news! Bank note forger arrested in New York City! Body snatchers plying their trade in Baltimore! Mining to resume on the Chrysolite!"

"Antonia." Mrs. Stannert returned, looking distracted. "Are you ready? It's time to board."

Antonia took a deep breath of mountain air, so cold it hurt her lungs, sharp like a knife, but it felt good, not bad. She was glad she had a warm blue coat with a bit of fur around her neck, and it matched the blue bonnet and her blue dress, so she guessed she looked like a city girl, all right. She didn't feel that way, but Mrs. Stannert just said, "Appearances, Antonia. You wear the costume, you become the part."

Antonia looked around, one more time. She saw Mrs. Stannert was doing the same. For just a second, Mrs. Stannert looked sad. Then she took Antonia's gloved hand in hers, and said, "Time to head West, into the sunset! I wonder what adventures await us in California."

As they boarded the train, Mrs. Stannert murmured, "Excuse me," as a man came down the steps, almost bumping into them. He backed up, lifting his hat, and moved aside to let them pass.

Tony watched him as he watched Mrs. Stannert come up the stairs. He had a black mustache and a little beard, looked a bit of a toff, looked like someone who'd come from somewhere far away. Then he looked at Antonia. She felt a jolt of...was it fear?

It was something all right.

She held Mrs. Stannert's hand even tighter, and ducked her head, glad that her face was hidden between the bonnet and the fur collar of her coat. For a moment, she felt like a little fox in a den, tail wrapped tight around its nose, preparing for winter.

She shook the feeling off. They were going now, she and Mrs. Stannert.

They were free.

Mrs. Stannert put an arm around her shoulders, guiding her into the train, into the future.

Epilogue

The traveler tipped his hat to the woman and girl boarding the train and patiently waited for them to move past so he could disembark. He'd had a long trip, longer than he had thought it would be. He was several months past the time he'd expected to be in Leadville, and in fact had gone so far as to buy a ticket and even had boarded the train about a month previous, before being called back. Work, requests, clients…they were always in need of his services, and he found it hard to say no. However, he had sent letters, money, and felt confident that all was well.

That girl, just now, though. There was something familiar about her. Her eyes? It had been such a quick look, a flash up and down. Little girls are shy, and well they should be. It was a dangerous world. He approved of the way the woman took the girl's hand and then wrapped an arm around the girl's shoulders, protective. That was good. He also approved of the woman in general—tall, dark eyes, dark hair, olive skin, with an air of command he rarely saw in the feminine sex. She had stared at him, not frightened, not shy, almost as if to warn him away, keep his distance from them both.

He descended from the train, carried his single bag off the platform and hailed a hack into town. Leadville called itself a city, but it wasn't New York, London, Vienna, or even Denver. Not as developed as he had hoped it would be. Still there was much money made here in the silver industry. And where there was money, there were always clients in need of his talents. He thought again of the young girl just now, how there was something about her that reminded him of the woman he was hoping to see again soon. She could even have been that woman's daughter. But no. Impossible. That woman and her daughter, they were here, in Leadville, waiting for him.

He had the hack stop at the Clairmont Hotel where he expected them to still be lodging. It was a fine hotel, he had to admit, for being here in these high, remote mountains. At the desk, he leaned over his cane and cleared his throat to get the receptionist's attention. The receptionist looked up from fiddling with the keyboard under the counter. It had to be a keyboard, because he heard the soft metallic jingle of keys on hooks.

"I am looking for a Mrs. Gizzi. She is a guest here. She took rooms back in June, with her daughter."

The receptionist scratched his side whiskers and eyed him. The traveler knew what he was thinking—here is an obviously well-off stranger, one who speaks with an odd foreign accent, probably from far away, probably come to investigate the famous silver mines for investment. What does he want with this woman?

That would be on the clerk's mind.

The clerk frowned, tried to look serious, and spun the guest register around to search through it. Lips pursed, he flipped back through the pages. "June, June, you say." He paused and jabbed at a line with his finger, looking up. "Found it! The Gizzis were here, but they left the hotel…" he paged forward, "at the end of August."

His heart sank. Could it be he had made a mistake, insisting they come here, rather than wait for him in Denver?

"Where did they go?"

The clerk shrugged, but avoided his eyes.

That told the traveler that he had to dig deeper, perhaps be a little unpleasant.

"I sent them many letters, in care of this hotel, all through summer and fall. What happened to those letters?"

The clerk made a show of opening and closing drawers, but it was clear it was all for show.

"No letters here for Gizzi. Sorry. Maybe they were returned?" He obviously hoped the questions would stop.

"Those letters contained monies for their continued lodgings in your fine hotel."

Another shrug. But on his forehead, a film of sweat was developing, ever so lightly.

He was lying. He knew something. Something he wanted to keep hidden.

"Could they be in town elsewhere?" asked the traveler. "Another hotel?"

"Could be," answered the receptionist. "We have lots of hotels in town, and rooming houses, places like that." He scratched his jaw and tried to keep his gaze steady on the traveler, but his eyes kept jerking to look beyond, as if hoping a guest would come so he could turn away.

He was a liar.

The traveller decided to sign in and stay at this hotel while he searched. It would be expedient to be in this liar's sight, a constant reminder of the web of lies he was weaving. Eventually, the liar would make a mistake, say something that doubled back on him.

If the woman and child were here in Leadville, the traveler would find them. If not, he would find that out as well. If this were the case, he would proceed to the next step and find out what had happened to them. Eventually, and it was always sooner rather than later for him, he would uncover the trail, no matter how obscure, how old, how hidden. Because that was what he did: search out what was lost and find it. Go after what was stolen and return it. Find what was in the dark and bring it into the light. That was what his considerable skills were focused on and what people paid him so well to do.

The traveler filled out the register, using his real name. There was no need to hide, not here. He despised lying in others. When, through employment or circumstances, he had to dissemble, to lie, he despised himself. But, business was business, and some-times it was required.

The receptionist spun the register around to read it, and the traveler braced himself for the inevitable butchering of his last name.

The receptionist tried. "Mr. de, uh, B-Brooo-eeee-gin?"

Wolter Roeland de Bruijn didn't even wince. "Brown. It is pronounced Brown."

Author's Note

As always, be forewarned: spoilers lie within.

First, let's deal with what is "truth" (always a relative term) and what springs from my imagination, starting with place and location. There is a Leadville, Colorado, which has a rich (and long) history of mining. And there was a silver rush in "Cloud City" (one of Leadville's nicknames) starting in the late 1870s. Many made fortunes in this time, including Horace Austin Tabor, the Guggenheims, David May, Charles Boettcher, and J. J. and Molly Brown. If you haven't been to Leadville, you're missing a grand experience. History infuses the high mountain air, the people are friendly, and the views are a treasure greater than gold.

In 1880, Stillborn and Tiger alleys existed, as did "the rows." The newspapers of the day used very colorful language to describe these areas; it helps to keep in mind we are viewing these descriptions through hindsight and our own frames of reference. Trying to "pin down" the exact configuration and location of the rows was an adventure for me and Lake County Public Library historian Janice Fox. From the 1880 census and city directory, we determined Kate Armstead lived in the rear of 137 West Second Street (or West State, if you prefer). I proceeded from there. The higher-class parlor houses were situated on West Fifth Street, while State Street (also known as Second Street) was the more notorious red-light district. The railroad depot was brand new in that timeframe. Evergreen Cemetery existed and had its "pauper fields": the Protestant Free and Catholic Free sections. At that time, there would have been few or no trees (they all having gone to other uses in the burgeoning city). Today, you can visit the cemetery and identify the free sections: no gravestones or markers, just undulating ground in all directions, dotted with new growth evergreens.

Thriving 1880 Leadville businesses mentioned in *What Gold Buys* include the Tontine Restaurant, the *Chronicle* offices and newspaper (and its newsies in their fancy brass-buttoned uniforms), Steve's Health Office, the Board of Trade Saloon, and the Grand Central Theatre. The "Undertaking" section of the city directory lists the Leadville Undertaking Company as well as Nelson and Company, and seven undertakers appear in the census, allowing me to slide in my fictional Alexander's Undertaking without issue. The Silver Queen, *The Independent*, the Stannerts' little blue house, and Susan Carothers' photographic studio are also part of my fictional world.

As for who is real in this milieu: Judge Updegraf presided over the county court in 1880, and I've tried to be careful in my treatment of him, as by all accounts he was an upstanding and honest sort. Kate Armstead lived in Coon Row and, according to the newspapers, was a force to be reckoned with. The architect and builder Eugene Robitaille lived on Fourth Street—right in Inez's neighborhood—and built some lovely structures, including the "House with the Eye," which is now a museum. Newspaperman Orth Stein (my fictional Jed Elliston's nemesis) was conducting investigative journalism and spinning tall tales for the *Chronicle* starting in the summer of 1880. In fact, Orth Stein's story of secret anatomy lessons appeared in great and enthusiastic detail in the August 10, 1880, edition of the *Chronicle* under the title "Cadaver Classes." I can hear fictional Jed gnashing his teeth even now.

Some of my references for Leadville and its people during this timeframe are:

Leadville: Colorado's Magic City by Edward Blair

History of Leadville and Lake County, Colorado (Volume I) by Don and Jean Griswold

A Social History of Leadville, Colorado, During the Boom Days, 1887–1881 thesis by Eugene Floyd Irey (thesis)

Leadville Architecture by Lawrence Von Bamford

Olden Times in Colorado by C. C. Davis

Tourist Guide to Colorado in 1879 by Frank Fossett

The online Colorado Mountain History Collection, which you can find on the Lake County Public Library website, is a fantastic resource for city directories, cemetery records, newspapers, photos, and maps.

My focus for this particular book—the "afterlife," in both physical and spiritual realms—owes its being to two inspirations. The first was the aforementioned newspaper article by Stein. The second was an e-mail I received waaaay back in 2010 from Myfanwy Cook of the Historical Novel Society. Myfanwy happened to mention that a fellow from Cornwall, England, came to Colorado in the late nineteenth century, died in Denver, and was shipped home in a glass coffin.

A glass coffin?

Hmmmm.

Thus began my research into life after death.

I've learned more about undertaking and embalming (plus the resurrectionist side of things) since then. For instance, did you know that embalming was the province of medical physicians (embalming surgeons) until the early 1880s? I didn't. But I do now, thanks to James Lowry, who very kindly responded to my out-of-the-blue inquiry. Embalming was refined during the Civil War, when the need for methods to preserve the dead so they could be shipped home for burial became important. The first embalming school in the U.S., the Rochester School of Embalming, opened its doors in 1883. However, even before then, some undertakers were forming "alliances" with embalming surgeons and adding that art to their skills set. One need only look at the plethora of undertaking/embalming advertisements and banner ads in the Leadville city directory and newspapers to realize: there was gold to be made in the trade. A lovely bit from the pen of a *Boulder News and Courier* journalist reinforces this supposition. The journalist visited Leadville in late August 1880 and noted that Leadville was a great place to live if one wished to make money rapidly, adding, "Its supreme attraction is for the heavy gambler in mining property, next for fast men and women, and those who wait upon their demands; then, for hotel and boardinghouse keepers, people who own a cow, washerwomen, doctors, undertakers, lawyers, mechanics, honest laborers, and tradesmen, about in the order named." So my fictional Alexanders were in an excellent position to make money, if only things had only turned out differently.

As to more ethereal side of the afterlife, efforts to communicate with those who had "traveled on" were quite common. Spiritualism was alive and well in Leadville in 1880s. Two self-reported fortunetellers (both women) are listed in the 1880 census, and there are numerous mentions of séances and mediums in the local newspapers. For instance, a *Chronicle* article of January 10, 1881, notes, "Leadville is, for a city of its size, overrun to an unusual extent with spiritualists, clairvoyants, and others of the ilk who either profess to be in intimate converse with the ghosts of the departed or to be gifted with an occult sense that reads with equal facility the hidden future and equally hidden past." A Leadville séance conducted in early 1880 by a noted spiritualist was attended by three journalists and a Methodist reverend. When it was over, the reverend told one of the reporters that "there were many of the acts performed which he believed he could account for as the deception of a scientific hand, and there were others that he attributed to the well-acknowledged gift of mind reading; but there were some things for the explanation of which he could offer no theory or solution…he admits himself mystified by the human mechanism and the miracles which can in these latter days be accomplished through aid of a brain and hand (*Chronicle*, April 3, 1880)." Some modern-day scholars now see the Spiritualism move- ment of the nineteenth and early twentieth centuries as closely entwined and allied with the early women's rights movement, which is fascinating territory in itself. For more about death, resurrections, undertaking/embalming, and the "afterlife" of body and spirit, I turned to:

Death in the Victorian Family by Pat Jalland

Burke & Hare by Owen Dudley Edwards

Stiff: The Curious Lives of Human Cadavers by Mary Roach

Embalming Surgeons of the Civil War by James W. Lowry (pamphlet)

The Principles and Practice of Embalming (Chapter 2: History) by Clarence G. Strub and L. G. Frederick

Buried Alive by Jan Bondeson

Celebrations of Death: The Anthropology of Mortuary Ritual by Peter Metcalf and Richard Huntington

Other Powers by Barbara Goldsmith

Radical Spirits: Spiritualism and Women's Rights in the Nineteenth-Century America by Ann Braude

For nineteenth-century viewpoints, you can't beat the books, newspapers, and circulars of the day. Regarding Spiritualism, for instance, the Internet is a goldmine. Two examples are:

The Herald of Progress (the July 16, 1880, issue is a nice example of what you can expect to find)

Seers of the Ages: Embracing Spiritualism, Past and Present: Doctrines Stated and Moral Tendencies Defined by J. M. Peebles (1869)

As to what was known/unknown about the human brain in 1880, and how physicians and psychologists viewed the interac- tion of brain and mind, again, turning to the documents of the day proved fruitful. Just search "brain" in any one of these to be treated to some interesting insights:

Rocky Mountain Medical Review: A Journal of Scientific Medicine, Volume 1 (1880–1881)

The Transactions of the American Medical Association, Volume 31 (1880)

The Mechanism of Man: An Answer to the Popular Question: What Am I? — A Popular Introduction to Mental Physiology and Psychology by Edward William Cox (President of the Psychological Society of Great Britain)

Now, moving on to Drina Gizzi, who "materialized" out of thin air and insisted on being put on the page, and Madam Labasillier, who did much the same...Who are these women? Where did they come from? Well, I did some exploring, but they didn't like to be pinned down:

Travellers, Gypsies, Roma: The Demonisation of Difference by Michael Hayes and Thomas Acton

Gypsy-travelers in Nineteenth-century Society by David Mayall

The New Orleans Voodoo Handbook by Kenaz Filan

Turning to Drina's daughter Antonia/Tony, I slid sideways into the newsie idea when my wandering eye snagged on the comment about the "brass-button uniforms" the *Chronicle* supplied to its newsboys. Also, long ago, I knew an elderly gentleman who sold newspapers on the streets of New York City when he was three years old (during the late 1880s, most likely). One reference leads to more, so this is just skimming the surface:

Children of the City at Work and at Play by David Nasaw

How the Other Half Lives by Jacob A. Riis

Calling Extra by Kristina Romero (a Young Adult fiction book with references listed in back)

Speaking of eyes, I did do some research into the genetics of heterochromia iridium (two different-colored eyes within a single individual). Sometimes the difference is due to injury/trauma; sometimes there is a genetic component. However, the genetics of eye-color inheritance is still somewhat of a mystery. To learn a bit more, check out these two online articles (very different in tone): *Scientific American,* "How does someone get two different-colored eyes?" from November 3, 2001, and "Heterochromia is very groovy mutation—maybe" by Esther Inglis-Arkell on *io9,* October 18, 2012. In both cases, be sure to read the comments. Verrrry interesting indeed. If you think you spot the comment that caused me to bolt upright in my chair and say, "Whoa!" contact me at annparker@annparker.net. If you are right, I will send you a special little something.

Finally, there is the matter of Inez and Mark Stannert's divorce and the final custodial guardianship of their son, William. I have been pursuing the realities of this particular situation for well over a decade now, and I must give my colleague Colleen Casey a standing ovation. She helped me unearth and pull together all the legal information for setting the legal foundations and commentary needed for these critical scenes. The information is all there, in the statutes, laws, and codes, and luckily for us, all that and more is now available online. My Google library is now populated with tomes such as

> *General Laws of the State of Colorado, Comprising that Portion of the Revised Statutes of Colorado, and the General Acts of the subsequent Legislative Assemblies of Colorado Territory for the Years 1870, 1872, 1874, and 1876, Still Remaining in Force, and the General Laws Enacted At the First Session of the General Assembly of the State of Colorado, Convened November 1, 1876…*(1876)

and

> *The Legal Relations of Infants, Parent and Child, and Guardian and Ward: And a Particular Consideration of*

Guardianship in the State of New York, Including Practice and Procedure in Surrogate's Courts, and in the Supreme Court, and County Courts, and the Superior Courts of Cities, in Matters of Guardianship; and in Actions Against Infants to Compel a Conveyance of Real Estate, and for the Partition of Real Estate; Also an Appendix of Forms for All Such Proceedings by G. W. Field (1888)

Okay, I'm now exhausted just from typing the titles of those two references. Suffice to say, Inez and Mark's divorce, the complications, and the discussions between Inez, her attorney, and Judge Updegraf were all as accurate as we could make them.

For those who respond to Inez's "riding off into the sunset" with, "Inez leaving Leadville? Nooooooo!" I assure you, she will eventually return to Leadville and in fine fettle. After all, consider: from November 1879 to November 1880 she has had quite a year, what with all those mysteries to solve and her very complicated personal life. Too, I wonder what Wolter Roeland de Bruijn will do, now that he has arrived in this very foreign (to him) City in the Clouds and the object of his search has vanished.

Hmmmm.

Shall we find out?

To receive a free catalog of Poisoned Pen Press titles, please provide your name, address, and email address in one of the following ways:

Phone: 1-800-421-3976
Facsimile: 1-480-949-1707
Email: info@poisonedpenpress.com
Website: www.poisonedpenpress.com

Poisoned Pen Press
6962 E. First Ave. Ste 103
Scottsdale, AZ 85251